"*Blind Trust* is a fun, sometimes quirky whodunit, full of everything a mystery lover is looking for, including a dash of romance. If you enjoy mysteries as much as I do, you won't want to miss Sandra Orchard's second installment in her Port Aster Secrets series."

—**Lisa Harris**, Christy Award finalist and author of *Dangerous Passage*

"Sandra Orchard weaves a clever web of suspense in this story of secrets, betrayal, and small-town intrigue. Seasoned with a sweet romance; a gripping, intelligent plot; and a few heart-touching surprises, *Blind Trust* will keep readers on the edge of their seats—and impatient for book three!"

—**Susan May Warren**, award-winning, bestselling author of *It Had to Be You*

blind trust

blind trust

a novel

SANDRA ORCHARD

Revell

a division of Baker Publishing Group
Grand Rapids, Michigan

© 2014 by Sandra J. van den Bogerd

Published by Revell
a division of Baker Publishing Group
P.O. Box 6287, Grand Rapids, MI 49516-6287
www.revellbooks.com

Printed in the United States of America

Library of Congress Cataloging-in-Publication Data
Orchard, Sandra
    Blind trust : a novel / Sandra Orchard.
        pages cm. — (Port Aster secrets ; bk. 2)
    ISBN 978-0-8007-2223-4 (pbk.)
        1. Counterfeiters—Fiction. 2. Commercial crimes—Fiction. 3. Family secrets—Fiction. I. Title.
    PR9199.4.O73B66 2014
    813'.6—dc23   2014000480

Scripture used in this book, whether quoted or paraphrased by the characters, is taken from the Holy Bible, New International Version®. NIV®. Copyright © 1973, 1978, 1984 by Biblica, Inc.™ Used by permission of Zondervan. All rights reserved worldwide. www.zondervan.com

This is a work of fiction. Names, characters, incidents, and dialogues are products of the author's imagination and are not to be construed as real. Any resemblance to actual events or persons, living or dead, is entirely coincidental.

14 15 16 17 18 19 20   7 6 5 4 3 2 1

For my parents-in-love, Greta and Peter,
for their supportive encouragement of my writing
and their penchant for nutmeg.

1

Diamond Heiress Escapes Murder Charges.

Kate Adams snatched a copy of the *Port Aster Press* from the newsstand next to the grocery store checkout. How could they drop the charges when Molly Gilmore confessed?

Kate's throat squeezed at the memory of finding Daisy's cold body.

The young clerk pointed to the newspaper. Tears stung Kate's eyes as she dropped it on top of the groceries she'd picked up for her elderly neighbor. Her dear friend and mentor was dead because of Molly Gilmore. If not for the sting Kate had devised, the police would still be calling Daisy's death a suicide. As if she would have killed herself when they'd been on the verge of a breakthrough in their herbal research project.

The clerk placed the newspaper on the other side of the register. Kate shifted so she could read the article as the teen scanned the groceries. *Insufficient evidence.* How could they say that?

Kate studied Molly's photo. No hint of the crazed glint

that had flashed in her eyes when she lunged at Kate with that syringe. Kate shuddered at the thought of how close Molly had come to killing *her* too.

Now that the syringe had conveniently disappeared, she prayed the judge didn't drop the attempted murder charges against Molly on grounds of insufficient evidence too. If attacking her with a hypodermic full of poison wasn't attempted murder, Kate didn't know what was.

Except the attempted murder charge was not enough to keep her behind bars. They let the woman out on bail, even though she practically had flight risk emblazoned across her Dolce pantsuit. In the photo, her face showed no trace of concern. And why should she worry? By trial time, her five-hundred-dollar-an-hour lawyers would have the charge whittled down to jaywalking.

Kate cringed at her negativity. Only Molly wasn't the hard-working young woman struggling to make ends meet that Kate had once thought. Molly hadn't shown a speck of remorse when her fatally flawed plan to poison Daisy and pin the crime on her ex was exposed. And sadly, with how powerful Molly's family money was proving to be, Kate feared Molly wouldn't be held accountable for her crimes either.

"That's $28.37," the clerk said, bagging the last of the groceries.

Kate handed over the three tens her neighbor had given her to pay for the items and continued reading: "A source close to Molly Gilmore claims the incident involving Kate Adams was a setup and that Gilmore was the victim of police entrapment."

"Ma'am."

Kate reached for the two bags of groceries, her gaze still pinned to the article. *Entrapment?* Molly was no victim.

Someone tugged the bags back.

"What—?" She looked up into cool gray eyes.

"Ma'am, could you come with me please?" The voice belonged to a security guard. At least that's what was embroidered on his crisply ironed shirt with chevrons on the shoulder. Since when did the store hire a security guard?

"Me?" she squeaked, sounding as guilty as a pilfering mouse. She cleared her throat and forced backbone into her voice. "Why?"

The line of customers behind her gawked, eyes rapt with morbid fascination. She recognized a couple of faces and felt her own face heat. In a town this size, whatever was going on would be common knowledge by suppertime.

The pimple-faced cashier held one of the ten-dollar bills she'd given him under a blue light and showed it to the towering guard who still had his hands on her groceries. "See? Counterfeit! All three of them."

A collective gasp sounded behind her.

"Good work, kid." The security guard released the bags to accept the evidence.

Heart pounding, Kate gaped at the bills. "My neighbor gave them to me to buy her groceries."

The guard nodded, but he didn't look like he believed her. "If you'll follow me, ma'am"—he shot a pointed look to the oglers behind her—"we'll sort this out in the manager's office."

"What should I do with the groceries?" the clerk asked.

The guard steered Kate toward the office. "Have a stocker put them back."

"No." Kate whirled around. "I need to take those to my neighbor. She's elderly and not feeling well. She needs—"

"Okay." The guard waved off the cashier, curled the newspaper into the top of one of the bags, and hoisted them off the counter. "Follow me."

Fevered whispers rose in their wake.

The guard closed the office door behind them and set the grocery bags on the manager's desk. From the front page of the newspaper, Molly's victorious smile mocked Kate.

Suddenly, she had the sinking feeling *she* was the one being entrapped.

Her breath came in gulps. What if the manager didn't believe her? Or worse, what if he did and the police went after Verna?

Kate dug around her purse for other cash, her credit card, something. She couldn't let her sweet old neighbor take the fall for trying to pass off counterfeit bills. How had Verna even ended up with a wad of counterfeit cash?

Kate zipped closed her purse. She must've left her wallet on the bed when she'd switched purses this morning. Chewing on her bottom lip, she eyed the guard. "Are you sure the bills are counterfeit? I mean, that cashier didn't look old enough to know the difference."

"No, ma'am. I don't know for sure." The guard positioned himself in front of the door, his expression impassive. "That's why we're waiting for the police to sort this out."

"The police?" She swiped slick palms down the sides of her slacks. "Is that really necessary?" She'd never liked the police. Not since her father died in police custody when she was ten. "I mean, I can pay for the groceries . . . some other way. My neighbor will be worried."

A loud rap sounded on the door.

Kate jumped at the sound, knocking a soup can out of one of the grocery bags. As she scrambled to stop it from toppling off the desk, the guard pushed open the door.

Detective Tom Parker strode into the room looking every inch her knight in shining armor, just as he'd been when he rescued her from Molly's attack with that syringe. Kate's knees went weak with relief. Tom was the one exception to her police aversion. Although he was not quite as tall as the security guard, with his dark hair, square chin, and piercing blue eyes, Tom's powerful presence dwarfed the younger man. And his warm smile loosened the knots in her stomach.

He'd never believe her guilty of counterfeiting. After how badly he'd felt about taking her into custody for her friend's murder three months ago, he'd make sure she wasn't falsely accused again.

Hopefully the fact that he wore his usual suit and tie instead of a police uniform would also stave off rumors of her being arrested. He glanced around the room, then turned back to the security guard. "Where's your counterfeiter?"

The guard hitched his thumb in Kate's direction.

"Miss Adams?" The surprise in Tom's voice reinforced the absurdity of the accusation against her, but a second later his face broke into a grin. "If you wanted to see me, you could have just called."

Her stomach somersaulted at his gentle teasing and at the disappointment that she hadn't called vibrating beneath his words. If only he knew how much she'd wanted to agree to that second dinner date he'd been vying for. But his warning that Molly Gilmore's lawyer might attack her character in the upcoming trial had her too worried Tom's reputation would be ruined. She knew all too well what guilt by association felt like. She could never willingly subject anyone to that kind of ridicule—especially someone she cared about as much as Tom.

Suddenly aware of the security guard's scrutiny, she schooled her expression. "Thanks. Next time I'll keep that in mind." Tom being a cop made the risk of being romantically linked ten times worse. If Molly's lawyers didn't try to shred Kate's reputation in their effort to make her look less of a victim, they'd certainly question Tom's objectivity as the investigating officer.

"You know this woman?" the security guard asked.

Tom chuckled. "Yes, she's known to the police."

The guard nodded, his expression smug.

"Because I was the victim of an attempted murder," Kate blurted. "Not because I'm a criminal." She knew Tom was making light of the situation to put her at ease. But he *wasn't* helping.

The guard's jaw dropped, and a smidgen of recognition lit his eyes.

Tom cleared his throat, wiping the grin from his face. "What do you have? I'm sure we can clear this up."

The guard handed Tom the money. "I believe you'll find these are counterfeit, sir. They failed our light test. She used them to pay for her groceries. She claims she received them from her neighbor."

Tom swung his attention back to her, one eyebrow raised.

"You can't think that I . . . ?" At the amused twinkle in his eyes, she let out a *humph*. "What kind of moron counterfeits ten-dollar bills? If I wanted to defraud someone, I'd at least go for twenties. More likely fifties or hundreds!"

The amusement in Tom's bright blue eyes intensified, but he held his mouth in a firm line. "You're not helping your case," he murmured.

She rolled her eyes. He knew she was joking. Then again—she slanted a glance at the guard—maybe this guy didn't. She cringed at the idea of him repeating what she'd just said.

Tom studied the currency in his hands. "These *are* counter-feit. Who gave them to you?"

"Verna Nagy, but she couldn't have known. Someone must have palmed them off on her." The newspaper poking out of the grocery bag drew Kate's attention. She passed it to Tom, Molly's picture face up. "Do you think she could be behind this? You warned me that her people might try to discredit my reputation—you know, 'try the victim'—to bolster her defense."

Tom scanned the headline, and the tick of his jaw muscle reminded her of how he'd blamed himself for Daisy's case unraveling.

The guard shook his head. "I haven't seen her in here."

"Could you excuse us for a moment?" Tom said to the guard.

"Of course."

After the door closed behind the guard, Tom turned her way, his expression empathetic but not encouraging.

Kate lifted her hand stop-sign style. "I know what you're going to say. It sounds crazy. But think about it. Molly tried to get back at her ex by poisoning someone. That's how she operates."

"Sure, but have you bought groceries for your neighbor before? Because what else would make Molly's people think you'd end up with the phony cash?"

"No, I haven't." Kate glanced out the office window toward the cash registers. "But . . . maybe the money didn't come from my neighbor. Maybe they got to that teenage clerk. I'm sure he's new here." She clasped Tom's arm. "I was reading the paper as I handed him the money. He could have easily replaced the bills I gave him with counterfeit ones."

"He just *happened* to have the exact denominations in counterfeit as you handed him?"

"No, I guess he wouldn't." Kate blew out a dejected breath.

"He wouldn't!" Her hope resurged. "If you search him or the register, maybe you'll find more."

Tom cast a skeptical look out the office window. "Wait here." He returned the newspaper to the desk, then let himself out of the room as the guard stepped back in.

Tom waited until the last customer in line exited, then showed the cashier his badge.

The teen nodded and opened the cash drawer.

Tom dug through the drawer, lifting removable parts. Now and again, he held a bill under the ultraviolet light. He said something to the teen, but the teen shook his head and turned out his empty pockets. Tom jotted something in his notepad, then stalked back to the office, grim-faced.

Kate's chest tightened. She knew Tom couldn't believe she'd counterfeit, but if the evidence pointed to her, he wouldn't ignore it. No matter how he felt about her.

Or didn't feel. After all, a guy could only handle so much rejection, no matter how well-intentioned her reasons. He still sat beside her in church, but he hadn't tried inviting her to lunch for weeks.

"Thank you for your alertness," Tom said to the guard. "I'll take Miss Adams into my custody."

Custody. She tried to swallow but couldn't choke down the disbelief balled in her throat.

"What should we do with these?" The guard motioned toward the groceries.

Tom reached for a bag. "We'll deliver them. I want to talk to this neighbor of hers."

"They're not paid for, sir."

Tom pulled out his wallet and handed the guard a twenty and a ten. "Will this cover it?"

"Yes, I'll get your change."

"Thank you," Kate whispered to Tom as the guard left the room.

"Don't thank me yet. We've had a rash of counterfeit complaints over the last few weeks. The Gilmore reach may be long, but I doubt this counterfeit operation was a setup to destroy your reputation."

"But you believe me, don't you? You know I wouldn't knowingly pass counterfeit bills."

"Do I?"

She knew he was teasing, but that didn't arrest the rush of memories of others who hadn't been, or stop the ache in her throat. She felt ten again, in line for lunch at her school's hot dog day and accused of trying to pay with a fake ticket. Called a crook, *just like her old man*. Chilled by the frosty doubt in even her teacher's eyes.

"Hey." Tom brushed his thumb across her cheek, compassion in his eyes. "*I* know you wouldn't."

Melting at the warmth in his voice, she sucked in a breath and shut out the memories.

"But the chief heard the call," he added. "We've been trying to track leads on this problem for weeks. He's not going to let the fact you were caught red-handed go."

"But if you tell him Verna Nagy gave me the money, he'll haul her down to the police station. The woman is eighty years old. She's got to be a victim here too."

"Criminals come in all shapes and sizes, Kate. People are rarely what they seem. Who knows what your little old neighbor lady could be hiding?"

"What do you mean she isn't the counterfeiter?" the police chief ranted.

Tom tapped down the volume on his earphone as he pulled behind Kate's car in her driveway. "It's complicated."

Kate's soulful green eyes lifted to her rearview mirror.

More complicated than he needed. He'd barely managed to regain Kate's trust after hauling her in as a suspect in her friend's murder investigation. But whether he liked it or not, she *was* now connected to his counterfeiting investigation, however inadvertently, and he had to follow every lead. He just hoped she understood it wasn't personal.

"I'm about to interview a possible suspect now," he said to the chief. "I'll be in touch." He disconnected before Hank could press for details. The man would not be happy to hear that Kate Adams was back on their radar. Her amateur sleuthing three months ago had caused the chief more embarrassment than he could stomach.

Tom waited for Kate to climb out of her yellow Volkswagen Beetle before getting out of his car. Her tousled red hair didn't look as fiery as usual, and her stooped shoulders betrayed her unhappiness at having to involve her elderly neighbor. He lifted the groceries from the trunk. "You want to introduce me to your neighbor?"

"Oh, Tom," she pleaded, sounding utterly miserable. "She's such a sweet old woman. There's no way she knowingly duped me into passing counterfeit bills."

Too many years in law enforcement had drilled reality into him, but he bit back his you'd-be-surprised-what-sweet-old-women-can-do remark. He hated to discourage Kate's exceptional faith in people. It had served her well when hunting down her friend's killer. If only Molly Gilmore's betrayals hadn't left it so tattered. "Okay, then we'll be up front with your neighbor. Tell her what happened and see what she has to say."

"Right." Kate strode across her yard, her flowery skirt flouncing with the let's-do-it attitude he'd grown to appreciate in her.

The bright August sunshine glinted off her hair, and reflexively his fingers tingled. He could almost feel the silky caress of her burnished red curls. In those moments when he let her take over his thoughts, he could still breathe in her lavender scent and hear the sweet ring of her laughter.

She stopped at the sidewalk. "Coming?"

He grinned at the determination blazing in her eyes. He should've tried harder to score that second date instead of biding his time until after Molly's trial. Just his bad luck she'd wind up in the middle of another one of his cases.

Verna Nagy's front door stood open with only a flimsy screen door between a possible intruder and the inside. A black and white cat met them on the porch and twined between their legs, purring loudly. Kate lifted him into her arms. "What are you doing outside, Whiskers?"

Tom rubbed the little fellow's neck. "Is this the cat that was cured by Grandma Brewster's herbal brew a few months back?" The police chief's German grandmother had been making natural remedies for townsfolk and their pets for as long as he could remember—a woman after Kate's own heart.

"He sure is." Kate nuzzled her cheek against the cat's fur. "You can't chalk *his* recovery up to mind over matter, can you, Mr. Skeptic?"

He feigned offense. "Hey, I never said the stuff doesn't work."

She dropped the cat to the ground and rang the bell. "You didn't have to." She winked.

At least she didn't take his skepticism about her cure-all teas personally. He admired her work as a researcher. He really did. It was the spin-off industries that preyed on people's quick-fix mentalities that caused him concern. In his FBI days, he'd had one partner who'd overindulged on a diet tea that not only stripped him of a few pounds but also landed him in the hospital.

A sprightly, white-haired woman peered at them through the screen door and pierced Tom with a glare. "I already have a vacuum. The no-good, overpriced one you sold me ten years ago."

"Excuse me?" Tom glanced at Kate. She hadn't told him the woman was senile.

Her eyes sparkled with laughter. "Verna, it's me, Kate. Your neighbor. I brought your groceries. And this is my friend, Tom. Detective Parker. He needs to ask you a couple of questions."

Verna's eyes narrowed as she studied his face. "You're not selling vacuums?"

"No ma'am."

She swung the door wide. "Come in then."

The cat leapt through the open door, leading the way inside the tidy little house. The air smelled like an odd combination of lemon oil and the spicy scent of the town's tea shop. The narrow-planked hardwood gleamed. Sunshine filtered through lace curtains, playing hide-and-seek with the elaborately gowned china dolls adorning the fancy Victorian furniture.

No sign of counterfeiting equipment, not even a computer. With no garage outside, that left the basement and bedrooms.

"You have a lovely house, Mrs. Nagy. May I have a tour?" Brazen, he knew, but it saved him the hassle of a search warrant.

The woman glowed. "Of course, of course."

"I'll just put away your groceries while you show him around." Kate fired him a warning scowl before slipping into the kitchen.

Photographs lined the hallway. "These your children?" Tom asked.

Verna peered at the pictures as if she'd never noticed them before. "My son Brian and grandson Greg. My husband passed two years ago."

"I'm sorry. Must be lonely for you. Does your son visit often?"

"Once a week. He's a good boy."

Tom made a mental note to check into her son's finances and make sure he was as good as his mother believed.

The bedroom housed nothing more than a bed and dresser. The spare room had a sewing machine and piles of fabric and half-finished articles. Mrs. Nagy squinted into the room and swayed a little. Then, as if she'd forgotten him, she strolled back to the living room, sank into her recliner, and clicked on the TV with her remote.

Tom trailed her, wondering how to wrangle his way into the basement without raising any suspicions, because from the looks of Mrs. Nagy, she'd make an easy front for a counterfeiter to exploit.

Kate came in waving a package of frozen fish. "Did you want this in the downstairs freezer?"

"Huh?" Mrs. Nagy looked up from the TV. "Oh, hello dear. When did you get here? Staying for tea?"

Kate paled. "Yes. I'll make us some." To Tom, she whispered, "I don't know what's wrong. I mean, she's forgetful sometimes, but never like this."

Tom relieved Kate of the package of fish. "I'll take this to the freezer. You make her a cup of tea and then we'll chat."

21

Kate nodded, thankfully oblivious to his motive for offering to take care of the fish. He took his time walking across the basement to the freezer, being careful not to move anything so any discovery couldn't be thrown out of court. The basement was devoid of furniture. Instead, shelves of home canning, coated in a thick layer of dust, lined one long cement wall, while the boxes stacked along the adjacent wall looked like recent additions.

He tossed the fish into the freezer and circled behind the stairs. A dust-free workout gym dominated the space. Her son's?

A large patch of dust was scraped from the floor beyond the workout area, as if something had recently been moved. Not likely by Verna, as frail as she seemed, but not without her knowledge either. With no outside exit on this level, no one could easily sneak into the basement undetected.

By the time Tom returned to the main floor, Kate was sitting next to Verna in the living room. The steam rising from the teacup in her hand intensified the spicy scent in the air. From the TV, a theatric judge lambasted a defendant for his overly trusting nature. Tom turned down the volume, debating how to interrogate Kate's neighbor. Showing signs of dementia, she wasn't likely the kingpin of a counterfeiting operation. But if she repeated his questions to the wrong people, he might lose his trail before he found it. Of course, she could be faking.

Tom took a seat kitty-corner from Verna. "Nice workout gym in your basement. Your son's?"

"Grandson's."

"He live with you?"

Verna glanced from him to the feuding couple standing in front of the TV judge and shook her head.

22

"Her son's wife walked out on the family," Kate whispered. "Greg and Brian had to move into an apartment. I think Verna's storing some of their stuff."

"Any idea why his wife left?" Maybe she didn't want to get caught up in her husband's illegal activities.

"She ran off," Verna hissed. "With some handyman drifter she had working on the house. I warned Brian he was traveling too much. She cleaned out their accounts. Mortgaged the house to the hilt and skipped town."

Sounded like Brian needed money to dig himself out of that mess.

Unless . . . The plaintiff in the TV courtroom echoed Verna's description. Tom cocked his head to Kate and mouthed, "For real?"

Kate shrugged.

Trying another tack, Tom asked the woman, "Do you get out much?"

"My ladies' mission sewing circle on Thursday mornings and church on Sundays."

A religious woman. More reason to doubt her as a viable suspect. Or it could be a front. He'd known plenty of criminals to hide behind a facade of uprightness. "Who takes you?"

She waved her hand in the direction of Kate's house. "The neighbor."

Kate frowned and shook her head that it wasn't her. "What about your groceries?" Kate asked. "Who usually picks them up?"

"I'm sorry, dear. I didn't mean to put you out."

Kate patted the woman's bony hand. "I don't mind shopping for you. I was just curious. I want to know you're being taken care of."

"My son hired a housekeeper who comes in. She picks up groceries sometimes."

"Do you do your own banking?" Tom asked.

Verna's attention drifted back to the TV as a red sports car veered into the driveway. Verna upped the volume on the remote.

Tom strode to the TV and hit the Off button. He wasn't buying the doddering routine. It was too convenient. "Mrs. Nagy, I'm Detective Parker. We need to know where you got the money you gave Miss Adams."

"Detective?" She turned her attention to Kate. "Are you in trouble?"

"Who's in trouble?" the lanky, fair-skinned sports car driver said through the screen, then pushed his way inside.

Tom recognized him from the photos in the hallway. From the rumpled suit, the man looked as if he'd been on the road for hours. From the look of his car, his wife hadn't wiped him out entirely. Tom extended a hand. "You must be Verna's son."

"Brian Nagy." The man clasped Tom's hand in an iron grip. "And you are?"

"Detective Tom Parker."

Nagy dropped Tom's hand like a hot potato and knelt at his mom's side. "What's going on? What happened?"

"Your mother came into possession of counterfeit bills, and we are trying to trace their source."

"Oh, Mom, I told you we need to get you into a nursing home. Things like this wouldn't happen." He glanced up at Tom as if he might convince her. "She doesn't want to go. I worry about her when I'm on the road. But I never imagined anything like this. Where did it happen? What are you going to do?"

"Your mother gave Miss Adams several counterfeit bills with which to purchase her groceries. We're simply trying to ascertain where they came from."

Nagy surged to his feet and pointed at Kate. "How do you know she's not responsible and trying to lay the blame on my mother?"

Kate gasped.

Tom patted the air in a calming gesture. "We're not blaming anyone, just trying to get some answers."

Verna's son gave a stiff nod and knelt next to his mother again. "Mom, do you remember where you got the money?"

Verna shook her head, but the frightened look in her eyes told Tom she was lying. The question was—why?

2

"I think your neighbor is protecting someone."

"You can't be serious." Kate stopped in the middle of her driveway and turned back to Tom, who'd taken the long way around from her neighbor's. The curtain at Verna's side window slipped closed, but a dark shadow remained—someone watching them.

Kate squirmed. Maybe Tom was right. *No.* "The woman was just scared of you," Kate insisted, as much to convince herself as him.

"Yeah, scared I'd arrest her son or grandson or housekeeper and maybe her as an accessory."

"You wouldn't." *Not an eighty-year-old woman.*

Tom pulled open his car door. "Kate, don't get in the middle of this. Okay?"

She flung out her arms. "I am in the middle of this." Before she let him leave, she had to convince him that Verna was innocent. "If Verna knew the money was counterfeit, she wouldn't have given it to me. I think she's just scared her son will follow through on his threat to put her in a home."

"I can understand why he feels the need. She seems pretty out of it . . . if she wasn't faking."

Kate closed the distance between them. "Are you really that cynical?"

"It's my job."

"Then why didn't you question her son?"

"I will. First I want to do a background check. Don't worry. I'll be keeping a close eye on him. If he's guilty, he's bound to try to hide the evidence."

Like someone had done for Molly Gilmore. Kate's fingers curled around the newspaper she'd picked up. She'd ferreted out her friend's killer but failed to get a conviction. She couldn't fail Verna too. "Wanna come in for a minute? I can make you coffee."

Tom raised an eyebrow.

Of course, he'd question her motives. She never drank coffee, not to mention she'd resisted all his recent invitations to go out with him. "You said you wanted to keep an eye on Verna's son." She motioned to Brian's car still parked in her neighbor's driveway.

He gave her a wry smile. "I'd love some coffee."

She led the way to the kitchen and tossed the newspaper onto the table.

Tom took a seat and scanned the article about the dismissal of Molly Gilmore's charges. Kate felt a little foolish for thinking that there might have been a connection between the counterfeit money and the Gilmores. As if a rich family like that would go to the trouble to frame her when they could just as easily buy off a judge with real money.

Kate dug out her grinder and a small coffeemaker from the bottom cupboard, then scooped beans into the grinder and punched the Power button. She willed the noise to drown out thoughts of her friend's death, but the high-pitched whir was no match for the voice screaming in her head. How could the judge let Molly get away with murder?

Kate slapped off the button. It wasn't fair. Daisy deserved justice.

Blinking back tears, Kate tipped the freshly ground beans into the coffeemaker. She still felt as though she'd turn around and find her friend sitting at the table, nursing a cup of tea. What would Daisy think of Tom sitting here?

Kate glanced over her shoulder at him and smiled. She'd probably say it was about time she had a man in her life. If only the circumstances were different.

As he read the newspaper article, she hit the Play button on her answering machine.

"You have ten new messages," the computerized voice chirped.

Ten? She rarely got that many calls in a month.

"Kate, what happened?" Julie's hushed voice demanded. She worked at the library and was probably trying not to be overheard. "It's all over town that the cops picked you up for shoplifting or something."

Kate fumbled the mug she'd plucked from the cupboard. "Shoplifting!"

Tom laughed. "You know how the grapevine goes. Tomorrow you'll be forgotten in favor of Farmer Harvey's two-headed calf."

"It was born months ago!"

"You know what I mean."

The second message came on. "Kate, I just heard," Patti said consolingly.

Kate slumped into a kitchen chair. "Even my new lab assistant has already heard."

"If you need bail money or anything," the message continued. "Just call. Well, I guess, you won't get this if you're in jail. I'll stop by the police station just in case."

Groaning, Kate slouched over the table and buried her head under her arms. "Tell me this isn't happening."

Mrs. C from next door, her hairdresser, and even Tom's dad left messages. She pushed from her chair to shut off the last of them.

The phone rang. She just stared at it.

"Aren't you going to answer that?" Empathy softened Tom's voice.

She shook her head. "Sooner or later, they'll give up calling. Don't you think?"

After the fourth ring the answering machine kicked on. At the beep a male voice rasped, "Miss Baxter, are you there?"

Her heart jerked at the name she'd been compelled to give up soon after her father's death.

"I think you're going to want to talk to me now."

The blood drained from her face and limbs, abandoning her to hazy memories she'd just as soon forget. Swaying, she grabbed the counter.

Tom snatched up the phone. "Who is this?" A second later he slammed it back down. "Who was that?"

"Wha—what did he say?"

"He didn't. He hung up." Tom clasped her arms. "Do you know who he was?"

She shook her head and Tom urged her back to the table.

"But he's called before?"

"Yes, when I was investigating Daisy's murder." She swallowed the fear wadded in her throat. "Left a message. Said he'd be in touch."

"Then you moved." Deep grooves slashed Tom's brow. "Was *he* why you changed your number?"

She nodded.

"You should have told me." The concern in his voice had an odd tightening effect on her chest.

"It was before you knew . . . about my dad, I mean." If only she'd never asked Tom to help her find out what really happened twenty years ago. It's not like knowing would change anything. Except maybe his opinion of her . . . for the worse. *Like father, like daughter.* The long-ago taunts of her classmates pulsed in her ears, their faces morphing in her mind's eye to those of the townsfolk who'd gawked at her when the security guard confiscated her groceries.

Tom rubbed her arm, banishing the unwelcome memories. "Do you know what this guy's calling about?"

"I don't even know who he is. No one has called me Baxter since Mom reverted to her maiden name and shuffled us halfway across the country to get away from the whispering."

"So this guy knows about your past."

"He must."

"But you have no idea who he is?"

"No." Kate surged to her feet and paced the kitchen. "Yes. *I don't know.* Maybe." She poured Tom's coffee, needing to focus on something ordinary. She spooned in sugar and trembled so badly that half of it spilled on the counter. She drew a deep breath. "A few days before the first call, a businessman mistook me for my mother at A Cup or Two." She added two more spoonfuls of sugar to Tom's mug.

He commandeered the spoon and set the mug aside. "And?"

"Don't you see?" She whirled away, snatched up a dishcloth, and scrubbed at the counter. "He knew my mom as a Baxter.

He must work for the pharmaceutical company that's trying to take over the research station." The same pharmaceutical company that had demanded Dad's arrest twenty years ago—the arrest that got him killed. Shivers wracked her body.

"Did you get a name?"

"Peter. I didn't ask his last name. I didn't want to talk to him. No one here knows about my father. I—"

"It's okay." Tom pried the dishcloth from her hand. "I'll churn the waters at GPC Pharmaceuticals, see if I can turn up an ID on this guy. Meanwhile, if he calls again, you need to talk to him, find out what he wants."

"Isn't it obvious?" She raked her fingers through her hair. "He calls on the day the whole town is thinking I'm a criminal."

Tom tilted his head. "Sorry, I don't get what you think he's up to."

"He wants to kill my research. Blackmail me with threats of exposing my family's secrets, at least their version of what they say my father did, while everyone's already convicted me of counterfeiting."

Tom gripped her shoulders. "First of all, what your father did has nothing to do with you. You have nothing to be ashamed of."

"How can I know that? For all our enquiries, the police department involved hasn't so much as produced his arrest record. We don't even know *what* he did, except for what the newspapers said GPC accused him of."

"Let's worry about one thing at a time."

"Which would you suggest?" She flipped over the newspaper that sported Molly's gloating smile. "That Molly will get off scot-free?" She motioned toward the neighboring house. "That poor Mrs. Nagy and I are caught in the middle of some counterfeiting ring? Or that I'm being blackmailed by some guy from my father's past?"

"Kate, you're not alone. Okay?" The warmth of Tom's voice melted a little of the fear icing her veins. "We'll let the courts handle Molly. I'll talk to Herbert at the *Port Aster Press* and ask him to put a stop to any rumors." Tom brushed a strand of hair from her cheek and tucked it behind her ear. He waited until she met his gaze before continuing. "You can keep an eye on Mrs. Nagy. And I'll see what I can dig up on this Peter guy. Okay?"

Kate nodded. *Yes. Verna.* She could help her dear neighbor and ensure neither of them were wrongfully accused. Kate swallowed, but an indefinable fear stayed firmly balled in her throat.

So the straitlaced detective wasn't so straitlaced after all.

Gritting his teeth, the man melted into the shadow of one of the giant oaks lining the sleepy street. The question was, did the detective have ulterior motives?

The man refocused his attention on Kate. He didn't like the nervous way she hugged herself as she watched the detective climb into his car.

The overconfident officer was an unwelcome complication. One that might not be so easily eliminated.

For the second time in the last ten minutes, the curtain shifted at the window of Kate's nosy neighbor's house.

The man slid into his car. This was as good a time as any to gauge the detective's game plan and, if necessary, devise a counterattack.

Now that he'd tracked Katy down, he planned to stick to

her like a burr on wool. And he could be a hundred times more prickly.

Kate Adams was a magnet for trouble.

Tom drew in a deep breath before pushing through the door of A Cup or Two. The local coffee and tea shop, and hub of town gossip, was *not* where he wanted to set straight the editor of the *Port Aster Press* on Kate's connection to a supposed counterfeiting ring in their community. But their resident newshound had beelined here the minute he'd heard the news. To get "community reaction," his secretary had said.

Sure enough, Tom found Herbert Harold III, owner, editor, and sole reporter of their local rag, in the center of a beehive of buzzing eyewitness wannabes. The man had already worn his pencil to a nub.

The last thing Kate needed was more unsubstantiated rumors. Tom had caused enough of those by hauling her into the police station during the investigation into her friend's death. That move had almost cost her the funding for her research. It was a wonder she still talked to him.

Tom nodded to Beth, the very pregnant owner behind the cash register—a friend of Kate's who was clearly flustered by the fuss—then strode toward the group crowded around a table and tapped Herbert's shoulder.

"I'd like to go on record," Tom announced.

The onlookers gasped.

Herbert spun around, his look of surprise instantly transforming to pleasure. He poised his pencil over his pad. "Yes, yes. Go ahead."

"Several of our residents have been victims of an unknown counterfeiter and may have inadvertently passed phony bills on to others. The police are asking anyone with information, or anyone who has received suspicious bills, to please contact us."

A round-faced woman he didn't recognize spoke up. "I heard Kate Adams tried to pass a phony hundred at the grocery store."

"And you are?"

The woman shrank back.

Typical. "The fact is, Miss Adams attempted to pay for a small amount of groceries with several *ten*-dollar bills. We investigated and are convinced that she too was a victim of this counterfeiter."

A flat-nosed soldier-type snorted. "Probably helps that she's dating a cop."

Yeah, I wish. Tom clenched his teeth and managed to refrain from glaring at the guy.

"Nonsense," blurted Mrs. C, the one woman present who could silence the crowd with a single word, having taught grade school to the majority of them in her forty-year career. If only she could convince Kate such talk was nonsense. Then maybe she *would* date him. "I'm the treasurer for the Women's Missionary Circle at my church. Even we've had a couple of phony bills in our donation basket in the last month or so."

"Doesn't Adams go to your church?" the cynic countered.

"She does, but not the mission meetings. They're during the day, when she's working."

But Verna Nagy attended those meetings. Tom bit back the urge to confirm as much in front of everyone. His more immediate concern was why the guy with the brush cut had it in

34

for Kate. His whiny voice didn't match the rasp of her caller, but Tom didn't recognize him from church either.

His stomach pinched. So how'd the guy know Kate attended church, or that they might be dating?

Tom scanned the rest of the shop and noted a vaguely familiar farmer-type guy—plaid shirt, leathered face, diesel-stained fingers—reading a paper by the stone fireplace in the corner. When their eyes met, the man immediately raised his newspaper, hiding his face from view.

Tom's internal radar spiked. The guy didn't fit Kate's businessman description of the caller, but he wasn't a regular either. Tom moved to the counter. "You know the guy in the corner by the fireplace?" he whispered to the owner.

Beth glanced briefly at the man. "He's been in here a few times. Drinks his coffee black and likes my blueberry muffins."

"A fairly new customer then?"

"He's been around a few weeks, maybe more."

Tom discreetly hitched his thumb toward the cynic. "What about the other guy?"

"Vic Lawton? He's harmless. His wife took the receptionist job at the newspaper when he lost his. I think seeing her boss here got him kind of riled." Beth shrugged. "You know how hard it can be on a guy's ego when his wife makes the money."

Yeah, but Tom didn't appreciate Vic taking out his frustration by badmouthing Kate. "One more thing. Has anyone tried passing off phony bills in here?"

"Not that I've noticed. Thank goodness!"

A Latina woman approached the counter. "Mr. Nagy sent me to pick up Verna's special tea. He said you'd have it ready."

At the mention of the Nagys, Tom gave the petite woman a discreet once over. She wore a pale blue, uniform-style dress and carried a fabric shopping bag. Her dark hair was pinned into a bun that made her look older than the faint lines on her face would suggest.

Beth leaned down and retrieved a small paper bag from beneath the counter. "Right here. That'll be four dollars."

As the woman pulled out a bill, she nervously glanced his way. "Oh, wait." She stuffed the ten back in her purse and laid a five on the counter instead.

Coincidence? Or had she been about to pay for her package with a phony ten-dollar bill?

She grabbed the bag and hurried out. The plaid-shirt guy left right behind her.

Beth's chuckle drew Tom's attention back to the counter. "What?"

Beth pointed to his weapon, visible beneath his open sport coat. "I think you scared her."

Yeah, he'd noticed. He fastened his button.

"Where she comes from, the police can't be trusted any more than the criminals. Maybe less."

"Who is she?" And why was that guy following her?

"Lucetta. She's Verna Nagy's housekeeper."

Tom's interest piqued even more at the direct connection to Kate's neighbor. "And she does Verna's shopping?" He angled his body to keep Lucetta and plaid guy in view through the large front windows.

"Verna's son usually picks up the tea blend."

"What's in it?"

Her gaze darted to the crowd still hovering around the newspaper editor. "I probably shouldn't say."

Tom didn't like the way she hesitated. "It's important."

She leaned over the counter and lowered her voice. "It has

herbs that enhance mental acuity. Brian's concerned his mother's succumbing to dementia."

Huh. Nagy's efforts to help his mother were impressive.

Lucetta entered the shop across the street.

"I've got to go." Given the woman's change of heart on paying with a ten-dollar bill, Tom wasn't ready to let her out of his sight.

Outside, Tom squinted under the late afternoon sun, looking for plaid guy. Keeping the door Lucetta went through in his peripheral, Tom glanced in the neighboring stores and down side streets, but the guy had disappeared.

Tom's cell phone beeped. He checked caller ID. *The chief.*

Letting out a groan, Tom leaned against a nearby lamppost to wait for Lucetta and hit the Talk button. "Yeah."

"You got any leads?"

"A few."

"And?"

"And I'll let you know if any of them pan out."

"*If?*" The distinct sound of a desktop being slapped punctuated the question. "The mayor is breathing down my neck on this. Bad press could change GPC's mind about expanding to Port Aster."

"More likely he's worried about jinxing the healthy raise he's counting on if the town doubles its tax base."

Lucetta exited the specialty shop and, with a furtive glance over her shoulder, hurried down the sidewalk away from him.

"I gotta go," he said, cutting off whatever the chief had been saying, and trailed her at an inconspicuous distance.

"Don't let that woman affect your judgment again. We can't afford any insinuation she's getting special treatment from the police."

"Understood." Tom disconnected before he said something he'd regret. One date. *One!* That could hardly be construed as special treatment. But it was too easy to treat Hank like his former school chum instead of his boss. A boss who could crush his career like a coffee cup.

His cell phone rang again—the bell drop ringtone reserved for his sister. "Tess, I'm kind of busy." He jogged across the street to catch up to Lucetta. "What's up?"

"I heard about Kate's run-in with the law."

"Why am I not surprised?"

Lucetta stopped to examine a rack of blouses outside a dress shop.

Phone pressed to his ear, Tom stepped to the edge of the sidewalk as if the call required his full attention.

"Yeah, I guess the Franklin sisters figured I should know what kind of woman my brother's been seen fraternizing with," Tess teased.

He groaned. "I trust you set them straight." To the old spinsters, Tom and Kate sitting together in church a few Sundays in a row no doubt meant they were practically engaged.

She laughed. "About the fraternizing? Or Kate's trustworthiness?"

"Tess, I don't have time for this. Is there a point to your call?"

A beat-up pickup pulled to the curb, blocking his view of Lucetta.

"Yes. After the Franklin sisters left, I did an inventory of the bills in my cash register and found a phony ten-dollar bill."

Tom pulled a notebook and pen from his pocket as he maneuvered to get a view of Lucetta. "Any idea which customer paid with it?"

"Yes, sort of. He didn't pay exactly. A teenage boy, Pedro,

brought in his aunt's antique tea set. He said she was interested in selling it and wanted to know what I'd pay."

"Weren't you suspicious that the set might be stolen?"

"Sure. He gave me her number to confirm. Which"—she continued before Tom could point out that the boy could have given her an accomplice's phone number—"I did a reverse look up on, on the pretense of looking up the item on the computer in my office. The number belonged to her landlady, who also happens to be a friend of mine. She confirmed Pedro's story, so I made him an offer."

"You paid *him*. So how'd you wind up with phony cash?"

"I didn't have the exact amount. I gave him three twenties, and he gave me a ten-dollar bill as change."

"How can you be sure that the bill in your register came from the kid?"

"That was the only cash transaction I'd done in the last couple of days, and the bill was on top of the pile."

Lucetta climbed into the pickup.

Tom quickly jotted down the license plate number, then, phone still to his ear, jogged the block back toward his car. "I don't suppose you happened to catch the boy's last name?"

"No, but his aunt's name is Lucetta."

Tom came to an abrupt halt.

"I remember her name because it's so pretty. Don't you think?"

Tom squinted at the pickup pulling away from the curb and the teen behind the wheel. "Was the kid Latino?"

"I assumed Mexican, but yeah, from somewhere in South or Central America would be my guess."

"And this happened today?"

"Yesterday afternoon."

Tom unlocked his car and tossed his notepad onto the passenger seat. "Thanks, Tess, you've been a big help." A note flapped against his windshield, anchored under his wiper.

He snatched it up and slid behind the wheel. He skimmed the words:

Are you reading your Bible? "The accomplice of a thief is his own enemy; he is put under oath and dare not testify." You can't protect her forever.

Tom's gaze shot to the street, the sidewalks, store windows. No one appeared to be watching him. The pickup had disappeared. Tom headed straight for Kate's, his mind racing. What did this guy want? Did he intend to hurt her? Tom caught sight of the pickup turning the opposite direction. *Forget it.* There'd be time enough to follow up on Verna's housekeeper and her supposed nephew later.

Five minutes later, he rapped on Kate's door.

She didn't answer.

But her car was in the driveway. She couldn't be far. With the way rumors were flying, maybe she didn't want to face anyone. Or maybe she was working out back in the garden.

He rounded the side of the house. The backyard was empty, but the patio door sat halfway open. Inside, the kettle whistled.

He jogged to the door, expecting to find her grabbing the kettle. "Kate?" he called through the opening.

No answer.

He stepped into the kitchen and snapped off the stove. Again he called. But still no answer.

No sound at all beyond the hammering in his chest.

3

You can't protect her forever. The words roared through Tom's head as he raced from bathroom to bedrooms to basement in search of Kate. Bracing himself in the center of the basement, he sucked in a calming breath and slowly turned, scanning every detail, doing his best to think like an objective cop. To stay detached.

It wasn't working.

He pounded up the basement stairs. *Her cell phone.* He pulled out his own and dialed her number. *Please, Lord, let her pick up.*

A ring sounded from the living room. *Argh! Why can't anything be easy with this woman?*

He found her cell phone on an end table being charged.

He returned to the kitchen. "She probably popped over to one of the neighbors," he said aloud, as if hearing it might make him believe it. Only . . . Kate wouldn't have left the kettle on the stove and the door gaped open.

He willed his heart to slow, forced himself to focus on the clues to where she might be.

An herb jar sat open on the counter next to a teacup and half-filled tea ball. From that position, Kate would've been able to see out the kitchen window. If she saw someone coming, she might have made a run for it.

Tom slipped out the patio door and scanned the neighboring yards.

Mrs. C waved to him from her garden.

He jogged over to the white picket fence separating the yards. "Have you seen Kate?"

Mrs. C tipped back her floppy hat. "Verna's grandson hollered for her as I pulled up."

Tom's fingers bit into the fence board. If Verna's grandson was connected to the counterfeiting, fear of being found out might make him do something *really* stupid. "Did you see which way they went?"

"No, I'd just gotten back from town and was head—"

Tom cut her off with a terse "Thanks" and headed for Verna's house. Peering through the side window, he debated the wisdom of knocking. He spotted Kate helping the older woman to a chair. No sign of distress.

But no sign of the teen either.

Tom tapped on the window. When Kate turned at the sound with nothing more than curiosity in her gaze, he took his first full breath since finding her house abandoned. He pointed to the front door.

A moment later Kate pushed it open. "Tom? What are you doing back here?"

You can't protect her forever. His adrenaline resurged. "You left a kettle screaming on your stove and your door standing open. I thought—" He pressed his lips into a grim line. She didn't need to know what he thought.

"Oh." Her cheeks flushed. "I rushed over here so quickly I—"

"Why?" He peered over her shoulder into the house. "What's going on?" The question came out more tersely than he'd intended.

Kate shifted as if she might block his entrance. "Why are you here, Tom? Verna's not in any condition to answer more questions right now."

Great, now he had her worried he was after Verna. "There's been another counterfeiting incident," he improvised. No reason to upset her with the note. "I need to talk to her."

Kate wavered a moment, then stepped aside. She lowered her voice as he joined her in the entranceway. "I'm not sure how much help she'll be. She's acting odd. Her grandson was here and didn't know what to do, so he asked for my help."

"How do you mean, odd?"

"Kind of giddy. Euphoric even."

"That's a bad thing? Maybe she'd just heard from an old friend."

"No, Tom. She's not just happy. She's seeing 'pretty' colors. Is surprised I can't see them."

He moved toward the living room where Verna sat smiling inanely at the air three feet below the ceiling. "It sounds like we need to get her to a doctor."

Kate halted him with a hand to his chest. "But if he sends her to the hospital, her son will use the incident as an excuse to have her removed from her home."

Tom covered Kate's hand still resting against his chest. "Kate, you *do not* want to come between this woman and her family." Especially when the woman's family might be counterfeiters.

Kate slipped her hand from beneath his and fussed with her necklace. "She doesn't seem to be in any physical distress."

"Yet." Tom steered Kate toward the kitchen to avoid being seen by Verna for a while longer. The room was bright and cheerful with white cupboards and two sunny windows, the exact opposite of his current mood. He needed to interview Verna about the tea set sold to his sister, to make sure ten-dollar bills weren't the only counterfeits being passed off at Verna's expense, but he didn't like the coincidental timing of this sudden downturn. "Have you checked her prescriptions for potential interactions, maybe with some of those herbal teas she likes so much?"

"I checked the kitchen cupboards, her bedside table, the bathroom cabinet. She doesn't seem to have any prescriptions. Her grandson said he'd never seen her take any meds."

Tom gave the room a cursory glance. "Where is he?"

"I told him I'd stay with his grandmother until I was sure she's okay."

"So he just left?"

"He's a kid. He was freaked."

Tom took a closer look at a plant on the kitchen windowsill. Beside it sat a dish with partially dried leaves. "What are these?"

"Catnip."

"Do you think she drinks catnip tea? That would explain her odd behavior."

"Actually, it doesn't affect people the same way as cats. Besides, I think she uses it as a hair rinse, not a tea."

"A hair rinse?" He couldn't help the you're-kidding-me tone that crept into his voice.

"Don't laugh. It works really well."

"I'll take your word for it." He tapped the canisters lining the counter. "What about these teas? Her housekeeper was just in A Cup or Two buying a special mix for her."

44

"I don't know about that, but none of what's here would explain the change either."

Tom shook his head. "I don't like it. For all we know, she could have a tumor pushing on her brain."

"I know, but . . ." Kate bit her lower lip. "She is so afraid her son will put her in a home."

"It might be for the best. She'd be safe from whoever's preying on her declining faculties."

"So you finally believe me that she wasn't faking about not knowing where the money came from?"

He shoved his hand in his pocket, feeling the paper he'd stuffed inside. Finding that note on his car had turned his priorities on their ear. "I don't know yet."

Kate's concerned gaze darted to the living room where Verna was now humming a ditty. "But you just said—?"

"Just because someone is taking advantage of her doesn't mean she's unaware of it. Does Verna have an antique tea set?"

"What does that have to do with anything?"

"A teenage boy sold one to my sister yesterday. Gave her a phony bill as change."

"You think it was Verna's set?" Kate skirted past him into the dining room and stopped in front of a curio cabinet. "It's gone."

Now he was getting somewhere. And if Verna didn't give her housekeeper permission to sell the tea set, he could add theft to the counterfeit charges. He met Kate's reflected gaze in the mirror behind the empty shelf. Her anguished expression said she didn't share his enthusiasm for the break in the case. "I'm sorry."

She let out a sigh that seemed to drain the last of her fight. "I can't believe Verna's grandson would do this to her."

"He didn't. A Latino teen named Pedro sold the tea set. Said he was Lucetta's nephew."

Kate gasped.

"I take it you know him . . . and can't believe he'd do such a thing?"

For a long moment, Kate didn't respond. She merely stared at the dust rings in the curio cabinet where the tea set had been. "Actually . . . that kid has always made me a bit uneasy."

The hair on the back of Tom's neck prickled to attention. "Uneasy how?"

"I don't know." The way Kate hugged her middle, as if guarding against whatever the kid might do, tripled Tom's unease. "I ran into him when I visited Herbs Are Us after Daisy died. He watched me with this smug look. That's when I figured Daisy got killed because she happened upon a grow-op, so I thought the kid might be involved." Kate unfolded her arms and threw a helpless glance toward the living room. "Now, it's just . . ."

"You don't want to believe Verna's housekeeper would do this to the old gal."

Kate shrugged. "I guess."

"Well, if we're going to get to the bottom of this, I need to ask her what she did with her tea set while she's still halfway lucid." He touched the small of Kate's back and gently prodded her into the room ahead of him.

A car pulled up across the street from Kate's house.

Tom groaned. "Terrific."

"What's wrong?"

He strode to the door. "You have company."

For once Kate was happy to obey Tom's growled "stay put" before he stalked out of Verna's house in full-cop mode. The last person she wanted to face was the *Port Aster Press*'s roving reporter. Following Molly's arrest, it had only been by the grace of God and a hospital security guard's zeal that the last reporter who'd tried to snap an exclusive photo had ended up in the drink along with his cell phone camera. Herbert was no doubt eager to make sure he didn't get scooped on the breaking news of her supposed spiral into crime. And unlike the last guy, Herbert came equipped with a real camera.

He turned from his car and all but collided with Tom, who even from her vantage point looked like an immovable force. Herbert must have gotten the same impression, because after a longing glance toward her house, he climbed back into his car and zoomed away, tires squealing in protest.

She half expected Tom to toss her a satisfied grin and feign brushing the dust off his hands, but he didn't even glance back at Verna's house, let alone return to start his questioning. Instead he scooted down her side yard.

Kate hurried to the kitchen in time to spot him slipping through her patio door.

As much as she trusted Tom, he was still a cop. It was one thing to search her house out of concern for where she'd disappeared to. But to nose around without her permission? What did that lunatic reporter tell him?

She hurried to Verna and knelt in front of her. "Will you be okay alone for a few minutes?" Guilt niggled her. She'd promised Verna's grandson she wouldn't leave. Of course, Verna hadn't seemed the least bit concerned when she left the room to talk with Tom.

"I'm fine, dear," Verna chirped. "No need to stay."

And she did look fine. Her eyes were clear, and the giddy quality had left her voice. Taking advantage of what might be her only opportunity, Kate took Verna's hand. "I couldn't help but notice that your fancy tea set isn't in the curio cabinet." Kate rubbed tiny circles over the woman's gnarled fingers. "Did you give it away?"

Verna patted Kate's hand with her other one. "Did you admire my tea set too? It was my mother's." Her gaze drifted.

"Yes," Kate said softly, hoping to draw her back to the conversation. "It was lovely."

"I gave it to Lucetta. The poor dear came to this country with nothing. I wanted her to have something nice."

"How kind." Considering how unkind Lucetta had been to turn around and sell such a precious gift. "Did she buy it from you?" That might explain how Verna ended up with the counterfeit cash.

"Oh, no. It was a gift. She doesn't have money to spare. She scrapes together all she can each month to send back to her relations."

"I see." Kate released Verna's hand and pushed to her feet. "I need to get home now, but I'll check in on you later, okay?"

"Visit anytime, dear. Anytime."

Kate hurried out the back door and across the yard to her house. She pushed open the kitchen's patio door and froze.

Tom stood in the opposite doorway, his gun aimed at something in her living room.

Her pulse raced.

He spared her an irritated glance. "I told you to stay put."

"What's going on?" she said in a squeaky voice, not daring to move and not entirely sure she'd asked loud enough for him to hear.

"I can explain," a female voice pleaded.

Patti? What was her new research assistant doing in her house?

Kate edged toward Tom, which earned her a glare that would've glued a lesser person to the wall. Patti probably had a perfectly reasonable explanation for being in her house.

"Well, you're in luck," Tom said to her. "Kate just arrived, so you can explain it to the both of us." He jerked his gun sideways. "Take a seat and keep your hands where I can see them. Kate," he said without taking his eyes off his target, "care to join us?"

She peeked around the doorway and startled at the sight of a six-foot *GQ* model taking a seat beside her plain, plump research assistant.

Tom lowered his gun. "Do you know these people?"

"I . . ." She swallowed, pressed a hand to her hammering heart. "I know Patti. She works for me. I'm afraid—"

"This is Jarrett, my boyfriend," Patti blurted. "I've told you about him." The young man waved at her.

Kate nodded at him and stepped into the room. "Yes, you have." She shouldn't be surprised that such a good-looking guy would be interested in Patti. The girl was sweet as pie. Kate drew a deep breath, willing her heart to slow. Of course, she'd have an easier time believing his affection was genuine if Patti hadn't recently inherited a wad of money. "But why are the two of you in my house?"

"I heard about your run-in at the supermarket. I tried calling. I even went to the police station, but they said no arrests were made, so I came here looking for you. Your car was in the driveway, so when you didn't answer the bell, I figured you were around back. You weren't, so I let myself in to leave you a note." She barely stopped long enough to draw a breath, then plunged on. "Once I got inside, I remembered that you

49

forgot to leave the test trial results before you left work, and I'd planned to work on the analysis this weekend. So I poked around your desk to see if I could spot them." She motioned toward Daisy's old rolltop.

Not to Kate's computer desk in the corner.

The thought of Patti poking through Daisy's files sent an uneasy ripple through Kate's chest.

"That's when this guy"—Patti jerked her thumb toward Tom—"showed up and pointed his gun at us."

Kate bristled at the thought of how scared Patti must have been. Not that Kate approved of Patti letting herself in, no matter how well-intentioned.

"Do you want to press charges, Miss Adams?" Tom said, his tone brisk.

Miss Adams? She understood the need to appear to have a professional distance between them, but did he have to sound so abrupt? "No, of course not. I believe her."

Tom holstered his weapon, then pinned his gaze on Patti yet again. "In the future, I suggest you wait for an invitation before entering a house."

Patti's cheeks reddened. "Yes sir."

Jarrett remained quiet throughout the entire exchange. Kate had almost forgotten about him until she noticed that he was staring at Daisy's desk. "Is something the matter?"

"Huh?" Jarrett looked up.

"With the desk?" she said tersely, ignoring the renewed hammering in her chest.

"Oh, no. Just admiring the woodwork. You don't see desks like that any more."

"Jarrett does carpentry in his spare time," Patti jumped in. "He's always noticing stuff like that."

Jarrett slid his arm around Patti's shoulders and gave her an adoring squeeze. Her cheeks bloomed under the attention.

Kate had no idea why else Jarrett would be interested in an old desk, but finding him in her living room uninvited didn't make her want to trust him. She slid a sideways glance at Tom. "I'm afraid I need to cut this visit short. It was nice to meet you, Jarrett. Patti, I'll email you that data this evening."

"Okay, sure. That'd be fine." She and Jarrett stumbled over each other rushing for the front door, as if neither could escape fast enough. "See you Monday."

Okay, now that was weird. Then again, seeing Tom adjust the gun in his holster . . . maybe not.

He locked the door behind them.

"Was the gun really necessary?"

"Finding two prowlers in your house after"—he wiped a hand across his mouth—"after everything that's happened? Yeah, I'd say it was necessary."

"Okay." She exhaled, trying to release the pent-up, freaked-out feeling of finding him pointing a gun at her assistant in her house. "I guess I see your point."

"Does she always talk like a runaway train? 'Cause she sure sounded guilty to me."

Kate chuckled. "She talks like one. And thankfully works like one too. She's helped me make up for a lot of lost time with . . . with everything that's been going on."

Tom nodded, sympathy for her loss radiating from his gaze. "Still . . . didn't you find her compulsion to explain Jarrett's unusual interest in Daisy's desk curious?"

Kate waved off the insinuation and headed back to the kitchen. "That's just Patti. Besides, after the way you held them at gunpoint, I'm sure she felt like she had a lot of explaining to do."

"You're too trusting." Tom's breath whispered across her ear.

Turning abruptly, she found herself with her nose to his chin. She retreated a step. "Being trusting isn't so bad."

"Just surprised me, considering how opposed you are to that pharmaceutical company's move to Port Aster the mayor's been championing. I take it you don't know who Jarrett is?"

She arched a brow and spoke slowly. "He's . . . my research assistant's . . . boy . . . friend."

"And the mayor's son."

"What?"

Tom smirked. "Yeah, kind of figured you didn't know. You want me to arrest them now?"

Kate gasped. "Do you think his father put him up to dating my research assistant to spy on me?"

Tom chuckled. "Didn't take you long to lose that trusting nature."

"Stop it. I'm serious. Do you think he knows I've been quietly trying to change a few board members' minds about agreeing to partner with GPC?"

Tom instantly sobered. "Your research assistant could've mentioned it. The mayor is determined to see GPC's move take place. I wouldn't put anything past him. Can you trust Patti?"

Kate shook her head. "I don't know who I can trust anymore."

Tom clasped her arms and dipped his head until their eyes met. "You can trust *me*."

"Can I?"

4

"Catch me, Uncle Tom. Catch me!"

Tom spun around just in time to see his nephew sail from his tree fort. Tom snatched him from the air, turning to absorb the momentum.

The giggling boy hugged Tom's neck. "I knew you'd catch me!"

The trust gleaming from the boy's eyes made Tom's heart float higher than the helium-filled balloons decorating the yard.

If only Kate shared his nephew's conviction. Maybe he should have told her about the note left on his windshield. Except its implication that she was guilty and he had compromised his integrity by siding with her would've only bolstered her *other* reasons for turning down a second date.

Tom plunked his nephew on the ground and shook off the frustration that had plagued him since leaving Kate's yesterday. This was Timmy and Terry's fourth birthday. No time to wallow. Kate was a suspect in his counterfeit investigation. Why should it matter to him if she trusted him?

Okay, the fact that he'd call her a suspect, when he knew she wasn't, reinforced why she didn't.

The terror in her eyes when she'd walked in on him holding her intruders at gunpoint replayed in his mind, echoed by the note's *You can't protect her forever*. What if next time the threat was real?

He needed her to let him stick close. He *needed* her to trust him.

"Catch me, Uncle Tom!"

He snatched his second nephew from the sky.

"Wow, that was some catch, *Uncle* Tom."

Tom's breath caught at the sound of Kate's voice. The sun glistening off her wavy red locks spilling over her shoulders and her wispy white dress made her look nothing short of angelic.

"Uncle Tom never lets us fall," Terry declared solemnly. "You try it."

Kate met Tom's gaze, amusement dancing in her eyes. "I'll take your word for it."

Tom set his nephew back on his feet, and the boy immediately tore off after his brother. "What are you doing here?"

Kate jerked back at the unintended edge to his question. "Your sister invited me to the party."

He should've guessed. Tess and Kate had become fast friends since he'd first introduced them.

"You can thank me later," Tess chimed in, setting a train-shaped cake on the picnic table. Leave it to his sister to play matchmaker.

Kate's cheeks turned pink. "I'm sorry. I thought you knew." She took a step backward, clutching a pair of brightly wrapped gifts a little tighter. "I can go."

"No." His heart kicked at the vulnerability shimmering in her eyes, knowing he put it there. "I want you to stay. I just . . . You caught me off guard, that's all."

She chuckled, still sounding apprehensive. "From that catch I just saw, looks like you get a lot of practice."

"But you notice I didn't let him fall."

"No." Her voice grew soft. "You didn't."

Tom relieved her of her packages. "I wouldn't let you fall either," he whispered, and her eyes brimmed with a wistfulness that caught at his heart.

His dad chose that moment to burst out the door with a bellowing welcome, but Tom thought he heard a faint "I know" before Kate ducked her head and turned Dad's way.

As Dad introduced Kate to Tess's husband's side of the family, Tom let his nephews tug him into a game of tag. Kate seemed to fit right in, chatting with his sister's relatives as if they were long-lost friends.

"Are you going to answer that?" Timmy asked.

Tom blinked and jerked his attention back to his nephew. "What?"

Timmy pointed to Tom's hip. "Your phone."

Tom swiveled 180 degrees to gain a measure of privacy and held the phone to his ear. "Detective Parker."

Dispatch filled him in on the latest piece in their counterfeit puzzle.

"I'm on my way." He pocketed his phone and pulled Tess aside. "I'm sorry. I've got to go."

"What about Kate?"

Tom checked the urge to say, "She's *your* guest." Truth be told, he appreciated his sister's little matchmaking scheme . . . this time. "Tell her I'll be back as soon as I can." She'd be safer here too, where their retired police officer father could keep an eye on her.

Six minutes later Tom pulled up to the front of Henry's

Hardware Store on Main Street. A yeasty aroma wafted from the bakery across the road. His stomach grumbled over missing lunch. Unfortunately, his stomach would have to wait a little longer. He pushed through the door of the hardware store and was greeted instead by the unappetizing smell of rubber.

Behind the counter, Julie Crantz—Kate's newlywed former roommate—hung up the phone. "That was fast!"

"I didn't expect to find you here. That new husband of yours got you working in the family store instead of the library now?"

"I'm just filling in while they're off at some hardware exhibition. He promised me I'd have no trouble."

Tom chuckled. "Famous last words. Show me what you found."

Julie pulled a twenty-dollar bill from the front of the cash register drawer and laid it on the counter. "I have no idea who gave it to me."

Tom snapped on a pair of latex gloves and held the bill to the light. *Yup, counterfeit.*

"How's Kate holding up with all of this counterfeit business?" Julie asked.

"Understandably upset," he said without glancing up.

"I'm sure she appreciates that you took the call and not some officer she didn't know, someone who wouldn't have been so quick to believe her innocence."

Yeah, she had seemed happy to see him at the time. Too bad her faith in him hadn't lasted. Or maybe it had. His thoughts skittered to Kate's whispered "I know" and the wistful look that had gripped a place deep inside him and wouldn't let go.

He cleared his throat. "When did you notice this was counterfeit?"

"One of my customers did when I gave it to her as change."

"I guess everyone's on the lookout for them since yesterday's incident hit the grapevine." Tom glanced around the empty store. "Any chance you can tell me who made cash purchases today?"

Julie blew a wayward strand of hair from her eyes. "You're kidding, right? Saturday is our busiest day. This is the first time we've had a lull."

"All regulars?"

"No, there were two or three customers that I didn't recognize, but no one who looked suspicious."

So much for the new lead. He noticed a camera mounted on the wall behind the counter. "Does that work?"

Julie tracked the direction he pointed. "Yes! I can't believe I didn't think of it." She beckoned him into a narrow cubby and turned on a monitor. "Here we go."

The camera had a bird's-eye view that spanned from the front window and door to the cash register and counter. Julie hit Rewind and images of customers skittered backward across the screen. She hit Pause and pointed to the screen. "There. That's the woman who alerted me to the counterfeit." Julie rewound further. "We probably should upgrade to a digital system. These tapes—"

"Stop there," Tom ordered. The black-and-white image was grainy, but there was no mistaking Brian Nagy, Verna's son. Tom hit the Play button and watched the man place some plumbing couplers on the counter and then pull out a bill. He couldn't make out the denomination. "Did Brian seem nervous to you?"

Julie squinted at the screen. "Not that I noticed."

Tom tapped the Rewind button again and watched as the morning's customers sped backward through their buying. At the sight of an unfamiliar businessman, he hit Pause and tapped the screen. "Do you recognize him?"

"Um . . . yeah, he looks familiar. Oh, I remember. I met him in A Cup or Two a while back. I remember because he knew Kate's mom and commented on their resemblance."

The guy on the phone. "Peter?"

"Yeah, that's right."

Tom squinted at the screen. Could Kate's caller be the counterfeiter? But if he wanted to blackmail her as she supposed, dropping a phony twenty in the hardware store wouldn't incriminate her. Still, Tom didn't believe in coincidences. He forwarded the video a few frames and hit Pause again. He could just make out the form of someone in a plaid shirt and ball cap outside the window behind Peter. The shirt reminded him of the stranger who'd disappeared from the coffee shop yesterday. The guy would have been standing by the barrels where the old-timers played checkers. But his head wasn't tilted down to watch a game. He seemed to be watching Peter inside the store. A lookout? Or a spy?

The vice-like grip on Tom's chest twisted tighter. It was bad enough this Peter guy was likely the person who'd left cryptic messages on Kate's answering machine. What was he supposed to make of some stranger lurking around town spying on Peter?

The tinkle of the store's bell over the door tugged Tom's attention from the screen.

Kate rushed toward them, her expression growing brighter as her eyes lit on the screen in front of them. "Did you get the counterfeiter on video?"

"What are you doing here?" Tom demanded.

Julie greeted Kate with a hug. "I called her as soon as I got off the phone with dispatch."

He should have known.

"What have you found?" Kate asked.

Tom's thumb hovered over the Fast-Forward button. The last thing he wanted to do was fuel Kate's fear, but he needed to know if she recognized the second guy.

Before he had a chance to decide how much to reveal, Julie blurted, "So far it could be Brian Nagy—I've heard he's a bit of a gambler."

"Really?" Kate shot him an overeager, sounds-like-our-man look. "Or?"

"Or that Peter guy who knew your mother. You remember him?"

Kate's face went chalky white, her gaze clinging to Tom's. "He was here?"

Julie's attention bobbed from Kate to him. "What's going on?"

"Nothing you need to worry about." He could worry enough for all of them. Her supervisor had confirmed last night that a Peter Ratcher was one of their GPC liaisons, and that he was back in town. Tom didn't believe in coincidences, and the fact that this Peter was here a day after Kate got that anonymous call was too coincidental.

Apparently Tom failed to disguise his concern, because the curiosity in Julie's eyes turned to alarm. "Kate?"

"I had another cryptic message on my machine," she admitted softly. "We think it might have been Peter."

Julie threw her arms around her friend all over again. "I'm so sorry. You should have told me. What can I do?"

"Let us know immediately if he returns." Tom waited for Julie to release Kate and then motioned to the tape player. "And I'll need a copy of this tape."

"Just take it. I'll throw in a new one."

Before hitting Eject, Tom tapped the screen at the guy in

the ball cap standing outside the window. "Do either of you recognize this guy?"

Both women shook their heads. "He looks familiar, probably a farmer I've seen around town," Kate ventured. "Why?"

"He seemed to be monitoring Peter's movements. I thought he might be able to tell us something." In light of this potential connection between a GPC employee and the counterfeiting, the presence of the mayor's son in Kate's house yesterday looked even more suspicious. Mayor Shephard King had made no secret of how determined he was to attract GPC to their community.

Tom had to admit that up until now, he'd dismissed Kate's concerns about GPC Pharmaceuticals as the overactive imagination of a daughter who blamed the company for her father's death. Now . . . he wasn't so sure.

Kate edged her cuff off her watch and glanced surreptitiously at the time as Tom's nephews oohed and ahhed over a thousand-piece Lego set. There were only three gifts left and still no sign of Tom. She never should have agreed to come back to the party while he tracked down Julie's customers.

Hearing that Peter had been one of them had unnerved her a little. The guy knew her darkest secret and had somehow found her unlisted number—probably by sweet-talking it out of one of her co-workers. Who wouldn't be worried?

Being accused of counterfeiting had already dredged up too many uncomfortable feelings.

Laughter broke out among Tom's relatives gathered around the twins in a circle of lawn chairs. Kate propped up her smile and tried to focus on the rambunctious pair tearing into another gift. She couldn't think of a single good reason why Peter would want to talk to her, but there were plenty of bad ones, starting with blackmail.

If there was one thing Mom had drilled into her, it was to never talk about Dad or mention their former last name. Kate instinctively smoothed the skirt of her dress, ensuring the proper impression she'd been programmed to project. But if Dad hadn't done anything wrong, as Mom had always insisted, why should they hide? Why hadn't they challenged the police department's treatment of her father?

If Peter knew Dad, maybe he knew what really happened. Her heart somersaulted at the thought. Just when she'd finally scrounged up the courage to search out the answer, she'd avoided the one person who might have it.

She sprang to her feet.

Tess caught her arm. "What's wrong?"

"I'm sorry. I have to go. I just remembered somewhere I need to be." If Peter tried to contact her again, it would be at her home. And this time she wanted to be there.

"But . . ." Tess's gaze trailed to her father before veering back to Kate. "Tom didn't want you to go home alone."

"That's because I was upset, but I'm fine now." Kate gave her a hug. "Thanks so much for inviting me. It's been fun."

Tess wavered. "You're sure you're okay?"

"I'm fine."

Ten minutes later, as Kate pulled her yellow Bug into Daisy's driveway—her driveway now—a smidge of that confidence slipped. She glanced around the neighborhood and her stomach flip-flopped. *Get over it already. It's not as if you're ten years old anymore and going to shatter over being called names. What is there really to be afraid of?*

Even if Peter threatened to expose her secret, would it really be that bad?

The image of Mom's haunted expression flared before Kate's eyes as her "no one can ever know" whispered through her mind. Kate shook the voice from her head and snatched her keys from the ignition. *Know what?* That's what she wanted to know. She'd kept her head down for too long already.

Brian Nagy's red sports car sat in Verna's driveway next door.

Kate hitched her purse up her shoulder, digging her fingers into the strap. The pleasant August afternoon suddenly felt a little too sticky. Brian never came by two days in a row. Something must be wrong with Verna again. He might need help. Kate strode toward Verna's house.

At the property edge her step faltered. What if Brian was there to get rid of evidence?

She should call Tom. He was probably looking for Brian right now to question him about his visit to the hardware store. Kate turned back and dug her phone from her purse. Except . . .

What if Brian *was* here because Verna had taken another bad turn? Tom showing up again would only upset her more.

Phone in hand, Kate eyeballed Verna's front door. She could pop over on the pretense of checking on Verna like any good neighbor would. If she happened to notice Brian up to no good, then she could call Tom. She zipped her phone in her purse and strode to Verna's door before she could change her mind a second time.

"Come in," Verna called at Kate's knock, sounding as chipper as ever.

Kate's heart thumped an erratic beat. Where was Brian? She let herself in, cocking an ear toward the basement for any telltale sounds. She might be able to warn Tom before Brian even knew she was here.

Verna was pushing herself up from her recliner as Kate poked her head into the living room.

"Oh, it's you, dear." Verna relaxed her arms and let herself drop back into the chair.

"How are you feeling today?" Kate hovered at the doorway where she could keep both the basement stairs and the hallway leading to the bedrooms in view. A spicy aroma hung in the air. Verna must've been baking.

The woman made a so-so gesture. "Water's giving me trouble."

"Water?"

Brian suddenly materialized in the hallway, a monkey wrench in hand, undisguised irritation creasing his face. "Oh, it's you." The lines slashing his brow rearranged themselves into a semblance of . . . gratitude? "I want to thank you. My son told me how you settled Mother down yesterday during one of her episodes."

"Episodes? This has happened before?"

"Unfortunately." He bent down and pulled a P-trap from a small paper bag. That must've been what Verna had meant about her water and what Brian had been at the hardware store to buy. "But don't worry, she's signed a power of attorney granting me the right to act on her behalf. I'm going to make sure she gets the help she needs, whether she wants it or not."

Behind Kate, Verna let out a soft humph.

Kate's heart ached at the thought of Verna being put into a home, but after yesterday, she had to agree that the dear needed some kind of help. "I imagine that'll take some time."

Brian lowered his voice. "She's been on the waiting list for a while. But between the counterfeit money swindle and now this, they can't help but see how necessary it's become."

At the mention of the counterfeit money, Kate's thoughts whirled back to her earlier suspicions. Was Brian overreacting to Verna's "episode" to divert suspicion from the family? Was he the one running a counterfeit operation and using his mother as a front? "What if she still refuses to go?"

"I'd have to apply for guardianship. I was hoping I could count on you to testify to her need for care . . . if I have a problem, I mean."

"Oh, I don't think I . . ." Wringing her hands, Kate glanced into the front room where Verna still sat. "I couldn't do that to her."

Brian stepped closer, the monkey wrench still clutched in his hand. "But now that you've seen how she gets, how can you not?" His knuckles whitened, and he seemed to be straining to keep his voice even. "She's not safe. I only want what's best for her."

"I'm sure you do." Kate backed up a step and shifted from one foot to the other. His concern seemed genuine, but that didn't stop her insides from zigzagging up and down like a roller coaster. "I'm sorry. I don't feel comfortable doing that. I'd feel like I was betraying our friendship."

"You've only lived here a few weeks," he argued.

"Exactly. So who am I to comment on her condition?" She wiped the ridiculous sweat from her palm on the side of her purse. "Couldn't you hire someone to live in?"

"I have. Lucetta agreed to stay with Mom until a room opens up at the home in town."

Kate swallowed her gasp, but not soon enough.

"What's wrong?"

"Um . . . Nothing, except . . . It's just . . . I was thinking more of someone trained as a caregiver." Lucetta had already sold the tea set. Kate cringed to think what other ways she might take advantage of Verna's generosity. "I'm sure they'll get along okay." Kate bit her lip. If Verna were her mother, she'd want to know what Lucetta had done, but "loose lips sink ships," as her grandmother used to say, and between the birthday party and the excursion to the hardware store, she hadn't gotten the chance to ask Tom if he'd questioned Lucetta yet. "She'll stay at the house?"

"Yes, aside from trips to the store and such, she'll be around all the time." He motioned toward the hall. "She's in making up the spare room for herself now."

Outside a car door slammed.

Brian glanced out the screen door. "Isn't that the police officer who was here yesterday? What's he want?" Brian shoved open the door and stepped onto the porch, his monkey wrench still gripped in a stranglehold.

Kate watched from inside the screen door. Tom acknowledged her with a stiff nod, clearly not happy to see her there.

"Afternoon," he said to Brian. "I need to ask you a few questions. May I come in?"

"What's this about?" Brian's tone grew unmistakably defensive.

Tom shot a pointed look at a curious neighbor watching the exchange from across the street. "Do you really want to talk out here?"

Brian jerked open the screen door. "Come in."

A woman's yelp, accompanied by the splash of water, broke the strained tension.

Brian stormed down the hall in a rant. Judging from the colorful Spanish words countering Brian's, Lucetta must've turned on a tap she shouldn't have.

Tom's fingers circled Kate's arm. "I need you to go home."

"But—"

"This is a police matter."

She closed her mouth, more hurt than shocked that he'd exclude her now.

"You have to live beside these people. I don't want to risk your presence affecting their attitude toward you. Okay?"

His genuine concern brought to mind his whispered promise at the birthday party—*I wouldn't let you fall*—and a smile tugged at the corners of her mouth. "You're right, of course."

But Lucetta appeared in the entranceway before she had a chance to escape. "Mr. Nagy say to make yourselves comfortable in the living room with Mrs. Nagy. He be back in a minute." She swiped at her damp pants with a hand towel as she turned away.

"Wait a minute." Tom introduced himself as Detective Parker. "Actually, I'd like to ask you a few questions if you have a moment."

The woman's gaze darted to the living room and back to them. "Me?"

"Excuse me." Kate moved past Lucetta and into the living room to give them some privacy. Well . . . to let them think she was giving them privacy. Verna had fallen asleep in her recliner, and since Brian was apparently fixing a water pipe, Kate hovered near the door where she could eavesdrop on the interrogation.

To her surprise, Tom started by asking Lucetta about Verna. "Has she started any new medication that might explain the change in behavior?"

"No, señor, but Mr. Nagy, he's worried she's losing her memory."

"I believe I saw you purchase a tea yesterday afternoon that is supposed to help with that. Has it?"

"Not so I've noticed. But I hope so soon. I don't want her to go away." Lucetta twisted the strings of her apron. "I need the work."

Kate couldn't see Tom from her vantage point, but she could imagine him nodding in that encouraging way he had that was so effective at drawing people out.

"I understand Mrs. Nagy gave you her tea set?" Tom said in a conciliatory tone.

"Yes." Lucetta's response was so soft, Kate scarcely heard it.

Tom didn't ask another question, and his silence seemed to make Lucetta even more nervous.

After a long moment, she added, "I didn't ask for it. I admired it, and she said I could have." Lucetta didn't lift her gaze from the floor.

"You admired it so much you had your nephew sell it?" Tom asked.

That drew Lucetta's gaze up. Her cheeks reddened. "You don't understand, señor. Where I come from, my people are very poor. Each month I send as much money to my brothers and sisters as I can."

"Have you sold anything else of Mrs. Nagy's?" Tom asked.

Lucetta hung her head. "Nothing. Please don't tell her I sold. I need this job."

"Your nephew made change on the payment with a counterfeit bill. Do you know how he might have gotten it?"

Lucetta's face paled. "No, señor. I don't."

Kate couldn't see her eyes, but her voice sounded frightened. Was she covering up for her nephew, herself, or—Brian stormed down the hall—maybe her boss?

5

The sun had just dipped behind the houses as Tom pulled out of the Nagy driveway half an hour after Kate excused herself from her neighbor's home. When he didn't pull into her place, she dialed his cell phone.

"You're leaving?" Kate let her disappointment sound in her voice.

"I got the impression you wouldn't want to see me."

She fell into the sound of his warm chuckle, but his brake lights didn't tap on. When it became clear he wasn't turning around, she let the curtain fall back into place. "I *wanted* to know if my neighbor's son or housekeeper is guilty of counterfeiting."

"That makes two of us. But I honestly don't know."

"You must have a suspicion."

"Brian claims he supplies his mother with eight fifty-dollar bills from her pension check at the start of each month. She could have gotten the smaller bills as change from anyone from the paperboy to the grocery clerk." He sighed, sounding utterly drained. "Lock your door and get some rest. I have some apologizing to do to my nephews for bailing on their party. We'll talk after church tomorrow."

"Wait. Did you talk to Peter?"

"I haven't tracked him down yet. But don't worry, I'll let you know when I do."

At the sound of a car pulling to the curb outside her house, she smiled and swept back the curtains. A silver Ford Escort parked in front of her neighbor's house across the street.

Tamping down her silly disappointment that it wasn't Tom, she grabbed the phone book. She could do better than wait for Tom to find Peter. She'd call every hotel in the Niagara region if need be. She was through waiting for another one of Peter's creepy calls. She'd find out what he knew once and for all.

❧

Tom slipped past the ushers at the back of the church and scanned the pews. Half the people sat quietly listening to the pianist playing a medley of praise songs. The others were hugging and visiting and still finding their way to seats. His sister and her husband had taken their overactive twins to the balcony, while Dad sat up front with Lorna for the third week in a row. As weird as seeing his dad sitting with someone else less than a year since Mom's death felt, Tom was happy to see him embracing life again.

The worship team assembled on stage, and the congregants still standing hustled to their seats. But there was no sign of Kate. Tom scanned every row again. It wasn't like her to be late.

Verna Nagy, flanked by her son and grandson, ambled down the center aisle pushing a walker. Not a sight he'd expected.

He hadn't been able to confirm Julie's aspersion about Brian's gambling debts, but apparently his ex-wife had cleaned him out. He'd gone from living in a nice bungalow to crashing in a dinky apartment on the outskirts of town. And his colorful description of his former bride would draw lightning bolts if repeated in church. Yet when Tom asked Nagy about his purchase at the hardware store, he hadn't betrayed a hint of guilt.

If he was the one who passed the bum bill, Lucetta or her nephew had most likely stuck him with it. Tom had confirmed her story about her poor relatives, which was all the more motive for *making* extra money by any means she could, including laundering counterfeit cash.

Since she occasionally picked up Verna's groceries, she could've easily slipped Verna counterfeit bills as change and kept the real change for herself. Then Verna could have inadvertently turned around and given those bills to the ladies' missionary circle or to Kate. Mrs. C had been reluctant to tell him who might have donated the counterfeit bills she'd found in the donation bucket, but she confirmed that Verna, along with a dozen other ladies, made regular contributions.

Since Lucetta got edgy when he mentioned her nephew, Tom suspected one or both of them were behind the scam. Either that or she was terrified of being deported.

Her nephew wasn't at the address she'd given him. Probably out with friends, she'd said. Didn't matter. He knew where to find the kid Monday morning. If the kid didn't show up for work, chances were his aunt had warned him to lie low.

And Tom could make short work of wrapping up this case.

Lyrics appeared on the screen behind the platform, and a couple of guitars, a keyboard, and a bass guitar joined the piano. Tom edged past the latecomers and checked the foyer for Kate, then the parking lot. He hadn't managed to track down Peter, even with the grainy image he'd lifted from the hardware store's surveillance video. What if he'd found Kate?

The possibility sent Tom striding toward his car, his heart in his throat.

Ten minutes later he swerved into her driveway. The curtains were drawn, the neighborhood quiet. Her yellow VW Bug didn't appear to have been moved since yesterday. But it wasn't like Kate to skip church. Unless . . .

Had she been worried that everyone would be whispering about the incident at the grocery store? She had to know that her church family wouldn't believe she'd knowingly try to pass off counterfeit cash.

He knocked on the door. After a minute, he pounded harder. The sun blazed through the trees, painting the street in mottled shadows.

"She could be in the shower," he said aloud, telling himself not to overreact like he'd done Friday. Or she could be in the basement throwing in a load of laundry or listening to music through her earbuds. He walked around to the kitchen door and knocked.

No response.

He cupped his eyes with his hands and peered through the glass. Was that a foot poking past the island that separated the kitchen from the breakfast nook?

He rapped the door again and slid it open at the same time. The foot disappeared behind the counter. A muffled sob made his heart stop. "Kate?" He rushed across the room and found her huddled against a cupboard, cradling a broken mug, tears streaking her face.

Hunkering next to her, he gently swept back her hair. "What's wrong?" His heart cracked at the pain in her eyes.

"I don't know what's the matter with me. I . . ." She looked at the porcelain shard in her hand. Bold letters proclaimed, "To the World's Greatest Friend." "I gave this to Daisy for her last birthday." Fresh tears sprang from her eyes. "I dropped it. How could I let her down like this?"

He eased the mug from her hand and then folded her into his arms. "You didn't let Daisy down. You solved a murder the rest of us didn't even believe had been committed." As Kate's tears soaked through his shirt, he faced the uncomfortable truth that he was the one she should be blaming. If he'd done his job right from the beginning, they might have had the evidence to ensure Molly's conviction. "I'm sorry you've lost your friend. So very sorry."

She lifted her cheek from his shoulder and patted the damp fabric. "It's been almost three months. I shouldn't still be crying like this."

He stroked her hair and offered an understanding smile. "You're grieving. And right now, grief is your friend. The best thing you can do to get through this is to let it take you wherever it leads."

"I feel like I'm losing my mind."

"Yeah, that's pretty normal."

She tilted her head and peered at him through moisture-rimmed eyes. "Is that how you felt after your friend died?"

The question hit him like a blow to the chest. "Yeah." The air whooshed from his lungs. Only he *had* been to blame for *his* friend's death. If he'd done his duty instead of letting his misguided loyalty to their friendship cloud his judgment, his friend would still be alive.

Kate dried her tears with her sleeve and pushed to her feet. "What are you doing here anyway?"

He took a step back and stuck his hands in his pockets. "I got worried when you didn't show up at church."

She ducked her head. "I meant to come, and then . . ." She reached for the dustpan and waved it at the shattered mug. "I fell apart."

"You'll get through this." He picked up the larger shards as she swept up the fragments.

The phone rang, and she jumped so badly half of what she'd swept up bounced from the pan.

Tom dropped his pieces into the trash bin. "Do you want me to answer that?"

"Would you mind?"

"Not at all." He lifted the receiver from the hook. "Adams' residence."

"Oh," said a surprised female voice from the other end of the line. "Is Kate there?"

"She can't come to the phone right now. May I give her a message?"

"Um, yeah. This is Patti Goodman, her research assistant. Could you tell her that the data she was going to email me didn't come through and ask her to resend?"

"Will do." He hung up and relayed the message.

Kate clutched her head and stalked into the living room. "I told you I was losing my mind. She was just being nice, pretending the email must have gotten lost in cyberspace. I completely forgot to send it."

He sat on the armchair closest to her desk. "You've had a lot on your mind." Her soft floral scent clung to his shirt and made him yearn for her trust all the more. He wanted to be here for her to lean on whenever she needed him. If only . . . "You've got to stop being so hard on yourself."

Kate rummaged through a stack of files. "At the rate I'm forgetting things, it won't matter what stunts GPC pulls, I'll end up sabotaging Daisy's research all on my own." She uncovered a USB drive and held it up in triumph. "Got it."

"I don't understand why you think GPC would sabotage the research. I'd think they'd welcome an opportunity to partner with you on something that looks so promising."

"Not when it jeopardizes sales of their most profitable drug. It wouldn't be the first time they've scuttled promising research."

He curbed his skepticism. Worrying about work was the last thing Kate needed right now. "What do you say I take you to lunch after you get that emailed?"

She bit her bottom lip.

He was so used to battling her determined side that her uncertainty tugged at his protective instincts. "My treat," he said for added incentive, unwilling to leave her alone all day.

Her eyes sparkled, and he marveled at how good it felt to be the cause. "Are you sure you won't get in trouble for fraternizing with a suspect?" she said teasingly, although he sensed a thread of genuine concern.

If he wasn't more concerned about keeping an eye on her, he probably wouldn't have asked until the counterfeiting case was wrapped up. There was bound to be more talk like Vic's at A Cup or Two if they were seen together. But . . .

"I'm willing to take the risk." He winked, drawing a beautiful flush to her cheeks.

"Okay, let me take care of this email and then we can go." She switched on her computer. "I'll just freshen up while this is booting."

After she slipped into the bathroom, he wandered around

the living room, a little stunned that she'd agreed so easily. He wondered if this counted as a second date. With this whole GPC move hanging over her, the upcoming trial against Molly for her attempt on Kate's life, and now this counterfeiting incident, it was natural that she'd shy away from adding any more complications to her life.

If only he could convince her that spending time with him was a good thing, not a complication.

❧

Strolling the grounds of the Niagara Parks Botanical Gardens, Kate pointed to a purple coneflower. "That's an *Echinacea purpurea*. Extracts from the plant can boost the immune system. But they also make good cut flowers, lasting for up to a week in a vase of water. They're lovely, don't you think?"

"Yes," Tom said, his voice husky. "Everything here is beautiful." Only he wasn't looking at the garden, he was smiling at her.

Heat that had nothing to do with the August sunshine crept to her cheeks. "Anyone ever tell you you're a flirt?"

"Never. But I've been told that I'm sincere, honest, and have exceptionally good taste."

"Ah, so that's why you drove thirty minutes outside of Port Aster? To find the perfect restaurant? Not because you were embarrassed about being seen with me?" She said it with a teasing lilt, but she understood how important it was to keep a low profile. Never mind the counterfeiting suspicions; he was a witness in the case against Molly for *her* attempted murder.

"Never." He captured her hand and the warmth of his touch melted the tension from her muscles. He led her along the cobbled path into the trees, away from the other visitors. "The truth is, I wanted you to myself."

His breath sent a tingly pleasure scurrying down her arms, raising goose bumps despite the warm temperature.

He squeezed her hand. "And I figured we could both use some time out from under the microscope of Port Aster's curiosity seekers."

Yes, escaping the speculations had been exactly what she needed. She relished his reassuring touch and his unwavering friendship despite her resistance, as necessary as it was. "I've had a lovely time."

"Really? Because I was beginning to think you were chiming off the Latin names of every other flower to avoid talking about us."

She hitched the corner of her mouth into a half smile. "That obvious?"

"Mm-hmmm."

"I'm sorry." She stopped at the pond and slipped her hand from his clasp. "I guess I don't have much experience with . . ." She fluttered her hand in search of the right word.

"Dating," he filled in, and the softly spoken word flitted around her chest, touching here and there like a tiny bird looking for the perfect place to nest.

"Is that what this is?"

Tom angled his body so he was facing her, his expression tender. "I'd like it to be."

Her heart leapt in response even as she braced for the impossibility. "I'd like that too . . ."

"I sense a 'but.'"

"It's just . . ."

He fluffed his hair. "You don't like my hair?"

She giggled. "No, your hair is gorgeous."

"Wow, thanks. Hmm, what other compliment could I fish for?" His gaze tangled with hers in a playful tug-of-war. He tapped his fingers on his lips. "You don't like the way I kiss?"

"I wouldn't know." She smirked, forgetting for a moment that he was a cop and she was involved in two too many of his cases.

"I could remedy that." He brushed his thumb along her bottom lip, releasing a flurry of butterflies.

She held her breath as his smoldering gaze drifted to her lips.

With a bittersweet smile, he dropped his hand to his side. "Except . . . you're still not sure you can trust me. What can we do about that?"

What? He wasn't going to kiss her? Of all the times to remember her half-joking question about whether she could trust him. She sucked in a sudden breath and jerked her attention back to his eyes. They were filled with a sincerity that tugged at her frenzied heart and drew her closer. "To be honest, these days I'm not sure if my own judgment can be trusted."

"I understand. No pressure. I promise. I care about you." The raw intensity in his voice trembled through her. "I want to help you however I can."

A frog poked its head out of the pond, sending ripples across the placid surface, much like the ripples churning in her chest. She nibbled her bottom lip. "I read somewhere that you shouldn't make any major decisions in the first year after losing someone close to you."

"A year, huh?" He made it sound like a life sentence.

She giggled. "I've already broken that rule by moving into Daisy's house and taking over her research project."

"Yeah, I did the same after my partner died. Left the FBI and moved back to Canada, to my childhood home no less."

"Any regrets?"

His gaze traveled over her face. "Nope."

Once again, heat surged to her cheeks. She snapped a leaf from a nearby shrub and fiddled with it. "You don't miss the excitement of working for the FBI?"

"Nope. Trying to keep you out of trouble keeps my adrenaline pumping more than enough."

"Very funny." She punched his arm.

He hugged her to his side, pinning her arm between them. "I'm serious," he said, all hint of cajoling gone.

She supposed after losing his partner to a bomber, dealing with her troubles looked pretty good. "So . . ." she said, falling back to their lighthearted banter. "Am I officially off the hook for counterfeiting yet?"

"You were never a suspect in my book. But I don't have any solid leads. I'm still looking for that Peter guy."

Her throat pinched. *Peter, right.* She didn't want to think about the fruitless night she'd spent calling every hotel in the book, at least a half dozen of which would neither confirm nor deny whether a Peter Ratcher was staying with them. "Let me call the research station's receptionist, Marjorie. She might know where the GPC reps hole up when they're in town." And why hadn't she thought of that last night instead of going cross-eyed working through the phone book?

Moments later she had the name of a lakeside hotel a few miles outside of Port Aster. "If this is our Peter, that's where he'll be."

"Great." Tom cupped her elbow and turned her back toward the parking lot. "I'll take you home and then pay him a visit."

"What?" She dug in her heels and dragged him to a stop smack dab in front of the wedding arbor, of all places. "No way. I'm coming with you. It's me he wants to talk to."

Tom's brow furrowed. "But I didn't think you wanted to talk to him."

"I didn't. But now I do. He knew my father. Maybe . . ."

"Maybe he'll be able to answer some of your questions?" Tom said softly.

She shrugged, suddenly afraid to hope she might get real answers after all these years.

"Okay, let's go." By the time Tom twined his car through the side streets and pulled onto the highway, he was glancing at the rearview mirror every few seconds.

"What's wrong?" Kate turned and peered through the back window. The highway was packed with the usual glut of tourists returning from a weekend over the river.

"Could be nothing."

"Or?"

"A silver Ford Escort, two cars back. I think it might be following us. I noticed one behind us when we headed to the restaurant."

Bile rose to her throat. "One parked in front of my neighbor's house last night."

Tom's knuckles whitened on the steering wheel. "See if you recognize the driver." He eased off the gas.

She twisted in her seat for a better look. "Why would someone follow me?" Her voice verged on hysterical, but she couldn't help it. "There have to be thousands of silver Escorts in the peninsula."

"I'm only interested in this one."

Heart thumping, she squinted at the car's windshield. "It's no good. There's a glare. I can't see inside."

"Okay, the next exit is ours. If he doesn't follow us, we'll get the license number." Tom pulled off at the harbor exit.

The car stayed on the highway, but as they peered at the rear bumper, a car zipped up the exit ramp beside them, blocking their view. "Did you catch any of the numbers?" Tom asked.

"Started with *B*, I think. Do you think it was Peter?"

"Probably not. Was an old car, not a rental."

Tom pulled into the hotel's parking lot, then reached across the seat and squeezed her hand. "You okay?"

"Yeah, it was probably just a coincidence. Right?"

His fingers clasped hers a little tighter. "You can never be too careful, okay?"

His concern rattled her almost more than the idea of someone following her. "Don't worry, Tom, Port Aster isn't like DC." He didn't like to talk about his stint with the FBI, but it had clearly left him a little paranoid.

He climbed from the car without responding.

A few minutes later, the hotel clerk rang Peter's room for them but got no response.

Kate let out a sigh. "Now what?"

The corners of Tom's mouth lifted, spreading into a full-blown smile. "We could walk by the water."

"You're enjoying this!"

He winked, then steered her toward the door. "What's not to enjoy? I'll take any excuse to spend more time with you."

She rolled her eyes. She knew he was teasing, but secretly she savored the truth in his gaze. If only she didn't keep landing in the middle of his cases, maybe things could be different.

They strolled toward the dock, but Kate didn't miss Tom's vigilant glances every which way. Thankfully, no silver Ford Escorts were anywhere to be seen.

Halfway to the dock, Kate spotted Peter sitting on a bench overlooking the harbor. She pointed and was all the more unnerved by how her finger shook. Her breath crowded in her throat. "That's him."

"Are you sure? You can't see his face from here."

She gathered her courage. "There's only one way to find out. Come on." Steeling her spine, she stepped in front of her father's former colleague. "You wanted to talk to me?"

"Miss Baxter!" He surged to his feet. "What a surprise. How did you find me?"

Tom extended his hand, sparing her from answering. "I'm Detective Parker. I'm here with Miss *Adams*."

"Detective?" Peter's Adam's apple bobbed. He looked to her, his forehead creasing. "Adams? But you *are* Gwen Baxter's daughter, right?"

"Yes, Mr. Ratcher, and I'm curious what information you have that convinced you I'd want to talk to you."

He slanted a glance at Tom. "It's kind of personal." At Tom's raised eyebrow, Peter added quickly, "About your father."

Kate's heart galloped at breakneck speed. "What?"

Peter hesitated.

"It's okay. Detective Parker is a friend. He's aware of what happened to my father."

Peter dropped back onto the bench. Kate sat next to him, angling her body to face him. Tom squatted beside her, the reassuring pressure of his leg calming her jittery nerves.

"I kind of got the impression when we first met in the coffee shop that you were embarrassed by my mentioning your family," Peter began.

Kate caught herself squirming, just as she'd done that day

when he'd addressed her by a name she'd been forbidden to utter for twenty years. Apprehension, not embarrassment.

"After I thought about it, I realized you probably didn't know the truth about your dad. I mean, I'm sure he told you and your mom, but with the way things went down, maybe you have your doubts?"

Kate fought to keep her tone neutral, even as her thoughts spiraled. "What truth would that be?"

"Your dad didn't steal any secrets. He was railroaded."

Kate forgot to breathe. Indignation at what GPC Pharmaceuticals did to her father warred with joy that her faith in his innocence was finally vindicated. An image rose in her mind of her dad pressing his forehead to the window of the police car, tears streaming down his cheeks. "I love you, Kate," he'd said as she ran to stop them. "Don't ever forget I love you." *Railroaded?* "How?" she whispered.

Tom covered her trembling hand as Peter went on.

"He'd just been to visit a village in Colombia where researchers from some obscure university were experimenting with an indigenous miracle plant. Your father had sent back glowing reports about its restorative properties."

"How—how do you know this?"

"He was my friend. I picked him up at the airport when he returned from his trip. I found him glued to a news report on the TV monitor in one of the restaurants. He said, 'I can't let them get away with this.'"

Kate clutched the edge of the bench. "Get away with what?"

"I don't know. He ranted on about innocent people. When I asked him what he was talking about, he said I was better off not knowing. That I should leave."

Tom squeezed her hand, the warmth of his touch loosening her death grip on the bench's seat. "Did he say why?" he asked Peter.

"Because of what he was going to do."

"What?" Kate gulped a breath. "What did he do?"

"Near as I can figure, he destroyed the plants he was supposed to bring back."

A dark cloud blotted out the sun. "Destroyed them," she repeated softly. What could Dad have possibly learned that made him destroy the plants? "But you said he believed they were beneficial?" His actions didn't make sense.

"Yeah, that's why management was furious when he showed up without them. The supervisor had security onsite faster than your dad could hand over his resignation. Only they didn't escort him from the building and bid him sayonara. They called the cops and accused him of stealing company property and secrets."

Kate's heart wrenched at the memory, even all these years later. "But he must have had a good reason for destroying the plants." Peter had to believe that too, or he wouldn't have said her father was railroaded.

"I figured he had something on GPC. Something they didn't want getting out. They used their corporate muscle to ensure he didn't make bail."

"They did that to your friend," Tom hissed, "and you didn't try to stop them?"

"He refused to see me after he was arrested. Said I couldn't afford to be seen with him. That they'd make my life difficult." Peter plowed his fingers through his silver hair, anguish bleeding through his words. "I had a wife and kid to support."

"So did your *friend*."

Kate cringed at Tom's emphasis on the word. "Why did

you think I'd want to talk to you now?" she interjected. "Your message said I'd want to *now*. Did you learn something more about why he destroyed the plants?"

Peter rubbed at his jaw. "Your father didn't tell you and your mother anything?"

"I was only ten!"

"Right, of course. Well, I spotted you in the lunchroom at the research center Friday and overheard you express concerns about GPC's proposed partnership with the research station jeopardizing your research project. A treatment for depression, wasn't it?"

"Yes." She slid a nervous glance Tom's way. As much as she hated GPC for what the company did to their family, she'd refrained from sharing her reservations about the proposed partnership too widely.

"So your call had nothing to do with the counterfeit money?" Tom asked.

With the revelation about her father, she'd forgotten Tom wanted to talk to Peter about his visit to the hardware store.

"What counterfeit money?" Peter looked confused, and she was pretty sure it wasn't an act. He hadn't so much as flinched at Tom's question.

Tom must've thought the same, because he only asked a few questions about Peter's hardware store purchase before revisiting what Peter had overheard at the research station. "Why did you think Kate would want to talk to you—a GPC employee—when she's opposed to their partnership with her employer?"

"Don't you see? GPC Pharmaceuticals has a tendency to silence dissension quickly and decisively."

Kate shuddered. Okay, so maybe her suspicion that she was

being framed as a counterfeiter wasn't so far off after all, except maybe it was by GPC. Smearing her reputation would go a long way to neutralizing her opposition to their move.

She glanced at Tom to see if he might be thinking the same thing.

His eyes narrowed, focused on Peter. "Did you tell anyone what you know about Kate?"

"No, of course not. Her father was my friend. I'd never betray him that way."

"When you were at the hardware store yesterday, an older guy in a plaid shirt, medium height, appeared to be watching you through the window. Any idea who he might be?"

Peter frowned and shook his head.

"Doesn't sound like someone you've seen working for the pharmaceutical company?"

"No."

"Would you mind coming down to the police station tomorrow morning and viewing the video clip just to be sure?"

"Yeah, I can do that." He glanced around, suddenly looking nervous. "I wouldn't put it past GPC to spy on me. I could never prove it, but I was sure they had someone watching me for months after Baxter died."

Kate shivered.

Tom squeezed her shoulder, and the warmth of his touch would have filled her with reassurance if not for the storm brewing in his eyes. "What do you think GPC will do if they learn Kate is Baxter's daughter?"

"You don't want to find out."

6

He pulled his fishing cap low over his eyes and meandered past the threesome on the bench overlooking the harbor. They were so intent on their conversation, not one of them glanced his way. Not even the detective—so much for his investigative training.

He stopped at the edge of the dock, not more than fifteen feet from where they sat, and pretended to search his tackle box for the perfect lure. He chose a rubber worm and speared it on his hook. Peter Ratcher knew too much. Maybe too much for his own good.

Definitely too much for Katy's.

Tom walked around Kate's house a second time, double-checking the position of the wood blocks he'd installed in every window to ensure they were secure, and still couldn't bring himself to leave. The locks wouldn't keep out anyone determined to get in. Not that he wanted to point that out to

Kate. He just couldn't shake the feeling she was in danger—immediate danger.

He hadn't spotted the silver Escort again, but that you-can't-protect-her-forever note had preyed on his mind all weekend. He found her in the living room watering the plant on the table behind the sofa.

"I'll be fine." She fluttered her free hand toward the window he'd just checked for the third time. "You're overreacting."

He didn't miss the way her hand trembled, though, or that she'd drawn the drapes over the sheers in the big bay window. "Do you always draw those curtains? Makes the room kind of dark." He scooped the watering can from her hand, before she drowned the plant, and teasingly lifted an eyebrow.

She snatched the jug back. "You're the one who's making me nervous. What could possibly make you think that GPC would care if I was a Baxter?"

"Because Peter felt the need to warn you." And whoever had been spying on him had a reason.

She headed toward the kitchen with the watering can. "Do you think he has anything to do with the counterfeiting?"

"No." Tom trailed her to the kitchen and leaned back against the counter. "His responses betrayed no hint of guilt."

Kate folded her arms across her chest. "He's a salesman. He's used to pulling the wool over people's eyes."

Tom mirrored her folded arms with his own. "I'm a former FBI agent. I'm trained to see through it."

She laughed at his imitation of her, and the sweet sound momentarily eased the tension that had knotted his stomach ever since their meeting with Peter.

"But didn't you get the feeling he was fishing for information?"

"Definitely. What I'm less sure about is whether he was

chumming the waters to see if you knew anything that could be a threat or to see if you knew something that would benefit him somehow."

"Yeah, I can't explain it, but even after he told me all that stuff about my father, I still don't quite trust him."

"That's probably good." Tom adjusted the bar bracing Kate's patio door. "Trust your instincts." *And me.* For her own protection, he needed to know if she planned to act on Peter's revelations somehow. Asking the wrong people questions could land her in a lot worse trouble than being accused of passing counterfeit bills. "Have you ever heard of this miracle plant your father supposedly collected on his trip?" *And never delivered.* He didn't say the last part aloud, but the pained look on her face said she'd heard it nonetheless.

She averted her gaze, fussed with the edge of a placemat on the kitchen table. "I don't even remember Dad being away before his arrest."

"You think Peter's lying about the whole thing?"

She snatched up a spray bottle and spritzed the ferns hanging by the patio door. "I don't know what to think." The wobble in her voice told him that Peter's story gnawed at her more than she wanted to let on. "When I combed old newspapers looking for information on my dad, I didn't come across anything about stolen plants. If the plants were as remarkable as Peter said, I'm sure the research community, at the very least, would have heard more about them in the last twenty years."

"There was a lot of upheaval in that area at the time. The political situation could've prevented a team from going back."

"Can't you talk to the arresting officers? Find out if my dad accused GPC of anything?"

Tom's heart clenched at the hopeful gleam in Kate's eyes. "There was no record in the system, Kate. The station he was taken to relocated last year. A lot of their records never made the move. I wouldn't know who to ask for. Even if I did, they'd probably be retired by now."

She slapped the spray bottle down on the table. "My father died in police custody. Someone's got to remember who brought him in." Her voice cracked.

Tom closed the distance between them. "You may not like what they have to say."

"My last memory of my dad is of him being hauled away in a police car. I want to know the truth."

He caught her hand and tilted his head to catch her eye. "But what if the truth isn't what you were hoping for?"

"At least I'll know."

He nodded, impressed once again by her determination. "It's possible that GPC Pharmaceuticals already knows who you are and is using Peter to scare you out of opposing them."

"By telling me they're corrupt?" The exasperation in her voice left no doubt how ludicrous that possibility sounded.

Tom shook his head. "By filling your mind with conspiracy theories, they could hope to marginalize you, convince any of the directors who might be swayed by your concerns that you're grasping at straws in a desperate attempt to avenge your father's death."

She jerked her hand from his clasp. "Is that what you think?"

He clamped his fingers around the top of the nearest kitchen chair and drew a deep breath. "Isn't your father's experience with GPC a big part of the reason you're opposed to their move here?"

A muscle in her jaw pulsed, confirming that he'd hit a nerve.

Not that he wanted to upset her. He was beginning to think there might be some validity to her concerns.

Monday morning Kate arrived at the research station before anyone else. She couldn't sleep. Or at least, she couldn't sleep without having nightmares. Every time she'd closed her eyes, she would see her dad wave from the window of a plane. Then she'd turn from the plane taxiing down the runway and step inside the airport, which morphed into a lab.

She swiped her fob over the electronic lock at the back entrance and stepped inside, pulling the door closed behind her. The squeak of her sneakers on the polished floor sent chills down her neck. She picked up her pace.

Overhead, the air vents groaned, and she nearly jumped out of her skin.

Okay, this was crazy. It was just the dream making her jumpy. She'd have to make herself some lavender tea before she got started. That should help soothe her nerves. She turned her key in the door to her lab and her mind reeled back to last night's dream. No, not a dream. A nightmare.

Every time she'd pushed through the lab door, her gaze had been drawn to plants at the window. She'd rushed toward them, thinking they were her father's. But just before she reached them, the room would explode into flames, and she'd wake up screaming.

Her palm was slick against the doorknob as she pushed open the door. The room was dark. The curtains drawn. Her gaze flicked to the table in front of the window. The only plants there were herbs they were using for their extractions. She let out a breath.

"What did you expect?" she scolded herself. Now that she'd put her silly imaginings to rest, maybe she could get some work done. She slipped into her office, adjacent to the lab, and turned on her computer.

The internet had been in its infancy when Dad died twenty years ago, but lots of universities had been connected. If she could figure out which university was doing the research that her father went to investigate, she might be able to figure out what got him all fired up against GPC Pharmaceuticals.

You're grasping at straws.

Kate shut out Tom's voice and clicked on her favorite search engine. She experimented with a variety of search words, but the number of potential hits was overwhelming. After scrolling through ten pages of results she clicked on a link that looked promising.

Nope, not even close.

A loud clunk sounded from the other room.

She glanced at the time at the bottom of the computer screen. No one should be here yet. No one could get into the building without a security pass, she reminded herself.

But the reminder didn't calm her racing pulse.

Her gaze flailed around the room for something to use as a weapon . . . just in case. She grabbed the paperweight decorating the corner of her desk and edged to the door. Taking a deep breath, she poked her head around the corner. "Patti?"

Her research assistant jumped, spilling coffee over the side of her hand. Crying out, she dropped a stack of files onto the workbench and lurched for the lab sink.

"I'm so sorry." Kate let go of her would-be weapon and grabbed a fistful of paper towels. "I didn't mean to startle you."

"You didn't. I mean, I knew you were here. I saw your car in the back lot." Patti dabbed at the splatters on her trendy, gold-trimmed jacket. "I guess I'm still jumpy from that cop surprising me at your house."

Remembering Tom's suspicions of Patti, or more particularly of her boyfriend Jarrett, Kate eyed the files Patti came in with. "What are you doing here so early?"

"I found discrepancies in the data you sent me. I wanted to run a couple more tests."

"Oh." Kate leafed through the pages to the flagged results and nodded. "Good catch."

"May I ask why you are so opposed to GPC partnering with the research station?"

"What?" Kate handed back the file. Why hadn't she noticed the subtle changes in Patti over the past few weeks? The new clothes, the thicker makeup, the funky new glasses. Changes to please her new boyfriend, no doubt. What else might she do to please him?

Kate gathered the beakers and test tubes she'd need for her next experiment. "I have my reasons."

"A lot of people think their coming here would be a good thing. They'd bring more jobs to the area, more housing starts for the researchers who move here, more money for local businesses."

"Is that what Jarrett told you?"

Patti's finger traced the rim of her coffee cup. "His dad, actually." She gulped down what was left of her coffee and tossed the cup into the trash. "I know you don't like him. But he makes a lot of good points."

"I like him just fine. I simply disagree with him."

"But—"

"Look, Patti, I have no desire to interfere with who you see outside the lab. Just don't let it interfere with your work here. Understand?"

Patti nodded, but the grim slant of her mouth said she wasn't happy about it. If Patti were dating anyone but Jarrett, Kate probably wouldn't have hesitated to share her reasons for opposing GPC's move. Unfortunately, she was dating the mayor's son, which meant Kate needed to watch what she said around her assistant.

Kate grabbed her lab coat from the wall hook. She hated that she'd become so easily suspicious of people since her mentor's murder, but the fact that a seemingly nice girl like Molly Gilmore could poison someone without any qualms proved to her just how guarded she needed to be. Patti might not intentionally divulge confidential information to her boyfriend, and by extension his very powerful father, but Kate had no doubt that the mayor would take advantage of Patti's employment to glean any inside information he could.

She shut down her web browser before Patti became curious about her web search too.

By 3:00 Kate's sleepless night had caught up to her. She turned on the gas, then took too long to light the match. The gas ignited in a whoosh.

"Go home," Patti said. "Before you blow us up. You're dead on your feet."

Kate fumbled her test tube at her assistant's choice of words—too unnerving a reminder of last night's dream. Gathering the broken shards, she stifled a yawn.

Okay, maybe Patti had a point. "You're right. I'll finish this tomorrow."

Kate arrived home shortly after 3:00, alarmed to find Lucetta lugging a suitcase from Verna's house. Had Verna given her something else that Lucetta planned to sell instead of to treasure as Verna intended?

Kate pocketed her car keys and cut across the lawn. "You leaving?"

Lucetta glanced up, tears in her eyes.

"What's wrong? Did something happen to Verna?"

Lucetta dropped the handle of her suitcase and swiped at her eyes with a tissue. "Mr. Nagy put señora in a home."

"I'm so sorry." Kate's heart ached for the dear woman. "I never imagined he'd manage to make arrangements this quickly." If only she'd tried harder to reason with Brian on Saturday, to ward off such a drastic move.

"She act crazy this morning. See things that not there."

"Oh no. Not again." What if Tom had been right and she did have a brain tumor or something?

"The ambulance take her to hospital," Lucetta went on, between scrubbing at her eyes. "Mr. Nagy said now that she critical the home have to give her a room."

"Surely he wanted the doctor to run tests first." How could Brian think of sending her to a home before finding out what was causing the behavior changes?

Lucetta crushed the tissue in her hand and reached for her suitcase once more. "All I know, he say she won't be back."

Kate's pulse quickened. Verna must be really bad, because she couldn't imagine the dear woman going into a home without a fuss.

Verna's cat twined around her legs. Kate lifted him into her arms and cuddled him against her chest. "What's to become of Whiskers?"

Lucetta shrugged. "Cats no allowed at the home. And Mr. Nagy never liked."

As if Whiskers understood, he let out a pitiful mew. Kate stroked his fur. "Don't worry, fella. You can stay with me." Kate jutted her chin toward Lucetta's suitcase. "How are you getting home? Did you need a ride?"

"No, my nephew come." Lucetta's gaze slid away as if she suddenly felt self-conscious.

Did she know that Tom hadn't been able to locate Pedro all weekend? Maybe he hadn't yet today either. Kate's fingers itched to text him a quick alert.

"You have Verna's spare house key still?" Lucetta asked. "So you get food for cat."

"Uh . . ." Kate took a second to register what she'd said, then used the question as an excuse to rummage through her purse. She dropped Whiskers to the ground and pretended to scrounge around in her purse as she thumbed a brief text to Tom from her phone. As soon as she hit Send, she shook her head. "I'm sure I do have the key, but it must be inside."

"If don't find, I be here tomorrow to clean." Lucetta let out a ragged breath. "After that Mr. Nagy probably let me go."

Kate felt sorry for the woman. With everybody cutting back on their expenses, she'd have a tough time finding more work. "If I hear of anyone looking for a housekeeper, I'll let you know," she heard herself say, even though in good conscience she'd have difficulty recommending her. For all she knew, the woman was a counterfeiter or aiding and abetting one.

Then again, maybe she should invite Lucetta to help clean

her walls and ceilings in preparation for some painting she'd
been thinking of doing. Might give her more opportunity to
uncover who Lucetta might be protecting.

A rusted gray-blue pickup rattled down the street and
swerved into the Nagy driveway. Herbs Are Us was painted
on the door with half of the letters flaked off, leaving only a
ghost of the letters. Pedro, his dark hair slicked back, jumped
from the driver's seat, wearing torn jeans and a dusty T-shirt.
His gaze collided with Kate's, and his step faltered. He reached
for Lucetta's bag. "This it, Aunt Luce? 'Cause the boss wants
the truck right back."

Kate squinted against the sun and studied the boy's rigid
jaw. Did he know who she was? Was that the real reason he
was in such a hurry?

Somehow she needed to stall him until Tom got here . . .
if he was coming. "Uh, you wouldn't happen to have change
for a twenty, would you?" Kate asked, hoping to get a glimpse
into his wallet.

Pedro reached toward the bulge in his back pocket. He didn't
look the least bit suspicious of her motive. In fact, he seemed
eager to help—which made perfect sense if he was about to
give her phony money for her twenty bucks. But then he must
not realize her connection to the counterfeit investigation.

Lucetta snapped open the handbag dangling from her arm
and an instant later, thrust four fives into Kate's hand.

Pedro scowled at his aunt but returned his wallet to his
pocket without comment.

"Thank you." Kate barely glanced at the money as she
tucked it into a separate compartment of her purse so Tom
could check it out when he arrived. "Um, it was nice of your
boss to let you borrow the truck," she said, trying a different

tactic to stall for time. "I imagine most of the migrant workers don't have driver's licenses that allow them to drive anything but farm equipment on the roads."

Pedro tossed Lucetta's suitcase into the truck's bed.

"Pedro have license," Lucetta said, although she didn't sound all that certain. She shot Pedro a look of alarm. Clearly she hadn't realized that Pedro's use of the truck might not be legal. But from the way she'd dashed the change for a twenty into Kate's hands, as if to stop her nephew from incriminating himself, Lucetta shouldn't be surprised.

🍃

Tom crossed another name off the list that his contact had given him and punched the phone number of the next person into his desk phone. Next to it, his cell phone vibrated, skidding into his empty coffee cup. He stacked the cup into the other three, but at the sight of Kate's name, dropped them in place and snatched up his cell phone. *Text message.*

He dropped the desk phone back into its cradle and clicked open the message: "Pedro here. Come quick."

Tom raced out of the police station, tapping Kate's number on his cell phone at the same time. Had the kid threatened her? His temper flared. If the kid laid a hand on—

The call rolled over to voice mail. "Kate, I'm on my way."

As he slid behind the wheel of his car, he realized he didn't know where she was. Pedro must've shown up at her work. Except the kid couldn't be that stupid. The security at the building was tight. He couldn't have just waltzed in. Kate must've gone home early. Unless she'd spotted him outside and was hiding in her lab.

He put a call in to dispatch. "Patch me through to the research station."

When he'd stopped by Herbs Are Us this morning, the kid had been polite and cooperative. When Tom asked to see the cash in his wallet, the kid had obliged without hesitation. Of course, his billfold had been empty.

"Go ahead," the dispatcher said a second before the call clicked over.

"Yes, I'm calling for Kate Adams. I don't know her extension."

"I'm sorry, sir, Miss Adams has left for the day," the receptionist responded.

"Do you know how long ago that was?"

"Twenty minutes perhaps."

"Thanks." Tom cranked the wheel a hard left and pulled a U-turn. Three minutes later he crawled down Kate's street so as not to scare the kid into running. When he caught sight of Kate's yellow Bug in the driveway, his heart settled back into a steady rhythm. At least he had the right location.

As he stepped out of his car, she emerged from behind her neighbor's house, head down, expression somber, carrying Verna's cat and a bag of food.

He hurried toward her. "What's going on? Is Pedro still here?"

Her attention snapped to him, and the smile that flitted across her lips jogged his heart into a whole other orbit. "No, sorry, I should have called you back. Have you questioned him yet?"

"Questioned?" Tom gave his head a mental shake. "Yes, this morning." He let his gaze travel over Kate until he'd satisfied himself that she was okay. "Did he threaten you?"

"No, nothing like that. He was picking up Lucetta was all." Kate rested the cat food bag on her hip. "How'd he respond to your questions?"

Tom relieved her of the bag. "His aunt had obviously filled him in. He was apologetic about giving my sister phony money. Even asked if he needed to give her good bills."

"Did you believe him?"

Tom hesitated.

Kate tilted her head, one eye narrowing. "What aren't you telling me?"

"He said he got the money from Verna, for hauling junk to the dump."

Kate frowned. "You can't still think she's a counterfeiter? Her son put her in a nursing home today."

"That was fast." Tom scratched the cat's neck. "You volunteer to watch the cat?"

"Yes."

"So you're okay? Your message sounded like you felt threatened."

That heart-jogging smile slid across her lips again. "Were you worried?"

He made a face. "What do you think?"

"I think I like it."

He blinked. "Huh?"

"That you care enough to worry about me." She nuzzled her cheek against the top of the cat's head.

Speechless, he stroked his thumb along her jaw. He hadn't thought about how lonely it would be to have no family to turn to in a crisis. To have no roommate to wonder where she was when she didn't come home, as her friend Julie used to. A yearning to be that person swelled in his chest.

She drew in a sudden breath.

Realizing he'd dipped his head toward her, he straightened quickly and tore his gaze from her lips. He'd promised not to pressure her. She was a material witness in an ongoing investigation. Now was not the time to entertain thoughts of tasting her lips. "I'd better get back to work."

Her lips curved south, making his heart kick. Was she disappointed?

Color bloomed in her cheeks as she shifted her attention to the cat. "Before you go, I need to give you something."

Tom followed her onto the porch and set down the cat food bag.

She dropped the cat inside the door and retrieved her purse before rejoining him. "I tried to stall Lucetta and Pedro by asking for change for a twenty. Pedro seemed eager to oblige, but Lucetta—"

"Wait a second. Pedro pulled out his wallet?" Tom clarified. A wallet that had been empty a few hours ago.

"Yeah, looked like he had lots of cash. But Lucetta whipped out change for me first, not looking pleased with him at all. I think she's covering for him."

Yeah, he'd thought the same when he interviewed her on Saturday.

Kate gingerly lifted four five-dollar bills from her purse. "I thought you might want to check over the bills she gave me."

Tom studied each bill closely. "I'll take them in for a closer inspection, but they all look legitimate." He tucked them into the inside pocket of his sport jacket.

"Hey, now I'm out twenty bucks."

"Don't worry. I'm good for it."

"You'd better be, because I know where you live." She gave him a playful nudge.

"You're welcome over any time." He smiled to himself. Maybe he'd have to hold on to the money for a while.

Clearly flustered, she turned her attention to the drooping flowers next to the porch. "Look at these. I keep forgetting to water them."

Tom mercifully let the change in subject slide without comment and started down the steps. "I'd better head out. I'm still on duty."

"Wait. Did you get the names of the officers who arrested my dad?"

"Yeah, two guys. Unfortunately both have passed on."

Kate let out a disappointed sigh.

"But I did find someone willing to search storage for the records. He said the original investigators both died soon after your father's death."

"Really?" Kate's eyes widened, lit with hope. "Do you think the deaths are connected?"

"They died in the line of duty."

"But maybe Dad told them what he had on the pharmaceutical company and GPC found out."

Tom misstepped, sideswiped by the image of his former FBI partner's car exploding. Yeah, bad guys thought nothing of offing an officer to kill an investigation.

7

The roar of an engine filtered through Kate's mind. She shifted uncomfortably. Her neck muscles spasmed. Dragging open her eyes, she massaged out the kink. Swirling colors floated in front of her. She blinked a couple times. Oh, right, her computer. She must've fallen asleep.

She tapped the computer mouse and the swirling colors disappeared from the screen, replaced by the webpage she'd been reading when she fell asleep.

Bending her head from side to side, she tried to relax her bunched muscles. How long had—? The sunlight slanting past the edge of the drapes suddenly registered. Her gaze shot to the bottom corner of her computer screen. Oh no, she was late for work!

She dashed to her bedroom. How could she have slept all night at her desk? She pushed a palm into the side of her back. Her body wasn't about to let her forget how stupid she'd been to not go to bed. She'd never even pulled all-nighters when cramming for university exams.

She'd just been so sure that if she pushed through the 213,632 matches the search engine spat out, she'd find some clue to what her father had discovered about GPC.

The phone rang. Patti.

"Are you okay?"

"Yes, my alarm didn't go off." Not a lie. She didn't mention that she forgot to set it because she never went to bed. "I'll be there soon."

"Hurry. The director just called, wants you in the conference room ASAP."

Great, and no time for a shower.

She twisted and squirmed, trying to reach the zipper on the back of her sundress. Every muscle screamed in protest. Giving up, she yanked it off and pulled on a skirt and blouse instead. She scrubbed at her eyes. They felt like she'd been plastered by a sandstorm.

Leaning over her dresser, she peered into the mirror. Talk about bloodshot eyes. She dragged a comb through her hair, then yanked it into a ponytail. All she could say was, good thing she worked in a lab. Too bad the director picked today for a chat. Hopefully this meant he was finally taking her concerns about partnering with GPC seriously. She took an extra minute to add a little makeup. If she had something to show for the sleep deprivation, she wouldn't care how she looked. But she was no closer to understanding what got Dad in trouble with GPC than she'd been yesterday morning.

There'd been protests over clear-cutting the rainforest, a scandal over the United States selling weapons to a rebel group, and a ream of other disasters. But nothing she could tie to GPC. She'd nodded off somewhere around a catastrophic mudslide and a village-destroying fire.

Grabbing her keys and purse, she eyed the kitchen. No time for breakfast. Her stomach grumbled. Okay, maybe just grab an apple. She snatched one from the crisper and headed out.

As she pulled open the front door, the roar of a lawnmower—the engine that had awakened her—filled the air. Thank goodness for Vic's Lawn Service. She waved to him as she rushed to the car.

Vic saw her wave. She could tell by the way his lip curled before he reversed directions on Verna's lawn. Apparently he was still sore that she hadn't taken him up on his offer to mow her lawn every week too.

She raced out of the driveway and reached the speed limit in record time.

Maybe hiring Vic would be smart. Thirty dollars a week wasn't a bad price. The dandelions turning to seed on her lawn certainly weren't going to cut themselves. Besides, he was a nice enough guy once you got past his somewhat negative attitude. And he did a decent job—showed up at 8:00 a.m. sharp every Tuesday morning.

Mrs. C had said he needed the work too, since he'd been laid off over a year and had a young daughter. Guess that would make anyone a little negative.

As she turned onto the street leading out of town, her cell phone rang again. "Work" appeared on the screen. She fit her Bluetooth mic into her ear and tapped it on. "I'm on my way. Do you know what this is about?"

"Not a clue. But he's not happy."

"*Great*. I need twelve minutes."

"I'll tell him, but Kate, make it eight."

She dreaded to think what the director wanted. The only times he summoned her to meetings were when funding was at stake. Would he cut her loose altogether because she wasn't on board with the plans to partner with GPC?

She prayed for calm, but peace eluded her. She eased her foot off the gas. Praying while breaking the speed limit wouldn't earn her any heavenly favors. Sailing past the nursing home, she made a mental note to pop in and see Verna, reassure her that Whiskers was well taken—

The air caught in Kate's throat. She'd forgotten all about Whiskers this morning, couldn't even remember if she'd let him in last night. "Please let him be okay," she added to her prayer.

A mile from the research facility, her yellow Bug sputtered. "No, not now." Kate gave the car more gas, but she kept on sputtering. Kate's gaze jerked to the fuel gauge. Way past empty. She'd just been too distracted with everything. She veered into the parking lot on fumes, parked in the nearest vacant spot, and dashed to the door closest to the conference room. At the sight of a black Cadillac, license plate KING 1, her heart jammed in her throat.

The only reason the mayor would be here would be to make sure the board didn't thwart GPC Pharmaceuticals' plans to move to town.

Please, Lord, please don't let this meeting include him.

The sun slipped behind a cloud, casting a long shadow over the walk. *Not good. Not good. Not good.*

This is what she got for skipping out on church on Sunday. She shook the silly notion from her head. Rationally, she knew God wasn't vindictive. That he didn't keep score of her failures and weigh them against her requests. It just felt that way sometimes.

She slapped her fob over the lock and yanked open the door. Voices—plural—emanated from the conference room.

"Where's your associate, Peter Ratcher?" the director asked.

"He had an urgent personal matter to attend to," came another voice.

"I see. Well, I can't imagine what's keeping Miss Adams. She's usually very punctual."

Kate swallowed hard and smoothed her skirt. Taking a deep breath, she lifted her chin and strode in. "Sorry I'm late, gentlemen." The AC hit her like winter's blast, equal in intensity to the stony nods of the men seated around the room's long table. She made a point of making eye contact with each person—the director, three board members, a man she didn't know but assumed was from GPC, the mayor, the police chief. She gulped. What was Hank doing here? And . . . the newspaper editor?

She sank into the nearest empty chair. The cold hard plastic bit through her thin skirt, tripling the chill rattling her spine. She schooled her expression. "What can I do for you"—she focused on the director—"sir?"

The chief slapped the table. "You can start by telling us what you're trying to pull."

Her insides jumped at his outburst. All eyes focused on her. She felt like shrinking into the floor. Why hadn't Tom warned her Brewster was on the warpath against her again?

Her cell phone rang. "I'm sorry. Let me just turn that off." She dug the phone out of her purse. Tom's name appeared on the screen. *Two minutes too late.* She turned off the power and used the momentary distraction to gather her wits. "I'm afraid I don't know what you're talking about, chief."

The director pushed a piece of paper across the table to her. "This letter you sent to the newspaper office."

"I didn't send a letter." She read the paper—a scathing diatribe on GPC and the mayor's supposed ulterior motives for inviting them to locate a division here. If they were true, no wonder he looked as if his shorts had been invaded by army ants. She slid the letter back across the table. "That's not my signature." She lasered in on Chief Hank Brewster, who'd suddenly stopped smoothing his too-bushy mustache. "I don't suppose you thought to check the paper for fingerprints before passing it around the table," she said, her voice surprisingly steady considering the Mexican jumping bean dance her insides were doing.

As Brewster stammered, she shifted her gaze to the man she presumed to be from GPC. The corner of his lip twitched up, but she didn't know how to read his expression—impressed by her counterattack? Or pleased to see her rattled?

Had the director—or Peter—filled the company in on her opinions? Was this their doing?

She dug her fingers into the chair's edge. Even if Harold had printed the article, the mayor's spin doctors would have had him coming out smelling like roses . . . while grinding her career to dirt.

"You didn't send this?" the mayor said, his tone low and foreboding.

"No."

"If Harold hadn't called for a rebuttal before printing it, the damage to my office would've been irreparable."

"Then I trust the person responsible will be appropriately punished." She swept invisible dust from the table in front of her—anything to mask the wave of jitters threatening to drown her. "Was there anything else, gentlemen?"

With a single finger, King pushed his trendy, black-framed glasses to the bridge of his nose, and something about his crooked smile made it difficult to believe his concern about bringing jobs to their community was as altruistic as he wanted people to believe.

"How do we know you didn't just change your signature so you wouldn't get in trouble?" Harold asked, waving his pen. Obviously he still hoped to wring a story out of this for his paper.

"If I didn't want to get in trouble, why would I sign my name at all?"

"I think we're done here, gentlemen," the director said in a hushed yet authoritative tone.

The police chief and Harold both rose and left without another word.

"Miss Adams, you may go too," the director said.

As she rose, the stranger at the other end of the table drew a file folder from his briefcase. She dallied, pretending to have trouble untangling her purse strap from the chair arm. But the man merely leaned back in his chair, as if to wait her out, which made her all the more curious—and worried—about what he was up to.

"*Gentlemen.*" She nodded to the table in general, then strode out.

The instant the door closed, trembling overtook her limbs. She might have dodged today's pruning, but clearly the weeding-out was far from over. She turned toward the lab and gasped. "How'd you get in here?"

"I'm sorry, Detective. Mr. Ratcher isn't here," the receptionist behind the thick glass in the research center's front lobby repeated.

"But when I called, you said that the GPC reps were meeting with the board of directors."

"Yes, but Peter Ratcher wasn't with them."

Kate, escorting Lucetta Lopez, came through the security door that separated the lobby from the labs. "Tom! What are you doing here?"

Lucetta's gaze dove to the floor. Clearly she still felt intimidated by him—or was trying to hide a guilty conscience. The money she'd switched with Kate had been legal tender, so he didn't have anything but circumstantial evidence to back up his suspicions. The moment he stepped away from the small window that allowed visitors to speak to the receptionist, Lucetta slipped past him and took his place.

He pulled Kate aside and lowered his voice. "Can we speak in private?"

"Of course." She waved to Lucetta as she swiped her card through the security slot. "Good luck. I'll see you this evening."

Tom followed Kate down the hall. "You're having her clean for you?"

"She's going to help me scrub walls and ceilings so I can paint."

"Since when have you been planning to paint?"

"Uh . . . I've been thinking about it for a while."

"A while?" he said skeptically.

"Okay, I thought if she worked with me, she might tell me what she knows."

"You think she's just going to admit to counterfeiting?"

"No, of course not." Kate lowered her voice. "But she might let something slip."

He blew out a breath. "I wish you'd leave the detective work to me." He cut off her argument by motioning to the lab doors.

"You have enough on your plate. What was she doing here anyway?"

"Applying for a janitorial position. I ran into her outside the conference room."

"Unescorted?"

Kate grimaced. "Yes."

"How'd she get past the front door security?"

"Said she grabbed the side door as someone was coming out. Probably Hank and Harold. They would've assumed she was an employee. Anyone who works here is more diligent about controlling access."

Tom flexed his fingers, drew them into fists. If Lucetta could slip in here, anyone could. And after what he'd just learned about the fate of Kate's father's arresting officers . . .

Kate directed him into an empty break room. "Okay, so why are you here?"

His mind replayed what else she'd just said. "Wait a second. Hank was here? As in Chief Brewster—Hank?"

"You didn't know? I thought that's why you called. To warn me."

"No, I didn't know." He closed the door to the room. "What did he want?"

"He was trying to get me in trouble for some letter to the newspaper I didn't write that exposed the mayor's supposed secret deals."

"Why would he think you wrote it?"

"My name was at the bottom!"

"What?" His concern escalated as she recounted a play-by-play of the morning meeting. Her being incriminated for counterfeiting could have been inadvertent, but this was deliberate. "Any idea who would do this? Or why?"

"To get me in hot water with the mayor, apparently, and with half the town who would never have believed a bad word about him if it'd been printed. Not to mention with my employer. Which makes me wonder if GPC was behind the letter. Peter knows I don't want GPC here. If he told his bosses . . ."

Tom shook his head. "Too big a risk that Harold would go straight to press without checking facts. A story like this could taint their credibility as much as the mayor's." Tom paced the small, windowless room. "Could be someone inside city hall who wanted to expose the mayor but feared for his own job. Your working here, coupled with your recent notoriety, makes you a convenient scapegoat."

"They'd have to know I'd deny it."

"Yeah, but after the letter's been printed, the damage to the mayor would already be done." It made sense, even if he didn't believe it.

She shrugged. "I suppose. It's less scary than thinking GPC has launched a campaign to derail me."

The door burst open. A young woman in a lab coat, carrying a mug, glanced from Tom to Kate to the coffeepot on the narrow counter behind them and then backed out of the room. "Sorry."

Kate moaned.

Tom brushed a tendril of hair from her eyes. "What's wrong?"

Her look turned sheepish. "Last time you showed up at my work, it was to arrest me."

He winced. Not his finest moment.

"If that lab tech, or Marjorie at reception, spreads the word that you came looking for me again, I can just imagine the rumors that will start flying."

He gave her a half smile and brushed his knuckles down her cheek. "That you've forgiven me?"

"No! That I'm guilty of counterfeiting."

His stomach soured at her "no," even though he was half-way sure it didn't apply to the forgiveness part. "No one will think that. Besides, Marjorie knows I came looking for Peter."

"Oh." The word sounded hollow, as if she was disappointed his visit hadn't been personal. As much as he'd like nothing better than to explore that feeling, he refocused on why he'd come in the first place.

"Do you know why Peter isn't here?"

"I overheard the director say he had an urgent personal matter to attend to."

Tom clenched his jaw. He knew he'd seen a flicker of recognition in Peter's expression when he viewed the video clip of the plaid shirt guy watching him through the hardware store window. He'd denied it, but chances were the guy worked for GPC too. And if GPC found out what Peter knew about Kate, they might've decided to take him out of the equation.

"What's wrong?"

"What makes you think anything's wrong?" he hedged.

"Because your cheek muscle always flicks like that when you're worried."

He scraped a hand over his jaw. Good thing she hadn't been around him in his undercover days. A tell like that could've gotten him killed. He nudged her toward a chair. "I need to tell you something."

She perched on the edge, her anxious gaze searching his.

He drew in a deep breath. There was no easy way to share what he'd learned. "I think you might be right about the officers who took your father into custody. One died as the result of a hit-and-run. The driver was never found. The other was shot during a drug raid along with his partner and the suspect."

"That's horrible." Her hand slid down to her throat. "And it does sound terribly convenient, doesn't it?"

"The report says that before he died, the detective shot his killer. Ballistics matched his gun." Tom winced at the hollowed-out look in Kate's eyes, the color draining from her face. He shouldn't have told her. Not here. Not in the middle of her workday. The murder happened twenty years ago. What good could come of dredging it up?

"But . . .?" she prompted.

He let out a breath. "In the crime scene photos, the detective's gun is in his right hand, but his holster was on his left hip."

Her face went even paler. "He was set up."

"Looks that way."

"Do you think my dad's—?" Her breathing quickened and he knew what she was afraid to ask. Was her dad's heart attack a lie too? Had he really been murdered?

8

After walking Tom to the lobby, Kate headed for her lab. Her shoes squeaked on the polished marble floor of the empty hallway, and a creepy feeling trickled down her neck. She couldn't shake the images conjured by Tom's revelation of the slain police officers who'd worked Dad's case, let alone Tom's warnings to watch her back. A door slammed behind her.

She spun around. The hall was still empty. *Get a grip. No one is trying to kill you.* She skimmed her thumb over the metal key to her lab door. This edgy, check-over-her-shoulder-at-every-sound paranoia would only make GPC gloat.

And she wouldn't give them the satisfaction.

She pushed the key into the lock. Somehow she'd figure out what secret her father discovered about them and make them accountable.

Her mind flashed to an image of an ambushed police officer. Her key jammed. If GPC could take out a police officer . . .

She shook her head, refitted the key. *The Lord is my protector. Please, Lord, lead me to the truth.* She pushed through the door.

"How'd the meeting go?" Patti asked without looking up from her microscope.

"Fine."

Patti snapped off the microscope's illuminator and swiveled her chair in Kate's direction. "So they're not shutting down our research?"

"No, of course not."

"You don't have to sound so shocked. You're the one who's been worrying this GPC partnership would ruin things."

She still was, on top of a gazillion new things to worry about. Kate massaged her temples. If she didn't get a full night's sleep soon, she'd wind up with a full-blown, weeklong migraine.

Patti must've read her mind. She pulled a bottle from her pocket and tipped a couple of pills into Kate's hand. "Here, these will help with the headache. You've got to stop worrying so much."

Kate examined the pills—extra-strength acetaminophen—then gulped them down with a glass of water. "Thanks."

Her supervisor walked in as she threw back the pills. "Let me guess. You're moonlighting."

She rolled her eyes. Darryl was one to talk, with his sideline of mushroom research.

"Up too late working on the computer," she explained.

The corner of his lips ticked up. "Perfecting your design, were you?"

"Huh?" She closed her eyes. Her head hurt too much to try to decipher what he was talking about.

He opened his wallet, pulled out a twenty-dollar bill and placed it on the workbench, smoothing the edges with his fingers. "Fooled my wife."

Patti gasped. "You know Kate didn't pass off that phony bill. Beth's her friend."

Darryl chuckled. "Kate knows I'm kidding."

Kate gawked at the bill. "You need to report this. Tom—I mean, Detective Parker—is trying to track down the counterfeiter, and every lead helps. Does Beth have any idea who gave it to her?"

"I said I was kidding." Darryl slapped Kate's back, jolting her brain into a new level of torture. "I ran this off the color printer. Wanted to see how realistic it'd look."

Patti picked up the fake, rubbed the paper between her fingers, and twisted it one way, then the other as she peered at the image. "It's actually pretty good."

"Don't be getting any ideas," Kate warned in mock scolding. Patti had inherited a fortune from her parents' estate. She probably didn't even need this job, let alone a few phony bills to make ends meet.

Darryl plucked the bill from Patti's fingers. "I don't know. Could solve all my financial woes."

Patti's jaw dropped. "You wouldn't!"

"No, he wouldn't." Kate pressed her palms to his back and pushed him toward the door. Not an easy task considering he was built like a linebacker and enjoyed pulling her young assistant's leg far too much. "Don't you have real work to do, Darryl?"

"I was going to ask the same of you. Where have you been? *Your detective* called looking for you this morning."

Massaging her throbbing temples, Kate ignored his goading. Darryl took far too much delight in the fact that *a cop* was interested in dating her, considering how many times she'd said cops couldn't be trusted. "I was in a meeting." She shooed him toward the door. "And the sooner you leave, the sooner I can get to work." She shut the door behind him, then rejoined Patti.

As they worked through their samples, her pain-dulled mind drifted over the various internet articles she'd read last night. Peter had said her dad had been watching TV in the airport coffee shop when he'd arrived, which suggested, assuming he'd told the truth, that something Dad saw had sparked his decision. She'd assumed it had been a news item. But maybe it was a documentary. Or just an image that had triggered a realization. Kate pinched the bridge of her nose, frustrated by how little the pain meds had done for her headache.

Patti straightened from hunching over the bench and stretched her back. "Can you believe Darryl actually printed a phony twenty-dollar bill?"

"Obviously has too much time on his hands." She'd have to ask Tom if he knew yet how the counterfeit bills were made. She doubted Lucetta had a computer if she was scraping to send money home every month. But Pedro likely had access to friends' computers. They'd think it a lark, too, to print off a bunch of counterfeit bills.

Counterfeit. *Counterfeit.* What if that's what Dad had discovered? What if the university research was a bogus cover story GPC used to gain access to the plant resources they wanted in Colombia? That would explain why her online searches didn't score a single university working on a research project for them at that time.

Except . . .

How could she prove it? They apparently never got what they were after. Which was weird. Why not just send someone else to retrieve more plants? *Unless . . .*

Her heart jitterbugged. Unless they'd really been after

something else, something that had been smuggled into the country along with the plants.

She clamped her pounding head between her hands and groaned. The whole scenario was starting to sound like a B movie—bad and unbelievable.

Tom's appetite soured at the sight of Hank and the mayor having lunch together in A Cup or Two. The mayor—a poster boy for tall, dark, and handsome, although he reminded Tom of a weasel—seemed to have the chief's unquestioning support, which, if the mayor was guilty of any of the allegations in that letter, didn't bode well for Hank's future.

Tom shoved the thought away as he bypassed the sidebar filled with canisters of herbal teas and ordered a coffee and muffin from the counter at the back of the store. Tom slanted another glance at his childhood-friend-turned-boss. Hank had too much to prove to this town. Becoming a dirty cop would just prove what the naysayers had been saying about his old friend since high school. Like father, like son. Criminal.

Hank waved him over. "Join us."

Tom nodded to King. "Mayor."

"Detective." King pulled out the chair next to him, and Tom reluctantly took a seat. "Any progress on the counterfeit case?"

"We've confirmed the counterfeit bills were printed on a color laser printer on a unique specialty paper."

"Laser?" King straightened his glasses and peered at him more intently. "Those aren't that common, are they? Should be able to narrow in on a suspect in no time."

Right. Tom tiredly peeled the paper from his muffin. *Some-*

one's been watching too many cop shows. "Without corroborating evidence to justify a search warrant, I can't simply check the memory of every color laser printer in town. The counterfeiter might not even live here."

"As my grandpappy liked to say, work is ninety-nine percent perspiration—" King's cell phone buzzed.

"And one percent inspiration," Tom mumbled, repeating the oft-used saying the mayor trotted out for every other inspirational speech he gave around town.

"Exactly!" King clicked off his phone with only a quick glance at the screen. "You've got your inspiration. Now find the people with that kind of printer and check them out. Most would be more than happy to let you. Don't you think? To prove their innocence."

"Yeah." Hank put down his sandwich. "If they agree to let you check, you don't need a warrant."

"And if they don't agree," the mayor added, "you'll have one more name for your suspect list."

Tom bit into his muffin to avoid the need to comment. Unfortunately, he already had more than enough suspects. But his prime ones—Pedro, and Lucetta Lopez—had already denied owning computers, let alone printers. And the hotel Peter stayed in only had ink-jet printers available to their clientele.

"It's important we maintain our stellar town image," the mayor went on.

Stellar? Tom choked on his bite of muffin. Three months ago the counter girl from this very tea shop had murdered Kate's friend and then tried to off Kate. He sipped his coffee to keep from saying as much. No need to agitate the man. "I'll do my best, sir."

"That's what I like to hear." He flashed one of his toothy campaign smiles.

Tom fought not to roll his eyes.

"The mayor is courting a couple of other major employers for the town," Hank shared.

"Really?" Tom wasn't sure how he felt about that. A lot of folks around here needed jobs, but . . . "You're not afraid we'll lose the small-town feel we've worked so hard to promote?" He motioned to the picture window at the front of the shop. The cobbled street. The wrought iron lampposts. The old-fashioned brick storefronts decorated with potted petunias of red and white and every shade of pink in between.

"We did that to attract tourism dollars, but the market's too seasonal. We need year-round employment for our citizens." His voice rose to stump quality as he seemed to realize others were listening in.

Oh brother. Does this man ever take a break?

"Hear, hear," cheered a guy who'd just walked in the door—the same guy who'd questioned Kate's innocence, and his ethics, the last time Tom was in here.

King waved to him. "Thanks, Vic." King lowered his voice and leaned forward. "There's a prime example. Vic hasn't had steady employment since the feed mill closed over a year ago."

"He seems to be doing okay," Tom countered. "Has his own lawn care business. I saw him mowing a lawn this morning."

"Doesn't pay enough, though. He's always looking for more work. Even contracts out to a janitorial service a couple of nights a week." King's gaze flitted across nearby tables, and he lifted his voice. "A man shouldn't have to work day and night to make ends meet."

A whispered frenzy of "So true" and "That's why I voted for King" rose around them.

An uneasy feeling settled in the pit of Tom's stomach. If Kate got her way and blocked GPC's move here, she'd become the town pariah overnight.

King winked at him, not the least bit ashamed at his blatant campaigning. Considering the next election would be this fall, he probably hoped to get at least one new business breaking ground in their town before citizens went to the polls. Tom hoped for Kate's sake that it wasn't GPC.

Apparently satisfied with his brief publicity plug, King returned his attention to his cell phone and tapped the screen. "Can you believe the gall of this woman?" King slanted his phone so Hank could read the text message. "I knew she was lying about the letter."

Tom tensed. Was King talking about Kate? He leaned over to try to see the screen.

Hank turned it for him with an almost gleeful look. "I told you that woman couldn't be trusted."

At the sender's name—Kate Adams—Tom pressed his lips shut and read,

I should've known someone as crooked as you would control the media too.

"That doesn't sound like Kate," Tom said.

"Wake up, Parker. Clearly, she's not what you think." Hank downed the last of his coffee, then clunked the mug on the table, wiping his mouth with the back of his hand. "Looks like we need to pay the research station another visit, Mayor."

"Wait." Tom stayed the mayor's hand and pulled out his

own phone to compare numbers. Just as he thought. "That's not her, see."

He showed the mayor her name and number in his contact list. "The numbers don't match."

"She must've gotten a new number."

"Since this morning?" Tom shook his head. "I contacted her at this number a few hours ago." At least she said she'd gotten the message. "Someone's setting her up."

"Why would anyone want to do that?" Hank snatched Tom's phone and glanced from his screen to King's.

"I don't know." Tom jotted the number into his notebook, his mind racing through several unpalatable possibilities. "But I'll do my best to find out who's behind this."

"Don't waste your time." Hank shoved his chair back from the table. "The counterfeiting case is top priority."

"Hold up there, Chief." The mayor slipped his phone back into his blazer pocket. "Wasn't this Adams woman the one caught passing phony money at the grocery store?"

"She's not a counterfeiter." Tom gritted his teeth. How had he completely lost control of this conversation? "Her story checked out," he said evenly, straining to not appear emotionally involved. "Not to mention she only has an ink-jet printer and no scanner capabilities."

King assessed him with a scowl as Tom, in an effort he hoped wasn't visible, held his gaze with an impassive look. "Then it looks like someone is going to a lot of trouble to make her look bad. Why do you suppose that is?"

"I don't know, sir. But clearly whoever sent this was privy to what went down in this morning's meeting."

With one eyebrow raised, the mayor slipped on his sunglasses. "Apparently, as were you."

Not about to be baited, Tom reached for his coffee, rather than respond.

"I don't appreciate being in the middle of whatever cat and mouse game this person is playing, so I suggest you find out who's behind the letter and text message. Wouldn't you agree, Chief?"

"Of course. Don't leave any stone unturned, Parker. That's an order."

Whoa. What just happened? As the pair walked out, Tom sat back, stunned. Here he'd been disgruntled with the whole conversation, and all of a sudden he'd been ordered—ordered, no less!—to find out what he'd wanted to find out anyway. Good thing too. With his growing suspicions of just what GPC was capable of, he had a bad feeling this cat and mouse game could turn deadly.

The instant Tom stepped through the library door, Julie's eyes sparkled his way. If she weren't Kate's friend, and married, he'd think she were flirting. More likely, flirting with the idea of being a matchmaker.

He smiled, then immediately nixed the reaction. He needed to run this investigation by reason, not emotion.

"How can I help you, Detective?" Julie asked as he reached the checkout counter.

On the bulletin boards behind her, brightly colored signs announced upcoming events and a large graph measured how many books each of the children in their book club had read to date in their summer reading challenge. Laughter drifted from the children's area to the right of the counter, where another librarian was reading to a group of youngsters.

"Do you keep a log of which patrons use your computers?" Tom scanned the faces of the youth monopolizing the half-dozen computers available to patrons. According to King's cell phone provider, the text had originated from an IP address matching the library's network, not a cell phone. The sender had identified him or herself as Kate and entered a bogus phone number, but he or she could've been anyone.

"The computers?" Julie repeated, looking a little dumb-founded. "Uh, sure."

"May I see it?"

"What's this about?"

"A police matter." No way did he want this getting back to Kate unnecessarily. No reason for them both to burn ulcers worrying about this guy's ulterior motives.

Julie grabbed a binder from the end of the counter. "We have really strong filters on our system. The kids aren't supposed to be able to access anything bad."

"It's nothing like that," he assured.

"That's a relief." She flipped open the binder to the book-marked page. "This is where people sign in. Summer is our busiest time. Lots of kids waiting to get on, so each one is allowed half an hour."

He began copying down the names, none of which, at first glance, set off any alarm bells.

"Want me to just photocopy the pages for you?" Julie spoke up.

"That'd be great." Tom shoved the binder back across the counter, wracked by sudden doubts this lead would pan out the way he'd hoped.

She snapped open the binder rings, pulled out two pages, then frowned.

"What's wrong?"

"A page must be missing." She pointed to the first entry at 11:00 a.m. "We open at 10:00, and like I said, we always have lots of people vying for the computers all day." She flipped back another page. "It's not here."

"Do you happen to recall who came in first thing this morning?"

"Actually, I didn't come in until noon. I'll ask Barb." Julie disappeared through a door marked for employees only, and it occurred to Tom that the text message could have been sent from a staff computer too. According to the tech rep he'd talked to on the phone, the network assigned the final sequential digit of the IP address in the order the computers logged on to the system, which meant the same computer could be assigned several different IP addresses over the course of the day, depending on how many times it'd been rebooted.

At the circle of computers, a teen called over his friend and pointed to something on the screen. They then traded places.

Clearly, identifying his text writer wasn't going to be as straightforward as he hoped.

Julie returned a moment later with his copies. "Barb says they had a problem with the computers this morning. No one got onto them before 11:00."

"Thanks. Could you tell me who had access to staff computers today?"

"That would be Barbara Owens and Mrs. Peabody and me. Oh, and we always have a couple of student volunteers, but they don't go on the computers. Anything else I can help you with?"

He scanned the sheets she'd given him. None of the names meant anything to him. As much as he hadn't wanted to worry

Kate with this latest development, he'd have to ask her to look them over. "A few of these are signed with only initials. Can you tell me who they are?"

"Yeah, our regulars—all kids. Tony Trace, Susan Leonard, Nikki Kite, and . . ." Julie tapped her pen on the counter as her gaze drifted to the far wall. Finally she shook her head. "Not sure who PL is."

Another librarian joined them. "Hey Barb, do you know who PL is?"

Barb glanced at the log book entry Julie pointed to. "Pedro Lopez, maybe. He comes in pretty often. Not usually on a weekday, though."

Pedro, yes! Kate had said the kid made her nervous. Tom snatched up the papers and hurried to the door. "Thanks!"

As he jogged back to his car, he reviewed potential scenarios. Kate had said Lucetta was hanging around outside the meeting room this morning . . . listening in? She could've asked her nephew to send the incriminating text. But why?

He'd assumed their letter writer and texter were one and the same. But how would either Pedro or Lucetta come up with all that semi-believable dirt on the mayor, let alone know his personal cell phone number? Unless . . .

Maybe Lucetta knew King's housekeeper. The help always knew everybody's dirt. Maybe they were really only after the mayor and figured Kate's name, as a research scientist, carried the authority needed to convince the paper to print their letter.

Yeah, he'd like nothing more than to believe Kate was an unwitting victim here, but his gut told him that was wishful thinking.

Then again, employers were always underestimating the intelligence of their house staff, and from his experience, the staff always knew exactly what was going on. Maybe the mayor's housekeeper decided the town should know too and elicited Pedro and Lucetta's help.

Sliding into his car, Tom glanced at the dashboard clock. Lucetta might already be on her way to Kate's for their cleaning spree. If Lucetta was behind both the counterfeiting and these messages, who knew how she'd react if Kate provoked her with a barrage of questions.

He turned in the direction of Kate's house. With any luck, Lucetta's nephew would give her a lift like he had the other day, and Tom could question them both at once.

Ten minutes later, Tom knocked on Kate's door for the third time. He'd seen her bedroom window blinds close as he pulled up to the house. She was in there.

The door edged open and Kate appeared behind the screen door, her red hair mussed, one eye squinted closed. "What are you doing here?" Pain tinged her voice.

He tugged open the screen door. "What's wrong?"

"Migraine." She plodded to the sofa and laid down, pressing an ice pack to the back of her neck.

"Can I get you a pain pill or something?"

She rolled her head his direction. "I've already taken all I'm allowed." She curled onto her side and moaned as if she'd been suddenly punched. Her breathing came in short gasps.

He dropped to his knees at her side, feeling as if he'd been punched too. "Try to take deep breaths." He picked up the ice pack she'd let drop and held it to the back of her neck. If hearing about the fate of her father's arresting officers had done this to her, then he really didn't want to mention the mayor's text message.

Her breathing evened out. "Thank you," she mumbled.

He brushed a strand of hair from her cheek. "I guess you canceled your plans with Lucetta?"

"Oh, no. I forgot. I need to call—" She pushed herself up to a sitting position and instantly clutched her head.

Tom nudged her back down and set the ice pack on the end table. "I'll take care of calling her." The questions he needed to ask Lucetta would be better handled in person, but not until he was sure Kate was going to be okay.

An old pickup rattled up the road as he pulled out his phone. "Looks like we're too late. I'll go out and let her know what's going on."

Lucetta was already to the porch by the time he stepped outside. "Oh!" She jolted back a step. "I didn't expect—"

"I'm afraid Kate will need to reschedule."

Pedro started to pull away.

Tom flagged him. "Hold up, Pedro. Your aunt's going to need a ride," he called out over the rumble of the kid's noisy muffler. "Kate's ill," Tom explained to Lucetta, walking her back to the truck. "She's sorry she wasn't able to notify you before you made the trip out."

"This happens," Lucetta said in broken English.

Tom paused with his hand on the truck door, keeping her from climbing in. "Before you go, do you happen to know who keeps house for the mayor?"

"No, he looking for a housekeeper?" she asked eagerly.

So much for that theory. "Not that I know of, no. I thought perhaps you might know who works for him."

"No, I not know many people."

He darted a glance Pedro's direction to see if his reaction gave anything away, because listening to Lucetta's choppy English, Tom realized it was unlikely she'd written the letter to the editor. "How about you? You know anyone connected to the mayor?" Tom asked Pedro through the open passenger window. A sickening combination of diesel fuel and rotten food wafted from the interior.

Pedro shook his head. His hands didn't tighten around the steering wheel. Not a single muscle so much as twitched at the question. Either he was a gifted liar or he had nothing to do with the mayor's text message.

"Were you on one of the computers at the library this afternoon?" Tom asked directly.

The kid snorted. "You kidding? The boss never lets us out early."

"It's nice of him to let you use the company truck to drive your aunt. Didn't he let you leave work earlier this week to pick her up?"

His eyes narrowed. "What's with all the questions?"

From the corner of his eye, Tom noted that Lucetta began to squirm. Anxious to get away, he could understand. But was it because he'd gotten too close to the truth? The only thing keeping Pedro from taking off was waiting for Tom to let his aunt inside the truck. Tom clasped the door handle as if to open it for her.

"I need to talk to anyone who used the library computers today. One was signed out to a PL. The librarian said that was you."

"Not today. Ask my boss. I didn't leave work until 5:00."

Tom opened the door. "Yeah, I'll do that."

Lucetta slid Pedro a nervous glance but avoided making eye contact with Tom. An ingrained reaction to the police? Or did she mistrust her nephew as much as he did?

As they pulled away from the curb, an animated discussion

erupted in the pickup's cab. But was Pedro vehemently shaking his head because he was innocent, or guilty? Tom text-messaged Hank. Pedro probably had no idea his boss was the father of the chief of police. They'd know soon enough if Pedro could've been in the library this afternoon or not.

When Tom turned back to the house, Kate stood at the front door watching him through the screen. "What were you talking about with Lucetta and Pedro for so long?"

He shrugged as if the conversation was no big deal. "I had a few questions."

A smile played on her lips. Surprising, considering how dragged out she'd been only minutes ago. Her pain medicine must have kicked in. "You know I can always tell when you're hedging."

He held in a smile. Could she read him so well? He changed to a subject he was willing to talk about. "How's the head?"

"See." She wagged her finger at him. "Like that. You're hedging."

With a chuckle, he urged her back inside. As much as he'd rather not worry her about the text message, he did need her to look at the list of names Julie photocopied for him. Besides, her friend was bound to mention his being at the library. He squinted at Kate. Was that what had prompted her to come looking for him? Had Julie already given her the inside scoop?

This time Kate plopped into an armchair instead of sprawling onto the sofa. "Is that what brought you here? You wanted to talk to Lucetta?"

Busted. He grinned. "That bother you?"

She rolled her eyes. "Julie called. What's going on? This have anything to do with the counterfeiting? She said Pedro was one of the names on the list you took."

"No, nothing to do with the counterfeiting." At least no connection that he could see, unless she'd been right about that being an attempt to set her up too. He might be able to build a case for criminal harassment. He sat on the edge of the sofa and unfolded the pages of names. "The mayor received a text message along the same vein as that letter to the editor. It originated from one of the library's computers. Any of these names stand out to you?"

She glanced at the top page. "What do you mean by stand out?"

"Are you familiar with any of the people, in either a positive or negative way?"

"What's it got to do with me?"

He shifted the top page so the two lay side by side. There was no easy way to soften the blow. "The sender used your name."

Her sharp intake of breath made his heart hitch, especially when she immediately began pressing her fingertips to her temple again.

"The mayor knows you didn't send it. But we don't have a good handle on the sender's motive. Is he just trying to rattle the mayor and thought using the name of someone at the research center—you—would work the best? Or is he really trying to get you in trouble?"

Kate traced her finger down the list of names. "Most of these people are kids. I recognize quite a few of the family names from church, but aside from PL, which I assume is Pedro, I don't really *know* any of them."

"You can't think of any reason why one of these people might have a grudge against you?"

She frowned. "No. The only person who's been annoyed with me is Verna's son when I refused to help him send her

131

to a nursing home. But now that she's in one, I can't see him still being irritated with me."

"And his name's not on the list." Pedro was still the most viable suspect, unless maybe one of these names meant something to the mayor. "You're sure there's no one else?"

"Not on the list." She closed her eyes and massaged tiny circles in the center of her forehead.

"Someone else has a grudge?"

Her breath seeped out in a weary sigh. "Yeah, Molly Gilmore."

9

After work Thursday afternoon, Kate finally got to the nursing home to see Verna. She'd planned to drop in Wednesday after work, but Tom had sidelined that plan when he'd insisted she revisit every last name on the library list for possible motives. Apparently Pedro's alibi had been solid, and the mayor hadn't raised a single red flag on any of the names either. Tom had been skeptical of her suggestion that maybe Molly Gilmore paid someone to incriminate her, but in the end, he'd visited every person on the list to judge for himself. And he still didn't know what to think.

Drawing a deep breath, she shoved the disturbing possibilities from her mind. The fragrance from vases of mixed flowers scented the air, but not quite enough to dispel an underlying liniment odor. In the main floor common area, a health care aide helped a frail woman into a chair next to a sunny window.

Kate smiled at the memory of Tom fussing over her on Tuesday night because of her headache. She couldn't remember the last time anyone had fussed over her. She had to admit it had felt pretty nice. Much nicer than his all-business focus of last night's visit.

Outside the home's locked wing, Kate peered through the window at the lost souls wandering the halls or sitting in wheelchairs mumbling to themselves. Her heart sank. How horrible for Verna to go from the freedom of living in her own home to being restricted from even stepping outside without supervision. Sure, the Alzheimer's patients needed security, but not Verna. She'd been a little confused was all.

A nurse pushed open the door and waved Kate in. "Mrs. Nagy is in the common room at the end of the hall."

Kate admired the woman's cheery voice, considering the sad state of her patients.

"Kate," Verna squealed the instant Kate stepped into the sunny room.

Two other patients dozed in their wheelchairs. A TV flickered in the corner.

Verna rose, more sprightly than Kate had ever seen her, and beckoned her to a couple of lounge chairs by the picture window overlooking the grounds.

Kate pulled her into a warm embrace. Verna still felt too frail, but her face had filled out. "You look wonderful. This place must agree with you."

"The food is good." Verna's blue eyes lit. "Best I've had in a long while. Never bothered much with cooking after my Robert died."

Kate sat in the seat across from Verna. "Didn't Lucetta cook for you?"

Verna wrinkled her nose. "I never much cared for her spicy dishes."

"So you like it here?"

"The nurses are nice."

"You think you'll be happy here?"

Verna spread her palms wide. "The Good Book says to learn to be content whatever the circumstances."

"You look content."

"I've had more visitors in the few days I've been here than the whole last month at home," she said, but Kate didn't miss the fact that Verna hadn't really answered any of her questions.

Kate let her gaze drift to the manicured lawn and flower gardens outside the window. "The grounds are beautiful."

A faraway look flitted across Verna's face. "It reminds me of our old farm."

"I didn't know you used to live on a farm."

"Oh, yes. It's out by old Mrs. Brewster's place. Overgrown now, I imagine. Robert and I used to love to go there for walks, especially along the stream. It's a lovely spot. Has some rare animals and plants too, because of how the hills protect it."

"Wow. I'll have to drop by there and explore sometime. Who owns the property now?"

"I do. My Robert always said we'd donate it to the town as a park when he passed on." Her voice turned wistful. "But I hadn't wanted to part with it just yet."

"That's understandable."

Verna grew quiet, her gaze drifting as if her thoughts had carried her to the property she loved. Her forehead creased, the smile slipping from her lips. "Don't suppose I'll get out there much anymore. I best talk to the mayor."

Kate almost suggested Verna let her lawyer take care of it, but she supposed her son would see to that.

Verna shook off her sudden melancholy and rubbed her

hands together like a child anticipating a treat. "How's my Whiskers?"

"He misses you." The night of her migraine, Tom said he'd found the poor thing meowing at Verna's door. Kate couldn't believe she'd forgotten about him in her rush that morning. From the way Whiskers had twined around Tom's legs last night, he'd clearly become the feline's hero.

"The poor thing." Verna's fingers stroked the armrest as if kneading the cat's fur. "I should be home soon."

Kate frowned. Did Verna not understand this was a permanent move?

Verna nodded as if she'd read her thoughts. "The doctor checked on me today. He's so pleased with my improvement. Said I should be able to go back home if I don't suffer another setback."

"That's wonderful! Have you told your son?"

She laughed. "He'd accuse me of hallucinating. The doctor said he'd talk to him."

Kate glanced at the other two patients in the room. Was Verna hallucinating? Or maybe wishful thinking. Her mind seemed perfectly sound.

The nurse strolled through the room and checked on each of the patients, then stopped next to Verna. "Would you like me to brew a cup of tea for you and your friend?"

"No thanks." Verna didn't so much as give Kate a questioning glance.

"Okay." The nurse winked at Kate. "Let me know if you change your mind."

The moment the nurse left the room, Verna leaned toward Kate. "Their tea tastes horrible. I miss my herbals."

"I'd be happy to bring some in for you."

"Would you dear? You have my key. They're in the blue containers on the kitchen counter."

"No problem. I can drop them by tomorrow morning on my way to work. I meant to ask too if you had any of that medicine for Whiskers that Grandma Brewster had given you when he ate that plant he shouldn't have?"

Verna's eyes teared. "He's doing poorly?"

Jabbed with regret at upsetting her, Kate quickly backpedaled. "He's probably just out of sorts. You know how animals can be. I just thought it wouldn't hurt to give him some as a precaution." She didn't mention that she'd found Daisy's aloe vera plant chewed this morning. Great to treat burns—toxic to cats.

"Oh, yes, the poor thing. But I'm not sure I have much of the tincture left. It would be in the cupboard next to the fridge."

"That's okay. I can always pick up more from Grandma Brewster." Considering how many other plants she might need to find safer homes for before Whiskers decided to sample them too, she'd be smart to have a full bottle of the remedy on hand.

"Are you sure? I don't want to put you out."

"I'm happy to. I can take a peek at your property while I'm there. I'd love to see what kind of plants grow there."

The wistful look returned to Verna's eyes. "My Robert doesn't farm it anymore. Hasn't in years."

Kate's heart sank again. Did Verna think her husband was still alive? She hadn't a moment ago.

"Well, you know what I mean." Verna's hand went to her throat. She rubbed her heart-shaped locket between her fingers. "He's been gone three years this month. He used to rent the one field out to other farmers. Seems to me we rented it to an Adams one year. Maybe your grandpa. Not sure if anyone rents it now. I guess I'd better ask Brian to check. Can't very well give the land out from under him before he gets his crop in."

Kate smiled. Except for the part about her grandpa renting the land—he'd been a farmer, but they'd lived in the next township—the woman was more lucid than Kate felt half the time these days. Would Tom theorize that her earlier episodes had been a ploy to throw suspicion off herself for counterfeiting?

Last night he'd said that no more phony bills had surfaced since Verna's admission to the home. A coincidence, perhaps. Or someone was trying to frame her. Or whoever had been using her to launder his phony bills was lying low for a while now that the police were investigating.

Either possibility was more palatable than believing Verna was a con artist.

"You have another visitor," the nurse announced cheerily, returning with Verna's grandson. He wore saggy jeans and a strategically torn T-shirt that would've made Kate's gran cringe, but Verna's eyes gleamed with appreciation at the sight of him.

The sandy blond teen ducked and gave her a kiss on the cheek. "Hi Gran. You look as beautiful as ever."

Verna's cheeks bloomed. She swatted his shoulder. "Go on with ya."

Kate marveled at the interplay. Most young men Greg's age would be out playing video games with friends or hanging with a girl. She stood and patted Verna's hand. "I need to head out. I'll bring by that tea tomorrow."

"Thank you." Verna fluttered her hand in farewell and then quickly returned her attention to her obviously much-adored grandson.

Kate's heart squeezed. How she missed her grandparents.

She wandered out of the building and noticed a couple walking the grounds hand in hand. That would've been her grandparents. They were so in love. A wistful sigh escaped her lips. She longed to have what they had . . . until she thought about what losing Dad did to Mom. The depression had grown worse with each year, until one day she couldn't remember ever seeing her mother happy. Snatching a few years of happiness didn't seem worth the price. Mom had said as much more times than Kate cared to remember.

An eerie feeling—like she was being watched—prickled her skin.

She glanced over her shoulder at the residents sitting on benches in front of the building, then squinted at car windshields in the parking lot. At the sight of the worn-out Herbs Are Us pickup parked on the street, she stopped short. What was it doing here?

Rock music boomed from the vehicle.

Rather than go to her car, she strolled down the path that circled the parking lot to get a better look. Pedro sat inside the truck, his head bobbing and his fingers tapping the steering wheel. He didn't seem to be watching for anyone. So what was he up to? Bringing Lucetta to visit Verna?

A moment later, Verna's grandson bounded out of the front of the building and headed straight to Pedro's truck. The instant he climbed in, the truck zoomed away.

Suddenly the young man's visit didn't seem so innocent.

Tom shifted in the front seat of his car for a better vantage point and his heart jerked. Ignoring Pedro's truck squealing

139

away, he leaned toward the passenger window. No mistake. The guy in the silver Ford Escort two rows behind Kate's Bug was spying on her.

And that fact disturbed Tom more than the new note burning a hole in his pocket. The note he'd found tucked under his windshield wiper after his shift ended. Unlike the last note, this one warned him to trust no one where Kate's safety was concerned, except that it sounded more like a veiled threat than the warning of a concerned citizen.

Tom climbed from his car parked at the curb and approached the Escort from behind. Dirt obscured the license plate, but the first letter looked like a B. Sitting in her car, Kate appeared to be searching for something in her purse and hopefully wouldn't notice him. He hadn't expected to find her here. As he left work, he'd spotted Pedro picking up Verna's grandson from the town's weekly farmers' market and had followed them on the off chance they might do something to incriminate themselves in the counterfeiting spree. Pedro might have alibied out on sending the text message, but seeing Kate's car in the parking lot when he arrived had been too uncomfortable a coincidence.

Two strides from the guy's rear fender Tom hesitated.

Their gazes collided in the car's side mirror.

The car's engine roared to life. In case the guy got it into his head to suddenly reverse, Tom veered sideways and instantly catalogued the driver's features—reddish-gray short hair, weathered face, square chin, plaid shirt. The same guy who'd been spying on Peter Ratcher.

Tom lurched forward, but before he could grab the door handle, the car streaked off.

Tom raced back to his car and pulled onto the street just as Kate turned right two blocks up. The Escort had disappeared.

The grip on Tom's chest eased a fraction. At least he wasn't following Kate . . . for the moment. But the fact this guy had been spying on both Peter Ratcher *and* Kate was bad news. Really bad news. He slowed at the first intersection and scanned both directions for signs of the Escort. How could the guy have given him the slip so fast?

Tom turned right in case the guy had anticipated Kate's turn on the next block and planned to cut her off. A silver Escort crested the hill ahead. *Got you.*

A kid on a bike barreled out of a driveway in front of him. Tom slammed his brakes, swerving wide.

The kid ramped onto the grass, his bug-eyed gaze fixed on Tom. The next second, the kid's bike slammed into a tree.

Tom sprang from his car. "You okay?"

At the end of the street, the gleam of brake lights turned left, back into Kate's path.

Tom quickly lifted the bike off the blond-haired boy, who didn't look much older than Tom's nephews. The kid hugged his scraped knees to his chest, and Tom hunkered down beside him. "What's your name, son?"

The boy shook his head. "Not supposed to talk to strangers."

"You're right. But I'm a police officer and I want to help you." Tom glanced at the empty front yards. "Where do you live?"

"No you're not." The boy edged away from him. "Off-fer-sirs wear uniforms."

"Yeah, I am." Tom flipped open his ID. "I'm after a criminal here and he's getting away."

The boy stared up at Tom open-mouthed. Or more precisely at his gun.

A woman dashed from the house, a baby propped on her hip. "What's going on?"

"Mama!" The boy scrambled to his feet and buried his face against the woman's stomach.

Tom introduced himself and filled her in on the mishap. "Now, if you'll excuse me, I need to go."

"He's after a bad guy," the boy said. "He's got a gun."

Sure, now he talks. Tom didn't stick around long enough to find out what the kid's mother thought about him revealing his gun to a four-year-old. Back in his car, he shifted into Drive and said, "Phone Kate," to his new voice-activated phone. At the sound of Kate's unruffled hello, his grip on the steering wheel relaxed. "Where are you?"

"Uh . . . driving."

"Driving where?"

"Nowhere at the moment. I stopped to answer the phone." Her tone turned playful. "I wouldn't want to be arrested for talking on the phone while driving."

His relief that she seemed okay rumbled out in a chuckle. "Smart move." But even as he asked her where she was, he strained to hear any telltale sounds that someone might be threatening her.

The ding of a railroad crossing signal sounded faintly in the background.

"I just left the nursing home," she responded, clearly hedging since she hadn't headed in the direction of her house.

Tom hung a left onto the next street and stepped on the gas. The town had only two railroad crossing signals. One out by the elementary school. The other out by Moyer's ravine. The one by the school was the closest.

The rattle and rumble of an approaching train grew louder in his ear. He hit his window button and as the window slid open, the blast of a train's whistle confirmed he was heading to the right crossing.

"Can we meet?" he asked, turning his car onto the road that intersected the tracks. He slowed at the sight of her car parked in the corner of the empty school parking lot. Too many years in the FBI had him thinking she was a sitting duck and scoping the rooftops for signs of a sniper.

"Uh, when were you thinking?"

Rolling his car up next to hers, he tried not to take her reluctant-sounding response personally. "How's now suit?" he asked, still talking into the phone.

She jumped at his sudden appearance, but better at him than some psycho in a Ford Escort.

"What are you doing here?" she said into her phone, then looked from it to him, clicked it off, and opened her window.

He came around and leaned over her door. "Trying to catch women talking on their cell phones."

She made a face.

"How about you? This isn't the way home."

This time, she ducked her head. "Pedro and Verna's grandson showed up at the nursing home. I decided to follow them. See what they were up to."

Tom laughed.

"What's so funny? I thought I might spot them doing something incriminating."

"I'm not laughing at you. I was following them too, until—"

The last few cars of the train rumbled past. The chime of the railroad crossing warning fell silent and the caution bar lifted. A car puttered past the school, the elderly driver craning his neck to look their way. Not the silver Escort, but it still made him edgy.

"How about I follow you home and we talk there?"

Pulling into her driveway, Kate took a deep breath and tried not to jump to conclusions, but Tom's tone had sounded so serious. This morning he'd said that the police department responsible for her father's arrest was couriering a copy of his file. *His arrest file.* He'd really been arrested, not just taken in for questioning, as she'd always wanted to believe. What if Tom had learned something really bad?

She hadn't known what to make of his pained look when he cut off his explanation back at the train crossing.

Tom parked behind her.

Bracing for the worst, she glanced in her rearview mirror. His furrowed brow and pensive expression only heightened her apprehension. He caught sight of her watching him, but didn't offer a smile to chase away her worry.

She grabbed her purse and slid out of the car. Any hope that today's visit might be a pleasant repeat of their Sunday afternoon walk at Niagara Parks vanished. With each passing day, he'd grown more distant, as if maybe he regretted his whispered *I care about you.*

He caught her elbow, his breath tickling the hairs of her neck. "What's wrong?"

Heat rushed to her cheeks. "Nothing, I—" She glanced around in hopes of noticing something else she might blame her frown on.

Brian Nagy came around from the side of Verna's house accompanied by a balding man in a business suit with a digital camera slung over his shoulder. Tom visibly tensed.

"Do you know who that guy is?" Kate asked.

Tom studied him a moment longer, then seemed to relax again. "Isn't he the real estate agent? Westby."

"That's what I was afraid of." Leaving Tom standing in the driveway, she stalked toward Brian. *Go easy*, a voice inside her head cautioned. Striving for a neighborly tone, she said, "What's going on?"

Westby turned his salesman smile on her as Brian said, "Exploring options."

"Options?"

"Now that Mother's settled into long-term care, we need to decide what to do with the house and properties."

"You'll see me around now and again showing clients the place," the real estate agent chimed in. "But we'll do our best not to disturb your privacy."

Kate checked the urge to mention Verna's plans to return home. If they weren't a figment of his mother's imagination, Brian would hear of them soon enough. "Um, Verna mentioned that she planned to donate her farm property to the town?"

"Donate it?" Westby's eyebrows connected with what remained of his hairline as his gaze swung to Brian.

"No! Why would I do that?"

"Your mom said that she and your dad had always planned to." Kate tilted her head, hoping to look nonthreatening. "Didn't she tell you?"

A whisper of acknowledgment flitted across Brian's eyes, but he didn't admit to it.

"That area is a unique microclimate," Kate pressed. "Probably home to several rare plants and animals. I'm sure the town will want to ensure that it's conserved."

"It's private property. None of the town's business." Brian's eyes narrowed. "Or yours."

She shrank back at his caustic tone. Then Tom stepped to her side, his solid presence bolstering her confidence. "It's what your mom wants," she said. "She told me as much not more than an hour ago."

"Nursing homes are more expensive than my mother realizes." Brian wagged a finger in her face.

"Excuse me. I need to get going." The agent beat a hasty retreat.

Brian scarcely acknowledged the man's departure, but at least he withdrew his wagging finger and crossed his arms over his chest. "I'd appreciate it if you don't fill Mother's head with impossible ideas. In fact, just stay away from her altogether."

Kate defiantly crossed her own arms. "I can't do that." At Tom's cautioning touch, she added, "I promised I'd deliver some of her tea tomorrow."

Brian dismissed the promise with a flick of his wrist. "I'll ask Lucetta to do that. If you'll excuse me." He gave them both a brisk nod, turned on his heel, and headed into Verna's house.

"Looks like you struck a nerve," Tom said.

"You don't think he'd sell the property without telling Verna, do you?"

"If he's got power of attorney, he might." Tom maneuvered her back toward her house. "Brian's wife really did clean him out, and even a basic room in a long-term care home isn't cheap. Sometimes we have to do things we don't necessarily want to do to protect a loved one's welfare."

Kate glanced back at the door Brian had disappeared through. "I'm not so sure it's his mom's welfare he's concerned about."

"That's a switch."

Kate's attention snapped back to Tom. "What do you mean?"

"Usually you're the one giving people the benefit of the doubt."

"I know, but I can't help it. He just . . ." She fitted her key in the lock, not really wanting to admit how she felt. "He rubs me the wrong way."

Tom didn't respond, but amusement danced in his eyes.

Kate sighed and trudged into her house. "You don't understand. Verna thinks she's coming home. Brian clearly hasn't talked to his mother at all about her wishes. And it's her property!"

"Unfortunately, if Verna gave him power of attorney, he has that right."

Kate dropped her purse and keys on the table behind the sofa. "I'm not so sure that she understood what she was signing. And something like that needs witnesses, doesn't it? Who'd he use? Lucetta and Pedro?"

"If you're concerned that he's not acting in her best interest or intends to abscond with his mother's money, you can call the Office of the Public Guardian and Trustee and they'll investigate."

"How long will that take?" She trailed Tom, who'd started checking her windows and doors again. "If he has gambling debts, like Julie said, he's bound to accept the first cash offer he gets. Maybe that's why there's been no more counterfeit bills surfacing."

"Whoa! How'd we switch to counterfeiting?"

"Don't you see? What better motive for printing money than covering gambling debts? Only now he doesn't have to, because he's got bigger crops to harvest."

The corner of Tom's mouth ticked up at her comparison. He edged back the window sheer and scanned the street. "Nagy's background check didn't show a high debt load, beyond what his ex-wife left him with, but if he's borrowed under the table, he *could* be grasping at creative ways to meet payments." Tom let the curtain slip back into place. "If you're worried about Nagy selling the place without Verna's consent, maybe before you call the OPGT, you should talk to her. Right now, I'm more concerned about the guy who's been following you."

"What?" Her gaze veered to the window. "What are you talking about?"

"I'm sorry, that's not how I wanted to tell you." Tom guided her to the sofa, but his tender expression only made her nerves jumpier than ever.

"Someone's following me? When? Where?"

"At the nursing home." Tom hesitated as if measuring his words. "The driver of a silver Ford Escort was watching you."

Her chest tightened. "The same car we saw Sunday."

"Yeah." Tom expelled the single word with a breath of frustration that only left her more rattled.

"Who is he? What does he want?"

Tom reached for her hand, but the warm strength of his fingers wasn't potent enough to slow her galloping pulse. "I've issued a BOLO for his car. Once we locate him, we'll get answers. All I know at this point is that he's the same guy who was spying on Peter Ratcher at the hardware store."

"So you think he's connected to GPC?" Kate gulped so loud Tom closed his other hand over hers.

"Unless you can think of anyone else who would be interested in following both of you."

She closed her eyes and tried to recall the man's image from the video. "He seemed vaguely familiar, but I don't think I've seen him around the research station. Do you think he could be behind the text message too?"

"I don't know." He squeezed her hand consolingly. "I think Julie would've said something if she recognized him, but I'll print off a still from the video clip and ask the rest of the library staff if they recognize him."

Suddenly feeling like a cornered animal, Kate sprang to her feet and paced. "Do you think he—?" She choked on the words.

But the empathy in Tom's eyes told her he knew what she was thinking. "Until we figure out who this guy is and what he wants, I'd rather you don't go out alone, or without at least letting me know where you're heading. You okay with that?"

Everything in her reared at the thought of letting this guy control what she did.

Tom must've sensed her reluctance. "There's something else." He reached into his pocket and pulled out a piece of paper. "This note was on my car this afternoon."

Where Kate's concerned, trust no one. Her life could depend on it.

10

"Stop!" Kate cried out, seeing visions of the tipping oak bureau pinning her to the wall.

Lucetta dropped her side of the bureau to the floor. "Sorry, I thought you had it."

As the would-be death trap teetered back onto solid ground, the note's *trust no one* warning screamed through Kate's mind. She gulped a breath. "It's no good. We'll have to pull the drawers. This thing is just too heavy." Only at this rate, they'd never get to washing the walls and ceiling in preparation for painting. Let alone get to chatting about counterfeiting suspects. "You start piling the drawers on the bed and I'll go see if I can find a big piece of cardboard that we can shimmy under the bureau so we can push it across the floor."

As she retrieved cardboard from her recycle box, she heard a car pull to the curb. She edged around the corner to peek out the kitchen window without being seen. Tom. *Perfect*.

When he didn't get out, she dialed his cell from the kitchen phone. "You just going to sit there?"

He laughed. "You saw that, huh?"

"Uh, yeah. You've got me downright paranoid." She moved so he'd see her in the window and offered a finger-fluttering wave. "I look every time I hear a car. I'm going to have an ulcer before the weekend's out."

"I'm sure you have a tea for that," he teased.

"Very funny. C'mon, we're trying to move furniture and in need of serious muscle."

"Be right there."

Kate unlocked the deadbolt on the front door on her way through the living room with the cardboard. She felt better having Tom here, but she doubted she'd manage to get Lucetta talking about anything remotely connected to the counter-feiting now. Of course, with some creep spying on her and leaving Tom cryptic notes, figuring out who was behind the counterfeiting had dropped from the top of her priority list.

"Here we go," she said, reaching the bedroom.

Lucetta lowered the bureau's top drawer onto the bed, her face pasty.

"What's wrong?"

With a trembling hand, she held out a framed photograph. "You know this man?" From the look on Lucetta's face, *she* knew him.

Kate's breath caught in her throat. She'd hidden the photo-graph of her father after Peter warned that she wouldn't want GPC figuring out she was the daughter of their most hated former employee.

Lucetta waved the photo in Kate's face. "Why you have his picture?"

Kate reared at the vehemence in her voice. "I knew him a long time ago."

"You know where he is now?" Her thumb drilled into the glass at Dad's throat.

Kate's own throat closed at the sight. "He's dead. He died twenty years ago."

Lucetta's eyes widened, and then she muttered something in a language Kate didn't recognize.

"How do you know him?" Lucetta had to be mistaken. She couldn't possibly have known him. She would've been twelve or fourteen at most when Kate's father died.

Pure hatred sparked in Lucetta's eyes. "He killed my mother."

As Tom stepped into Kate's house, a shriek swiped his breath. He charged toward the sound.

"You call me a liar?" Lucetta stormed from the bedroom. "I no work for you."

Tom grabbed her arm. "Whoa. What's going on?"

Kate lurched through the door, her face ashen. "Wait, I'm sorry. Please don't go."

Lucetta teetered on the balls of her feet, her eyes narrowed in his direction, then shrugged off his hold.

"What's going on?" he repeated, this time redirecting the question to Kate.

The pained look in her eyes told him this was serious. "She says my . . ." Her voice hitched. "She says Mike Baxter killed her mother."

"What?"

"*Si.*" Lucetta nodded. "Gringos came to our village looking for her. She . . . How you say?" Lucetta fluttered her hand, her gaze searching the air. "Like old lady Brewster."

"An herbalist?" Kate asked.

"*Si*. Gringos want to know how she make people well."

Kate's frightened gaze collided with Tom's. The story fit Peter's.

"They settle in our village," Lucetta continued. "Build us new huts. Give us children sweets."

"And this man"—Kate lifted the photograph clutched in her hand—"he was with them?"

Lucetta shook her head. "He came later."

"These men," Tom interjected. "Were they interested in one plant in particular?"

"*Si*. Amendoso."

"Amendoso?" Kate repeated.

Judging by Kate's frown, she'd never heard of it, which also fit Peter's story.

Tom urged the pair to sit, his mind reeling. What had her father gotten himself into?

Lucetta shuffled to the living room and perched on the edge of a side chair while Kate joined him on the sofa.

"Is the plant native to your country?"

"*Si*." Tears shimmered in Lucetta's eyes. "Mama said plant rare. When Mama picked leaves, she always careful to only pick speckled leaves and not overpick. Then the gringos—"

"They came to your village and took the plant?" Kate filled in, shooting Tom a quick glance, obviously desperate to understand what happened but sounding afraid at the same time.

"Yes, when I a girl."

Lucetta didn't look much older than Kate. Her village could be the one Baxter had visited.

Lucetta sliced her hand toward Kate's photograph. "Then

this man came. He talk to Mama and to other gringos. He only stay a few days and took seedlings Mama give him."

"He left?" Hope rose in Kate's voice. "But you said he killed . . . ?"

"The fire start after he left. Mama and gringos try to save the plants. But they burn. They all burn."

Kate seemed to crumple under the weight of Lucetta's words.

"If the fire started after he left, then why would you think he had anything to do with it?" Tom asked.

"Men in village caught him."

"Mr. Baxter?"

"No, man mister pay to drive him. But he say gringo paid him to set fire too."

"Mr. Baxter paid him?" Tom clarified.

"*Si*, he say same person paid him to drive paid him to burn plants."

Kate's teeth dug into her bottom lip as she vehemently shook her head. "He lied. Someone must've paid him to lie."

Lucetta's eyes narrowed. "How you know? What is mister to you?"

Tom moved between Kate and Lucetta, before Kate said something she shouldn't. "Perhaps it'd be best to put off the cleaning for another day."

"She not answer my question!"

Tom pulled out his wallet. "How long have you been here? I'll pay you for your time."

Lucetta's gaze slid from Kate to his wallet. "Not long."

He handed her the twenty he still owed Kate. "Then this is for your travel. Kate will be in touch to set up another time, okay?"

"If I don't get other job." She accepted the payment and headed for the door.

The sound of him clicking the lock behind Lucetta propelled Kate into action. She dashed toward her desk. "The fire. That must be what Dad saw on the TV in the airport. He must've realized his boss paid his driver to go back and burn the plants, believing Dad would deliver the only surviving ones in the world, with all their healing properties."

Tom closed the distance between them and gently clasped her arm. "You don't have to do this, Kate."

She jerked from his grasp. "Yes, I do. He was my father." Her voice cracked. "I need to clear his name." She clicked on the internet icon on her computer, her hands shaking. "The other night I found an article about a fire that destroyed a remote Colombian village around the same time as Dad's arrest." She fixed her gaze on the computer screen, her fingers flying over the keyboard. "Did his arrest report come in?"

"No, it'll be Monday now." He let out a long sigh. "Kate, I don't like the idea of you having Lucetta here again. Clearly her bitterness runs deep. If she figures out that's your father in the photo, who knows what she might do."

"You think she'd take revenge on me?"

"It's not uncommon," he said gently, not wanting to frighten her, while at the same time needing her to take the threat seriously. She had too many directed her way. By the time the chief cancelled the BOLO on the Escort, they'd stopped more than two dozen cars. Not one of them harbored the man who'd followed her. The man who might still be out there waiting for her.

Kate didn't seem to hear his response. She leaned closer to the computer. "This is it. The article I told you about."

Tom skimmed the article. "I suppose that could be Lucetta's

village. The timing fits. But it doesn't say anything about re-searchers being killed or rare plants being destroyed."

"Reporters rushing to report breaking news tend to miss a lot of details," she said, clearly not about to be swayed.

"But if the arsonist pointed a finger at a gringo, that's a big detail to miss."

"Maybe GPC bribed the police to squash the story."

A chill crawled down Tom's spine at the prospect of what GPC would do if she reopened it.

"That has to be what happened," she said, the confidence in her voice growing. "Because if my dad was really guilty, they'd have no motive to squash the story. It was one more strike against him. The truth was only a threat to them if *they* paid the guy to torch the lab."

"Your dad worked for them. I doubt they'd have wanted the negative publicity either way."

Her shoulders sank.

Tom scanned the article again, knowing how important believing in her father's innocence was to her, but all they had to go on was Peter's say-so and a vague article. Of course, the fact he still hadn't been able to locate Peter since he stopped by the station to view the video clip Monday suggested not only that she was right, but that GPC was *still* covering their tracks. And that's what worried him more.

"My dad did *not* kill those people," she said adamantly.

"I'm sure that's true. I'm just not sure we can prove it."

"We have to try. GPC needs to pay for what they did to Lucetta's village. To my family." She shoved her chair away from the computer desk and picked up the photograph of her father. Her fingers lovingly traced his image. "My mother never recovered from losing him. I'm not even sure she ever really believed he was innocent." She swiped at a tear. "For twenty years, I was forbidden to talk about him, as if he never existed, or worse, as if I should be ashamed of who he was."

Tom folded her in his arms, speechless at the depth of pain in her voice, the shame she'd buried so deep he'd had no inkling of how much it affected her. "I'm sorry, Kate."

"My dad deserves to be remembered," she mumbled against his shirt. "He was a good man."

Yes, Tom suspected that's exactly why her father took the secret to his grave—to protect his wife and child. As long as the secret died with him, the rest of his family wasn't a threat to GPC. Except . . . her mother must've known something. He could understand moving to escape the whispering behind their backs. But changing their name was extreme—as if she knew they'd be in danger if they were found.

Just as Peter had warned.

❧

Flames licked toward her like hungry lions.

"No!" Kate's scream jolted her awake. Drenched in perspiration, she flipped on the light and stalked to the bathroom.

The nightmare had been just like the one from earlier in the week, only the fire wasn't in her lab, but in Lucetta's village.

He killed my mother.

Kate cringed at the memory of Lucetta's words. She leaned over the sink and frowned at her reflection in the mirror. At the red hair and green eyes she'd inherited from her father. Reminders that had always brought sadness to Mom's eyes. Did Mom know what really happened? Or had Dad pushed her away the same way he had Peter, thinking she'd be safer?

Then when he died, maybe she'd never been able to get past the hurt that he didn't fight hard enough to clear his name. Or did she really think he was wrong to keep those plants from GPC? That he was guilty?

Because if she believed he was innocent, why didn't Mom fight to clear his name the way Kate had fought to clear Daisy's?

Something inside Kate gave way. She snatched a towel and scrubbed the perspiration from her face, wishing she could scrub the question from her mind as easily. Because only one answer made sense: Mom didn't believe Dad was innocent.

Kate slumped onto the edge of the cold tub, buried her face in the towel, and sobbed. *Lord, why did I have to go and dig up the past when I'd finally put it behind me?*

Why couldn't knowing he loved me be enough?

She dragged the towel down her face and shoved the unwelcome emotions back inside. Deep inside. Tom hadn't abandoned her after learning about her dad the way Mom had always warned that people would. But no one wanted to hang around an emotional basket case for long. That was one lesson Mom had taught her well.

Kate headed to the kitchen to brew a cup of tea.

Whiskers followed her, mewing pitifully.

"I know I fed you last night. You can't be that hungry." She jostled his still-full food dish. "Look, you didn't even eat it, silly. No wonder you're hungry."

Whiskers sniffed the bowl, then sat back on his haunches and yowled.

"What's wrong? Did Verna soften your food with something? Milk maybe?" Kate poured some milk over the kibble.

Whiskers didn't seem impressed.

"You miss your mistress, don't you?" She lifted the cat and

was alarmed by how much weight he'd lost. "You're skin and bones." She ruffled his fur. "You have to eat, baby." Remembering the plant she'd caught him nibbling, she gave herself a mental throttle. "I'm sorry, Whiskers. I forgot all about fetching Grandma Brewster's special mixture for you."

The sun peeked over the horizon, shining a bright swath across her kitchen floor. She set Whiskers down and pulled the kettle off the stove. "No time like the present, I suppose." She peered out the window. No sign of a silver Ford Escort staking out her house. Tom wouldn't object to her scooting next door just for a sec. She quickly dressed, grabbed the key, and hurried out. At the sight of Vic's truck in Verna's driveway, she stopped short.

He never mowed her lawn on Saturdays. Always Tuesdays. She cocked her head and suddenly clued in to what else was off.

No sound of a lawnmower engine. She scanned the yard but couldn't see him anywhere. Movement behind the far bedroom window—the *open* bedroom window—caught her eye. Would Vic rob Verna's house so brazenly?

Kate slipped back inside and grabbed her cell phone, then stole across the yard for a closer look. Whiskers scampered out behind her and meowed loudly. "Shh," she scolded, which only made him meow louder. Eyeing the open window, Kate scooped Whiskers up and muffled his whine with her hand. When the sound settled into a purr, she peeked over the edge of the windowsill.

Vic stood in the center of the room, holding a long pole to the ceiling. A long pole with a paint roller attached.

She felt a rush of shame that she'd so easily assumed the worst about him.

Dropping Whiskers onto the lawn, she let herself in the

back door. "Vic, it's just me. Kate from next door," she called as she walked to the room he was painting. "I just have to pick up Verna's cat medicine." She glanced around the room. "Looking good."

"Work cheap too." He dipped his roller in the tray of white paint. "Lucetta said you might need some painting done?"

"Oh." She tried not to squirm. She hated to turn him down after already refusing his offer to take care of her lawn, but if Tom didn't like the idea of Lucetta in the house, he probably wouldn't be too keen on Vic being there either.

"Never mind," Vic said, the ice in his words chilling the room.

"No, I'd be very interested in using your services. It's just . . . I've decided to put off the painting for a while."

"Sure." He didn't sound like he believed her.

"Um, where'd you see Lucetta?"

"She was cleaning the walls when I stopped by to quote the job."

Relief washed over Kate. Silly, really. What did she think? That Vic had bumped into Lucetta outside, spying on Kate's house?

The woman was not going to launch some sort of nefarious attack simply because Kate had a twenty-year-old photograph of her mother's supposed murderer. Probably no one intended to attack her at all. Spook her out of complaining about GPC, maybe, or out of trying to solve the counterfeiting.

She scrunched her nose at the smell of Vic's paint. Brian seemed awfully eager to sell this place. A whole new tension knotted her stomach. She'd been uneasy about calling that government office Tom had mentioned without proof, especially since Brian could justify needing to sell at least one property to pay for his mother's care. Poor Verna. Kate sighed. All this, because she'd gotten caught with those phony bills. If only she could prove where they came from, maybe this whole nightmare would end.

Kate returned to Verna's kitchen to fetch Whiskers's medicine, but the jar wasn't where Verna said it should be. Kate searched the other cupboards but still couldn't find it. She surveyed the counters one last time. Someone had spilled a bottle of something. She tapped a damp finger to the small green leaves and looked at them more closely. Basil. Lucetta or Brian must've knocked the bottle from the cupboard. Kate grabbed the dishcloth and wiped up the mess then headed back to her house. She'd have to drive out to Grandma Brewster's to pick up more of the remedy.

Back home, she rang up Tom to let him know her plans. The call went straight to voice mail, so she left a message and then made herself breakfast.

After an hour lapsed without him calling back to veto her plan, she discreetly peeked from every window in the house to ensure the guy in the silver Escort wasn't lurking about, then headed to Grandma Brewster's.

Once she hit the winding back roads, Kate rolled down the windows, absorbing the sights and sounds of the lush mixed forest.

When she reached Grandma Brewster's road, one of the few in the region still unpaved, she rolled the windows back up to guard against the rising dust. Towering beech trees blotted the sun, casting the road in deep shadows. A few minutes later, Kate pulled into the driveway—if you could call the sparsely grassed swath that led to the house a driveway.

Grandma Brewster's quiet hum emanated from behind the house. Kate pushed through the small iron gate and entered a garden-lover's dream world. Sunlight danced over herbs of every description and color, from dense low-lying mounds of oregano to gangly wisps of dill. And the aromas! Kate closed her eyes and inhaled. Mint, basil, sage, coriander . . .

Grandma Brewster's deep-throated laugh jerked her from her reverie. "Inspiring?"

Kate smiled, feeling an instant kinship to this dear woman. "Yes."

For the next half hour, Grandma Brewster walked Kate through the garden, expounding on her eclectic collection of herbs and their various uses. Although the woman, with her heavy dark skirt and hairnet-plastered gray hair, had to be pushing ninety, she was more spry than many half her age, bending easily to tug a weed here and there.

"I visited Verna a couple of days ago," Kate said once they'd come full circle and Grandma Brewster had fetched the tincture for Whiskers. "She mentioned that her old farm adjoins your property. Is that it there?" Kate pointed to an orange survey marker that looked as if it had been added recently.

"*Ja,*" Grandma Brewster said in her thick German accent, even as she shook her head.

"What's wrong?"

She motioned to the survey marker with a gnarled hand. "They'll destroy the plants."

Kate noticed the path leading from Grandma Brewster's garden down the meadowy hill into a stand of trees that must flank the stream Verna had mentioned. No doubt Grandma Brewster collected a few plants from along the water that wouldn't thrive in her garden. "Verna had planned to donate the land for a park. But her son doesn't like the idea."

Grandma Brewster simply nodded. At her age, there was probably little that fazed her anymore.

"I think I'll wander down and take a look before I leave. Do you mind if I leave my car parked in your drive?"

"*Nein*," Grandma Brewster said and disappeared inside.

Kate tucked the tincture into her pocket and headed down the hill. As the path dipped into the trees, the air didn't cool as she expected. Instead it grew thick and muggy like the air in a tropical rainforest. Intent on reaching the stream she could hear babbling below, she picked her way along the steep incline littered with damp, decaying vegetation.

Thorny raspberry bushes clawed at her pants, while overhead the songbirds went eerily silent. Perspiration trickled down her back, triggering an uneasy shiver.

The bushes rustled behind her. She pivoted on her heel, expecting to spot a squirrel or rabbit.

Only shadowy bushes and thick, straight tree trunks filled the hill. She continued downward, but the feeling of being watched prickled her skin.

Alert to every change in sound, she circled her fingers around the cell phone in her pocket.

No one followed you.

Were you even watching your rearview mirror?

Terrific. Not only was she talking to herself, she was disagreeing with herself!

Tom and Grandma Brewster were the only people who knew where she was, and she was pretty sure she could trust Grandma Brewster.

Spotting the stream, she silenced the voices and scrambled down the rest of the hill. The variety of plants growing along the banks was incredible. She pulled out her cell phone and snapped a few pictures. She recognized all of the plants, or at least their plant families, until she came to a serrated, broad-leafed plant with peculiar spines poking from its main stalk. The small cone-like flowers bore characteristics of the Asteraceae family, but the leaves were a bizarre cross between a fleshy cacti and gargantuan dandelion leaves. Unsure if it was poisonous, she didn't dare pluck a leaf to show Grandma Brewster. So she took pictures from every angle, anticipation building with each at the rarity of her discovery.

A twig snapped behind her.

She spun around, losing hold of her cell phone in her haste.

As she scrambled to recover it, a gunshot cracked the air.

11

What was she thinking driving alone to Grandma Brewster's? Tom shoved his lawnmower back into the garage and returned her call. "Where are you now?"

"I . . . Grandma . . . Tom?" Her phone cut out.

Tom grabbed his keys. "Dad, I've got to go. I think Kate might be in trouble." He gunned the gas and soon reached the town limits. The back roads twined through the hilly terrain like a snake. No wonder her phone had cut out.

At the top of the next hill, he checked his phone's reception and tapped Kate's number again. Two seconds later, it rolled to voice mail. Cutting it off, he kicked the gas.

Veering left at a Y in the road, Tom stomped on his brake. What was Pedro doing out here?

Tom coasted to a stop behind the beat-up truck the kid always seemed to be borrowing from his employer.

As Tom circled the truck, he cocked his ear toward the trees. There was no evidence Kate had been inside or that the truck had collided with her yellow Bug. A faint trail led from the truck into the woods. Tom checked the urge to follow it. His first priority was finding Kate.

As he turned back to his car, sunlight flashed through the trees on the other side of the road. Shifting sideways for a better look, he spotted a shiny silver surface. The hood of a car?

Two shots sounded from the valley behind him, followed by a blood-chilling shriek.

Drawing his gun, Tom raced toward the sound along the faint trail leading from the truck. Branches slapped his arms as he plowed through the bushes.

The hedgerow opened onto a wide rolling meadow with a stand of trees beyond.

"Kate, where are you?" he shouted, his heart hammering in his chest.

An angry male voice exploded into expletives.

Tom raced across the meadow toward the sound. The instant he plunged into the woods, a suffocating heat closed in on him. Something or someone crashed through the thick underbrush to his right. He veered right, only to catch movement through the trees to his left.

"Kate," he shouted again, backing against a tree for cover.

"I'm here." She bobbed into view at the brink of a steep incline.

At the sight of her unharmed, his breath swooshed from his chest. "What happened?"

"Pedro and Verna's grandson tried to scare me into leaving. Said I was trespassing."

"Tried to scare you. How?" He choked at the image of Kate on the business end of a gun.

"Oh, you know, waving around their guns, acting tough." She sloughed off the confrontation as if it were all in a day's walk through the woods, but the wobble in her voice told a different story. "Of course, they clammed up when I told them Verna said I could be here, and then they tried to shoot a rabbit, and I yelled at them. They ran off when they heard you."

Tom reached for her hand and tugged her the rest of the way up the bank. "What are you doing out here? You said you were going to Grandma Brewster's, not traipsing all over the countryside."

"This is Verna's land. Weren't you listening? Brian's already had it surveyed. He must've been plotting to sell it for a while."

"Okay, but we have more pressing concerns right now."

Maneuvering her behind him, Tom scanned their surroundings. "Did the boys run off in opposite directions?"

"No, together."

Not what he hoped to hear.

"Did you hear what I said?" Kate yanked on his shirt to get him to look at her. The fire in her eyes betrayed both fear and determination. "Verna's son had the land surveyed weeks ago. No wonder he got so angry when I said Verna wanted to make it a park."

Tom pried her hand from his shirt, only half listening as he tugged her in the direction he'd last seen movement.

"He probably sent the boys to scare me off before I could find a rare plant or animal that could force his hand," she went on.

"Shhh," Tom whispered as they stepped out of the woods into the meadow. Spotting her plaid-shirted stalker disappearing over the ridge near the road, he quickly turned and clasped her arms. "Head up to Grandma Brewster's and wait there until I return. Go." He released her and raced the other direction after the guy.

By the time Tom crested the ridge, the guy was barreling

away in his car. But through the spiraling dust, Tom caught the license plate number.

A quick search on the number yielded a name: Michael Beck, a resident of Niagara Falls. Tom jotted the address into his notebook, then put a call in to the station requesting another BOLO.

Kate huffed up behind him.

"I told you to wait at Grandma Brewster's," Tom growled, his insides still twisting over how close the guy had gotten to her.

"What's going on? That wasn't Pedro and Greg you were chasing."

"No." He let out a pent-up breath. "It was the guy in the silver Escort."

"Here?" A hint of panic pitched her voice higher as her gaze darted left, then right, and she took a step closer to him.

"I spotted his car"—Tom pointed to the tracks across the road—"over there just before the gunshot."

"Did you get the plate number?"

"Yes. Hold on a sec."

He punched his dad's number into his cell phone.

"Kate okay?" Dad asked the second the call connected.

"Yeah, I need a favor."

Kate's arms curled around her middle, and Tom's heart crammed up into his ribs at the thought of what could've happened if he'd gotten here any later. "I need you to find everything you can on a Michael Beck." Tom rattled off the guy's address and plate number.

"What's this for?"

"He owns the car I saw following Kate."

"I'll get right on it." The urgency in his dad's voice tightened the knot in Tom's gut, but if anyone could figure out what this guy was up to, Dad could. Forty years on the police force had taught him more than a few shortcuts and given him plenty of favors to call in.

Tom opened the passenger door for Kate. "Get in. I'll drive you to your car."

"You still have no idea why he's following me?"

"No." His response came out more gruff than he intended. But how was he supposed to track this guy down and keep her safe at the same time? "Until I do, I want you to stay at my dad's place."

Her foot slipped off the car's running board. She pivoted to face him. "I can't do that."

"Why not?"

"Because you live there, too. People will talk."

"Your safety is more important." He needed to find Peter Ratcher. Find out what he knew about Michael Beck. "The department doesn't have the resources for a twenty-four hour security detail. Hank wouldn't approve one anyway. Not without a direct threat."

"Exactly. For all we know that guy could be a PI working for Molly's lawyers. Do you really want him to catch the lead detective 'bunking up with Molly's victim'?"

"Get in," Tom ground out through gritted teeth, then slammed the door shut behind her.

🌿

Kate swallowed the lump that had risen to her throat on the drive back to town. Okay, so maybe she'd been a tad extreme in protesting Tom's offer. She turned onto her street with Tom's car on her tail.

Clearly, he was worried. But the fact the guy in the woods drove a silver Escort could've been a coincidence. How could Tom have gotten a good enough look at him to know he was the same guy that had been watching her at the nursing home? Maybe he was just a prospective buyer. If some stranger had chased her, she would've run too.

She shook her head. She'd seen one too many silver Escorts around lately for her comfort. But apparently the idea of taking refuge with Tom scared her more.

She parked in her driveway and grabbed the tincture she'd picked up for Whiskers.

Mrs. C waved from her rose bed. The woman was like a mailman—neither hail, nor sleet, nor scorching heat kept her from tending her pristine garden. At least with Mrs. C on neighborhood watch, Kate needn't worry about anyone sneaking around undetected.

Then again, Patti and Jarrett had done just that last weekend.

Tom pulled in behind her car and beelined to the small picket fence separating her yard from Mrs. C's. "Could you let us know if you see any strangers watching Kate's place?"

Mrs. C tipped up her wide-brimmed hat and gave him a sympathetic smile. "I'm afraid we'll be getting a lot of those now that Verna's son has put her house up for sale. Why, I've already seen a couple of cars sitting out in front of the place."

Kate pressed a hand to her increasingly queasy stomach. Anyone could sit outside the Nagys' house under the pretense of being an interested buyer, while really spying on her.

"Did you happen to see a silver Ford Escort?" Tom voiced her fear.

Mrs. C squinted up at the sky as if searching her memory. "Not that I recall. Why?"

"He's someone who I thought might be interested . . . in the place."

"Well, I'll be sure to let you know if I see him." Her head tilted and a mischievous glint lit her eyes. She waggled her finger between them. "You two dating?"

Kate's jaw dropped. Mrs. C's question came out of nowhere. And more surprising than that, Tom didn't seem the least bit ruffled by it. Kate's cheeks flamed as his palm came to rest at the small of her back. "She's not ready to call it that yet," he said in a stage whisper and winked.

Mrs. C laid a finger aside her nose and gave a crisp nod.

As soon as she'd gone, Kate turned on Tom. "I'm not ready to *call it that yet*?"

His grin swirled through her chest, doing strange things there.

She crossed her arms in a vain attempt to suppress the effect. "You only encourage her, you know."

His hand grazed up her back and swept the hair from her shoulders. "You're cute when you're mad."

She rolled her eyes to smother the fireworks his touch had set off in her chest. "Weren't you going to try to find that car, *Detective*?"

"Are you staying home?"

Staying home? Alone? After some guy had maybe followed her into the woods? Not to mention that she was haunted by new questions about her father's death. *No thank you.* "I promised Julie I'd meet her for lunch. Then . . ."—there had to be something else—"oh, I thought I'd drop in on Verna." As much as Kate didn't want to be the one to tell the dear woman, Verna needed to know what her son was doing with her land. *There has to be some way we can stop him.*

". . . Okay?" Tom said.

Kate shook the thoughts from her head. "I'm sorry. What did you say?"

"I'll drive you."

"As nice as that sounds, you can't spend your day chauffeuring me around if you want to find the guy who's been following me."

He arched an eyebrow, a glint of amusement twinkling in his eye. "Where else would I find him?"

"He's not going to follow me if you're with me."

"I can either drive you or tail you," Tom said, his tone unyielding.

Any other day his my-way-or-the-highway attitude would've irked her. But after the morning she'd had, being chauffeured by an armed bodyguard—a ruggedly handsome one at that—sounded pretty good. Really good, if she was honest with herself. "Okay, you can drive. Thank you," she added softly. "Let me take care of Whiskers first. Then we can go."

Twenty minutes later Tom parked in front of A Cup or Two. "Wait," he ordered as she reached for the car's door handle. He rounded the car and glanced up and down the street before opening her door.

"What do you think he's going to do, shoot me?" she joked, but the twitch in Tom's cheek and serious look in his eyes wiped the smile from her face. She'd convinced herself that if the guy had wanted to hurt her, he would have done so already. But Tom obviously didn't think the guy following her was just a PI.

"Let's get inside," he said firmly.

Julie turned from the counter with a steaming mug in hand. "Perfect timing. I got us a table in the corner." Her gaze lifted above Kate's head. She smiled. "I'll grab another chair."

Kate quickly filled a cup with a selection of herbs, chose a muffin, and stood in line for the harried new waitress behind the counter.

"You go ahead and sit down." Tom took her cup and muffin. "I'll take care of these."

She slid into the chair opposite Julie.

"So Tom's taking care of your order . . ." Her friend's eyes twinkled as she lifted her tea. "I noticed his car in your driveway last night too. I guess you two are getting serious, huh?"

"Oh, yeah," Kate deadpanned. "He asked me to move in with him."

Julie spluttered tea halfway across the table. "What?"

Kate sopped up the dribbles with a napkin, straining to hold back a grin.

"You're not serious?"

"Perfectly."

"C'mon, you're pulling my leg." Julie grabbed Kate's left hand and examined her empty ring finger. With a humph, she added, "You wouldn't."

"No, I wouldn't." If her best friend reacted this way, she could imagine the rumors that would have been flying by the end of tomorrow's church service. The pastor would have declared a shotgun wedding. A chuckle burbled past her lips at the image of Tom saying "I do" with the pastor holding a rifle pointed at his chest. "He wants me to stay with his dad until he can figure out who's following me."

"Someone's following you?" Julie's voice rose so high that heads turned.

"Shh, will you?" Kate leaned forward and lowered her voice. "I don't want the whole town to know. It's probably nothing." She flinched, wishing she really believed that. "Some guy in a silver Ford Escort has been watching me."

"Who is he? Why's he following you?"

"I don't know." Kate fiddled with her napkin. "We think he followed me onto Verna's farm property this morning." Tom seemed so certain this guy was connected to Peter Ratcher and GPC, but she wasn't convinced. "The time before"—she gasped at the sudden realization—"was connected to Verna too. I was visiting her at the nursing home."

"Maybe her son hired someone to spy on you. Didn't you say he was pretty ticked after you told him Verna wanted to donate her farm property to the town?"

"Yeah, I just had the same thought." Good thing she didn't threaten to report him to the OPGT to his face. Kate decided not to mention that Verna's grandson and Pedro had threatened her too, or Julie would be insisting she sleep on *her* couch. "I feel so sorry for Verna. There's got to be something I can do to stop her son from selling her properties out from under her."

"Are you sure you're not just latching on to another cause to avoid dealing with your feelings?"

Kate let out an exaggerated humph. "Tom's practically glued himself to my side. You can hardly accuse me of *avoiding* him."

One side of Julie's mouth turned up, her gaze lifting.

An uncomfortable feeling plunged to the pit of Kate's stomach. "He's behind me, isn't he?"

His amused voice tickled her ear. "Glued to your side." He set her tea and muffin in front of her, then settled into the chair Julie had dragged over, moving it even closer.

"I wasn't complaining," Kate clarified.

He stopped his mug midair, a smile that loosed butterflies in her stomach curving his lips. "Glad to hear it."

The rumble of his words stirred the butterflies into a frenzy. Julie cleared her throat. "I have an idea."

Kate blinked. "Huh?"

"To keep Verna's son from selling her land. You're a botanist. If you found some rare plant on the land, you could submit a protection request, like they did for the nesting bobolinks."

"I did find something!" Kate grabbed her cell phone and showed them the photos she'd snapped of the strange plant. "I have no idea what it is. I meant to ask Grandma Brewster if she knew."

"I'm sure you'll figure it out, and if it turns out to be rare"— Julie smacked her hand on the table like a judge's gavel— "you'll have your case."

Tom didn't look nearly as enthusiastic about the idea.

"What's wrong?"

He pursed his lips.

"What?" Kate repeated, growing more unnerved by his reaction by the second.

"The last thing you should do right now is draw more attention to yourself by getting in anyone else's bad books."

"I don't care what Brian thinks of me. His mother's wishes should come first."

"Did you care when those boys showed up with guns?"

Julie's eyes bulged. "Someone threatened you with guns?"

"No. Tom's exaggerating. I ran into a couple of teens in the woods playing with air rifles. They weren't doing anything illegal."

Tom caught her wrist. "Doesn't mean they're innocent."

"Kind of new to sell for scrap, isn't it?" The dealer popped the Escort's hood and studied the engine. "Your insurance company write it off?"

"Yeah, you know how it goes. Costs more to repair than the car's book value," Michael Beck hedged. Truth was, he'd pulled the plates and deliberately backed the car into a tree a mile back, hoping the ruse would buy him more time. Sure, he could've gotten a lot more than two hundred bucks if he'd traded it in on another car rather than wrecking it. But he couldn't risk buying a new car under the same alias. The police would be onto him the instant the car's new registration hit the system.

The dealer headed inside to punch a few numbers to decide on a value, or so he claimed. More likely making sure the car wasn't stolen.

Michael glanced at his watch. He couldn't risk going back to the apartment. If the detective got his license plate number, he'd have someone watching the place by now.

The dealer came back with an offer of two hundred dollars. Michael dickered him up to two-fifty, then hitched a ride to Niagara Falls and stopped at the credit union where he'd purchased a safety deposit box under another alias. He retrieved the new driver's license and cash, then closed the metal box with a clank.

Time to change strategies.

12

Kate did her best to ignore Tom's brooding as they waited outside Verna's locked ward. "I'm not going to stay away from Verna just because my visiting might rile her son."

"I know. But be careful what you say. A mother is not going to believe a neighbor over a devoted son. Not easily."

"I thought you'd welcome the opportunity to question Verna, considering this guy showed up at *her* property today."

Tom clasped her hand, the warmth of his touch immediately arresting her growing frustration. "Trust me, your safety is my top priority. I don't intend to overlook any angle." The sincerity in his eyes dispelled any doubts. His cell phone beeped. "Excuse me." His thumbs flew over the miniature keyboard.

"Hutchinson find him?" Kate asked, assuming the message was from the officer Tom had sent to stake out Beck's apartment.

"Not yet." The anxiety in Tom's tone left her nerves more frayed than his concerns about Brian Nagy.

Kate took a deep breath, inhaling the soothing aroma of the lemon balm tea she'd brought for Verna from A Cup or Two.

The same smiling nurse who'd greeted her Thursday opened the door. "I see you brought your own cup of tea today." She acknowledged the still-texting Tom with a nod.

"It's for Verna, actually." Kate handed the nurse a package of tea leaves. "This is for her too."

The nurse peeked into the bag. "I'll put it with her other one."

"So Lucetta did bring in Verna's tea from home? I forgot to double check."

"Her grandson actually." The nurse turned down a different corridor than yesterday. "Verna's still in her room. She was very agitated this morning."

Kate turned to Tom. "I so hoped Verna would be able to return home."

Tom brushed his thumb over the back of her hand. "I know."

Her heart fluttered at his support, so steady and sweet.

Verna sat in a padded chair, back to the door, face turned to the window. The nurse went in ahead of them and rubbed her palm across Verna's stooped shoulders. "You have company."

Kate sniffed the air. "Did she have lunch in here?"

"No, that's her tea. We thought it might calm her."

"They're all gone," Verna wailed.

Kate hurried to her side. "What's all gone?"

Verna's eyes seemed to look right through Kate. "The cats. They're all gone."

Kate gently rubbed the dear woman's arm. Sadly for Verna, it must seem that way. Kate turned to ask the nurse if she might bring in Verna's cat for a visit, but she'd already slipped away.

"I'm taking good care of Whiskers for you, Verna," Kate reassured her. She ducked her head at Tom's empathetic expression. He pushed a chair beside Verna as Kate offered the cup of tea they'd brought.

Verna waved away the cup and sprang to her feet. "They're all gone," she wailed.

"Maybe Brian mentioned his plan to sell her property," Tom whispered close to Kate's ear.

She cringed. The news would have crushed Verna. Kate helped Verna back to her chair. "It's okay. Tell us what you're missing and we'll find it."

Verna shook her head. "Too late."

Kate slanted a helpless glance in Tom's direction, but he'd slipped out of the room too. She patted Verna's hand. "I'll be right back." Tom returned as she reached the door. "What's going on?"

"Brian hasn't been here since the day before yesterday, so unless her grandson told her about the house going up for sale, it's more likely her meds that set her off. But since we're not family, the nurse can't tell us what she's on."

Verna spun toward them. "What are you whispering about? Did you take them?"

Kate's heart wrenched for the poor confused woman. She sat beside her and reassured her that they hadn't taken anything. Any hope of asking about Verna's house and property had disappeared the moment Kate saw how unsettled she was. As Verna chattered on about nothing in particular, Kate mentally reviewed the herbs in Verna's tea that might have reacted with her meds.

A few minutes later, Brian Nagy appeared at the door.

Kate stiffened, expecting a reprimand for being with his mother.

Instead Brian offered her and Tom a congenial smile. More than congenial.

"Nice of you to stop by and see my mother," he said as if

there'd not been a cross word between them—which made her even more wary. Apparently Brian's son hadn't told him about her visit to the property yet.

He pressed a kiss to his mother's wrinkled cheek.

Verna's eyes momentarily sparkled as she patted his face. "My dear boy."

"Brian," Kate ventured. "Did the nurse tell you about your mom's sudden change in behavior?"

"Yes, I came as soon as I got the nurse's message."

Moving out of Brian's way so he could sit next to his mother, Kate asked, "Did they say what they think caused the change?"

"The doctor here put her on Haldol."

"An antipsychotic?" With the symptoms Verna had exhibited, Kate wasn't surprised, just disappointed.

"The nurse says Mom may not have taken her last dose at the right time, or if she hasn't had enough fluids, or had too many, that can affect absorption. She put a call in to the doctor."

"Good to hear." Kate and Tom slipped out of the room to let mother and son have their privacy. "That was weird. I expected him to be annoyed to see me there. But his smile verged on exultant, don't you think?"

Tom hurried her down the hall, keeping his voice low. "Maybe he figured his mother's lapse vindicated his decision to sell the house."

"It certainly prevents me from lobbying her for help to protect the land."

From the front door of the nursing home, Tom scanned the parking lot, then quickly shepherded her to the car. "I don't suppose that'll change your mind about trying to block the sale."

"No." She tempered the answer he didn't want to hear with a sweet smile. "But you can take me home now."

"So you can figure out what the plant you found is?" he asked wryly.

"Yup." She might not be able to prove Brian was the counterfeiter, but with a bit of luck she might be able to stop him from commandeering his mother's estate against her wishes.

Tom's cell phone rang again as they climbed into the car. "That's Dad," he said at the distinctive ring. "Hopefully he's got something we can use on our Escort driver." He flicked the phone to speaker. "What'd you find?"

"It's all bogus. I could only trace him back a couple of months. Before that he didn't exist."

Tom's gaze shot to hers, skyrocketing her own alarm. "What do you mean he didn't exist?"

"The identity's fake. He laid down enough of a trail so a cursory check wouldn't raise suspicions. But his credit card, his utility and phone bills, even his driver's license, none of them date back more than two months."

Kate's throat closed in. "Since Molly's arrest."

❧

Against his better judgment, Tom walked Kate to her door. The woman was too stubborn for her own good. He'd spent the entire drive from the nursing home emphasizing how dangerous this guy could be. "Assassins—not PIs—use fake IDs."

She fitted her key into the lock. "Don't you think you might be blowing this way out of proportion? Like Beth's dahlias."

He cringed at her reference to the time he'd raced from her hospital room with a potted dahlia, certain it contained explosives. "Paranoia saves lives."

"If what your theories are doing to my blood pressure doesn't kill me first."

He stayed her hand on the doorknob. "Then change your mind. Stay at my dad's, where we can protect you." He'd re-issued the BOLO on the silver Escort more than three hours ago—this time with a license plate number—but they still had nothing. If the guy went underground . . .

"I can hear Mrs. C now. *Scandalous!*"

If the situation hadn't been so serious, Tom would have laughed at Kate's perfect imitation of the old gal. But the tremor in Kate's chin betrayed her own unease. "Mrs. C knows my dad would never allow anything remotely scandalous under his roof. Your reputation will be perfectly safe."

She nibbled at her bottom lip. "What about Verna's cat? I promised I'd take care of him."

The fact that this independent, strong-willed woman was grasping at so flimsy an excuse should have worried him, but he was too relieved. "Whiskers can come too."

Kate tilted her head and peered into his eyes in that way she had of covering up her uncertainty and tugging at his heart. "How do I know this isn't a sly attempt to assure yourself a dinner date every night?"

"Trust me." He skimmed his palm across her back, appreciating her slender figure. "That's purely a fringe benefit."

Her cheeks turned a gorgeous shade of pink. "See, that's why I can't."

He frowned, thrown by how quickly their banter had veered off course. "You can't because I enjoy spending time with you?"

She twisted the key in her hands. "People would talk."

The vulnerability in her voice nearly unraveled him. But after the glimpse she'd given him of how much gossip had hurt her as a child, he sensed there'd be no reasoning her fear away. If he wanted to keep her safe, they had to find this guy. *Today.*

Tom slipped his hands beneath her hair and cradled her neck. "It's okay. I understand." The gesture was meant to be supportive and understanding, but he wasn't prepared for the warmth that radiated through him when her eyes tangled with his. Shimmering gold and auburn flecks in those bottomless green depths drew him closer. Invited him to linger.

Her gaze dropped to his lips and his pulse quickened.

Dipping his head, he leaned closer, focusing on her heart-shaped lips lifting into the sweetest of smiles and anticipating their even sweeter taste.

"Take it inside," shouted a crusty old man walking past with his dog.

Tom jerked back.

The blush in Kate's cheeks deepened.

"Okay, I see your point," he said about her concern people would talk and chuckled to mask his irritation with his lapse in attention. He needed to be focused on finding the guy who was following her. Giving rein to his feelings would only cloud his judgment. Something he couldn't afford. His partner's death had taught him that lesson too well.

He pushed open the door and put some much needed distance between them. "Just please don't go anywhere, not without calling first. I'll be in touch as soon as we have him." He glanced down the hall, then toward the kitchen. "I'll walk through the house before I leave just to be safe." Only, she wouldn't be. Not until they tracked this guy down and found out what he wanted.

After church Sunday morning, Kate joined the others outside for lemonade on the lawn. She chuckled at the sight of Tom's nephews dragging him off for piggyback rides.

"I see you two made up." Julie gave Kate her patented googly-eyed matchmaking look. "I saw you sitting together in church."

Kate smiled at Tom galloping little Timmy around the lawn. Only she was really thinking about the kiss they'd almost shared outside her house yesterday afternoon. He was everything she'd ever dreamed of in a man. Caring, thoughtful, protective, good with children, not to mention handsome and capable of making her insides do somersaults with a single glance.

Aside from being a police officer, which, considering the way her life had been going lately, she was learning to get over, he was pretty close to perfect.

"Oh yeah, you've definitely made up," Julie chirped as if the credit should all be hers.

"Made up?" Kate shook her head out of the gauzy mist of yesterday's almost kiss. "We never had a fight."

"He must've been annoyed that you refused to stay at his dad's."

"Shh." Kate glanced around to ensure no one had overheard. "He said he understood."

"I'm sure he did. But it couldn't have been comfortable for him sitting outside your house all night to keep watch."

"What?"

Julie chuckled. "You didn't know? When Ryan and I passed your house at midnight last night, Tom was sitting in his car across the street."

"I had no idea." Her gaze drifted to where she'd last spotted him. He was loading his other nephew onto his back. She should be irritated at him for staking out her house. But a warm fuzzy feeling that he'd been that worried about her ousted all the others.

Julie elbowed her. "If you ask me—which for some reason you don't seem to do anymore—he's a keeper."

Um-hmm. If only she could steer clear of involvement in his cases.

"Did you figure out what that plant was you found yesterday?"

"Unfortunately, no. Couldn't find anything like it in any of my books or online."

Julie clapped her hands together. "That's great! So that proves it's rare!"

A couple of heads turned their way.

"Shh." Kate's heart rate quickened at the sight of Brian Nagy's real estate agent moving away from the group of men he'd been talking with and pulling his phone from his pocket. "It doesn't work that way." Kate shifted closer to the agent in hopes of eavesdropping on the call, as she suspected he'd been doing on their conversation.

But just then the rookie police officer Tom had enlisted to stake out Beck's apartment approached Tom, carrying a thick manila envelope. Tom straightened, letting his young nephew hop to the ground. Taking the envelope he slanted an anxious look in her direction.

Her heart skipped a beat, as much from the realization that he'd been aware of exactly where she was as from the concern in his gaze.

"Excuse me," she said to Julie. "I've got to go." She reached Tom just as the officer strode away. "Did they catch the guy?"

"Huh?"

"Beck. Wasn't that—?"

"No. I mean, yes." Tom rolled the large envelope in his hand. "Hutchinson was watching Beck's place, but Beck never showed."

"So what's in the envelope?"

A sigh seeped from his pursed lips, his grip on the rolled envelope tightening. "Your dad's file."

Dad's file. Nervous energy streaked through her chest, but words escaped her. Her fingers tingled, but she couldn't bring herself to reach for the envelope. This was the moment of truth, the moment she'd been longing for—and dreading—for twenty years.

The crowd's attention seesawed between watching Hutchinson climb into his cruiser and eyeing her speculatively.

Tom touched the small of her back. "Let's go to your house."

The tenderness in his voice wrapped around her like a sweet embrace. "People are going to say you're protecting me, you know."

He tucked her dad's file under his arm and looked so deeply into her eyes that her heart felt as if it were freefalling straight into his warm, strong hands. "And I'm going to keep on protecting you. Okay?"

"Thank you," Kate whispered, nibbling her bottom lip.

Tom hated to see her so vulnerable. When she'd been rallying to clear Daisy's name, she'd been self-assured, fighting him at every turn. But now, ever since the day she landed in the middle of his counterfeiting investigation, it was as if something had broken inside her.

She hadn't lost the will to fight . . . not exactly. She was still fighting to prove Verna's innocence, and to save Verna's land, but she wasn't the same somehow.

They drove to her house in silence. Kate held her father's file on her lap. Every few seconds, she skimmed her fingers across it.

He hadn't really expected the small police detachment to have the file after twenty years. He was even less optimistic that it had the answers Kate was looking for.

About the twentieth time her fingers swept the envelope, the obvious smacked him between the eyes. All this anxiety she was radiating—it wasn't about the counterfeit money. She was petrified of what she might find inside that envelope.

"Are you sure you want to read the file, Kate?"

"Of course." Her fingers stopped their restless sweeping, and she rested her palm on the envelope. "I need to know the truth."

When they reached the house, she carried the packet to the kitchen table. "Do you want me to fix you a sandwich first?"

Pretty sure she was grasping for an excuse to put off looking at the file, he shook his head. The sooner they reviewed the reports, the sooner her torment would end. He slit the envelope and pulled out the pages. Her dad's photo sat on top of the stack.

Kate stared at the photo, frozen. The family resemblance was remarkable. They shared the same green eyes, the same red hair, even the same oval-shaped face, although her father's chin was a little more square.

She tentatively reached out and touched her dad's cheek, and Tom noticed another characteristic they shared—a tiny mole at the right temple.

"You okay?"

She swallowed. "Yes. Sorry." She set the photo aside and looked at the next sheet of paper—an itemization of her dad's possessions upon processing.

They perused Peter's witness statement, which matched the details he'd shared with them. His supervisor's statement alleged that Kate's father had been sent to Colombia to bring back samples of plants, but he never delivered them, even though customs records confirmed he declared the plants upon arrival.

Kate gasped. "So he did bring them home."

"According to his supervisor, he stole them to sell to their competition." Tom shuffled through the pages. "Let's see what your dad had to say to the allegations." He paused. "That's odd."

"What?"

"Your father's statement isn't in the file."

Kate let out a long sigh, her entire body deflating. "So we still don't know his side of the story."

Tom read the investigating officer's notes aloud, but when he turned over the page to continue, the notes abruptly ended midsentence. "This file is messed up big-time. Half the detective's notes are missing too." He leafed through the remaining pages. "There's no charge sheet. No arrest warrant."

Kate tugged the next page—the coroner's report—toward her and drew in a ragged breath. Cause of death: heart attack. At the request of the family, no autopsy was performed.

"Did you see your father's body?"

"No." Her fingers jittered over the words as if she might erase them, undo what happened. "Mom didn't want me to remember him that way. Why?"

Tom shook away the sudden crazy notion. "No reason. They just never noted who confirmed his identity."

"We had a small graveside ceremony, and as soon as I finished my school year, we moved to my grandparents'." Kate's gaze drifted to the wall, unfocused. "I remember asking Mom if we could stop at the cemetery and leave flowers before we left. It didn't seem right to move so far away from Daddy without doing something. I used to sneak there after school sometimes and talk to him."

Tom's heart ached at Kate's wistful remembrances. He wanted to gather her in his arms and soothe her pain. Except that wasn't what she needed right now. She needed him to keep his head. His heart was already too entangled. He gathered the pages and stuffed them back into the envelope. "I'm sorry there wasn't more."

A scrap of paper fluttered to the table, a name and number scribbled on it. He added the paper to the packet, making a mental note to follow up on it later.

Kate sighed. "The last thing my dad said to me was, 'Remember I love you, Kate. I will always love you.'" Her voice hitched. "I guess that's all I really need to know."

Unable to hold back any longer, Tom gathered her into his arms. More than anything he wanted to give her the answers she longed to hear. That her father was innocent. That the arrest had been a horrible mistake. That her search hadn't been in vain.

Inexplicably, his mind flashed to the explosion that took his former FBI partner's life. Why would he think of that now? He was long past expecting Kate to betray him the way his partner's double-crossing girlfriend had.

But hadn't his partner said the same of Zoe, the woman

who'd wooed him for information then planted a bomb in his car?

Tom stiffened. The name on the scrap of paper that fell out of the file. Z. Cortez. *Zoe Cortez*. What did Kate's father have to do with the spy who killed his partner?

13

Walking the corridors of the research station toward her office, Kate felt as if her legs were encased in cement. She hadn't slept at all. No, that wasn't true, because more than once she'd woken up screaming, haunted by nightmares of fires and her father and counterfeit money. It had brought the female officer bunking in her spare room running. The woman had come as a favor to Tom, not in any official capacity, but still, the idea of having a bodyguard in the house had only made her feel more unsettled. But with her stalker still at large, agreeing to have her there had been the only way to keep Tom from spending another night sleeping in his car outside the house.

"Lord," she prayed aloud, as she had much of the night. Only unlike Tom's comforting embrace, God's solace hadn't come. "Was I wrong to dig up the past? I wanted so much to believe Dad was innocent. But the files only raised more questions. What am I supposed to do?"

A researcher unlocking his office looked up. "Were you talking to me?"

"No. Sorry. Talking to myself." Embarrassed at being overheard, she hurried to her lab. She needed to put her father out of her mind, focus on what she could do—her research and helping Verna. Since she'd had no luck identifying the plant she'd hoped would be the ticket to securing protection for the property, maybe her better chance of stopping Brian was to prove he was their counterfeiter.

"Hey," Patti glanced up from her workbench as Kate pushed through the door. "I was beginning to wonder if you'd need another wake-up call." She frowned. "But it looks like you never went to sleep."

Kate finger-combed her hair. "Been having trouble sleeping."

"Know what you mean. I had nightmares for months after my mom died. It was as if by reliving her last hours I might be able to do something differently so she wouldn't die."

Kate nodded. She didn't have the energy to explain that her restlessness wasn't connected to Daisy's death. Not to mention she didn't want anyone beyond Tom to know the truth about her father—what little she really knew.

Patti reached across the bench and held out a file. "I did find something that might cheer you up."

Cheer her up? She doubted anything could push past the grinding pain in her head, or her heart. Kate flipped through the pages—articles downloaded from the internet, all in Spanish. "What are these?"

"Info about that plant you emailed me a picture of Saturday afternoon. Since I couldn't find anything on it in English, I tried translating the description to French, Russian, and Spanish, and hit upon this."

"You can read all those languages?"

Patti adjusted the slide on her microscope. "Nah, I used the translation tools."

Kate squinted at the unfamiliar words but couldn't decipher more than two or three. "So how do you know this is relevant?"

"Look at the photo on the last page."

Kate flipped to it and gasped. She pulled up the photo of the plant from Verna's property on her cell phone screen and compared the two images. "They're nearly identical."

Patti grinned. "Near as I can figure, the guy who wrote the article is a missionary or priest or something in Central America, based on how many times he uses *dios*, the Spanish word for God, and *amen dios*. Not sure what that means. Must be like our *amen*. I tried using the translation tool to translate it all to English, but my computer locked up."

Patti chattered on, but the words became a background noise of gibberish.

Amen dios. Amen. *Amendoso*—the plant Lucetta's mom gave Dad?

Kate's heart fluttered. They couldn't be the same plant, could they? Those woods *had* felt unusually tropical. But sheltered enough to sustain a tropical plant through the winter?

"I figured you could ask Juan to translate it for you." Patti's voice filtered past the questions racing through Kate's mind.

"Who?"

"You know, Juan. Building two. Studies peaches."

No, she didn't dare ask anyone from the research station to translate this. If by some crazy coincidence this was the same plant that cost Dad his life, she couldn't risk the news getting to GPC.

"Or maybe that Lucetta woman you mentioned last week could."

Kate's throat thickened. She definitely could *not* show this to Lucetta. "Could you do me a favor and not mention this to anyone?"

Patti gave her a strange look.

"It just seems pretty rare. I want to learn more about it. How to protect it without risk of curiosity seekers destroying its habitat." Thank goodness she never told Patti where she found the plant or why she wanted to identify it. Not when Dad lost his life trying to keep it out of GPC's hands.

Patti shrugged. "I guess that makes sense. I'll call Jarrett."

Kate lurched. "No! I don't want you to tell *anyone*."

"Jarrett already knows."

No, no, *no*. Kate clutched the edge of the bench. If Jarrett told his father, what would the mayor—?

She shook the thought away. There was absolutely no reason why Jarrett would have said anything. No reason, if he had, why the mayor should connect the plant to GPC Pharmaceuticals . . . if it was connected.

Kate shuffled through the stack of papers Patti had printed off on their mystery plant. The website's address—the only English on the pages—was printed in the footer. She turned on her computer. Maybe she could get an online translation tool to decode the article. While she waited for the computer to boot, she called Julie. "Can you recommend an online translator that won't freeze up my computer?"

"For what language?"

"Spanish to English."

"Why don't you just ask my aunt Betty at the B and B? All those years working on her parents' fruit farm beside the migrant Mexican workers, she got pretty fluent. She can read it too. At least as well as any online tool. What's this about anyway?"

"I'll fill you in later."

If only she could show Lucetta the plant and find out if it was the same as the one Kate's dad had gone to Colombia to see. Learn how Lucetta's mother used it. But she didn't dare. Not when Lucetta was already suspicious about why she had a picture of the man she blamed for killing her mother.

She flipped off the computer and grabbed her car keys from her purse before remembering that she'd let her "bodyguard" drive her to work this morning at Tom's request. "Grrr. I knew I shouldn't have agreed." Visits to the intern placements were almost due again. She could have used them as an excuse to slip out, stop by the B and B on the way, maybe even drop by Grandma Brewster's to see if she knew anything about the plant.

Tom would've been furious. He didn't want her going anywhere until they located Beck. But surely her stalker would expect her to be in the lab all day.

He wasn't going to show. Tom glanced at his car's dashboard clock. Kate had already been inside the research station for forty-five minutes, and for all Beck knew, she wouldn't emerge again until quitting time. It'd been a long shot expecting him to show up here, but they couldn't spare the manpower to stake out Beck's apartment any longer. And Tom would rather spend his day off watching Kate's back than sitting outside an apartment building half an hour away.

He pushed back his seat and pulled out her father's arrest file. The scrap of paper with a number for Z. Cortez sat atop the rest. The area code matched DC's, but reverse lookup on the internet hadn't yielded an address. For all he knew the number was no longer in service or belonged to someone else now. But what if it didn't? What if the person who picked up the phone on the other end was the woman who betrayed his partner? What did he do then?

The woman had disappeared without a trace after the bombing. What were the chances this scrap of paper would lead to her? She would've been a teenager at the time of Kate's father's arrest.

Tom turned his phone in his hand. Yeah, what was he thinking? There was no way a twenty-year-old arrest was connected to Ian's killer. Zoe probably wasn't even the woman's name.

So why not call? Nothing to lose. None of their other leads were panning out.

The phone rang. Once. Twice.

He suddenly felt like a caged animal. If this turned out to be the same woman who got his partner killed . . .

He crushed the paper with her number scrawled on it, wishing it was her neck and hating the ugly emotions burgeoning in his chest, choking off all sense of—

"Hello," a female voice said. Not Zoe's. The woman had a British accent.

"I'm calling for Zoe Cortez. She there?"

An odd scuffle sound interrupted the woman's response. "Ah, no, she's not in at the moment. May I take a message?"

If this was his partner's Zoe, there was no way she'd respond to his message. More likely she'd skip town the instant she found out he was onto her, which if she had caller ID, might be what that scuffle sound had been.

"No, that's okay. I'll call back. Thanks." He clicked off the phone with a groan. *Lord, I need your help. Lead me to this guy so I can protect Kate.*

The rear door of the research center opened and Kate strolled out.

What was she doing? He'd told her to call him if she had to go anywhere. As he reached for the door handle to remind her as much, his cell phone rang. Kate held a phone to her ear. Okay, so he couldn't yell at her yet. He settled back in his seat and watched her through his windshield.

When she bypassed her yellow Bug and opened the door of a white Honda, he clicked on his phone and started his engine. "Where you going, Kate?"

"Hey." She glanced around as if she'd sensed from his question that he might be watching, then slipped inside the car without noticing him. "I'm going to Landavars Greenhouses to pick up some herbs. But I'm borrowing Patti's car, so you don't have to worry about anyone following me."

"Is that the only place you're going?"

"Uh, no." She fixed her phone on the dash and turned on the car. "I need to drop off some paperwork at Betty's B and B." Her voice rose with excitement as she pulled out of her parking space. "I might have a lead on that plant I found, but it's all in Spanish. Betty said she'd translate it for me."

"That's awesome. I'll—" Movement in his side mirror caught his attention. "Listen, be careful. I'll catch up to you as soon as I can." He clicked off as a tan Toyota Corolla coasted behind his parking spot, Michael Beck at the wheel, his gaze fixed in the direction Kate had just turned.

Tom rammed his gearshift into Reverse and stomped on the gas. His fender clipped the rear end of the Corolla, but Beck didn't stop.

Tom shoved his stick into Drive and swerved onto a parallel lane, racing him to the end. But instead of turning out of the parking lot after Kate, Beck veered left across the bridge leading to the lilac garden. A dead end. Tom grinned. Beck obviously wasn't from around here. Tom careened after him, screeching to a diagonal stop in the center of the bridge.

The Corolla pulled a donut in the parking lot, then jerked to a stop, and Beck bolted from his car.

"Stop! Police!" Tom shouted, racing after him.

"Okay." Beck lifted his arms.

But momentum, adrenaline, and a chestful of anger at what he'd put Kate through hurtled Tom straight into him. He whirled him around and rammed his back against the nearest tree. Fisting the guy's plaid shirt in his hand, Tom pressed hard against his chest.

The guy didn't put up a fight. In fact, he kind of smiled. Tom was struck by the sense he knew him, and not just because he'd seen his face a hundred times on that video clip. The red tinge of his beard stubble was testimony to his former hair color. "Who are you?" Tom locked on his green eyes, and his heart jerked. "You're supposed to be dead."

Kate stashed the sage Patti had asked her to pick up in the Styrofoam cooler in the trunk and then headed to Grandma Brewster's. As she'd done all morning, she continuously monitored her rearview mirror.

A black car appeared. The same black car she'd noticed on her way to the greenhouse. Her pulse quickened. Gripping the steering wheel, she scouted her options. As she cleared a four-way stop, another car pulled in behind her. Seeing her opportunity, she swerved into old Mr. Surely's farm, circled behind the barns and exited the two-hundred-plus-acre block via the back farm lane. No other car in sight.

Tom would be proud of her. She sat a little taller and stepped on the gas. In record time, she pulled into Grandma Brewster's driveway. She grabbed the last page of the stack Patti had printed off—the one with the photo of the plant—and opened the door.

The black car swerved into the driveway behind her, and a male voice called out. "Thought you could get away from me, huh?"

14

"I am dead. You understand?"

Tom loosened his hold on Michael Beck, aka Mike Baxter, and stared. He couldn't help himself. The eyes, the hair, the telltale mole on his temple—this was Kate's dad. And he'd shoved him up against a tree trunk. Tom released his grip, a thousand questions buzzing through his brain. "*No*, I don't understand. You were stalking Kate. Had her scared half out of her mind. What were you thinking?" His indignation welled up so fast, he plowed his fingers through his hair to arrest the urge to give the man a good shake. "How could you abandon your wife and daughter, let them believe you were dead?"

"Shh." The man glanced around, and even though there wasn't another soul in the secluded lilac garden, he kept his voice steely low. "It was the only way to keep my family safe. Then and now. If you care about Katy as much as I think you do, you won't tell her."

"Are you nuts? She's been tormented by your arrest, your supposed death. She needs to know you're alive. I can't *not* tell her."

"She can't know." A flicker of regret crossed his stone-faced glare. "Her safety depends on it."

Tom's heart lurched. "What are you talking about?" He'd let her drive off without a tail, thinking Beck—Baxter—was the only immediate threat. He whipped out his phone.

Baxter grabbed his arm. "What are you doing?"

Tom jerked free of his hold. "Calling her to make sure she's okay."

"I didn't mean she was in imminent danger."

A research station truck pulled up to the bridge and a burly-looking guy jumped out of the cab. "This your car, mister?" He hitched his thumb toward Tom's car blocking the one-lane bridge into the lilac garden.

"Yeah." Tom resisted the impulse to pull rank and tell him he was interrogating a witness. Kate's undead father didn't need any more attention directed his way. "Sorry about that. I'll move it now." To Baxter, he warned, "Don't move. I'll be right back. Then I want answers." Tom parked his car beside Baxter's Corolla and waited for the security guard to finish his rounds of the area before confronting Baxter again. "Okay, start talking."

"First I need your promise that you won't tell her."

Tom jabbed a finger into the man's chest. "All I'll promise you is that I'll do whatever it takes to keep her safe from *whoever* might hurt her." His jaw clenched at the possibility that might mean keeping her father's secret. To let her keep thinking her father was dead when he knew the truth was the worst kind of betrayal. He ground his teeth until they hurt. "Why are you here? Why have you been following her?"

"I had to make sure she was safe."

"*Safe?* Sounds to me like you've put her in more danger by coming here."

"I've been a ghost for twenty years. No one's going to recognize me, let alone connect us, if you don't give me away." He snapped a twig off a tree and crushed it in his hand. "But when I saw the newspaper coverage of Katy's attempted murder, I was afraid they'd figured out she was my daughter."

Katy. Her father poured such love and heartache into the affectionate nickname, Tom felt for him. "The attempted murder had nothing to do with GPC Pharmaceuticals."

Baxter shook his head as if he couldn't believe that.

"Kate exposed Molly Gilmore for killing your daughter's colleague in a twisted ploy to get revenge on a lover who'd spurned her." Tom's voice cracked at the memory of how close he'd come to losing Kate. He shut down the thought and cleared his throat.

Baxter squinted at him. "You believe that?"

"Trust me. Molly Gilmore is one warped woman. After she killed Kate's colleague, she decided she wanted the guy back and tried to frame Kate for the murder."

"But the woman who was killed—Daisy—she'd discovered something. Right?"

"Yeah."

Again, Baxter cast furtive glances around the perimeter and lowered his voice. "Something GPC wasn't happy about?"

"Kate thinks as much," Tom admitted, but even she hadn't gone so far as to blame the pharmaceutical company for Daisy's death. "What did you see in Colombia that turned you against GPC?"

"You know about my trip?"

"Your old buddy Peter Ratcher filled us in."

Baxter snorted.

"You don't trust him?"

Baxter flung the crushed twig to the ground and ripped off another. "I don't know if I do or not."

"He knows Kate's your daughter. He told her about your arrest. That you were trying to do the right thing." Tom got into Baxter's face. "If you don't trust him, I need to know."

Baxter patted the air in a calming gesture. "It's okay. I took care of him."

"What do you mean you took care of him?"

"I hacked into his accounts to buy some time, keep him preoccupied rebuilding his identity."

"That's why I haven't been able to get ahold of him?" Tom blew out a breath. "Here I thought he'd recognized you in the video clip of you spying on him at the hardware store. And—"

"You what?" Baxter clamped his head in his hands as if it had suddenly exploded with pain. "Did he recognize me?"

"He didn't say so, but I thought I saw a flicker of something."

Baxter groaned and slumped back onto a bench, his eyes hollowed out. "If he's already told someone . . ."

"Told someone what? That you're alive? Based on a grainy video clip . . . after twenty years? Who'd believe him?"

"True, but it'd be just as bad if he tells them Kate's my daughter."

"He's not the only one who's connected her to you. The daughter of one of the fire's victims recognized your picture in Kate's house and accused you of destroying her village."

"You know about the fire?" Baxter's voice broke. "Kate knows?"

"Did you pay the guy to set it?"

"No! GPC was behind it. Why do you think they wanted to bury me when I didn't deliver? The plant is like bananas. It doesn't grow from seeds. Destroy all the plants, lose the species forever." Baxter's expression soured. "Except I was supposed to deliver the Golden Goose."

"Yeah, what did you do with the plants?"

Baxter shook his head. "I can't tell you that."

Tom squinted at him, not sure what to think. Just because this man was Kate's long lost father didn't mean he didn't swindle his employer and sell the plants to the highest bidder. "Why are you really here?"

"It's complicated."

"Uncomplicate it." Tom planted a foot on the bench beside him. "What really happened twenty years ago?"

"I was cooperating with the police to expose GPC. The police 'arrested me'"—he made quotation marks in the air—"for my own protection."

"You mean like witness protection?"

"That was the plan. Only my wife couldn't bear the thought of never seeing or speaking to her parents again." The deep lines carved in Baxter's face said he hadn't borne not seeing his wife and daughter any easier. He fisted his hand against his forehead, his eyes squeezed tight, as if he was fighting back a rush of emotion. He swallowed hard, dropped his hand. "The police staged my death so that GPC would think they didn't have to worry about me."

The missing reports in his arrest record now made sense. "So your wife knew you didn't really die?"

"Yeah." Baxter blew out a breath, then got up and paced. "I'm sure she thought I'd come back eventually, once the court case was over."

"But your family buried a body."

"A casket." Baxter's gaze lifted to some faraway point. "A couple of months later, Peter started going by my house. The detectives were worried he'd draw the truth out of my wife, that maybe GPC was using him." Baxter choked on the explanation, clearly struggling to recount what happened next. He pressed his palm to his mouth a moment, briefly closed his eyes. "The detectives figured my wife needed to believe I was *really* dead because if GPC figured out I wasn't, they'd threaten her and Katy to lure me out of hiding."

The emotion had seeped from Baxter's voice. It sounded dead—not unfeeling like it'd been an easy decision to dupe his wife that way, but like he'd shut off the part of him that was *allowed* to feel. A survival strategy Tom knew too well from his FBI days.

"Peter claimed he felt guilty for not doing more to try to help you."

"We couldn't take the chance. So the police told her I died . . . for real, this time."

"That's when she moved back to her parents'?"

Baxter scrubbed a hand over his face. "Nothing to keep her at our home anymore."

That also explained why she didn't want to take Kate to the cemetery, why she'd battled depression for years. Tom fought to keep his own emotions in check. "So what happened? Why didn't you testify against GPC?"

Baxter grew restless again and continued pacing. "Shortly after my wife moved away, the detectives investigating GPC died under suspicious circumstances. My lawyer advised me to drop the case." Baxter's expression twisted as if he'd swallowed a bitter pill. His breath came in shallow, angry huffs. "He said that some companies are just too big to topple. That if the police continued to investigate my allegations, GPC would figure out I wasn't dead. And my family would be in jeopardy."

Tom braced his hand on a tree limb. "So you disappeared."

"Yes." Baxter slumped back onto the bench. "Once the detectives were killed, I knew my family wouldn't be safe if anyone knew I was still alive. So *I* staged my death for the benefit of my handlers." He leaned forward, recounting his story now like a casual observer who had no emotional connection to what transpired. "They never recovered the body, of course. I bounced through several identities, compiled what evidence I could against GPC, anonymously feeding it to the appropriate authorities whenever I thought it might make a difference." His nostrils flared. "It never did."

Tom rested a foot on the edge of the bench, leaning his forearm on his knee. "So why come out of hiding now?"

A car turned onto the dead-end road leading their way and slowed at the bridge. Baxter eyed it suspiciously.

A young woman jumped out sporting a digital camera with a large zoom lens.

Baxter sprang from the bench and hurried to his car.

Tom blocked him. "Wait, where are you going?"

The woman on the bridge glanced their way but focused her camera on something in the treetops.

Baxter reached past him for the door handle. "I've got to go."

"What am I supposed to say to Kate?"

Baxter gulped a breath, deep pain in his expression. "Nothing."

Tom let him climb into his car, knowing he couldn't leave until the woman with the camera moved her car off the bridge. He braced his hands on the roof and leaned down to speak to Baxter through the driver's side window. "How can I contact you?"

"Leave a light in your front window. I'll contact you."

Tom snorted. "You've got to be kidding. Don't you have a cell phone?"

Baxter looked at him as if he were an idiot.

"Right, you prefer to leave notes," Tom bit out, fed up with Baxter's cloak-and-dagger routine. He still hadn't gotten a straight answer on why Kate would still be in danger after all these years.

"Your responses to my notes told me what I needed to know."

"What's that?"

"You're a good man."

Tom shook his head. Not that good—as a cop, anyway—not if Baxter had been watching him undetected. Of course, twenty years of being a ghost had given the man lots of practice. Tom glanced over his shoulder to the bridge. The woman was climbing back into her car. "How do you think your being here will protect Kate?"

Baxter started his car and shifted into Drive. "It won't. That's your job."

Heart racing, Kate peered in her rearview mirror at the black car that had her blocked in Grandma Brewster's driveway. The trees and bushes lining the driveway suddenly didn't feel all that serene.

The driver—Jarrett King—hopped from the car. She gulped. The mayor's son, Patti's boyfriend. The only other person who knew about her interest in the rare plant.

Stuffing the picture she'd brought to show Grandma B into her back pocket, she climbed from the car and turned toward him. "What are you doing here?"

"Kate?" Jarrett sounded shocked. "Why are you driving Patti's car?"

Kate pressed a palm to her chest. "Oh." He'd thought she was Patti. "I borrowed it." She closed the car door, expecting him to get back into his car and drive away. Instead he slammed his own car door closed and stalked toward her. "What—" she cleared the squeak from her voice. "Was there something else you wanted?"

"Huh?" His head ticked sideways. "Oh, no, not from you. I'm picking up some concoction my mom ordered."

Kate couldn't help letting her breath escape in a rush. Clearly this whole business with Michael Beck had her way too jumpy. "You go ahead. I came to ask Grandma B a few questions. I could be awhile."

"About that plant you had Patti researching?" His voice rose excitedly.

"Um, yeah."

"Where did you find it?"

"Uh . . ."

"*Ach*, I thought I heard someone." Grandma Brewster bustled through her garden gate, sparing Kate from answering. Her heavy gray stockings were rolled down to her ankles, or maybe she hadn't gotten around to rolling them up just yet. "You here for your mama's tincture, *ja*?"

"That's right," Jarrett confirmed. "Is it ready?"

She reached into the large pocket of her apron and pulled out a small bottle. "*Ja, ja.*"

"Thanks." Jarrett handed her a ten-dollar bill and took the bottle. Turning back to his car, he nodded Kate's way. "See you around, Ms. Adams."

She sincerely hoped not around here but smiled anyway.

She waited until he pulled out of the driveway, then reached for the picture of the plant she'd stuffed in her back pocket.

Grandma Brewster was intently studying the ten Jarrett had given her.

"Is something wrong?"

"*Nein*. It good." She removed her glasses and tucked the money into her apron pocket.

Kate imagined everyone was looking at their money a little more carefully these days. She showed Grandma B the picture she'd brought. "Do you know what plant this is?"

The older woman studied the picture a moment. "Not from here."

"I saw something like it down by the creek."

Grandma B squinted at her and then back at the picture. "*Ja?*"

"Yes. I would have picked a sample, but since I didn't know what it was, I didn't want to risk it without a pair of gloves." She'd made that mistake once as a kid while collecting leaves for a class project. She'd never itched so badly in her life—thanks to the poison ivy she'd pressed into her book.

"Show me."

About to turn back to her car for a pair of gardening gloves, Kate remembered she was driving Patti's car. "Do you have a pair of gloves I could use?"

Grandma B pulled a bright floral-patterned pair from her apron pocket.

"Great. Follow me." Kate led the way down the same path she'd taken a few days earlier, and despite the uneven terrain and fifty-plus-years age difference between them, Grandma B kept right up with her.

The stark change in humidity as they entered the forest caught her by surprise again. Thankfully she'd worn a light cotton blouse with her capris today, although her open-toed sandals weren't the smartest footwear for traipsing down a creek bank.

Grandma B took up a sturdy branch and used it as a walking stick, but otherwise she showed no sign of slowing.

"It's over there." Kate pointed to a small patch on the far bank of the creek.

A twig snapped to her right, and a frightening déjà vu feeling snapped to attention every hair on the back of her neck.

She peered through the trees, half expecting to see Greg and Pedro, or maybe Jarrett, and praying it wasn't Beck. After the last time, how could she have been so stupid as to leave her purse with her cell phone in it back at the car?

Grandma B, apparently oblivious to the visions of ax murderers parading through Kate's head, squatted in front of the patch of *amen dios*, or amendoso, or whatever it was, and uttered an unintelligible repertoire of German-sounding exclamations.

Kate wasn't sure what to make of the reaction and was too intent on safeguarding their flank to ask. She'd never forgive herself if she endangered Grandma B.

Grandma B pulled on her gardening gloves and gingerly handled the plant—testing the turgidity of the stem, tracing the veins of the leaves, examining their underside before plucking a sample.

She let out another rush of guttural sounds at the sight of the milky sap that seeped from the break.

"What are you doing here?" a male voice sniped.

Kate nearly jumped into the air at the sudden appearance of Brian Nagy's real estate agent and another man, also in a business suit.

"Oh." Kate paused to catch her breath and give her careening pulse a chance to slow. They obviously weren't stalking her in that getup, which meant the guy must be an interested buyer.

"Well?" Westby's narrowed eyes drilled into her, his forehead wrinkles inching their way up his bald head.

"Um," Kate mumbled, which even to her own ears sounded like a way-too-guilty stall tactic. He knew exactly why she was here, or at least could guess.

"Picking plants for my tinctures," Grandma Brewster piped up.

Kate's pulse went from a wild rampage to a halting stop. If Westby found out which plant she wanted to protect, he'd probably have it eradicated by nightfall. But seeing the bouquet of coltsfoot clutched in Grandma B's hand, Kate remembered to breathe.

"Good for coughs. Loosen"—Grandma B patted her chest as if searching for the word.

"Phlegm," Kate filled in. "The tea is very effective. Some commercial cough syrups use the plant."

The other man grabbed Westby's arm and hissed something in his ear.

"She's harmless," the agent assured. "Just our local homeopath. A good one too. My wife's used her tinctures a time or two."

The other man hissed something back, and Westby turned an apologetic look toward Grandma B. "I'm sorry. Now that the property is being sold, you won't be able to wander about picking plants anymore. Understand?"

"*Nein.*" Grandma B narrowed her eyes. "Fifty years I do. I don't hurt nothing."

"I know, but you are trespassing."

"*Nein*, Verna say okay."

"I'm sure she did," he said impatiently. "But she's selling it. You understand."

Kate clasped Grandma B's elbow. "C'mon, let's go back to the house." She tugged the older woman away from the plant she didn't want the men to notice.

The potential buyer with the beady eyes was already scrutinizing her far too intently for her peace of mind. Her skin crawled at the thought of the unfriendly city slicker taking over her neighbor's property.

Grandma Brewster let out an indignant harrumph but started walking.

Westby gave Kate a surprised look. Clearly he hadn't expected Brian's sworn-to-block-the-land-sale neighbor to be on his side in this particular battle.

Once she and Grandma B were out of earshot of the two men, Kate turned to Grandma B. "Did you get a sample of the plant?"

Grandma B dropped her handful of coltsfoot, and with a smile teasing the corner of her lips reached into the giant pocket of her apron and produced the other plant she'd picked. *"Ja!"*

Kate laughed. "What made you hide it?"

Grandma B dropped the plant back inside her pocket and shrugged, but Kate wondered if she'd been thinking exactly what Kate hoped to prove—that this was a rare plant that needed its habitat to be preserved. And if potential buyers were already scouting the property, the sooner she figured out what plant they had, the better.

Tom strode up the B and B's driveway and rapped the door knocker. He eyed the street as he waited for Miss Betty to answer. For the past seventy-two hours, Kate's father—her supposed stalker—had been the focus of the danger seeming to surround her. Now, Tom had no idea where the true danger might lurk.

Kate pulled the door wide and her face lit with a welcoming expression that on any other day he would've been thrilled to see. Today, her joy only made the secret he harbored flare accusingly in his chest.

"Oh, Tom, I have fantastic news! Betty is able to translate those webpages Patti printed, and from what we've gleaned so far, the plant is a miracle plant."

Miracle plant? That's what Peter had called the plant Baxter never delivered to GPC. Did Kate's father know it was here? Tom fisted his hands. Of course he did. It was probably what had brought him here. Tom jerked back a step, sideswiped by another possibility—that the plant was what brought GPC here too.

Betty bustled toward them, carrying a plate of freshly baked cookies. "Detective Parker . . . " Her bird-like voice tapered off in a delighted twitter. "How nice of you to join us."

She handed Kate a dainty china plate that complemented the high ceilinged, richly ornamented entrance and motioned them toward the dining room. "Can I get you a cup of tea too, Detective?"

"No, thank you. I'm fine."

Betty hurried off to the kitchen yet again, while Tom joined Kate at the massive dining room table papered with computer printouts. He perched on an antique chair upholstered in an uncomfortable floral needlepoint.

Kate pulled a few pages toward them, her words tumbling over each other. "This is the information Patti found, and Betty's agreed to translate it." She paused for an instant to catch her breath. "But you'll never believe what else."

The excitement on her face, in her eyes, tightened the knots coiling in his gut. "What?"

She lowered her voice. "I think it might be the same plant Lucetta's mom gave my dad."

Tom pressed his lips into a tight smile. Yeah, no wonder Baxter had refused to tell him what he'd done with the plants.

"I don't know for sure, of course." Kate rushed on. "But it's from Colombia, and the name is so similar to what Lucetta called it. I don't think I should ask her, though. What do you think?"

"No. Definitely not." The last thing he needed was Lucetta taking her vendetta against Kate's father out on Kate. And this discovery was just the kind of thing that might set her off.

"Yeah, I'd just as soon not have to face her again."

Hearing the rattle of teacups heading their way, Tom lowered his voice. "If this is the same plant, Kate, you do *not* want word about it getting out. Can you trust Betty to keep what she learns to herself?"

Kate gathered together the pages awaiting translation. "I'd planned to ask her, yes, because I don't want Brian and his real estate agent learning of the discovery and destroying the evidence before I can file a conservancy petition."

Everything in Tom reared like a horse at the edge of a cliff. "No, you can't. If—"

Betty came in with a tray of tea, cutting off his explanation. "Oh," she muttered to herself, setting the tray on the table. "I forgot the sugar. I'll be right back."

"Of course I will," Kate insisted, before he could finish what he'd been about to say. "The whole point of finding and identifying the plant was to save Verna's property."

"What about GPC Pharmaceuticals?"

"What about them?" She tapped the edges of the papers on the table, though with a little less confidence than a moment ago.

"Kate." Tom stilled her hands, let the question sink in. "Your father went to a lot of trouble to keep that plant out of GPC's hands. If they catch wind of your discovery . . ."

Her eyes widened. "I'd been so excited about getting the proof I needed to help Verna, I hadn't thought beyond—" A strangled gasp cut off her words. "Do you think that guy—Beck—who followed me into the woods already knows?"

Tom shook his head, although he wondered the same thing himself and planned to ask *her father* next chance he got. "Beck's harmless."

"You found him?"

"This morning." Tom shifted uneasily. "He's not with GPC. He won't bother you again."

"Who is he? What did he want?" she quizzed him excitedly, oblivious to how difficult it'd been for him to grind out as much as he'd already told her. He needed time to figure out how he could handle the questions without betraying her trust, or her safety.

As Betty poured Kate's tea and shared how delighted she was to help with the translation, Kate snuck him anxious looks, clearly eager to hear everything he'd learned about the man who up until an hour ago they'd been sure posed a serious threat.

Except that he still did—just not in the way they'd thought.

And considering Baxter's less-than-forthcoming answers to his questions, the more information Tom could glean about the plant, the better picture he'd have of GPC's motives.

Betty skimmed the top page of the stack Kate had made.

"This is the journal of a missionary. He learned about the plant in a remote Colombian village where the local medicine woman made a tea from it to cure his dysentery. He says he drank the tea three times a day for three days. It not only cured his dysentery but also lessened symptoms of several other ailments." Betty sipped her tea. "Hmm, I wonder if it would help with my arthritis."

"Isn't the alfalfa tea I gave you helping?" Kate asked. "You need to give herbals time to work. They're not usually quick fixes."

As Kate and Betty got sidetracked discussing the merits of alfalfa tea, Tom mulled over what Betty had read so far. There had to be more to it. Folk remedy stories like what she'd read were a dime a dozen. "Sounds to me like marketing copy for the kind of cure-all ads you see in magazines or those 'discover the secret' headlines you see all over the internet—too good to be true. Are you sure Patti didn't just land on a Spanish version of one of those sites?"

Shaking her head, Kate finished jotting down what Betty had translated. "There weren't any 'buy' links on any of the pages. But you're right, it would take, at the very least, a controlled double-blind study to convince the scientific community of its value."

Let alone to incite GPC to do what Peter Ratcher claimed.

Kate didn't voice that last part, but when their eyes met, Tom knew she was thinking the same thing. Except for this "rare" plant to end up here, mere miles from where her grandparents had lived, Baxter had to have sent it somehow. Had he secretly profited from it too? Just because he was Kate's dad didn't make him innocent.

"Listen, Betty," Kate said. "I need to get back to the lab.

Could I leave these with you to work on and pick them up later?"

"Of course, you go on. I should be finished by the time you get off."

"It's important that you don't mention anything about this to anyone else, okay?"

Betty walked them to the door. "I understand."

As they stepped outside, Tom braced himself for the inevitable questions about "Michael Beck." The muscle in his jaw twitched, reminding him how easily she'd read his unconscious tell before. He pursed his lips. A year of small town living had left him sorely out of practice at the art of misdirection. His gaze swept over Kate's soft hair and even softer eyes, lingered on the smile lines that spoke of her sweet temperament. A hard lump balled in his throat. She was the last person he wanted to hide anything from, but he'd never had so much at stake.

"So what's the deal with Beck?" she asked the instant Betty closed the front door after them.

Tom's cell phone rang. The chief. "Sorry, I need to take this." He'd never been so happy to get a call from his boss.

"Parker," Brewster barked. "Sorry to call on your day off, but I figured you'd want to know we got another counterfeiting call."

Perfect—just the kind of excuse he needed to put off his explanation to Kate. "Where?"

"A Cup or Two. I sent Hutchinson."

Tom swallowed a groan. The rookie was way too eager. "I'll be right there." He pocketed his phone and gave Kate an apologetic kiss on her cheek. "Sorry, we'll have to have that conversation later."

The blush that bloomed where his lips had touched sent a

matching warmth through his chest. He winced. Apparently he'd forgotten what she'd think of him if she discovered the secret he harbored. *Lord, please let her father be wrong.*

Kate drove to the research station, brimming with too many emotions—a giddy schoolgirl rush at Tom's parting kiss, relief that he'd caught her stalker and she could stop looking over her shoulder, and anticipation at being able to save Verna's land . . . tempered by a strange mix of excitement and trepidation that she might have stumbled onto her father's miracle plant. She felt as though understanding this plant would somehow connect her to him.

Marjorie, the receptionist, jumped out of the way as Kate plunged through the side door. "Goodness. What has a bee in your bonnet?" She clasped Kate's arm, a consoling look overtaking her surprise. "It's all that whispering after that police car showed up after church yesterday, isn't it?"

Kate cringed at the reminder. With what had happened since, she'd just about managed to put the incident out of her mind.

"You need to know that no one pays any mind to what Nella says. The woman would never deliberately hurt a soul, but her mouth is about as reliable as a leaky faucet."

Kate rubbed her arms. She hadn't heard what Nella said, but just imagining made her skin crawl.

"If anything," Marjorie prattled on, apparently in no hurry to get started on her lunch. "Verna's sudden admission into a home makes *her* look guilty, not you . . . in a way."

Kate groaned. *Hardly.* It made Verna look like an unwitting victim.

"Trouble just seems to be finding you lately. Lord knows that whatever you did to get the mayor so riled last week sure got those GPC execs all fired up too. I heard you'd made Verna's son mad too—that true?"

"Probably, yeah." *Terrific.* "I need to get to work." Kate started down the hall before Marjorie could commiserate anymore. Her tally of Kate's woes was downright depressing.

Patti and Jarrett exited the lab as Kate rounded the corner.

"Jarrett's taking me out for lunch. I'll be back in half an hour." Patti's brow furrowed. "Hey, where's the sage?"

Kate's grip tightened on the small brown paper sack carrying her mystery plant—instead of the sage she'd volunteered to fetch. "Uh, the box is still in the trunk." She handed Patti the keys. "Would you mind bringing it in after you finish your lunch?"

Kate pushed open the door without waiting for a response. The last thing she wanted to deal with was a round of twenty questions with Jarrett over her visit to Grandma Brewster's.

She turned on her computer and pulled up a database. She could input the plant's characteristics and hopefully narrow in on its plant family and ultimately its genus and species.

Her inbox chimed notice of a slew of unread emails—not unusual for a Monday. Most were usually spam. She clicked it open to make sure there was nothing urgent.

One email purported to be from a friend traveling in Europe whose purse was stolen. Delete. Another from a lawyer in the UK, claiming she'd just won twenty thousand pounds sterling in a lottery. All she had to do to claim her prize was supply her banking information. Delete. The next one was from Tom—"Detective Parker," the sender line read—must be his work email. The subject said, "Good News." Hopefully he wanted to fill her in on what happened to her stalker. She lifted her hand to where his breath had tickled her cheek as he'd whispered reassurances.

She felt a little guilty now for taking so long to forgive him for handing her over to the chief during Daisy's murder investigation. How had she ever doubted she could trust him?

She clicked open the email.

"Kate, take a look at this," it said, followed by a link.

She clicked it, and in the millisecond after her finger tapped the mouse, a tiny voice inside her said, *What if it's spam? Like the email from the friend supposedly robbed in Italy.*

She yanked the FireWire connection from the back of her screen—the one that connected to the new backup drive she'd recently installed. "Lord, please let the email be legit, please."

A red light at the top of the monitor flickered. Why would the computer's webcam click on?

The website opened. Only it wasn't a website. She was looking at herself looking at her computer with flames flicking at her face.

How did he do that? Words blipped on the screen, too small and too quickly for her to make them out. They blipped again and again, growing larger with each blip.

You'll pay. You'll pay. You'll pay.

She clicked the X in the corner of the screen. Nothing happened. She clicked Escape once, a second time, a third time. The words came faster, larger, a darker red. *YOU'LL PAY.*

15

Beth, the proprietor of A Cup or Two, shot Tom a pleading look as he entered the shop, then tipped her head toward the back corner where Hutchinson was grilling a middle-aged woman and her preteen daughter.

"What happened?" Tom asked Beth quietly. The shop wasn't that busy, but a couple of tables had patrons stealing glances in Hutchinson's direction.

"Vic Lawton's daughter came in to buy a couple of teas and muffins to take back to the *Port Aster Press* office. Her mom's the receptionist there." Beth folded and refolded the napkin she was holding, "The girl paid with a ten that was obviously counterfeit. She got really upset when I pointed it out, but I didn't accuse her or anything. I figured she'd had it sloughed off on her without realizing it." Beth slid a sympathetic glance in the mother's direction. "But Trish said she got it from her mom and insisted on calling her mother to prove it, who then insisted on calling the police." Beth lowered her voice. "I'm afraid her boss will milk this story for all it's worth. You know how he gets."

Yeah, he'd demand to know what the police were doing to stop the counterfeiter and get the mayor more riled than ever. He was still irritated that they hadn't been able to trace the source of his text message. "Thanks," Tom said.

As he turned from the counter to join Hutchinson, Beth caught his arm. "And Tom, I've overheard them mention Kate's name a couple of times already."

A foul taste slid down his throat. "Okay, good to know."

Tom joined Hutchinson and introduced himself to the mother and daughter.

"Mrs. Lawton claims she has no idea where the bill came from. She shopped at several downtown stores yesterday afternoon but doesn't recall getting a ten as change from any of them."

"Do you have a computer and printer at home, Mrs. Lawton?" Tom asked.

The woman's posture turned prickly. "Are you suggesting we printed the money?"

Tom raised an eyebrow. "I wouldn't be doing my job if I didn't ask. And I'm sure your boss would be the first to point that out, wouldn't you agree?"

She begrudgingly conceded as much. "Of course we have a computer and printer. These days my daughter could hardly do her schoolwork without them."

"But our printer's been out of ink for weeks," her daughter chimed in. "It ran out in the middle of printing my last essay for school at the end of May. Dad told me I'd have to finish printing it at school because we couldn't afford to buy more ink."

"It's highway robbery what printer companies charge for ink," Mrs. Lawton added. "You're welcome to come to the house to look if you don't believe me."

The last part was clearly a challenge she didn't expect him to take her up on. Her first mistake.

Tom smiled congenially. "Thank you, we appreciate that. Does now suit?"

Mrs. Lawton let out an exasperated huff. "I really need to get back to the office."

"I can show them," the girl piped up.

"We won't take long," Tom assured.

"Okay, fine." Mrs. Lawton waggled a finger at her daughter. "Then you come straight back to the newspaper. I don't want you getting into any more trouble."

The mention of more trouble piqued Tom's curiosity, but he opted to wait to quiz the daughter without her mom around.

The Lawtons lived within walking distance of the tea shop, so the officers accompanied the girl on foot.

"Must be kind of boring having to spend the day at the newspaper when your friends are out playing," Tom said off-handedly.

"At least I only got grounded for a week. My friend got grounded for the rest of the summer."

Tom whistled. "What'd you girls do to deserve that?"

"Went bike riding with a couple of boys after telling our parents we'd be swimming at the public pool."

"Ah, yes, I can see how that would worry them." Tom's cell phone rang just as they reached the house. Caller ID said NSA—the National Security Agency—not the kind of call you kept waiting, even if it was probably only his buddy calling to catch up. "You go ahead," Tom said to Hutchinson. "I'll take this out here and then join you." He clicked on his phone.

"Why'd you call Zoe Cortez?" Zeb barked in his ear.

"Hello to you too," Tom said to his friend—a friend who'd helped him track down more than one person during his FBI stint, his partner's murderous girlfriend being the glaring exception. He shoved aside the resentment that had dogged him for eighteen long months. How on earth had he found out about the call?

The truth hit him like a battering ram square to the chest. "You knew where she was all along? And didn't haul her in?"

"I can't talk about the investigation. You know that."

"Well, she's connected to a case I'm working on."

"Yeah, right. You forgetting who you're talking to? They told you to leave your partner's murder investigation alone."

"And I did." Against his better judgment. Not to mention it took quitting the FBI and leaving the country to make it stick.

"Well, keep leaving it alone."

Tom bristled at his friend's stonewalling. The only reason he didn't rip into his buddy for keeping his knowledge of her whereabouts from him was that they clearly had her in their sights. "The Zoe Cortez I'm looking for is connected to the arrest of a GPC Pharmaceuticals employee twenty years ago." Why hadn't he thought to ask Baxter about her? "Do I have the right Zoe?" Tom tasted the answer in the back of his throat.

"Leave it alone, Tom."

Tom looked at the neat, wartime bungalows lining the quiet street. The kind of street where he and his friends would've played ball hockey as kids. But instead of getting a nostalgic feeling, he found himself remembering a raid on a terrorist sleeper cell on a street much like this one. He hunched forward, gripping his phone tight to his mouth. "You're telling me we're talking about the same person."

"I'm telling you to leave it alone."

Sweat slicked his palms. "I can't. She really is connected to a case I'm working on."

"Then un-connect her." Zeb hung up.

The order made Tom's blood boil. Now that Kate's dad had revealed himself, he had no reason to follow up on Zoe. But he wanted to. More than ever. And it would be next to impossible if the NSA was monitoring everything linked to the woman. What could Zoe possibly have to do with national security?

Unless . . . the lab had been experimenting with the amendoso plant for—he choked on the thought—biological warfare.

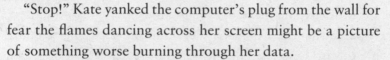

"Stop!" Kate yanked the computer's plug from the wall for fear the flames dancing across her screen might be a picture of something worse burning through her data.

Patti raced into the office. "What's wrong?"

"I . . ." She sucked in a deep breath, shoved away the image of her face bursting into flames, and willed her racing heart to slow. "I'm not sure. I think my computer's been hacked or infected or something." She pressed Tom's number a second time.

"You calling IT?"

"No, not yet." As Tom picked up, Kate pulled the phone from her mouth. "Patti, could you give me a sec?"

Patti backed out of the room, pulling the door closed.

"Kate, what's going on?"

"The email you sent. I clicked the link without thinking. It burst into flames."

"What? I didn't send you an email. You're not making sense."

"It said, 'You'll pay,' and they were watching me. The

flames . . ." Her voice broke. "He could see me through the webcam. I'm sure of it. How did he get in here?"

"Don't touch anything. I'm on my way." The wail of a police siren serenaded his words.

"I don't even know who this Beck person is. Why does he want to make me pay? For what?"

"Beck didn't do this."

"It's got to be him. He's been following me for days. Clearly he wants to frighten me. But why?"

"Kate," Tom said softly.

"If it was Brian or Molly, it would make some sense. At least I'd understand why he's ticked." Her voice crept higher. "But—who is this guy?"

"Kate," Tom repeated more loudly.

Somewhere in the back of her mind she sensed herself edging toward hysteria, but she couldn't stop. "Why doesn't he just tell me what he wants?"

Minutes later the office door burst open and Tom strode toward her, equal parts empathy and fury smoldering in his eyes. He folded her in his arms. "Katy, I'm not going to let anyone hurt you."

The husky promise unraveled what little composure she had left. Her dad used to call her Katy. She burst into tears.

Tom's arms tightened around her. "Tell me what happened."

"I was staring at myself on the computer screen." Her words were muffled against his shirt. She straightened and swiped the tears from her eyes with the back of her hand. "Then flames erupted. It was like I was Lucetta's mother. That's what flashed through my mind. I know it's crazy. There's no way Lucetta could've hacked into my computer, but that was my first thought. My dad killed her mother and I had to pay."

Guilt festered in Tom's chest. With a few assurances he could alleviate Kate's doubts about her father. He dropped his hold on her shoulders and backed up a step, hating the feelings that roiled inside of him. The walls of the small office seemed to close in on them. What little sun slipped through the miniscule chest-high window disappeared behind a cloud.

He shifted his attention to her computer. Everything in him wanted to tell her the truth, to take away the pain shimmering in her gaze. But it was exactly that kind of emotional thinking that he couldn't afford.

If her father was right about GPC, revealing his existence to Kate could cause more harm than good. Except knowing that didn't make him feel any less cruel for keeping her in the dark.

Her research assistant poked her head through the door. "I called IT. He's here."

Tom raised a hand to block the entrance and further contamination of his possible crime scene. "Sorry, we're going to want one of our computer forensic investigators to trace the source of this intrusion."

"Are you serious?" The anything-but-geeky-looking tech swiped a palm across his sun-bleached hair. "I didn't know the research they did here was so valuable. Cool!"

"Someone stole our research?" Patti's voice lifted with the same edge of panic he'd heard in Kate's earlier.

"We have our backups." Kate patted a portable hard drive that they had yet to check for corruption.

As the IT tech opened his mouth, probably to point out as much, Tom cut him off. "I'll need a list from you of anyone with remote access to this computer and any usage information you have."

"Sure thing."

Patti gasped. "You think someone *on the network* sabotaged her computer? Not a hacker?"

"The attack wasn't random. That's all we know at this point."

Kate's fingers dug into the back of the desk chair she was leaning on. "Did you notice anything weird on the computer this morning?" she asked Patti.

"Weird how?"

"Like, did the webcam light come on?"

Patti frowned at the computer screen. "Not that I noticed."

"Well, if you don't need me," the IT guy interjected, "I've got other work to do. I'll get you that list."

Patti clasped the doorknob. "I guess I'd better get back to work too."

"Patti, wait," Kate called out. "When Jarrett came to take you for lunch, did he go on the computer?"

"No." A moment later the gist of what Kate was really asking penetrated, and Patti's eyes flared along with her voice. "*No!* He wouldn't sabotage our research." She drew in a breath as if she would blurt out more, then abruptly exhaled and yanked the door shut behind her.

"I had to ask." Guilt laced Kate's voice. "He saw me at Grandma Brewster's and . . . I don't know . . . he seems way too interested in the plant I found on Verna's property."

"Wait a second." Tom's brain reeled through everything she'd just said. "When did he see you at Grandma Brewster's?"

She ducked her head. "This morning. I was out that way and I thought she might know the plant. And I needed a sample if I'm—"

"You went back onto Verna's property?" Tom clenched his fists. Keeping this woman out of harm's way was fast becoming a full-time job.

"With Grandma B," Kate said defensively. Then, like a dam had burst, her words tumbled over each other. "I have to act quickly if we're going to save Verna's property. The real estate agent was already showing it to a buyer who seemed really serious."

This was worse than he thought. The property wasn't even listed yet. The buyer had to have inside information. "Did they see you?"

"Yeah, but they didn't know why I was there. Grandma B pretended to be collecting herbs for her tinctures."

Tom shook his head. He didn't like it. Given their first meeting with the real estate agent, Westby was bound to be suspicious of her reasons for being on the property.

"Never mind about that right now. I need to know who hacked into my system and if they stole or corrupted any data. That Beck guy must be good on computers to hide his identity so well."

"Beck didn't do this," Tom muttered, sitting down to examine the computer.

"How do you know?"

"I—" She looked at him expectantly, and his insides felt as if they'd been blasted with pepper spray. "I can't tell you. You're going to have to trust me."

She didn't protest, just nodded, and her trust only intensified the burn in his gut. Her father was alive. *Alive.* And he was keeping that fact from her. Tom shoved away the thought. He didn't have a choice. Not really. He plugged in the computer, ensured that the computer's wireless connections were disabled, then flipped it on.

Flames filled the screen, only now his face, not Kate's, was the shadowy mirage being consumed. Except in his mind's eye, he saw his partner's face and the all-too-real explosion that took him out.

He wouldn't let the situation get that far with Kate. He had let his friendship with his partner mess with his priorities, and he couldn't let that happen with Kate. Yes, he wanted her to trust him. He wanted much, much more. But that didn't matter right now. She might hate him if she ever found out about her father, but at least she'd be alive to hate him, and he'd have done everything in his power to keep her safe.

"YOU'LL PAY" flashed on the screen.

"Turn it off. Please." Kate's voice came out shaky. She hugged her waist and stared at the warning dancing with flames.

Tom tried a few key sequences, and after a couple failed attempts, he managed to bring up the code powering the message.

"What's that?" she whispered.

"The program that the link installed on your computer. It's actually not as sophisticated as I thought it'd be."

He contacted her email provider to have them trace the IP address that had spoofed his email address and that of the link's webpage, although he didn't hold out much hope the info would net him a real person. "I'll get one of our computer forensics guys in here to check for data corruption, spyware, malware." Tom's insides churned. If the message could be believed, she wouldn't escape unscathed, which had him worried the guy planted something in the system that was waiting to be activated.

Kate dug her teeth into her bottom lip. "Do you think it

could've been Lucetta? I mean, if she figured out it was my dad who killed . . ." Her voice faltered.

Tom clasped her arms. "Your dad didn't kill her mother. Lucetta said herself that the fire didn't start until after he left."

"But"—Kate motioned toward the screen—"the flames. It can't be a coincidence. It doesn't matter if Dad did or didn't. If Lucetta thinks he did, and figured out I'm his daughter, she'd want to make *me* pay."

Tom nodded reluctantly. It was the most logical explanation, even if he couldn't imagine the petite housekeeper, who didn't own a cell phone, let alone a computer, being capable of pulling this together. "I'll talk to her. And to Nagy. He has the most vested interest in seeing you derailed."

"The mayor too." Kate grew more animated, a little righteous indignation eclipsing her fears. "He looked pretty keen on seeing me fry last week for my supposed letter to the editor. And his son Jarrett seemed to be showing up everywhere I was today."

"Trust me." He caught her by the shoulders and instantly thought better of the intimate gesture. He averted his gaze, unable to meet her eyes. *Trust me, right.* He dropped his hands. "I won't leave any rock unturned."

He heard her gulp and forced himself to look at her. Between her red-rimmed eyes and quivering chin, she looked way too vulnerable for his comfort.

"I'd like to take you up on your offer," she said shakily.

"Offer?"

Her gaze darted to the computer, and she hugged herself as if the webcam might still be spying on her. "To stay at your dad's."

"Oh." Not a good idea. Never was, but especially now. If

he was going to keep his head in the game, he couldn't afford to be distracted. Never mind what seeing her hurt eyes across the breakfast table would do to his resolve to keep her father's secrets. "Uh, I think it would be better if Officer Reed stayed on at your place. She said she'd be happy to. We're actually doing her a favor, because her superintendent had her apartment building fumigated today."

Hurt flashed in Kate's eyes, slicing his heart swifter than a punk with a switchblade. Yeah, it would definitely be better for everyone.

16

"Looks like we might be in for a storm," Kate mumbled as Tom pulled up to the front of the library where she was meeting Julie to have supper with her.

Tom squinted at the bullet-gray sky. "Yeah."

He'd been responding to her questions in monosyllables ever since she'd suggested staying at his house. And he'd gotten pricklier than a porcupine, especially after the phone call from his dad, which didn't exactly make her feel too good about admitting to needing him.

"You going to be okay?" he asked.

She hitched her purse over her shoulder and reached for the door handle. "Sure. I'm fine."

"Good." He didn't rub her arm and give her that empathetic look she'd come to expect. In fact, he didn't look at her at all. His gaze drifted over her shoulder to the park. "Stay put at Julie's house until Officer Reed picks you up after her shift, okay?"

"I know." She really didn't like being babysat, but after seeing her image swallowed in flames this afternoon, she was too edgy to argue. So edgy that she was actually glad she hadn't driven herself to work this morning after all. Of course, what she'd wanted to do was hang out with Tom at the lab while the police department's computer forensics investigator analyzed her computer, but something more urgent had come up for Tom to nix that idea, and since she'd already had plans to share pizza and a movie with Julie tonight, she gave Tom the out he'd seemed to want.

"You're being ridiculous," she muttered to herself, stepping onto the sidewalk. *He's preoccupied. Stop taking his reticence so personally.*

A chilly wind swooped around her as she marched toward the library. Even knowing Tom would keep watch until she entered the building, she slanted glances toward the nearby bushes and the shadowy corner of the building. A poster announcing the mayor's ribbon cutting for the grand reopening of the butcher shop flapped on a telephone pole, reminding her of her suspicions of his son Jarrett.

Patti hadn't said much when she returned from wherever she'd disappeared to while Tom checked the computer, and Kate regretted not saying more to bridge the rift. But the truth was, she didn't trust Jarrett, and she couldn't pretend she did for the sake of her working relationship with Patti. He might not have had anything to do with the computer attack, and maybe he wasn't even spying on her for his dad, but something about him just didn't feel right.

At the library door, she forced herself to turn back to Tom's car and wave. He didn't smile when he returned the gesture. Her heart pinged annoyingly as she plunged into the building.

"You're late." Julie pushed her chair under the desk and gathered her purse and a DVD.

"I had to stop at your Aunt Betty's"—Kate lifted the ream of papers in her hand—"to pick up the translation she did for me."

Julie frowned. "Does that mean you don't want to watch a movie?"

"No, a movie is just what I need." She'd hoped to go over the translation. She would've even spent some time testing the sample she'd picked up from the property . . . if Tom hadn't nixed her idea of waiting with him at the lab for his forensics guy.

As they headed for the door, Kate sniffed. "What's that smell?"

Julie shrank a little, clearly embarrassed, and pushed her nose into her sweater. "You can smell it?"

Kate wrinkled her nose. "What'd you do? Tangle with a skunk?"

"Not me. Ryan's dog. I'd hoped the smell would've dissipated by now. I think I've gotten so desensitized I don't notice anymore."

"Does the house smell too?"

Julie twisted her mouth into a sheepish half smile. "Afraid so. You want to do pizza at your place instead?"

Kate pushed open the library door and inhaled deeply of the cool evening air. "Definitely." She tucked her papers under her arm and pulled out her cell phone. "I'll just let Officer Reed know that she doesn't need to pick me up."

"Hey, isn't that Tom's car?"

Kate glanced up from texting Officer Reed to the black sedan parked half a block up the street. "Yeah." She looked around, her intestines stomping a Mexican hat dance on her stomach. He must've seen someone spying on her.

"There he is." Julie pointed toward the park where Tom stood amongst the shrubbery with his back to them.

Hiding?

Julie shifted, squinting. "He's talking to someone. Uh, isn't that the guy on the surveillance video?"

Kate's stomach somersaulted. Beck? Tom said he was harmless. That she didn't have to worry about him. Kate caught sight of the disheveled gray-haired man, confirming Julie's ID. What was he doing here? Spying on her again? Her mouth suddenly tasted tinny. Swallowing, she hit Send on her text message and headed toward Tom. "C'mon, let's find out what's going on."

They hadn't walked more than three strides before Beck suddenly about-faced and plunged into the hedge maze. Tom turned their way, looking none too happy. "What's wrong?"

"Was that Beck? Was he following me again?"

"No." Tom raked his fingers through his hair. "I mean, yes, it was Beck. No, he wasn't following you."

"What's going on? Why did he run off when he saw me coming?"

Tom's gaze flicked past hers, not stopping to rest, and that muscle in his jaw did its telling little dance. "It's complicated."

Kate fought to contain her growing annoyance with his non-answers. She bit back the impulse to inform him that she was pretty sure she was smart enough to figure out *complicated*. But catching sight, in her peripheral, of Julie fidgeting, she just said, "Whatever. I thought you'd want to know that Julie and I will be at my house tonight. I already let Officer Reed know."

"That's good. Thanks." He nodded, then squinted toward the maze as if hoping Beck hadn't abandoned him completely. "Watch yourself. If there's any sign at all that someone's tried to get in, get back in your car and call me."

"What's going on?" Julie squeaked.

"I'll fill you in on the way," Kate said. "Let's go." By the

236

time she finished her explanation, they'd driven three blocks past the pizzeria. "Hey, we forgot to pick up our pizza."

"I didn't forget." Julie flipped on her turn signal and headed toward Kate's street. "It won't be ready for twenty more minutes. I figured I'd drop you home so you could get started on baking a batch of those muffins that taste like donuts that I love so much. Then I'll run back and pick up the pizza."

"Ah, so avoiding skunk smell wasn't your only ulterior motive for eating at my house."

Julie shifted into Park. "What can I say? I miss your baking."

"You know, now that you're married, you really should learn how to bake. They say food's the way to a man's heart." In their six years of sharing an apartment, Julie had only tried baking once. Once being one too many times.

Julie tossed off the idea with a flick of her wrist. "I've already caught my man. But I bet Tom—"

"Let's not go there." Kate hurried inside with Julie on her heels.

"Haven't you noticed the way the man looks at you? He can't take his eyes off of you. Well, except back there in the park. Seriously, you need to stop playing hard to get before you lose him."

Yeah, didn't work. Whiskers circled Kate's legs, purring. She set the translated pages on the table and picked him up. "You're feeling better, aren't you?"

Julie strolled around the main level, glancing at windows, checking behind doors. "Everything looks copasetic. I'll get our pizza."

"Okay, see you in a bit." After giving Whiskers a good cuddle, Kate poured fresh food into his bowl, then set to work on the muffins. She added the flour and milk and melted butter to the bowl, but when she pulled the salt, cinnamon, and nutmeg bottles from the spice cupboard, the nutmeg bottle was empty.

She glanced out her side window to see if anyone was next door at Verna's. Not seeing a car in the driveway, she grabbed Verna's house key and hurried across the yard. She'd bought Verna a new bottle of nutmeg on that ill-fated shopping trip. Verna wouldn't mind her borrowing some.

Kate let herself in the back door. The house had a stale, shut up smell. And thanks to the dark gray clouds blocking the sun, the kitchen lacked its usual cheeriness. She shook her head. It lacked Verna. Tamping down a rush of sadness, she opened the spice cupboard.

The bottle would have lasted the most ambitious baker a good six months. But it was practically empty. She shuffled the other bottles aside, thinking it must be the old bottle.

Something clonked in the other room.

Her heart jumped to her throat. Holding her breath, she slowly turned.

Whiskers romped into the kitchen.

"Whew, you scared me. I didn't know you snuck past me when I came in."

Whiskers meowed, tail held high, body quivering proudly.

Kate pulled a chair to the counter to dig deeper in the cupboard.

"What are you doing trespassing in here?" Brian Nagy slammed into the room.

Nearly jumping out of her skin, Kate sent a couple of bottles toppling from the shelf. Flailing wildly, she tried to grab them before they hit the ground and broke, but her foot slipped off the edge of the chair, sending her toppling too.

Brian grabbed her by the arm and jerked her back onto two

feet on the chair, as his other hand deflected the rest of the spice bottles to the back of the counter. "What do you think you're doing?" He yanked her off the chair with a hard shake.

"I—I'm baking and ran out of nutmeg. I knew Verna had—"

His fingers squeezed her arm painfully. "You've got some nerve. Get out!" He shoved her toward the door.

She backed away from him, her hands feeling their way along the counter. "I just needed some nutmeg. I wasn't—" She snapped shut her mouth at the sight of his bulging neck veins.

"You can't just barge onto someone's property like you own the place."

Oh. His real estate agent must've told him about her being at the other property.

He snatched up the spice bottles that had rolled across the counter, stepped on the trash can pedal, and tossed them in.

"Hey, there's nothing wrong with those."

He scowled at her, his face redder than the paprika he'd just turfed along with the nutmeg she'd been after. "What are you still doing here?"

Whiskers meowed loudly, twining around her leg as if to hurry her up so he could escape too.

"I'm sorry," she demurred. "I shouldn't have assumed you wouldn't mind."

"I *mind* plenty," he fumed, and reaching over her head, he slapped open the back door.

She scooped up Whiskers and held him against her pounding heart.

"Keep your nose out of my business or you'll be sorry!"

One step on the back stoop, she matched his glare. "Is that a threat?" Clearly he was no longer talking about her borrowing a pinch of nutmeg.

At his look of utter hatred, her heart beat in her throat. She should've just walked away. Why'd she have to—

He jabbed a sharp finger into her shoulder. "Missy, you're the one trespassing. You better believe it's a threat."

"Yoo-hoo!" Mrs. C waved cheerily from her yard.

Nagy snarled in her direction, then retreated into the house, letting the door slam shut.

Thank you, Lord, for neighbors. Kate hurried back to her own yard, dropped Whiskers onto the porch, then joined Mrs. C at the fence.

"Everything all right?" Mrs. C asked.

"I just meant to borrow some nutmeg from Verna's kitchen, but Brian . . ." She waved off the episode as if it were no big deal even though her insides were still shuddering and her arm still hurt where he'd grabbed her. "I shouldn't have presumed."

"Don't mind Brian. I'm sure he's overwrought with his mom's decline. Property tax bills came in today. After the way his wife left him, he doesn't have much money to cover extra bills now that his mom's government pension will go toward her care."

Kate ducked her head. "Yes, I hadn't considered the strain he must be under." Maybe it was no wonder he'd be upset to hear she'd been snooping around the property he hoped to sell. Not that it made him selling it right.

Mrs. C patted her hand. "Hang on a minute and I'll lend you my nutmeg." She hurried into her house and returned a moment later with a bottle. "Here you go. No hurry getting it back. I don't bake much these days."

"Thanks, I appreciate it." Through the gap between their houses, she spotted Brian's sports car speeding off. She stuffed her hand into her pocket and fiddled with Verna's key. She probably should've returned it, considering.

She resumed her muffin making and had just finished washing up the mixing bowl and pulling out plates and glasses when the doorbell rang. Seeing Julie through the peephole, she unlocked the door.

Julie held the pizza box up with one hand and danced a DVD in the air with her other. "You left our movie in the car." She sniffed the air. "Mmm, those muffins smell good."

"They'll be a few more minutes."

"And then you have to dip them in sugar and cinnamon. Don't forget. That's what makes them taste extra good."

"I'm sure you won't let me forget."

Julie twirled past with a wide grin and led the way to the kitchen where she set the pizza box on the table. She inhaled again, a giddy expression on her face. "What is it that makes them smell so good?"

"The nutmeg and cinnamon. If you baked once in a while, you'd know that," she teased, reaching for the DVD. "What movie did you get us?"

"*Suspicion* with Cary Grant and Joan Fontaine. They're married and she thinks he's poisoning her."

"Oh, yeah, that's a good one." Kate put the kettle on and tipped open the oven door to check on the muffins. The aroma that wafted out reminded her of her visit with Verna. "That's weird."

"What?"

"Just talking to myself." Kate couldn't quite dismiss the thought. She chewed on her thumbnail, bothered by the impression. "When I visited Verna at the nursing home, there was a nice aroma in the room. The nurse said from her tea, but I think it was nutmeg."

"In tea? I've never heard of anyone putting nutmeg in tea."

Kate's gaze fell to the image on the front cover of the DVD of a frightened Joan Fontaine looking at Cary Grant. She gasped. "Beth wouldn't."

"Beth wouldn't what?"

"She wouldn't put nutmeg in Verna's tea . . . but Brian might!" Her heart hitched at the possibility. *Nutmeg psychosis.* Kate picked up the DVD. "It would explain Verna's mild euphoria the weekend before last, then her sudden agitation and confusion later. Hallucinations are even a symptom of acute poisoning."

"You think Brian poisoned his own mother?"

"It explains everything—including the near-empty bottle in her cupboard! The effects wear off after a few days, which explains why she looked so much better after going to the nursing home. That is, until her grandson delivered a new batch of tea." Brian's exultant smile flashed through Kate's mind. "The next time I saw Brian there, he'd seemed almost pleased to see his mother confused and agitated. How had I not guessed it sooner?"

"Whoa, you better be sure before you start accusing him."

"That has to be what he did. He's probably been using her to fence counterfeit money for him, all the while feeding her just enough nutmeg to keep her a little off balance."

Julie plucked the DVD from her hand. "Don't you think the doctor would pick up on that?"

"Not if he's not looking for it. She's old, susceptible to dementia. He saw what Brian set him up to see. After Tom came to talk to Verna about the incident in the grocery store, Brian must've upped the dose." Kate whirled toward the oven and yanked out the muffins. "We have to get to the nursing home. C'mon."

Julie snagged one of the muffins, only to drop it again and blow at her fingers. "Can't we eat first?"

"Not without risking Verna consuming even more nutmeg." She pushed Julie toward the door. "I'll drive."

Julie dragged her feet. "Are you sure this is a good idea? What if Brian finds out?"

Kate's arm tingled where he'd clutched it less than an hour ago. She lifted her chin. "If my theory's right, he'll be sitting in jail."

Tom had waited until Julie's car was out of sight before following Kate's father. The chance meeting had been way too close for comfort. Never mind how frustrated his hedging at her questions about "Beck" was making her.

Where did he disappear to? Tom glanced at his watch. The computer forensics investigator had agreed to meet him at Kate's lab in twenty minutes. He didn't have time to play hide-and-seek. But he needed straight answers about who was most likely behind this latest threat, not to mention about the plant Kate found and how on earth Baxter was connected to Zoe Cortez.

A zillion questions had been running through his mind since the call from his NSA buddy.

Tom circled the hedge maze, then expanded his search to the picnic area. If Baxter would give him a phone number, it'd be a whole lot easier.

The temperature had dropped into the sixties, and with the gathering storm clouds, the area sat empty. Tom scanned the faces of a group milling around the bandstand where a bluegrass concert was scheduled to soon begin.

Baxter peeled himself off a bench and veered into the rose garden.

Tom meandered after him, feigning interest in the large pink blossoms.

"You wanted to talk to me?" Baxter said without turning to look at him.

"Yeah, and this time I want straight answers. Why is GPC trying to locate here?"

Baxter pinched off a dead rose blossom. "I don't know."

"But you have suspicions."

"What makes you say that?" Baxter tossed the question like a boxer testing his opponent's reflexes, gauging for weak spots.

Tom discreetly caught him by the wrist and gave it a hard twist. "We're done playing games. I need answers, or your daughter will end up exposing exactly what I think you're really here for."

"What are you talking about?" Baxter said under his breath. Only his pasty white pallor said he knew.

"You knew the plant was in Port Aster, didn't you?"

His gaze darted about. "We can't talk about this here."

A couple walking hand-in-hand headed toward them.

Still holding Baxter by the wrist, Tom jerked his chin toward the street. "We can talk in my car."

Baxter shook his head. "Can't risk it."

"They think you're dead, remember? No one's going to suspect anything." Tom dropped Baxter's wrist before the couple got any closer. "Start walking out of town. As I drive up, stick out your thumb." Tom walked away without waiting for a response and prayed Kate's father cared about her enough to obey. He glanced at his watch. Weller would be getting to the research station soon to look at Kate's computer. He didn't have a lot of time.

Baxter left the park at a brisk pace. Tom waited until he reached the end of the town's sidewalks and moved onto the shoulder, then started his car. As instructed, Baxter hitched a thumb in the air as Tom approached.

The guy had the passenger door open before the car came to a full stop. "I'm in. Go!"

Tom headed toward the research station. He'd worry about how to get Baxter back to his car later. "Start talking."

"I shipped the seedlings to my wife's father from the airport. He was a farmer. I'd hoped he could keep them alive until we took GPC down. But after the way things went, I didn't dare contact him." He drew a quick breath and barreled on. "I figured he'd probably destroy them for the family's protection. My wife may have changed her name, but GPC knew she moved here. You can bet they watched their every move for months."

"So when GPC announced plans to set up here, you were afraid they'd found the plant?"

Baxter grabbed the dash. "Have they?" The panic in his voice sent Tom's pulse skyrocketing.

"Answer the question," he ground out, not about to lose control of this interrogation to Baxter's agenda.

Baxter's gaze drilled into the side of Tom's head for what seemed an eternity, but Tom kept his attention fixed on the road, refusing to give ground until he got the answers he needed.

Finally Baxter sat back and turned his attention to the passing scenery. "Not at first. I thought the proposed move had to do with that Daisy woman's research." He fussed with the hem of his shirt, repeatedly rolling it in his fingers, then smoothing it straight. "My father-in-law has been dead for years. I never imagined—" He suddenly straightened. "Is it in those woods you chased me from?"

Tom ignored the question. As long as he knew something Baxter wanted to know, he had leverage. "What did GPC plan to do with the plant?"

"It is, isn't it?" Baxter let out an exhilarated sound. "I can't believe it survived."

Tom jerked the steering wheel a hard left to veer into the research station. "Is that all you care about? We're talking about your daughter's survival here."

The disgust in Tom's voice snapped Baxter back to cold reality. "Does GPC know? Does Katy?"

Tom's throat tightened at Baxter's strangled question. "What's GPC want with the plant?"

"Are you kidding? This plant healed more diseases than ten Nobel Prize winners combined. If they controlled it, they'd control the entire pharmaceutical industry."

"But it's a plant. They can't patent a plant." When Baxter didn't respond, Tom added, "They can't, can they?"

"No, but if they could figure out exactly what chemicals in it have healing properties, and synthesize them—they could patent those."

Tom shifted into Park at the curb outside the front doors of the practically deserted main building. "And by destroying the only source of the plant, they guaranteed themselves no competition."

"Yeah."

"But by hijacking the plant, you deprived the world of the cure." Tom shifted in his seat to face him. "Which is worse?"

"It wasn't supposed to happen that way." Indignation simmered in Baxter's gaze. "They destroyed a village to capitalize on the secret. Innocent people died."

Tom's thoughts veered to the name and phone number of his partner's murderer in Baxter's police file, and the NSA's cease and desist call.

The NSA wasn't interested in pharmaceuticals.

"What can you tell me about Zoe Cortez?"

Baxter started at the name. His gaze flicked to the side-view mirror. His fingers curled into his shirt again as an unmarked police car pulled up behind them.

"That's the computer forensics investigator I'm supposed to meet," Tom said. "I've got to go inside and get him started on analyzing Kate's computer. Stay put. I'll be back in a few minutes."

As quickly as he could, Tom had security escort him and Officer Weller—the department's newly qualified CFI—to Kate's office. He gave Weller a quick rundown of what happened and said he'd be back in a few minutes. He hadn't been inside more than ten minutes. Fifteen tops.

But when he got back outside, Baxter was gone.

Twilight had slid toward night, and the building's outdoor lights clicked on, throwing disturbing man-like shadows from every tree and shrub around it. Tom rounded the building, peered into the orchards, jogged through the gardens. "Mike," he hissed. "Where are you?" He waited expectantly, but Baxter didn't emerge. *Terrific.*

Tom jumped in his car and circled the lanes crisscrossing the grounds, then drove a few miles back toward town. There was no sign of the man. He must've hitched a ride, gone after the plant. A loud clap of thunder shook the car. Rain pinged the windshield. He wouldn't likely succeed in this weather.

Tom's cell phone beeped. A text message from Weller that he'd found something.

Tom squinted into the distance, then pulled a U-turn to return to the station as his mind replayed Baxter's reaction to the mention of Zoe Cortez. Baxter had definitely recognized the name. Then resumed his fidgety habit of rolling the hem of his shirt.

Tom slammed his hand into the steering wheel. How had he missed it? Zoe's name had made Baxter downright edgy.

What did that mean for Kate? How could Baxter just up and disappear without giving him more information to go on to keep his daughter safe?

Outside the research station, Tom peered again into the darkness as a disturbing feeling seeped over him—he'd been as wrong to trust Baxter as his dead partner had been to trust Zoe Cortez.

17

"They're not just going to hand over your neighbor's tea for no reason," Julie hissed as they waited outside Verna's locked ward for someone to let them in.

Kate shushed her as an aide answered their knock. "Follow my cue."

"The residents are having dinner now," the aide explained. "Would you mind coming back in half an hour?"

She'd already started to pull the door closed again when Kate jutted out her foot to block it. "Actually, we're here to collect the herbal tea Verna Nagy's grandson brought for her."

The aide didn't ease off her hold on the door. "I'm afraid I can't h—"

"It's very important," Kate cut in. "We believe there was contamination in the mix that might explain her turn for the worse."

"That's terrible. Wait one moment. I'll need to consult the nurse." She pulled again at the door, then looked pointedly at Kate's foot still blocking it.

Kate immediately stepped back, and the aide hurried off, the door closing between them.

"I don't like this." Julie paced from one side of the wide hall to the other, rubbing her hands up and down her arms as if the building were an icebox rather than a comfortable seventy-five degrees. "What if Brian visits tonight and she tells him you took the tea?"

"Unless he's guilty, he's not going to make a fuss."

"It's his being guilty I'm worried about."

The aide reappeared with two paper sacks—the one Kate had brought in and the one Verna's grandson had presumably delivered. "Here they are."

"Thank you. It would probably be better if you don't mention to Verna or her family that we've taken them. We don't want to cause undue stress before these are analyzed."

"Not a problem. The doctor recommended she avoid them for a few days anyway. We'll take good care of her."

Julie laughed as they dashed through the rain to her car. "You're good. I can't believe you got her to just hand them over."

"Verna has you to thank for the rescue. If you hadn't asked me to bake those muffins and then brought over that movie, I might not have figured out what was going on. C'mon, let's hit the lab so I can prove my theory."

"You're not going to believe what I found in the computer's trash bin," Weller called from Kate's office adjoining her lab.

Shedding his wet coat, Tom dismissed the security guard who'd escorted him back to the lab and then peered over the shoulder of the computer forensics investigator.

Weller clicked on the file and a scanned image of a twenty-dollar bill popped up on the screen.

Tom's throat instantly dried. This was not good.

"Looks like your girlfriend's been playing you." The guy zoomed in on the image with a you-are-so-cooked chuckle, making Tom regret playing the "it's for a friend" card to get Weller here after hours.

Tom pulled out his notepad and pen and thumbed to the page where he'd recorded the serial numbers of the other counterfeit bills. "Number doesn't match any bills we've recovered so far." He jotted it down for future reference.

"Doesn't matter. I'm going to have to take the computer in to the station now. Log it in as evidence. Get a warrant for its examination before I go any further." Weller moved the mouse to the X in the corner.

"Wait." Tom jabbed his notepad back into his pocket. "Her hacker could have planted the file."

Weller's hand hovered over the mouse.

"C'mon, what'll it hurt to quickly check?" Tom squelched the impulse to remind him he'd come out tonight as a favor and that the department didn't even know he was here. The last thing Tom needed was Weller thinking he was trying to cover something up.

Weller pressed a few buttons. "Nah, not a plant. The file was created and then trashed over a week ago."

"Before or after the grocery store incident?"

Weller compared the dates. "After." He punched a few more buttons and brought up a screen full of information. "There's a record of one copy of the file being printed." He glanced at the printer sitting next to the computer and then back to the screen. "On that printer."

Tom stifled a groan. "Okay, pack it up." He had no choice. The evidence had to be protected. He retreated to the adjoining lab room to collect his thoughts just as the hall door burst open and Kate rushed in. The sight of her bedraggled, rain-drenched hair gave his heart a kick.

"Tom, I'm so glad you're still here. I've figured out who's doing the counterfeiting."

"The counterfeiting?" He glanced at her friend Julie hurrying in behind her. "Where's Officer Reed? I told you not to go anywhere alone."

Kate skidded to a stop halfway across the room as Weller let out a snort from the doorway to her office, her computer in his arms. "What's he doing? He can't take that!"

"It's evidence, ma'am," Weller answered for him, the angry scar that slashed from the corner of his mouth to his jaw line, courtesy of a domestic violence call gone bad, making him look more than a little intimidating.

"Set it down a minute, will you, Weller?" Tom said, not thrilled to have to confront her with what they'd found in front of an audience. He motioned Kate to take a seat.

Julie, carrying two small paper bags, took up sentry beside her.

"Who do you think is behind the counterfeiting?" Tom asked, ignoring, for the moment, her question about the computer and the fact she'd come out without her bodyguard.

"Brian Nagy." Kate's eyes lit as she grabbed one of the bags from Julie. "And as soon as I run a couple of tests on this, I'll be able to prove it."

Weller let out another snort.

Tom threw him a scowl.

"What's with the computer?" Julie asked, clearly reading the escalating tension between him and Weller.

"Yeah." Kate eyed Weller suspiciously. "You said the IT guy could scan it here so I wouldn't be without."

Yeah, so much for using Weller's zeal to his advantage. Tom

checked the urge to reach for her hand. He couldn't afford to show undo prejudice in front of the detective. The man had only recently received his certification and was way too keen to prove himself. Tom let out a sigh. "That was before he found an image of a twenty-dollar bill in the computer's deleted files and a record of it being printed on your printer."

Julie gasped.

"You think I—?" The hurt that flashed in Kate's eyes cut him off at the knees. The laugh that followed sounded forced. "That was Darryl. He wanted to see how easy it would be. He showed Patti and me after he did it. Ask them."

"I believe you." Tom held her gaze steady, willing her to believe him. "But you understand that we'll need to take it into evidence until we can prove that it's not connected to the case."

She chewed her bottom lip, clearly fighting the impulse to argue.

"Now tell me." He hooked a finger on the top of the bag she held and peeked inside. "How will this prove Nagy's our counterfeiter?"

As if he'd flipped a switch, she bobbed forward with scarcely restrained energy. "He's poisoning her."

"Poisoning who?"

"Verrrrr-naaaaa." She enunciated slowly as if to compensate for how slow on the uptake he was. "With nutmeg in her herbal tea."

Beside her Julie nodded as if Kate was making perfect sense.

"Nutmeg?" Tom repeated, dodging the skepticism that tried to creep into his voice. He was pretty sure nutmeg was what his mom had always used in her pumpkin pies, and they never killed anyone. At the sound of a snicker, he shot Weller a silencing glare. "But Kate, nutmeg isn't a poison."

"In high doses it is." Peeling off her wet coat, she rattled off all the symptoms, which admittedly did match Verna's.

"If Brian wanted his mother out of the way, why poison her with nutmeg?" Surrounded by counters overflowing with herbs of every description and test tubes and contraptions for siphoning who knows what out of the plants, he shouldn't be surprised that she'd imagine such a scenario. "And what does poisoning Verna have to do with counterfeit money?"

"Don't you see?" Impatience with his apparent denseness pushed Kate's voice higher as her hands flew into motion gathering petri dishes and tweezers and microscope slides. "He doesn't really want to hurt her. He just wants control of her assets. The symptoms from overconsumption of nutmeg are perfect."

Tom sniffed the bag of tea. "Because they make her look like she has dementia?"

"Yes!" She grabbed his arm in her excitement, victory flaring in her eyes. "Which gave him the perfect excuse to coerce her into signing a power of attorney giving him authority over her assets."

"Then once he has what he wants," Julie piped up, "he can let the symptoms wear off."

"That's why she seemed so much better soon after she went into the nursing home," Kate finished breathlessly.

"Okay." Tom still wasn't sure how any of this proved Nagy was a counterfeiter.

"But I must have spooked him when I brought up Verna's plan to donate her farmland to the town," Kate rushed on. "Because he—well, his son—took more tea to her, remember? Then shortly after that she got all agitated and confused again."

"A credible theory." Tom rolled the top of the paper bag closed.

"But how can you prove it?" Weller grunted.

"The bottle of nutmeg I bought for Verna last week is practically empty."

"You went in her house?" Tom's voice spiked along with his anxiety that she'd been so reckless.

At least she had the good grace to look sheepish about it. "I shouldn't have, I know. I was baking and . . . Never mind that." Kate took back the bag and tipped a small portion of the contents into a clear glass dish on her workbench. "This is the tea Brian's son brought to the nursing home. When I test it, I'm sure we'll find it contains significant amounts of nutmeg."

Tom nodded. The plan would be ingenious, but . . . "Even with attorney privileges, any proceeds from the sale of Verna's property would have to go toward her care first. I don't see what he ultimately gains."

"If he controls her money," Julie chimed in, pulling her chair over to where Kate had set to work, "he's going to be able to sneak payments to himself left, right, and center."

"Okay, say you're right," Tom said as Weller huffed impatiently. Tom motioned him to cool his jets. "How does this implicate him in the counterfeiting?"

"He must have been using Verna to fence his money," Kate said without looking up from the dried herbs she was meticulously separating with tweezers onto individual microscope slides. "Only Verna didn't know. By making her look doddering, he probably figured the police wouldn't suspect her. Julie, could you grab me a rack of test tubes?"

"Not only that"—Julie set the requested test tubes on the

bench—"he's a traveling salesman. Who knows where else he could be spending the phony bills."

Tom grinned at their exuberance. They made a compelling case.

Kate frowned at him. "You don't think it's possible?"

"Sure I do. That's why last week I checked with the police detachments in the areas where Brian travels."

Her tweezers stopped mid-tweeze. "And?"

"There has been a slight increase in reported counterfeiting."

"See!"

Weller cleared his throat. He was leaning against the doorframe, arms crossed. "Where'd you get the sacks of tea?"

"From the nursing home," Kate said.

Weller shook his head.

Kate set down her tweezers. "What's wrong?"

"The evidence won't stand up in court," Weller barked as if any idiot should know as much. "There's no warrant, no chain of custody. Even if there's nutmeg in that"—he flicked his finger toward the herbs she'd spread out—"there's no way to prove how it got there."

"Well, I couldn't just leave it there and let him keep poisoning her!"

Tom touched her arm. "He's not saying what you did is bad, Kate. Just that it won't give us enough to arrest him."

"But once you're certain it's him, you can look for other evidence. Right?" Julie insisted.

Kate's brow suddenly furrowed. "But Verna might not get better soon enough to stop Brian from selling the property." She looked at him pleadingly. "Can't you talk to that Office of the Public whatever-it-was and get them to put some kind of stay on Brian's powers until you get your proof?"

Weller let out another of his unhelpful snorts. "Not likely. Maybe if that receptionist who gave her kid the phony five worked for Nagy instead of the paper you'd have something."

"Izzy Lawton, Vic's wife?" Kate's eyes lit. "She had a phony bill?"

"Yeah," Tom said cautiously, trying to anticipate where she was going with this new information. "But we checked her home computer and printer. They were clean."

"Her husband works for Brian Nagy! He mows Verna's lawn. And last weekend, he painted a couple of her bedrooms."

Tom grabbed his coat and smirked at Weller. "Now we're getting somewhere. You run your tests and I'll track down where Nagy stays when he's out of town. His laptop was clean, but he could have printed the counterfeit bills while on the road."

"We still have to take this computer in," Weller reminded him.

"You go ahead." Tom sent Kate an apologetic look. He didn't doubt her alibi about the file on her computer, but taking in the machine would make it a whole lot easier to convince the chief he wasn't playing favorites.

The lights flickered as rain lashed the windows harder than ever.

Julie glanced out. "The storm's getting worse."

"Yeah." Tom opened the lab door for Weller, then turned to Kate. "Why don't you leave the testing until tomorrow, and I'll follow you two home? Officer Reed will be—"

"Not yet. Please." Kate lifted a hand, scarcely sparing him a glance before returning her attention to the eyedropper she was using to dispense something into a test tube. "We need to know if I'm right about the nutmeg before you bring Brian in."

"Did you even tell Reed you were coming here?"

"Sorry. No, I forgot."

"Forgot? Do you think whoever sent this afternoon's threatening email is just—?" Tom bit off the rest of the lecture and texted Reed. This was no time to relax their vigilance. It would be tomorrow before Weller got back into the computer to see if he could find anything that might lead them to her hacker. He hit Send on the message to her bodyguard and fired another email to the research center's internet company, which still hadn't gotten back to him on an IP address for his spoofed email.

A loud crack rattled the windows. The lights flickered again.

Julie hunkered down on a stool and pulled her sweater tightly around her. "I hate storms."

"I'm sorry to drag you out in this, Julie," Kate said.

"Oh, you owe me big-time." Julie pressed a palm to her growling stomach. "I'm starved. You better pray that new cat of yours doesn't eat the pizza, or my muffins."

Kate made a goofy face that warned not to count on it and Tom laughed.

Laughing felt good after the day they'd had. If they could tie Nagy to the counterfeiting and poisoning his mother, maybe half Kate's problems would be resolved. He hated seeing the dark smudges under her eyes, the tired stoop of her shoulders. Yet she was holding up well, considering. His heart pinched at the strain her questions about her father had added. Questions he could answer. Except he couldn't.

He rubbed his palm over his mouth. After her father's disappearing act, he wasn't sure what to believe. And who was behind the threatening email?

Could be Nagy. Tom wouldn't put it past him, especially if Westby had warned him Kate was snooping around the property. His chest went tight at the thought of what could've happened to her out there today. He moved to the window and watched the trees whip wildly in the wind. Lightning slashed the sky. Hopefully her father made it back to town before the storm hit. Tom didn't want to think about why the man had taken off on him. Not tonight. He pressed his fingertips to the bridge of his nose and prayed trusting him hadn't been a mistake.

He turned his back to the window. "How often does Nagy visit his mother?"

Kate set her test tube into a machine and turned on the power. "I don't know. Why?"

"I'm trying to figure out how much time we have before he realizes you're onto him."

"I told the aide not to say anything to the family."

"That's not going to stop him. If Nagy's doing what you think he's doing, you can be sure he's making sure she keeps drinking the stuff." Kate clearly had no idea how difficult she was making it for him to protect her.

She squirmed under his pointed stare, but given the choices, he knew her well enough to know she'd do the same thing again. Her cell phone rang.

Tom didn't like the worry that flashed in her eyes when she glanced at the screen. "Who is it?"

"Mrs. C." Kate clicked on the phone and said, "Hello."

"Kate," Mrs. C said so loudly Tom could hear her from halfway across the room. "I wanted you to know I have Whiskers. I heard him yowling outside when the storm started."

"You're sure it's Whiskers?" Kate looked at Julie, her forehead crumpled as if straining to remember something.

"Of course. Don't worry, dear, you can just pick him up when you get home."

Kate's face turned pasty. "Someone was in my house."

18

Kate asked Julie for a rain check on dinner and caught a ride home with Tom so Julie could drive straight home too. By the time Kate and Tom got to Kate's house, a black-and-white police car already sat in the driveway. Officer Reed, her unofficial bodyguard, jumped out of the police car and hurried toward Tom's, holding the hood of her rain poncho low against the howling winds.

Tom rolled down his window. "Any sign of an intruder?"

"Just got here. Haven't walked the perimeter yet." She looked past Tom and nodded at Kate.

"We'll do it together." Tom rolled up the window and held out his hand to Kate. "I'll need your house keys. I want you to stay in the car until we make sure the place is clear."

A jagged flash of lightning sliced the sky, followed by a bone-rattling clap.

"Yeah, okay." Kate handed over her keys, trying to ignore the green-eyed monster that wondered why he didn't trust her to stay out of trouble but didn't question letting Sophie Reed traipse around looking for a bad guy.

Kate peered through the rain-sluiced windshield at them striding together toward the dark house. Tom suddenly stopped and lifted his arm in her direction.

The car beeped and all the door locks shot down with a thunk.

Kate jumped. She couldn't help it. What few frayed nerves she'd managed to hold together until now unraveled in one beep. She shivered uncontrollably.

Lord, why are you letting all this happen to me? The wind whistled an eerie response. Rubbing her hands up and down her arms to stave off the chill, she watched Tom and Officer Reed's flashlights bob in opposite directions around her house. *Please, Lord, keep them safe.*

Thunder rumbled, long and low, like a growling dog.

She hoped that was a "yes."

Lights started coming on in the house. First in the kitchen, then in the living room. The front door opened, but Tom didn't motion her in. He left it standing open, and one by one bedroom lights came on. She let out the breath she'd been holding when the last light came on and no wild shouts accompanied it.

She jumped from the car and dashed for the front door.

Tom emerged from the hall as she stepped inside. "I told you to stay in the car until—"

"I saw all the lights come on. I knew it would be safe." Her voice petered out on the word *safe*. She sniffed the air. "That's gas. Can you smell the gas?" Her voice edged higher. "He was trying to kill me?"

Tom caught her by the shoulders. "Calm down."

"Calm down?" She shook off his hold. "Don't tell me to calm down! He tried to gas me." She gulped air, but none seemed to make it to her lungs. "He must've seen my car in the driveway, and no lights on, and assumed I was sleeping."

"No, Kate." Tom looked like he wanted to take hold of her and give her a good shake. "Your oven's pilot light blew out. That's all. Probably blown out by the storm."

"The pilot light's inside, not outside." Her heart raced a mile a minute. Was that an effect of the gas? Should they even be in here?

"The wind's from the east tonight—not typical—so you probably haven't felt before how badly it drafts across the kitchen floor. Don't worry. The pilot light valve on these old stoves doesn't give off much gas, just enough for you to smell something's wrong. Reed's relighting it now."

"Oh." Kate gulped. She'd panicked over nothing. And from the frown between Tom's eyes, she'd freaked him out too. He probably thought she'd shatter completely any second. She took a deep breath and pulled herself together. "Okay," she said with a calmness that surprised even her. "If he didn't come here to gas me, what did he come inside to do?" She glanced around the room. "Nothing seems to be missing or vandalized."

Tom motioned her to the sofa.

She shook her head, still too antsy to sit. He was being too . . . too . . . professional. Why couldn't he just hug her and tell her everything would be okay?

Except it wouldn't be. And he knew it. Someone had violated her home. What was to stop him from doing it again? Only next time she could be here! She moved down the hall to check the other rooms.

Tom trailed her, dripping water from his rain-soaked clothes. "Are you certain the cat was inside when you left?"

"Yes." She handed him a dry towel from the linen closet. "Whiskers was sitting at the living room window scowling at us. I remember it distinctly."

Tom made a frustrated noise as he followed her to the next room.

At the sight of him standing in her bedroom scrubbing his head with a towel, her heart did a totally inappropriate little dance.

"There's no sign of forced entry," he said, draping the towel around his neck. "Is it possible you left a door or window unlocked?"

"No way. I've been too paranoid to open windows."

Apology swam in his eyes, but his arms stayed pinned to his sides.

She turned to her bureau. "And I know I locked the door."

"Who else has keys to the place?" His voice sounded strangely tight, as if it was eating him up inside to not be able to figure out how someone got in.

"No one that I know of." She opened a couple of drawers. Nothing seemed amiss, and that made her feel more edgy than ever. What did this guy want?

She gasped, remembering. "I never changed the locks when I moved in after Daisy died."

Irritation replaced the apology in Tom's eyes. "So her nephew has a key."

"No, he returned it to me when he left town. But . . ." She bit her lip. How could she have been so careless?

"He could've given one to Molly Gilmore," she and Tom said at the same time.

They'd been engaged. Until Edward discovered Molly was an aunt-killing crazy woman.

Kate's breaths came in short gulps. How was she supposed to sleep here when someone out there had a key and could sneak in at any time? "Surely Edward would've warned me if he'd given Molly a key."

Tom nodded, but not very convincingly.

Officer Reed knocked on the bedroom door, making Kate jump. "Pilot's lit. Figure out what this guy wanted yet?"

Kate shook her head. "Can't even figure out how he got a key."

"Do you keep one hidden outside in case you lock yourself out?"

"No."

"But Daisy might have." Tom strode down the hall and out through the back patio door.

From the window, Kate watched as he turned over every rock and flowerpot within a six-foot radius of the door. At least the rain had stopped.

"Hey," Reed said from behind her. "Do you mind if I have a slice of that pizza? I missed supper."

"Help yourself." Kate pulled out three plates and napkins and set them down beside the DVD Julie had brought over. She'd have to return it to her tomorrow along with some of the muffins she'd been looking forward to. Looking at the table, Kate tilted her head.

"What is it?" Reed asked.

"Something's missing, but I can't . . ." Kate squinted at the DVD, her suspicions of Brian Nagy poisoning his mother once again roiling through her chest. She looked to the counter where she'd mixed the muffin batter, tracked her steps back from the time she got home. She glanced toward the living room. She'd been carrying . . . "The translation." Her breath caught in her throat. "He took the translation."

"Translation of what?" Reed asked.

"Found how he got in." Tom held up a key as he closed the patio door behind him. Only he didn't look the least bit happy about finding it.

Kate's heart skittered at the pained look in his eyes, as if he should've anticipated this happening.

Reed cleared her throat. "This translation that's missing, who knew you had it here? And who'd want it?"

"Um." Kate's voice came out shaky. "Only Tom, Julie, and Julie's aunt Betty knew about it. No one who'd care, except . . ." She locked gazes with Tom, her heart hammering in her throat. "My research assistant." Whose boyfriend had seemed far too interested in the mysterious plant.

The plant that got her father killed.

🌿

"Put your notebook away," Tom told Officer Sophie Reed after sending Kate to check her desk and computer for anything else that might've been stolen. "It'll be safer for Kate if no report is made of the robbery." Pinning the robbery on Kate's supposedly dead father was the last thing he needed—and they just might if he was stupid enough to not wear gloves. "Understand?"

"No, I don't." Reed tilted her head. "You asked me to stay with her because some guy's stalking her. This could be our first clue to catching the guy and you don't want it reported?" The uptick in her tone suggested he needed his head examined.

Yeah, I probably do. He mentally wrestled over how much to reveal. He still needed her help watching Kate's back. "I was wrong about there being a stalker."

Her eyebrow lifted.

He looked away with a strangled groan. "It's complicated."

"Clearly." Reed tipped her notepad closed and stuffed it in her pocket, looking none too pleased. "I've got half an hour left on my shift, and then I have to return the squad car. I take it you plan to stay until I return?"

"Yeah, I'll be here."

Reed tugged on the rain poncho she'd slung over the laundry tub when they came in. "I'll swing by the hardware store too and pick up a couple of new deadbolts."

"Thanks, I appreciate it."

She waved to Kate as she opened the front door. "I hope you know what you're doing, Tom."

Yeah, so did he. He shut the door, then turned to Kate. Her long hair hid most of her face from view, and the light from the desk lamp highlighted colors he couldn't recall seeing before—the bronzy color of oak leaves in autumn and the orangey-red color of the flaming sun just before it dips below the horizon—the same color he'd seen in her father's beard.

His chest tightened. To think a week ago, all he'd wanted was to win Kate's trust. Now he seemed to have it, and he felt like the worst kind of betrayer. If someone knew something this big about his dad and kept it from him, he'd be furious—no matter what the person thought he was protecting him from. And after the disappearing act Kate's dad pulled earlier this evening, Tom wasn't so sure the man was as concerned about Kate as he wanted him to believe.

"I know what you're thinking."

Tom jolted.

Kate had stopped thumbing through the papers on her desk and was staring at him. "You think GPC somehow found out about my discovery and sent someone to dig up whatever proof he could find."

Tom shrugged noncommittally. "Something like that." From the moment he'd mentioned the plant to Kate's father, the man had latched onto it like a kid with a new toy. He clearly couldn't wait to play with it. No wonder he'd scrammed the second Tom went into the research station. "You have other ideas?"

"Yes." She tapped a pencil against her chin. At least she'd stopped trembling. In fact, she looked confident, determined.

Tom hitched his hip on the side of her desk. "Let's hear them."

"I think you should check on Jarrett's whereabouts this evening. Ask the neighbors if they saw his car on the street. He was unusually curious about the plant and knew about the translation." She hesitated.

"What is it?"

"If whoever came in wanted to scare me out of looking into the plant, don't you think he'd have left a threatening note or something?"

"Not if he didn't want to risk being exposed." Like her father. Tom looked away. "I'll pay Jarrett a visit after Reed gets back." *Right after I track down your father.*

Kate pushed her chair back from the desk. "I guess we'd better fetch Whiskers from Mrs. C's."

Raising a hand to stop her, Tom stood. "I'll go. I could really use a coffee. How about you put some on and heat up the pizza?"

Her stomach gurgled at the suggestion, sparking a grin. "Sure, I can do that." She caught his arm before he reached the door. "Tom." Her voice hitched.

He brushed the back of his fingers across her cheek. "Hey, it's going to be okay."

The trust in her eyes made his heart stagger. "Thank you for being here. For caring. For—" She swallowed, dropped her eyes. "For not giving up on me."

"Never." The word came out gravelly. He let his hand drop to his side even though every fiber of his being wanted to draw her into his arms. If he was going to keep her safe, he couldn't act on emotion. He stepped out the front door. "Lock it behind me," he said before closing it, and he listened for the click of the deadbolt before pulling out his cell phone to call his dad. He needed to talk to Baxter. After telling his dad to set the signal light in their front window, he texted Reed and asked her to check on Jarrett King's whereabouts just in case his suspicions were wrong.

The rain had stopped, but thunder continued to rumble in the distance, much like his unsettled thoughts. He should've been relieved when Kate realized her burglar stole the translation, but he was too furious.

Revisiting how vulnerable she'd looked, Tom blew out a breath. The burglar had to have been her father. And her father would never hurt her.

A twig snapped to the left of the house.

His hand automatically went to his gun as he scanned the area. The streetlights scarcely pushed back the darkness so that he couldn't make out anything more than the cars parked in the driveway and the outline of the trees beyond.

A shadow detached itself from the tree closest to the house.

Tom drew his gun. "This is the police. Put your hands in the air."

The man's hands shot up as he took a step closer. "It's me."

"Baxter?" Tom slid his weapon back in his holster and then yanked the man around the corner of the house out of sight of the front windows. "I have half a mind to haul you into jail after this stunt. Kate feels utterly violated." Tom's fingers tightened on the front of Baxter's jacket. "Probably won't be able to sleep for weeks, thanks to you. What were you thinking?"

"What are you talking about?"

"The translation you stole. Did you honestly think I wouldn't know?"

Baxter shook himself loose of Tom's hold. "You got the wrong man."

An icy chill that had nothing to do with his damp clothes slid through his chest. "It wasn't you?" This changed everything.

Baxter's expression twisted in pain. "Is Kate hurt?"

"No. She wasn't here at the time. But emotionally . . ." Tom shook his head. "I don't know."

"What's this translation thing about?"

"The plant. Some Spanish priest blogged about it."

Baxter's eyes slipped shut and he leaned heavily against the side of the house.

"Who did this?" Tom seethed, certain Baxter knew.

"I don't know. I got here just as the cop car left and hung around hoping to get you alone to find out what was going on."

Tom caught him by the shirt again and pinned him hard to the wall. "You must have some idea."

Baxter's shoulders lifted a fraction, then dropped.

Tom shook him. "Do you want to help your daughter or not?"

"That number in my arrest file," Baxter breathed.

Tom glanced around the corner of the house to ensure no one had closed in on them in the dark. "Zoe's?"

Baxter nodded. "Did you call it?"

"Yeah, I got her roommate."

Baxter clamped his head in his hands. "What have I done?"

Tom yanked Baxter's hands away from his face. "What's Zoe got to do with this?"

A screen door slapped shut next door. "Come on, Whiskers," Mrs. C sing-songed from her front porch. "Let's take you back to your new mistress."

"I gotta go." Baxter clutched Tom's shoulder. "Keep my Katy safe." The raw yearning in his face cut to the core.

"Tom?" Mrs. C's voice shrilled from the sidewalk. "Is that you?"

Realizing she must've heard them, Tom stepped into view. "Yes, I was coming to fetch Whiskers for Kate." He glanced back at the side of the house. Baxter hadn't moved. Tom had never seen an expression so tortured.

"Give her my love," Baxter whispered, then slipped through the trees and away.

Tom felt like his heart had been knifed. He'd like nothing more than to give Kate her father's love. She deserved to know she was loved by her father—and, Lord help him, by *him*—but how could he look into Kate's eyes, knowing her father was alive, and remain silent?

He tipped back his head. *God, show me how to be your man here. Show me what's right. Because I don't know anymore.*

Tom stared at the starless sky as if he might see a flash from heaven, a sign, something.

Instead Mrs. C came up the driveway with Whiskers in her arms and cocked her head. "You got a lot weighing on your mind by the looks of it." A gleam lit her eyes. "Should we expect an announcement in church next Sunday?"

"An announcement?" he muttered dumbly, before registering the meaning behind that matchmaker's gleam.

"I can see the signs. And once a fellow gets to your age, he can't afford to dillydally, or some other young man will come along."

Relieved she'd misinterpreted his sky-gazing, he managed to tease, "Are you saying I'm old?" as he tried to ignore the effect of the sudden image of him dropping to one knee in front of Kate.

"Just saying . . . why dillydally when you know what you want?"

What did he want?

Kate. *Yes.* But at the thought of keeping her father's secret from her, he could scarcely stomach looking at himself in the mirror, let alone meeting Kate's trusting gaze. A text-message alert spared him from dwelling on that thought.

"You best get Whiskers inside now." Mrs. C transferred the cat into Tom's arms. "And remember what I said about dillydallying." With a finger to the side of her nose in silent salute, she trundled back down the driveway.

Kate swept open the door and took Whiskers into her arms as if he were the long-lost prodigal. "You poor thing, being locked outside in that horrible storm," she cooed.

The brush of her arm reminded Tom of the comforting hug they'd shared this afternoon, and he suddenly felt jealous of the silly cat.

Kate led the way to the kitchen where she set Whiskers in front of a fresh bowl of food.

The air smelled like coffee and pizza and cinnamon. "You baked?"

Kate smiled. "Warmed up the muffins and dipped the tops in cinnamon and sugar."

"Mmm, sounds delicious." He noticed a smudge of the

sweet mixture on her cheek and, brushing it onto his finger, helped himself to a taste. "Sweet."

The flush in her cheeks made him feel a foot taller. And lower than dirt. He had no business flirting with her. How ironic that she'd warm up to the idea of spending time with him just when it was more important than ever that he keep a tight rein on his emotions. If he'd paid more attention to his judgment than his friendship with Ian, his former FBI partner might still be alive.

"Sit." Kate nudged him toward a kitchen chair and set a plate of pizza and mug of coffee in front of him, then bounced into the chair beside him. "I have a plan."

The gleeful declaration sent a shiver down his spine. He knew better than to shut her down without hearing her out. Last time he did, she went ahead anyway, and her plan almost got her killed.

He swallowed a steaming gulp of coffee to fortify himself. "Let's hear it."

"Okay, so whoever stole the translation is going to want to find the plant, right?"

"Probably."

"For sure. Think about it. If Jarrett stole it, after he—"

Tom held up his hand. "Jarrett didn't steal it."

"How do you know?"

"I asked Reed to look into his whereabouts tonight. She just texted back that he and Patti had dinner at The Wildflower and then went to the movies. There are witnesses." Tom scooped up a slice of pizza and took a bite.

"He could have slipped out unnoticed and then gone back. I don't live that far from the theater."

"But as far as Patti knew, you were going out with Julie for supper and would likely have the translation with you."

"Hmm. I never thought of that." Kate frowned at the paper on the table in front of her and crossed out a word.

"What's this?" Tom turned the paper for a better view.

"My suspects."

"Lucetta?" he read from the top of the list.

"Sure." A proud glint lit Kate's eyes that made her look so cute, he wanted to . . .

He dropped his gaze to his plate.

"I started thinking about all the things that have been happening to me, like the counterfeiting and the nasty letter about the mayor I was supposed to have written to the newspaper."

"And the text message," Tom added. The mayor was still haranguing him about tracking the guy down.

"Yeah, and then that creepy email this afternoon and the robbery tonight. I was trying to see if there might be a way they're all connected."

Tom scanned the list of strikes against Lucetta. "Sold Verna's tea set. Needs money to send home. That goes to motive for counterfeiting. But blames your father for her mother's death. How do you figure that plays in?"

"She was furious when she found my father's photo. If she thinks I'm hiding something, which if she came in here and found the information about the plant, she now *knows* I am, who could blame her for wanting to get to the truth? Except that creepy fire on my computer—I don't know how she would've pulled it off, but it had revenge written all over it." Kate shuddered.

Tom fought to keep a neutral expression and a clear head, when what he really wanted was to load her in his car and get her as far out of town as he could as fast as possible. "Hopefully Weller will find something to shed light on that. But Lucetta couldn't have known you had the translation either, and from how undisturbed the house is, it seems that whoever let him or herself in knew exactly what he was after."

"She might've hoped to find more info about my father. Oh!" Kate sprang to her feet and ran to her bedroom.

"What is it?" Tom trailed after her.

Kate sat on her bed, a photo pressed to her chest.

Tom didn't have to see it to know it was the picture of her father. He steeled himself against the sight of moisture gathering in her eyes.

"I thought Lucetta might try to see if anything's written on the back, but it doesn't look like she took it out of its frame."

Tom pried the photo from Kate's hand and returned it to the drawer. "It would be better if that's not out where Officer Reed might see it."

Kate sniffed. "Maybe Lucetta saw the translation on the table first and forgot about her original plan, or maybe she got spooked and didn't want to risk getting caught."

"It's credible." Tom caught her by the elbow and urged her out of the bedroom, back toward the kitchen. "Trouble is, I couldn't get a search warrant to check anyone's possessions for the papers without information about the plant becoming a matter of public record. And I don't think that's such a good idea, considering all the trouble your father went to trying to keep it out of GPC's hands. He must've had a good reason."

At the kitchen doorway, she whirled to face him. "That's where my plan comes in!"

"Your plan?"

"Like I started to say before, whoever took the translation is going to go after the plant. Soooo"—she flounced into the kitchen and took a seat—"we keep the area under surveillance and nab her when she shows up."

Needing time to think, Tom refilled his mug from the coffeepot before joining Kate at the table. "Assuming Lucetta is your thief, how would she figure out where the plant is?"

"Her nephew saw me in Verna's woods. He probably told her. She'd put two and two together."

He sipped his coffee. It'd be a tough area to keep under surveillance, especially when they had no sharable reason to involve law enforcement. And even if they did, the less people who knew about the plant's significance and whereabouts, the better. "Who else is on your list?"

"Michael Beck. The guy in the silver Ford Escort."

"It's not him."

"How do you know?" Irritation piqued her tone.

"I'm not allowed to tell you that. Believe me"—he set down his mug—"I would if I could."

She stared at him a moment as if she thought she might wear him down, then glanced at her list again. "Brian Nagy, of course. For poisoning Verna. He clearly needs money, so he's got motive to counterfeit, and he or his mother are indirectly connected to at least three counterfeit purchases that we know of since he pays both Lucetta and Vic Lawton."

"And he's angry at you for interfering with his mother's property, which might have prompted the nasty email." Tom drained his cup of coffee. "But he wouldn't have known about the translation either."

"No, but he might've noticed I wasn't home and decided to come on a fishing expedition to see what I'd found to go to

275

town council with." Kate fussed with his empty mug. "After his real estate agent told him I was at the property."

Tom tensed, not liking her nervous fidgeting. "How do you know Westby told him?"

"Brian told me I should mind my own business."

"He threatened you?" Tom half rose out of his chair, then forced himself to calm down. "Where? When?"

Kate's head dipped and she twisted the mug faster. "Earlier this evening, when I let myself into Verna's house to borrow the nutmeg."

"He saw you?" Tom dragged down his voice. "Kate, if he's really poisoning his mother, he's got to already be thinking you're onto him." Tom plowed his fingers into his hair. "Oh, Kate, what have you done?"

19

The sun shone brightly the next morning. Not the kind of weather Tom had hoped for. Too perfect for a little *gardening*. He hoped he wouldn't regret asking his dad to watch Nagy instead of the plants on Verna's property. Although he suspected Baxter would be thoroughly checking them out.

Tom leaned over Weller's worktable in the station's computer forensics lab. "You got anything for me yet?"

"Give me a break, will ya? I've only been at it for ten minutes. Why don't you go harass Kate about getting you the nutmeg proof?"

"Because you know as well as I do that the judge would throw the evidence out of court."

"Sure, but Nagy won't know that," Weller said, all the while peering at what looked like Greek on the computer screen and punching keys. "Suggest the judge might go easier on him if he comes clean now."

"First I need enough for an arrest warrant."

Weller wheeled his chair over to the fax machine and

snatched up a page. "This just came in. The research station's internet provider confirmed the sender's IP address belongs to Brian Nagy."

"Yes! Any evidence he corrupted her data—something substantial I can charge him with?"

"I thought you were building a criminal harassment case against him. Wasn't he the guy following Kate? 'Cause the *you'll pay* message—"

"No," Tom bit out, not wanting to get into who'd been following her.

"Okay, I can get a warrant for *his* laptop, see if there's evidence of plans to follow through on the threat."

Tom pulled out his cell phone to check in with his dad. "You still have eyes on Nagy?"

"Yeah, he's just getting in his car now." The sound of an engine starting accompanied his dad's words. "Carrying a stack of papers."

Kate's? Tom rushed out to his car. "Which way's he heading?"

"Your way. Toward Main Street."

Tom pulled out of the police station's parking lot and idled next to the library at the edge of the business district.

"He just turned onto Main," Dad reported.

"Okay, I see his red Mustang."

Nagy pulled into the real estate agency's parking lot and climbed out of his car carrying a ream of paper.

Perfect. Tom waited until Nagy went into the building, then parked behind Nagy's car, blocking him in. By the time Tom let himself in the side door, Nagy was waving the papers in Westby's face.

"This is what she's going to use against us," Nagy ranted. "You saw her there. If we get rid of this stuff, she'll have nothing."

Westby slapped down Nagy's arm. "You idiot," he hissed. "You can't dig that out. That's the whole re—" The agent's gaze slammed into Tom's. "May I help you?"

"No, go on, don't let me interrupt."

Nagy spun around, his face white. He quickly tried to stuff the papers inside his jacket.

Tom held out his hand. "I'll take those, thanks."

Nagy straightened. "What are you talking about? These are mine."

"Oh yeah?" Tom scrutinized the top page, confirming his suspicion. "You translate them yourself?"

"Uh, no." He shot Westby a glance.

The agent took a step back, hands raised in a you're-on-your-own gesture.

"A friend did," Nagy improvised.

"Friend have a name?" Tom stepped closer, crowding Nagy's personal space. He enjoyed a moment of satisfaction when sweat popped out on Nagy's forehead.

"I don't have to answer your questions," the man blurted, not sounding all that certain.

Tom pulled handcuffs from his pocket. "You're right. We'll save them for the police station."

"You're arresting me? On what charges?"

Tom clapped a cuff on Nagy's wrist and snagged the papers he held. "We'll start with possession of stolen property." Tom yanked Nagy's arms behind his back and clapped on the second cuff. "Let's go."

Once outside, Nagy resisted going farther. "What about my car?"

"Your car's the least of your problems." Tom glanced inside it. "But we probably shouldn't leave your laptop on the seat where anyone might be tempted to steal it. Want me to grab it?" Might as well save Weller the trip when the warrant came through.

Nagy fought against Tom's hold.

"Okay, don't say I didn't warn you." Tom covered Nagy's head with his hand and urged him into the backseat of his unmarked cruiser.

"I'm not saying anything," Nagy spat, but as Tom climbed in the front, he added, "Okay, you can grab the laptop."

Nagy had left the car unlocked, so Tom grabbed the laptop bag and then clicked the auto lock on the door. The man couldn't afford to have his one remaining asset stolen. Not with where he was going.

"I'm not saying anything," Nagy repeated when Tom returned with the bag.

"That's your right." Tom drove back to the station in silence to give Nagy a little more time to squirm over his predicament. He parked in view of two officers struggling to escort a mean-looking suspect inside and bit back the urge to threaten to throw Nagy in the same cell.

"If you're going to arrest me for walking into your *girlfriend's* house," Nagy seethed as Tom opened his door, "then I demand you arrest her for trespassing in mine."

Straining to keep his cool, Tom pulled Nagy out of the backseat. "Don't you mean your mother's house? Somehow I don't think she'd mind, given that she gave Kate a key. But I'll be sure to ask her."

Nagy snorted. "She's not fit to answer questions, so the house is under my control. And Miss Adams should just learn to mind her own business."

Tom led him inside, beyond irritated with the guy's over-confidence. "Yeah, she likes sticking her nose in people's business, doesn't she? Really irks people."

"Yeah."

"Like how she defended your mom against the counterfeiting allegations, took care of your mom's cat when she went into the nursing home, asked you to talk to the nurses about her meds when your mom took that sudden turn for the worse." Tom let out a disgusted snort. "What kind of woman does stuff like that?"

Nagy clamped his mouth shut.

Tom flagged the desk sergeant. "Weller got a warrant for Mr. Nagy's laptop?"

Weller appeared around the corner. "Right here."

"What's going on?" Nagy struggled against Tom's hold. "What do you want with my laptop?"

"Interrogation room open?" Tom asked the desk sergeant.

"Use C."

Tom motioned Nagy into the six-by-six room with nothing but a table and a couple of metal chairs in the middle and a two-way mirror on one wall. "Sit."

Tom sat opposite him and read him his rights.

"I don't need no lawyer. I'm not guilty of anything she didn't do to me first."

"Uttering threats?"

"I told her to mind her own business. So what? What's that got to do with my laptop?"

For someone who had nothing to hide, he seemed awfully worried about them looking at his laptop.

"All I want to do is sell a piece of property so I can take care of my mother. Is a judge going to throw me in jail for that?"

"You think the judge will be as understanding when we play

that little software program you sent Kate? With his face burning on the screen and blood-red letters flashing 'You'll pay'?"

"Huh?" Nagy was a pretty good actor, because he looked like he had no idea what Tom was talking about. "I didn't send her any program. I don't even know her email address."

"So you're saying we won't find any record of it on your computer?"

"No."

Tom laid the fax sheet from the internet provider on the table between them. "According to this you did. The email originated from your IP address."

"Well, I didn't send it!"

"Then I guess our computer forensics investigator won't find anything on your computer."

Nagy's leg took up a nervous bounce. "Our apartment has wireless internet. Anyone could've sent something from it."

Tom gritted his teeth, prayed Weller found something on the computer. "You password protect your wifi?"

"Sure, but my kid knows the password, which means half his friends probably know it."

"Any of them have a grudge against Miss Adams?"

"How am I supposed to know?" Nagy drilled his finger into the table. "I'm telling you that I didn't do it."

Tom sat back in his chair and scraped his unshaven jaw. As much as he hated to admit it, he believed the guy. And if Nagy *wasn't* behind the threat, then whoever was, was still out there. Tom glanced at his phone, uneasiness rippling through his chest. He thought he'd have heard something from Kate by now. She said she'd try to isolate the nutmeg in the mix first thing. He texted her. "You okay?"

Tom laid his cell phone on the table and looked at Nagy,

who'd grown increasingly fidgety over the prolonged silence. "Tell me about the counterfeit money."

"What are you talking about? The money my mother gave Kate?"

"And your lawn mowing service. And your housekeeper's nephew." Tom leaned back and crossed his arms. "And the money you used to pay for your plumbing supplies the Saturday before last."

"That wasn't counterfeit."

"Are you sure?"

"What are you trying to do? Pin all your unsolved cases on me because I upset your girlfriend?"

"Watch it!" Tom tamped down his anger, uncomfortably aware of the video camera behind the two-way mirror. He tugged at his collar, wishing there was a window they could open in the stuffy room.

It felt like the Molly Gilmore interrogation all over again. Nagy wasn't singing like Tom had hoped. Not even sweating. And the reality was that if the computer search came up empty, they had nothing strong enough to give him more than a court appearance notice.

Tom's phone vibrated on the table. He glanced at the screen, then at the mirror behind him. *Kate's here?* He strode to the door in two short strides. "Excuse me a minute."

Weller stood in the hall.

"Where's Kate?"

Weller handed him a counterfeit twenty.

Tom gave it a cursory glance. "What's this?"

"Kate's supervisor and her assistant both verified her story about the deleted file on the computer. They claim it was a prank."

"I never doubted it," Tom glanced past him to Hutchinson escorting Kate their way. She wouldn't be happy to learn he didn't have enough to hold Nagy. Tom lowered his voice. "Tell me you have something I can use in there."

"I'm still reviewing his internet searches," Weller said. "But it doesn't look like he sent Kate the email."

Just great. "Then bring in the kid for questioning."

Kate beamed as she and Hutchinson joined them. But the tired lines and dark smudges around her eyes gave away the toll yesterday's cyber threat and break-in had taken on her. She proudly held out a paper. "That's the list of everything in Verna's tea, including dangerously high levels of nutmeg." She covered the page with a second one. "And this is the official ingredient list from Beth of what should've been in the mix. No nutmeg."

"Good work."

"I suggested we pick up the comparative at the tea shop," Hutchinson said.

Weller shook his head. "A lawyer will get that evidence thrown out in a heartbeat."

Tom curled the papers in his hand. "But so far Nagy hasn't asked for one." He winked at Kate. "You can wait in the next room if you like and watch the interrogation." At least then he'd know she was safe.

"I'd love to." The look in her eyes—a mix of gratitude and confidence in him—took away his breath.

He tipped the papers in salute. "Thanks for this."

"C'mon." Hutchinson caught Kate by the elbow. "You can wait in here."

Tom strode back into the room, shaking his head at Nagy.

"What?" Nagy's gaze darted to the papers in Tom's hands.

284

Tom straddled the chair opposite him and laid the papers on the table with a disturbed sounding tut.

"Why'd you put nutmeg in your mother's tea?"

Sweat broke out on Nagy's upper lip. "I don't know what you're talking about."

Tom waited, confident he'd given Nagy enough rope to hang himself with.

"I—" Nagy's fingers rat-a-tatted over his lips as if trying to hold back the lie Tom suspected was coming. "A jar tumbled out of Mom's cupboard when I was collecting her tea to bring to her. It was a spice—could have been nutmeg. Some may have spilled into her tea."

"Some?"

Nagy fidgeted. Glanced at the mirror behind Tom's head. Swallowed. "How was I supposed to know it would hurt her?"

"What makes you think it did?"

"You just said—" Nagy clamped his mouth shut.

"In high doses, it causes nutmeg psychosis with symptoms similar to dementia. But you already knew that, didn't you?"

Nagy stared at Tom with the look of a scared kid arrested for the first time. Then he planted his hands on the table and surged to his feet. "Are you accusing me of poisoning my mother? How dare you!"

"Sit down." Tom narrowed his eyes at Nagy until he sat, then laid out the scenario much the same way Kate had speculated.

Nagy grew paler by the second.

"A blood test should confirm elevated levels in your mother's blood," Tom concluded. He made a mental note to order one if Hutchinson, watching the interrogation through the mirror, wasn't already on it.

The last of the color drained from Nagy's face. "I want my lawyer."

Tom reined in the grin that tugged at his lips. "Yeah, thought you might."

Kate stood by the two-way mirror in the adjoining room and waited uncertainly. After what that other detective had said about their evidence, she was pretty sure that it couldn't be good that Brian had asked for his lawyer.

"We can wait in the hall," Hutchinson suggested.

Tom and the other detective were having an animated discussion, and Tom seemed surprisingly pleased. He must have read her concern on her face, because his expression swiftly changed.

"Hey." He touched her cheek, glanced at Hutchinson still standing nearby, and let his arm drop, catching her hand instead. "It'll work out. You'll see." His reassuring hand squeeze buoyed her hopes.

"But you said our evidence wouldn't stand up in court."

Tom smiled. "Didn't you hear him admit to putting nutmeg in her tea?"

"Yeah, but not deliberately."

Tom waved the sheet of paper the other detective had handed him. "The trail of internet searches into the toxicity of nutmeg found on Nagy's computer suggests otherwise."

"Really?" She chewed on her bottom lip. "But he'll argue he looked it up after spilling the nutmeg."

Tom grinned. "The search dates back to three months ago—around the time he learned of a buyer interested in his mother's property. I'm sure that'll be enough to convince the judge to revoke his power of attorney."

"Oh, Tom, that's wonderful!" Without thinking, Kate threw her arms around him. Then, realizing how bad hugging him in the police station might look, she started to pull back.

But Tom unashamedly closed his arms around her and let out the most contented-sounding sigh.

Feeling like she'd come home, she returned his hug. In his arms, she felt safe, cared for, not alone—things she hadn't felt in a very long time, probably not since before her father's arrest twenty years ago. But more amazing than that, she felt cherished. *Lord, thank you for bringing this man into my life.*

He pulled back just a little and tenderly cupped his hand at her neck. "You did good."

She snuck a glance in Hutchinson's direction, but he'd disappeared. The hall was empty save for them. Tom's thumb brushed her jawline, sending a wonderful ripply feeling through her chest.

"If not for you, Verna could have lost everything to Brian's schemes."

Kate shuddered at the suggestion. "I'm glad she's feeling better, but she thinks Brian hung the moon. This news is going to devastate her."

"It's a good thing she has friends like you to cheer her up." The affection in Tom's gaze left her breathless. That and the way his gaze dropped to her lips.

A ruckus down the hall broke the magical moment.

Tom dropped his hand and took a step back. Kate pressed her back to the wall, wishing she were invisible.

Weller had Greg Nagy by the arm. "He was coming cooperatively until he saw you two."

Greg yanked against Weller's hold. "I want to talk to my dad."

"You explained his rights, that he's not under arrest, we only wish to question him?" Tom asked Weller. At his nod, Tom said to Greg, "I'm afraid your dad's in custody. Would it be okay to invite your mom to sit in instead?"

Greg's face went white. "He didn't do it."

If Tom questioned what "it" Greg referred to, he didn't let on. "Why don't you tell us how it happened and we'll get this mess sorted out."

Greg snatched his ball cap from his head and curled it in his hand. "Oh man, he's going to kill me."

Tom motioned toward an empty conference room. "Why don't we sit in here and you can explain what happened?"

As Weller escorted him in, Kate whispered, "I guess I should go?"

"No. Stay." Tom caught her by the wrist, his fingers reassuringly caressing the tender underside. "I suspect this concerns you."

The warmth of his invitation—or maybe the depth of his concern—did funny things to her heart. "If you're sure it's okay."

Tom paused at the door. "Greg hasn't been charged with anything. We're just talking."

Kate noticed he didn't lower his voice and wondered if the reassurance had been as much for Greg's benefit as hers. As she stepped inside the room, Weller reiterated to the sixteen-year-old his rights and asked him if he was sure he was okay with answering a few questions, on tape, without a parent or attorney present.

"We could invite your pastor or perhaps an uncle to join

you instead," Weller offered. "Because you need to understand that what you say can be used in court."

"I understand. I'm not stupid," Greg groused. "I'll tell you everything."

After hearing his dad was in custody for what appeared to be his own crime, Kate didn't imagine the boy was all that anxious to call any adult who might deride him.

Greg signed the required waiver Weller presented without hesitation. He didn't even wait until Tom took a seat before he started spilling his guts. "It was Pedro's idea. He—"

Tom stopped him with a raised hand. "Which part *exactly* was Pedro's idea?"

"Sending her the email." Greg darted a sheepish glance her direction.

At least he seemed ashamed of himself. That was a start, but her stomach still churned at how much he must hate her to be party to such a thing in the first place.

"I was ranting about her being on Gran's property because Dad promised me a dirt bike when the deal went through, and I was afraid she'd mess it up."

The fact that childish greed, not hate, had motivated him probably should've made her feel a little better, but it didn't. In a way, it was more scary.

"So there's already a buyer interested in the property?" Tom asked, and Kate scrambled to catch up to the conversation.

"Sure. Some real estate guy stopped by Gran's months ago." Greg slapped his ball cap back on his head and relaxed a little, apparently believing he was off the hot seat.

"When was this?"

"April, I think." Greg fussed with the brim of his hat, shifted it sideways. "But she said no right out. He tried to tell her how much money she'd make, but she said she didn't need it and shut the door on him."

"And you told your dad?" Tom guessed.

"Sure." Greg took off his cap, scratched his head. "Mom had just cleaned him out. I figured if Gran sold the property, she might lend Dad enough to get another house instead of the lousy apartment we're in." Greg yanked his cap back on his head. "I can't even fit my exercise equipment in it. Half our stuff is in boxes in Gran's basement. Dad would get the money eventually anyway."

Kate squirmed at the boy's bluntness. Here she'd convinced herself Greg *enjoyed* visiting his grandmother.

"Okay, so Pedro had an idea?" Tom prodded.

"Yeah, his aunt told him about a picture she found in her house." He hitched a thumb Kate's way.

"*She* has a name," Tom said sharply. "Miss Adams."

Kate's heart fluttered at his implication that Greg had better use it, that he must treat her with respect. She'd never known a man who cared so much about how people treated her, who cared so much about *her*.

"Sorry." Greg ducked his head.

"Go on."

"So he came up with the idea to try to scare her—Miss Adams—away with a fire program. I don't know why he thought it would scare her, but he said it would work. He's always finding all kinds of weird programs online. Anyway, I was worried we'd get caught, but he said he could make it look like someone else sent it."

Tom wrote something on the notepad in front of him and handed it to Weller, who then left the room.

"And the text message?" Tom quizzed the now squirming

young man. "The letter to the editor? Did you do all that to scare her too?"

Greg looked believably baffled. "We didn't do that. I swear. I don't know anything about that stuff."

"Do you know where your friend's getting the counterfeit money?"

"You mean what Pedro gave that antique lady?"

"For starters."

Kate swallowed a chuckle. Tom's sister wouldn't appreciate being called "antique."

"He said Gran gave it to him for hauling some junk away in his pickup. I never heard about any more." He repositioned his ball cap. "You gonna let my dad go now?"

"He has to talk with his lawyer before anything happens."

Greg fidgeted in his chair and snuck a glance at Kate. "Am I under arrest?"

"What you and Pedro did was serious. How can we be sure you don't intend to follow through on the threat?"

"I won't." Greg lifted shaky hands, palms out.

"What about Pedro? Sounds like he holds a grudge against Miss Adams."

"I don't know."

The uncertainty in Greg's voice sent a fresh streak of jitters through Kate. She shared a quick glance with Tom.

"Okay, sit tight," Tom said to the boy, then motioned her to join him in the hallway.

"What happens now?" she asked after Tom pulled the door closed behind them.

"I sent Weller to pick up Pedro. We'll see what he has to say."

"Do you think he'd really follow through on the 'you'll pay' threat? It's not as if *I* did anything to Lucetta's mother."

"He won't after I get through talking to him." Tom rubbed her arm, chasing away the chill that had swept over her.

"Greg won't go to jail, will he?"

"No, since no data was damaged, it's not an indictable offense."

"I'm glad. I mean, I think he needs to face consequences so he doesn't pull something like this again. But I don't think he deserves jail." Kate leaned back against the wall and blew out a breath. She hadn't realized how tense she'd gotten in there. "At least I don't have to worry about opening my emails or anyone lurking in the shadows. You'll let Officer Reed know that I won't need a bodyguard anymore?"

He hesitated.

"You said that Michael guy who was following me is harmless. Right? So if I don't have to worry about Pedro—"

"Yes, I'll let Reed know."

"Whew. What a relief. Verna's land will be protected, and I can go back to my research." The director had been livid when he found her testing Verna's tea mix this morning instead of working on her project. She'd ended up booking the day as vacation.

The telltale muscle in Tom's jaw flexed. Not a good sign.

"What's wrong? Don't you believe Greg?"

"No, I do."

It took a moment for the gist of what that meant to sink in. "So . . . we're still looking for a counterfeiter."

"No, *we're* not looking for a counterfeiter—that's my job." Tom's sudden smile reached inside her and filled all her empty places. "You've done what you set out to do—convinced me your neighbor is innocent."

She returned his smile. "I guess this means no one could

accuse you of fraternizing with a suspect anymore?" Butter-flies fluttered in her stomach at her boldness, or maybe at the pleased glint in his eye when he realized what she was really hinting at. She bit her lip. Never mind him being a witness in Molly Gilmore's attempted murder case. Kate didn't want to put her life on hold any longer. Tom cared about her, and she wanted to spend time with him, time totally unconnected to any police investigation, open or shut.

She shoved away niggling questions about that letter to the editor. No real harm had been done anyway.

Tom took her hand and gave it a feather-light caress with his thumb. "Would you have dinner with me?" His gaze dropped to her lips, sending her heart thundering. "We can celebrate."

"Yes, I'd like that."

A dimple appeared in his cheek. "Is 8:00 okay? I work until 7:00."

"Perfect."

He gave her hand one last squeeze, then took a step back as Hutchinson turned the corner, escorting a silver-haired man in an expensive-looking charcoal suit. "Brian Nagy's lawyer," Hutchinson announced.

Tom opened the door to the room where Brian was waiting.

Kate spotted her stolen papers on the corner of the table. "Oh, can I take those?"

"Not yet," Tom answered under his breath and waved her back, but not in time to stop Brian from seeing her.

He charged toward the door, pointing an accusing finger. "This is all your fault. If you hadn't stuck your nose where it doesn't belong, I wouldn't have had to—"

"Not another word," the lawyer bellowed, yanking the door closed on Brian's rant.

But Brian's voice only rose. "She ought to be charged. She can't stop me from doing what I want with the property. She's got no right."

Tom shot her an empathetic look and ushered her out of earshot. "Just forget about him. We'll make sure he doesn't bother you anymore."

Kate's thoughts veered to the amendoso plant. What if Brian could somehow legally stop her from accessing it? She'd never figure out what made it so special, or why her father had risked everything to keep it from GPC.

She stole a glance at Tom. He wouldn't want her to go anywhere near the Nagy property after Brian's outburst. But what if Brian got it into his head to destroy the plants so she'd have no grounds to press for its protection?

"Okay?" Tom prodded. "Just forget about it."

Kate let out a resigned sigh. "You're right. Of course." But she couldn't forget. She wouldn't.

20

After delivering Brian Nagy to holding, Weller clapped Tom on the back. "You must be relieved for Kate."

"Yeah."

Weller's head cocked. "You don't sound relieved."

Tom curled his fingers around the papers Nagy stole from Kate's place. Weller was kind of perceptive for a computer geek.

"She's out of danger, right?"

"Yeah." He hoped. As long as she didn't get it into her head to do something with the plant. If GPC Pharmaceuticals was behind the offer to buy Verna Nagy's land, they wouldn't be happy if Brian lost the power to approve the sale. No telling what they might try next.

Weller chuckled. "What's the matter? You afraid you've run out of excuses to spend time with her now?"

Tom's thoughts veered to the dinner date she'd agreed to tonight, and he couldn't stop the grin that tugged his lips. "No, no problem there." He glanced at the papers rolled in his hand and his expression sobered. *Until she asks again for these back.*

Chief Brewster cut around the corner. "I just heard you don't think Nagy is our counterfeiter. What's your next move?"

"Uh." Tom looked to Weller, who shot back a don't-look-at-me frown.

"What about the mother of that kid who passed bills in the coffee shop? Did you check her work computer?"

"No, just her home computer and printer."

Brewster scowled. "She works for a newspaper for crying out loud. If anyone knows how to print stuff, she would."

"We'll get right on it," Tom said, before Brewster started fuming about the mayor breathing down his neck.

"Fits the pattern," Weller said after Brewster strode off. "Your girlfriend said Lawton's husband worked for Verna Nagy, right?"

"Right." The corner of Tom's mouth hitched up at the thought of Kate really being his girlfriend.

"So he might have passed phony bills to her, as change, instead of the other way around."

"Would explain why the bills she passed were smaller denominations than typical. Let's get the warrant and get over there."

An hour later, warrant in hand, they walked the block and a half to Main Street. As they neared the newspaper office, Tom slowed their pace.

The clock tower struck three, and a moment later, Herbert Harold III left the newspaper office and strolled toward A Cup or Two as he did every afternoon. Eavesdropping on the latest gossip was how the newspaperman scooped most of his stories.

"Okay." Tom motioned Weller to follow. "This is one story I'd prefer Herbert not break before the evidence is secure."

Mrs. Lawton glanced up from her L-shaped reception desk

in the center of the large, open room. Her eyes widened in what seemed like surprise, not distress. "Detective Parker, are you here to see Mr. Harold? Because you'll find—"

"I came to talk to you."

"Oh." She closed down the screen she'd been working in on her computer and swiveled her chair to face him. "How may I help you?"

"We need to do a routine elimination I neglected when your daughter was caught with the counterfeit bills." He noted the large laser color printer at the far end of her desk.

"Elimination?"

Was that a shiver he'd seen? Of course, the air conditioning was cranked up in here. Could be an innocent shiver. "Yes, we checked your home computer, but not your work one. We—"

"Oh, say no more." She rose and motioned him toward her chair. "Be my guest. I understand completely."

Tom didn't know whether to be disappointed or suspicious at her zealous cooperation. Now that he thought about it, she had played it cool when her daughter was caught passing a counterfeit bill. Why hadn't he picked up on that at the time? As he recalled, she'd been in a hurry to get back to work too. To delete the evidence?

If she didn't know much about electronic footprints and she'd already deleted any incriminating files, she might think the search now would prove her to be squeaky-clean.

Except she eyed Weller warily when he took her seat instead of Tom. But maybe it was just the scar down Weller's jaw that put her a little on edge.

Scanning for a conversation starter, Tom picked up a "Hire a Handyman" business card from the corner of Mrs. Lawton's desk. "This your husband's business?"

"Yes, help yourself to a card. He does lawn cutting, painting, dump runs, anything you need."

"Good to see a man with initiative." Tom perused the shelf behind her desk, stacked with paper—basic 20-pound bright white copy paper, not the specialty paper forensics had identified in the fake bills. Then again, he wouldn't expect her to keep her stash out in the open. "Business going well?"

"Up and down." She straightened the stack of cards, her gaze slanting toward her computer screen and Weller's fingers dancing across her keyboard.

"I imagine it's hard not having a regular paycheck to count on." Tom poured a healthy dose of empathy into the observation.

She nodded. "The uncertainty gets to Vic. He used to be a happy-go-lucky kind of guy. Now he takes everything personally."

"How do you mean?"

Color splashed across her cheeks. Clearly she hadn't meant to reveal something so personal. Her gaze flitted around the room, as if seeking a place to land. "Like when our neighbor rejected his offer to clean her windows and hired someone else instead."

A vendetta could explain the attempt to cause Kate trouble with that letter to the editor. Vic had likely offered to mow her lawn, seeing as he was doing Verna's next door.

Tom casually hitched one hip on the edge of the desk and leaned forward, resting his forearm on his thigh. "I guess he'd be happy if GPC Pharmaceuticals moved here," he fished. "Get a chance to be hired into a stable company?"

"Oh, yes. He was so upset when Miss Adams tried to kibosh that. Never took so much interest in my job as the day she sent that letter to the editor about the mayor."

Tom straightened. "The forged letter, you mean?"

Mrs. Lawton ducked her head at the edge in his tone. "Well, yes."

Hoping to set her at ease once again, Tom picked up the family photo perched on the corner of her desk. "VIP" had been carved into the frame—a nice reminder of the "very important people" in her life. "You have a lovely family."

"Thank you."

Officer Weller caught Tom's attention with a discreet hand gesture that meant he found their proof.

Unfortunately, Herbert chose that moment to return.

"Oh, Mr. Harold, I'm so glad you're back." Mrs. Lawton grabbed her purse from her desk drawer, avoiding eye contact with Tom. "I didn't want to leave while these gentlemen are here, but I need to pick up my daughter from the library and drive her to the dentist."

Pinning Tom with a glare, Weller jerked his head toward her as if to say, "You going to arrest her?"

"Thank you for your cooperation," Tom said instead. He needed to see the evidence before making the arrest. The woman wasn't exactly a flight risk.

"What's going on?" Herbert bellowed.

"Oh." Mrs. Lawton jumped and fluttered her hand toward the computer. "Uh, I'm sure they can explain better than me. I really need to go."

Herbert waited for an explanation as Mrs. Lawton rushed out.

Weller handed him the search warrant. "We need to take this computer and that printer to the station for forensic evaluation."

"Forensic evaluation?" Harold's eyes flared—half shock,

half the excitement of a bloodhound on a scent. "What's this about?"

Weller disconnected the printer. "Has anyone else used this computer recently?"

"No, there's only Izzy and me here, and I have my own. What's she done?"

"We can't comment at this time." Tom glanced at the appointment book Izzy Lawton left lying open on her desk. Several personal appointments were penciled in for the week. But no notation of a dentist appointment. So where was Isabelle Lawton running to?

* * *

Kate threw her shovel and a five-gallon bucket into the trunk of her car. At the sound of a car door slamming, she shot a nervous glance to the street.

Just another neighbor getting home. She blew out a breath. Bail hearings took at least a day, didn't they? She shut the trunk and straightened her shoulders. Of course they did. If she had more time, she'd have preferred to find a comparable habitat to move the amendoso to before digging it up, but by then Brian might be out on bail.

This way if she left enough of the plants behind, Brian need never know that she took some. She hoped. Her insides twisted nervously. She prayed that Tom was right that with Verna feeling better, Brian wouldn't get a chance to sell the property. And since she'd already taken today as a vacation day, it was the perfect day to go. No one would expect to see her until Tom arrived at 8:00 to take her to dinner.

Her heart fluttered at the memory of the look he'd given

her in the police station. She pressed her fingertips to her lips. He'd be so upset if he knew what she planned to do. But as long as Brian was still in custody, there really was no danger.

It wasn't as if GPC knew about the plant. If they did, they would have dug it up themselves long before now.

Her pulse jittered unevenly. Okay, maybe she should at least tell someone where she was going.

Remembering the muffins Julie had been expecting, Kate hurried back into the house to grab them. Julie was the perfect confidante since she already knew all about the plant.

A few minutes later, Kate parked in front of the library.

"Hey, are those my muffins?" Julie called as Kate stepped out of the car.

The DVD slid across the lid of the muffin container, and when Kate overcorrected to keep it from falling as she shut the car door, the DVD skidded the other direction.

Julie lunged to its rescue. "Good timing. I was just heading to the park for a late lunch."

"Great, I'll join you."

Julie looked Kate up and down. "What are you doing in that getup?" She motioned to the grass-stained jeans and "grow where you're planted" T-shirt. "Didn't you have to work today?"

Kate started toward a park bench. "Long story. The director walked in as I was testing Verna's tea, which I proved contained nutmeg, by the way."

"That's great!" Julie sat down and pried open the muffin container. "Did they arrest Brian Nagy?"

"Yes, and I ended up booking the day off as vacation to appease the director."

"Smart." Julie brought a muffin to her mouth, then abruptly

pulled it back and eyed it warily. "Are you sure there's not too much nutmeg in this?"

Kate laughed. "It's loaded!"

"Right," Julie said wryly and took a big bite. "Mmm, I don't care if they kill me, they're too good to pass up. Thanks for bringing them by." She savored a second bite as Kate wavered over what to tell her about her little rescue mission.

"Was Brian behind that threat on your computer too? Is that why Tom's let you out without your bodyguard?"

In the light of day, with no rumbling thunder or pelting rain, she could scarcely conjure up the fear that had dogged her last night and that had compelled Tom to commission Reed to watch out for her. "That was more of a prank, courtesy of Brian's son. So yeah, we're not worried about anyone lying in wait to attack me." She shivered. No one might be lying in wait, but that wouldn't stop the fire nightmares.

"What a relief." Julie popped the last piece of her muffin into her mouth and picked out a second. "Mmm. You know, if you baked these for Tom, he'd be begging you to go out with him."

"Who says he hasn't?"

"Are you serious?" Julie squealed, almost dropping her muffin. "And it's taken you this long to tell me? And you're sitting there in that getup when you should be getting your hair done?" She grabbed Kate's hands and examined them. "And your nails."

"What's wrong with my nails?" Kate snatched back her hands. "Tom likes me just the way I am." Her mind drifted back to the hug they'd shared earlier.

Julie turned sideways on the bench, bumping her knee into Kate's. "I want details."

"We hugged, that's all. It was nothing." *Nothing?* Then why did her heart stir just at the thought of the tenderness in Tom's touch?

Julie wasn't buying it either. She grinned knowingly at Kate. "Uh-huh. Didn't I tell you he liked you? I knew from the day you came home from the police station with his cell phone number scrawled on the back of his business card. I guess you're over your hangup about cops, huh?"

"This cop, anyway." Although come to think of it, she hadn't gotten the heebie-jeebies at the police station today. Tom made her feel safe.

"He's great with kids too." Julie put her muffin down like it was getting in the way and rushed on. "You've seen him with his nephews after church. They adore him."

"*Julie*, he asked me to dinner. Not to marry him."

"Just saying." Julie fluttered her hand with that gleam in her eye. "You can't tell me you haven't thought about it."

Kate laughed. "Apparently not as much as you have." Although she had to admit, she kind of liked being called auntie by Tom's nephews. She pictured her friend Beth's permanent smile these days, her tummy bulging with new life. How she seemed to unconsciously cradle it with her palm.

Realizing that her hand had dropped to her own stomach, Kate casually tried to reposition it before Julie noticed and made a federal case of that too. Except the thought of having a family with Tom filled—

"Earth to Kate." Julie waved a hand in front of Kate's face. "Still with me?"

"What?" Kate let her exasperation with Julie's theatrics sound in her voice.

Julie leaned back in her chair and laughed. "You are so over the moon, you can't even remember you're in the middle of a conversation with a lowly earthling."

Kate swatted her arm. "I'm not."

"You are. And I love it. It's so good to see you happy."

Kate hugged herself. "I am."

"So . . ." Julie squeezed her hand. "You going to do what I said and get your hair and nails done?"

Kate rolled her eyes. "No, I'm going to rescue a few samples of that plant I found on Verna's property."

"Why? Surely, Brian won't be allowed to sell it if they're charging him with trying to poison his mother."

"He was so mad at me for interfering, I wouldn't be surprised if he destroys the plant just to spite me."

Julie shook her head. "Don't you think you might be over-reacting?"

"Maybe. But to be honest, I'd like the chance to study the plant." She swallowed the sudden lump in her throat. Maybe studying the plant would help her understand what compelled her father to let the police take him away rather than give GPC the plants in exchange for his freedom.

"Well, be careful. I'm sure Tom wouldn't like to know you're going out there by yourself."

No, he wouldn't. She stuffed away the niggling voice that said she shouldn't go without telling him. "I'll be fine."

21

Tom scanned the windows as he pulled up behind Hutchinson's squad car parked in front of the Lawton house. Isabelle Lawton had lied about her daughter's dentist appointment. No surprise there. Weller had found proof that she'd printed over a thousand dollars' worth of counterfeit ten- and twenty-dollar bills, probably figuring stores didn't scrutinize the smaller bills as carefully.

Hutchinson opened Tom's door. "No car in the driveway."

"Could be in the garage. Check it out, then cover the back, in case she gets it into her head to run again." Tom didn't expect her to give them any trouble, but he'd been surprised by her type before.

By the time he reached the front door, Hutchinson was at the garage window. "No vehicle. Still want me to go around back?"

"Yeah, I see movement inside."

Hutchinson took off at that, and Tom rapped on the door.

Trisha Lawton opened it. "Oh, hi. Detective Parker, right?" She pushed a hank of black- and blonde-streaked hair behind

305

her ear and chewed on a chipped purple nail. "Um, can I help you?"

"Is your mother home?" Tom asked, watching her body language carefully for any hint of lying.

"No, she docsn't get off work until 5:00." Trish pulled a pink cell phone from her back pocket. "I can call her for you."

"That's okay." He didn't want to get her daughter in the middle of this. "How old are you?"

"Fifteen. Why?"

"Any relatives in the area?" They'd want to bring both her parents in for questioning, and if her dad turned out to be complicit in the scheme, she'd need somewhere to go.

"My aunt lives down the street."

A familiar-looking dark-haired teen appeared behind her. "What's up?"

"And you are?" Tom asked.

She gave him a look that said, "What cave have you been living in?" "Addie King. The mayor's daughter."

"Hello." Tom's cell phone rang. Figuring it was Hutchinson, he checked the screen. Dad. Looking at Addie, he tilted his head. "You have a cell phone?"

"Sure. Who doesn't?"

Yeah, and he bet she had her dad's number programmed into it. His phone rang again. "Excuse me a second." He half-turned before pressing Connect. "What's up?"

"Got a flat tire out on Sixteen Road, and I left the spare in Tessa's garage when I had to make room for all those boxes she had me deliver this morning."

"And you need me to bring it out to you." Tom watched the girls drift back to the living room.

"If you can spare the time." Dad sounded apologetic.

Addie snatched up a cell phone that had been lying on an end table, where anyone in the house could've glanced through the numbers saved on it. Like Izzy Lawton.

"Xavier is out of town," Dad went on. "I hate to ask her to close up the shop and load up the boys to run it over."

"No problem. I just have to finish what I'm doing first." He disconnected and then called to Trish, "Patricia?"

"Yeah?"

Yup, that explained the "VIP" on the family photo on Isabelle Lawton's desk—Victor, Isabelle, Patricia—and maybe the "PL" on the sign-in list at the library. "Do you ever use the computers at the library?"

"Sure, for the internet. We had to disconnect ours after Dad lost his job."

"Your parents too?"

"Nah, Mom has it on her work computer."

"How about your dad?"

She shrugged. "Sometimes he'll do a quick search of the job ads when I'm on."

Or send the mayor a text message. Tom smiled to himself. So the Lawtons were counterfeiters, and also likely behind the backhanded harassment against Kate. Now he just had to find them.

Standing at the edge of Verna's property with her shovel and bucket, Kate glanced up at the sky. Clouds had rolled in. If she didn't hurry, she might get caught in a downpour. She hurried down the hill and across the meadow to the stand of trees that flanked the spring-fed stream. The sky grew darker by the second. Maybe going in now wasn't such a great idea. She peered through the trees at the shadowy trail. The patch was only a couple of a hundred yards in. She'd be in and out in no time.

She plunged ahead. Mosquitoes dive-bombed her. Yanking her hoodie over her head to keep them from feasting on her neck, she picked up her pace.

The ping of metal hitting rock sent a chill through her veins. She froze and listened.

The sound of shoveling rose from the direction of the creek. Maybe Grandma Brewster was collecting samples. Even as the thought crossed Kate's mind, she knew it was wishful thinking. Grandma B collected leaves and flowers. She didn't dig things up. Then again, maybe she needed the root of some plant for something.

Kate edged closer, using the trees for cover so whoever was digging wouldn't see her. Ten yards farther she caught a glimpse of the digger and stifled a gasp.

He—definitely not Grandma Brewster—was digging up the amendoso and shoving the plants into burlap sacks.

Her fists clenched. He was going to destroy them. The plants wouldn't survive just anywhere.

Everything in her wanted to run out and demand he stop his wanton destruction, but even with him stooped over a shovel, she could tell he outweighed her by a good fifty pounds and had the height to match. If he decided to make trouble, she'd be neck deep in it.

She studied him for a moment. She couldn't see his face, but his build reminded her of the guy Tom had chased out of here the day she happened upon Greg and Pedro—Michael Beck, or whatever his real name was.

Tom had assured her she didn't have to worry about Beck. But what if she was wrong and this was someone else? Or what if Tom was wrong?

The man shuffled to the last few plants still in the ground and stomped his spade into the dirt.

She couldn't just stand there and let him destroy them all. She pulled out her cell phone and scrolled through her contact list as she stepped forward. "Stop!"

The guy whirled around, sheer panic glazing his eyes.

Eyes that seemed vaguely familiar. But behind her leaves crunched.

"No!" the guy shouted.

Then blackness swallowed her.

22

Mike roared toward his daughter's attacker. The guy's shovel glanced off Mike's back as he plowed straight into the guy's gut and backed him against a tree. He grabbed the guy's arm and slammed it hard against a low-lying branch until he dropped the shovel.

The guy grabbed him by the neck and drilled his thumbs into Mike's windpipe.

Desperately prying at the guy's hands, Mike kicked and twisted. Dots danced before his eyes. He couldn't utter a sound.

A rifle shot cracked through the tree above their heads, spitting bark.

His assailant's arms shot up. Mike gasped for air. He recognized the guy from the tea shop. He had to be connected to GPC. Who else would come out here with a shovel?

A squat woman in a ratty cardigan and dark, heavy skirt stepped into the clearing, sighting them down the barrel of her rifle. "Don't move."

Lifting his hands, Mike's gaze veered to Katy. The sight of his precious daughter's body crumpled in the dirt tore at his soul. Impulsively he stepped toward her, but the old woman motioned him away with the muzzle of her gun. "She needs help," he argued, even though he wasn't the one who should give it to her, no matter how much he longed to take her in his arms.

Hands still in the air, Katy's attacker eyed the burlap bags Mike had filled.

Katy began to stir.

The instant the old woman's attention turned, Mike snatched up the bags and the phone Katy had dropped and sprinted through the trees. The old woman would make sure Katy was okay.

The other guy crashed through the underbrush after him, a bullet kicking up the dirt behind them.

Mike ran five miles a day, but he could hear the other guy closing in fast. Mike cleared the trees and picked up his pace across the meadow. Behind him, the guy breathed heavily. Rain stabbed Mike's face. Weighed down by the sacks, he slowed on the hill up to the road.

The guy lunged for a sack, catching it at the base and going down to his knees.

Mike plowed his heel square into the guy's chest without a second's remorse, considering what the creep did to his Katy, and sprinted the rest of the way up the hill. He threw the sacks into the passenger seat of his car, turned on the ignition, and gunned the gas just as her attacker stumbled across the ditch.

Watching the road with one eye, Mike thumbed through the contact list on Katy's phone. At Tom's name he hit Connect. He barely heard Tom's hello past the roar in his ears. "Katy's been attacked. She's with an old German woman in the woods."

Tom invited him to leave a message.

Voice mail. Mike cursed under his breath as he waited for the beep. He repeated what he'd said. "Didn't see what the guy was driving. Wearing a gray windbreaker, jeans, early forties, dark hair. Make sure she's okay, then get him."

A silver pickup rounded the bend behind him, gaining fast.

Mike clicked off the phone and lowered his window. Once he lost this guy, he couldn't risk them using the phone's GPS to track him down, which was likely how they'd cornered Katy. He chucked the phone out the window.

Rain battered the car.

Mike fought the steering wheel to stay on the winding road.

The truck swerved into the other lane and squeezed him against the guardrail.

A car appeared ahead of them.

The truck veered back into its lane, and Mike took the opportunity to surge ahead. But the instant the car passed them, the truck was back on his side, shouldering him off the road.

Mike cranked hard to the left to avoid the ditch. The truck clipped his back end. Trees raced around him. His map book flew off the dash and winged the side of his head. The car banked the ditch and cartwheeled down the ravine.

He must've blacked out because the next thing he knew, the car was on its roof and he was suspended by his seatbelt. Blood rushed to his head—what little wasn't pouring out of him. His legs were wedged under the crumpled dash. And—*Lord, no!*—he couldn't feel them.

The guy appeared at the passenger window, tried to yank open the door.

Terrified, Mike slapped down the lock.

The sound of the guy at the door faded as darkness crept

over him. Then a crash shattered the fog clouding his mind. Chunks of glass blasted through the window. The guy cleared the edges with the rock in his hand, then reached through the window and cursed. "Where are they?"

The plants. He wanted the plants.

The guy lifted his hand holding the rock.

Mike twisted away too late. Pain exploded in his head. Then nothing.

Standing on the side of the road next to his dad's disabled car, Tom ended Hutchinson's call confirming Isabelle Lawton was now in custody and immediately returned Kate's. He pulled up the hood of his jacket against the spitting rain. Why wasn't she answering?

Glancing at his watch, he prayed she hadn't gotten cold feet about tonight's dinner plans. They could really celebrate now that they'd found their counterfeiter. "You managing okay?" he asked his dad, who already had the spare tire fitted in place.

Kate's phone went to voice mail.

"Returning your call," he said, then clicked off and listened to the message she'd left. At the sound of her dad's voice instead of hers, his heart slammed into his ribs. *Katy . . . attacked . . . in the woods.* He raced to his car. "I've got to go. Kate's been attacked." Tom choked on the word. *Please, God, let her be okay.*

His dad dropped his wrench and jerked to his feet. "Where?"

"Verna's property!" Tom jumped into his car.

Eight minutes later, squinting through the intensifying downpour, he spotted Kate's car and parked behind it. Racing down the hill, which was already slick from the rain, he spotted two figures staggering from the woods. Kate and . . .

Grandma Brewster stopped her with a slash of her arm and raised what looked like a rifle.

Tom skidded to a halt, arms raised. "Whoa! Kate, it's me, Tom."

Kate said something to the old woman, who slowly lowered the weapon.

This time Tom closed the distance at a slower lope so as not to get Grandma Brewster antsier.

"Tom, how'd you know I was here?" Dirt was smudged on Kate's left cheek. Leaves and twigs were tangled in her hair. But she didn't look cut or bruised. She pressed a palm to the side of her head.

At the sight of her wince, he scooped her into his arms. "Never mind that. Let's get you to the house. Where are you hurt?"

"My head. Someone knocked me out."

Anger surging, he picked up his pace. "Did you see who it was?"

"No, I didn't even know he was behind me until it was too late. But I saw his partner. It was Beck."

The accusation in her voice bit at his conscience. If she only knew that Beck/Baxter/her father was the last person who'd ever hurt her. Nagy's real estate agent must've alerted their buyer—GPC, if Tom's guess was right. Baxter must've figured out what was going on. He glanced at Grandma Brewster, who'd matched his swift pace despite her age and long skirt, wet from the pelting rain. "Could you describe the men?"

"One was older, gray hair, beard. The other"—Grandma B slanted her head, seeming to size him up—"like you, but skinny."

"How do you mean like me? My height? Dark hair? Clean shaven?"

"*Ja.*"

Tom paused halfway up the hill to catch his breath and reposition Kate in his arms.

She pressed her palm to his chest. "I can walk."

He brushed his lips across her forehead. "I like carrying you."

The sweet smile in her eyes loosened the knot that had been strangling his gut since Baxter's call. "The bouncing kind of hurts my head."

"Oh." He lowered her feet to the ground. Her pupils were equal size and no more dilated than he'd expect in the fading light. He fanned a hand over one eye, then the other—something he should've done at the bottom of the hill to rule out a severe head injury. Thankfully, her pupils reacted to the change in light normally. He wrapped an arm around her waist. "Why did you come here?"

"To dig up some of the plants. But Beck—or whatever his name is—beat me to them."

Tom bit back his irritation with the pair of them.

"Had 'em in burlap sacks," Grandma Brewster added. "The younger one looked like he wanted 'em." She walked ahead, then suddenly stopped and lifted her rifle.

At the top of the hill, Tom's dad shot his arms into the air.

"It's okay. He's here to help," Tom said.

"Kate okay?" Dad called down the hill as the old woman lowered her gun.

"She needs to see a doctor. Could have a concussion."

"I'm fine," Kate protested even as the climb grew steeper and she leaned more heavily into him.

315

"We'll let a doctor decide." His heart had felt like it ripped from his chest at the news of the attack. He wasn't taking any chances. "I can't believe you came out—"

"Save the lecture." Dad strode to Kate's other side and lifted her free arm over his shoulder. "I can take her to the hospital. The police radio's buzzing. A car went off the road at Turner's Hollow." Dad caught Tom's gaze above Kate's head. Insistence flared in his eyes. "You need to go."

Realizing the victim might be Kate's attacker, Tom gave her one last hug. "Promise me you'll stay with Dad until I get back."

"I won't let her out of my sight," Dad vowed.

23

Tom swerved onto the road as details of the accident came over the police radio. A tan-colored Corolla had careened off the embankment.

His heart sank. *Kate's dad.*

Tom floored the gas. *God, please don't let him die. Not before Kate can talk to him.*

The rain had stopped, but the roads were still slick. In minutes he reached the hairpin turns of Tucker's Hollow. As he rounded the first curve, the ground to the right seemed to fall away, no longer hemmed in by trees. The purple-gray sky opened up over him.

One more bend in the road and he caught his first whiff of the sickening smell of burning fuel and tires. He pulled behind the yawning doors of an empty ambulance.

Firefighters in protective gear were already hauling hoses and equipment down the embankment. Tom headed after them.

The car's rear bumper exploded and every firefighter dropped to the dirt as if he'd been shot. Tom kept running, his gaze fixed on the burning vehicle. *Oh, God, not again. Please, not again.*

Someone grabbed his shoulder and held him back as firefighters turned hoses on the flames. A scream—his scream—cut through the swooshing in his ears.

The guy who held him gave him a hard shake. "You know this guy?"

Tom blinked. He stared at the figure suspended by his seatbelt in the upturned car. Not his former FBI partner.

Kate's dad.

Firefighters quickly beat down the fire, then one of them reached through the window. "He's still alive!"

Thank you, Lord.

A giant power saw roared to life, and the firefighters went to work on the crushed door.

Tom turned away. Kate wasn't expecting this. Never in a million years would she expect this. But how could he keep this secret and ever look into her eyes again?

He trudged partway up the hill out of the way of the rescuers and pulled out his phone. Broken glass and yards of battered metal lined the crushed vegetation Baxter's car had pitchpoled over.

Dad answered on the first ring. "How bad?"

"Bad. How's Kate?"

"Waiting to see a doctor. Don't worry about us. You do what you have to do."

Tom glanced toward the vehicle to see a firefighter hunched over Kate's dad from the backseat, holding his battered head immobile as another worked to free the man's legs.

This was exactly the kind of attack Baxter had feared. What they'd been trying to protect Kate from. He wished he could have reunited them one last time.

Dad had given Kate the phone, but Tom's whirring thoughts

couldn't make sense of her words. Before he knew it, the fire-fighters were snapping a c-collar on her dad and moving him carefully to a backboard. His clothes dripped away in molten strips, baring raw, mangled flesh. "Kate, honey, I need to go. I'll call you again as soon as I can." He didn't wait for her response before disconnecting.

Firefighters hustled her dad up the hill and into the ambulance.

"Is he going to make it?" Tom asked one of the paramedics.

"We're doing everything we can." The default response. The paramedic climbed into the back of the ambulance. "You know him? He got any medical conditions we should know about?"

"I—" He swallowed, shook his head. "Sorry. I don't know."

The doors snapped closed. How had he let it come to this?

Kate would never forgive him. Was that why he had this overwhelming sense that his life had just hurtled out of control along with Baxter's car? Because if he told Kate the truth, she might not ever be able to trust him again. Or forgive him.

Or love him.

The ambulance veered onto the road and away, siren wailing.

His mind spun backward like a film unspooling in his head. His FBI partner stomping back to his car, telling him he had it under control, that he knew what he was doing. Then *boom*, the earth shook. Burning metal spewed in a hundred different directions.

And his friend's life vaporized.

The psychologist had assured Tom that he'd done everything right, that Ian reaped the consequences of his own choices. But deep down Tom hadn't believed her. There had to have been more Tom could do. If he couldn't change outcomes, why do the job?

He could rationalize decisions all he wanted, but he couldn't undo what he'd done. Sometimes, mercifully, he could forget.

"Hey, you hear what I said?"

Tom focused on the uniformed officer standing in front of him. "What?"

"This was no accident. The shattered plastic from the car's parking light is strewn on the road. Based on its location and the tire skid marks, looks like someone rammed the car off the ravine."

He'd figured. Tom jogged back down the ravine to the car. "You find any burlap sacks?" he asked the officer photographing the scene.

"No. Lots of dirt, though, and this." The officer held up an evidence bag with an amendoso plant. "Not like any weed I've ever seen. You think this guy dug up someone's pot garden? A sure way to make an enemy."

That thought gripped Tom's chest like a vice. Baxter had only one enemy—GPC. And now they'd connected him to Kate.

Tom scanned the swath Baxter's car had plowed. The other guy must've grabbed the sacks. And any hope of tracking footprints had been obliterated by the dozen firefighters, paramedics, and officers tromping up and down the hill.

Leaving a couple of officers to work the scene, Tom drove to the hospital.

Family engulfed him the instant he walked through the ER doors. He returned Timmy and Terry's boisterous hugs, then turned to his dad. "Did something happen to Tess and Xavier?"

Dad caught a hand of each of the twins. "No, I figured Kate shouldn't be on her own tonight, but she couldn't reach her friend, Julie, so I called Tess. Of course, as soon as Tess heard what happened, she came right over."

Grateful for his sister's big heart, Tom scanned the waiting room. "Where are they?"

"With the doctor. Kate asked Tess to go in with her. She's pretty shook up. The reality of everything has finally hit her."

Tom cringed at how much darker the reality was than she knew.

Dad settled the twins back on a play mat with a couple of cars. "How's her . . . Mike?"

"It doesn't look good. And it was no accident. I definitely don't want Kate going home alone."

"Tess already invited her to spend the night at their house. I said we'd pick up her car later and bring it around."

"Good. I need to go check on"—wary of listening ears, he glanced at the people lining the chairs of the waiting room—"the victim. Don't let Kate leave before I see her."

Before the words were out of his mouth, Kate rushed to his side. "I'm here. Are you okay?"

Tom swallowed her in his arms. "Me? You're the one with the head injury."

"The doctor says I have a slight concussion, not too serious. But you sounded so distraught on the phone."

He clung to her, soaking in her loving concern. He didn't deserve it. Not with her father fighting for his life a room away and him keeping the fact from her. He heaved in a breath and relaxed his hold.

"What is it? You look like you just lost your best friend."

His heart crunched into his ribcage at how close to the truth he feared that was, or would be if he told her who'd been driving the wrecked car.

Dad mouthed, "I'm sorry," and ushered Tess to the chairs. Yeah, so was he.

"Did the victim survive? Is he someone you know?" Kate pressed.

"Yes, I should go check . . ." He needed to try to convince her father to tell her who he was. He had no idea if Baxter would survive his injuries. This could be their last chance to see each other.

Kate gave him a supportive side hug. "I'll wait for you."

"That's not necessary," he heard himself say, hating himself for it.

"I want to be here for you, Tom. I can't explain it, but from the moment you called, I had this strong sense that you really needed me. That you needed to know I'd be on your side tonight."

He cupped her face. "I love you. You know that, don't you?"

Her lips spread into a heart-crushing smile. His gaze became entangled in a dance between her eyes and lips. Slowly, he dipped his head and brushed his lips over hers, absorbing their sweet softness.

The babble of the waiting room faded to nothing. Nothing but him and Kate and the feel of her arms around him.

He drew her closer and deepened the kiss.

His knees weakened at her utter surrender. He didn't deserve her. And more than life itself, he wanted to. He wanted to be a man she could trust and believe in—something revealing the truth about her father might irrevocably jeopardize.

But if he didn't, he could never be that man.

She pulled back, tilting her head, and gave him a strange look. She reached up and thumbed dampness from his cheek. "You're crying." Something akin to awe reverberated in her voice.

He tightened his embrace and buried his face against her neck. "I never imagined I could feel this way about anyone. I never want to hurt you. Never. You have to know that."

Her fingers stroked a reassuring rhythm along his back. "I know, Tom."

The blare of a code blue over the hospital's PA snapped his head up. Suddenly hyperaware that anyone could be watching, he scanned the faces around the waiting room. What if her father's attacker was among them? Waiting. Watching.

There was no telling how Kate would react to his revelation. He deserved nothing less than to be screamed at, but giving away that the victim meant something to her was precisely what her father had been so desperate to avoid. For her own protection.

The paramedic from the scene flagged Tom. "Your friend's stable. They'll probably let you in now."

"Thanks." Tom clasped Kate's hand and tugged before he lost his courage. "Come with me."

"Hey, where are you going?" Tess hurried after them, Dad and the twins on her heels.

"You go on and get the boys to bed. I'll bring Kate by in a while. Okay?"

A gleeful "way to go, brother" twinkle lit Tess's eyes before she gave Kate a warm hug goodbye.

Knowing better, Dad squeezed Tom's shoulder.

Tom expelled a breath. "Pray she gets a chance to speak to him before . . ." His voice cracked.

"I will. And . . ." Dad glanced at the people lining the waiting room. "I'll watch your back."

***

Kate paced the empty waiting room on the burn ward, her heart aching for Tom and his friend. He still hadn't told her who the victim was, but clearly he was dear to Tom.

Sinking onto a chair, she closed her eyes and revisited his kiss, the tears on his cheek, his whispered words of love, and her heart soared once more. *Love.* Could it really be? Seeing someone he cared about so near death would make him not want to hold back, as she'd been doing. If only her love could take away the pain crushing his heart.

He returned with two cups of steaming coffee and handed her one.

"Any word on your friend?"

He shut the door, giving them absolute privacy, then set his coffee on the corner table and sat beside her. "There's something I need to tell you."

The gravity in his voice made her heart hammer. Her coffee sloshed over her fingers. She set it on the table and snatched up a napkin.

Like a fog lifting, the situation suddenly became clear to her. The way he'd avoided answering her questions about the victim. His reassurances of love. The victim wasn't his friend . . . It was hers.

Oh, please, God, no. Not Julie.

Tom clasped her hands, squeezing so tight her fingers began to lose sensation, but she didn't mind. His grip was a lifeline. An unspoken promise that he wouldn't let her fall. His soulful eyes searched hers, awash with apology and sympathy.

"Is she going to make it?" Kate whispered.

He blinked. "What?"

"Julie. She's the victim, isn't she? That's why . . ."

Tom crushed her in his arms. "No! Oh, Kate, I'm sorry. No. I didn't mean to let you think that the victim was your friend."

She gently pushed against his chest, and when he released her, she looked him in the eye. "Then what's going on? Just tell me."

His Adam's apple bobbed. But she couldn't imagine any worse news he could tell her. She had no family. He and Julie were the most important people in her life, and he was sitting right in front of her, perfectly healthy.

Or was he? Was this not about the accident at all?

"There's no easy way to tell you this, Kate." His voice sounded rough, agonized.

Her spirit plummeted. She clasped his hands. "Just tell me."

His shoulders sagged. New lines creased his forehead. "Your father . . ." Tom swallowed.

Kate braced herself for what could only be a horrible revelation about her father's guilt, and yet at the same time she felt oddly touched that Tom should agonize so over telling her.

Tom closed his eyes, then slowly lifted his eyelids as if they were leaden. "The man driving the car that went over the ravine is in critical condition. He's suffered internal injuries and a head injury and has third degree burns down his legs. He's in a coma."

She nodded, because he seemed to be waiting for some response, but she didn't understand why he was telling her this or what it had to do with her father.

"The crash wasn't an accident. Someone rammed his car."

She gasped. "Why would someone do that to him?"

"Because he knows things he shouldn't." Tom closed her hands in his. "This man revealed himself to me a week and a half ago and swore me to secrecy for your protection."

"Mine? Why?"

"He feared that if you knew who he was, you wouldn't be able to conceal that knowledge, and that would put you in danger."

"I don't understand. Why me?"

"Because your father knows things about GPC Pharmaceuticals, bad things, and if they were to discover that you're his daughter, they might assume you know too. They might assume you have access to proof he was never able to reveal twenty years ago."

As Tom's words whirled through her head, her mind stuttered at his word choice. "*Knows?* You mean knew. He *knew* things about GPC." When Tom pressed his lips together, a cold sensation crept over her body.

"Your father didn't die in police custody, Kate."

She stared at him, trying to make sense of what he was saying. "He's alive?"

Tom nodded, agony in his eyes, which made no sense.

"He's alive," she repeated, a little louder this time, hope swelling within her. "Where? Can I see him?"

Tom's hold on her hands tightened. "Kate, listen. We don't know who we can trust. You can't do or say anything that would give away that this man is more to you than a casual acquaintance. Even to show that much might be dangerous."

This man? "You mean . . ." The hope that a moment ago had made her feel lighter than air balled in her chest and dropped like a stone to the pit of her stomach. "You're telling me the man in the coma is . . ." She gulped air.

Tom clasped her shoulders in a steadying grip. "Your father. Yes."

Something exploded inside her. She pushed him away and surged to her feet. "You knew he was alive and you didn't tell me! How could you? How could you?"

"Kate, I—"

She cut him off with a slash of her arm. "There's no excuse. My father's dy—" She balled her hand against her mouth. "I

326

could have talked to him. Spent time with him. Now . . . I may never get that chance."

Tom reached for her arm, but she sloughed off his grasp. "Don't touch me. I want to see my father. *Now.*"

He gripped her upper arms with a steel force she couldn't break and waited until she met his gaze. "You can see him. Talk to him quietly when no one else is in the room. But you have to remember what I said. You can't give away what he means to you. Your life, and *his*, could depend on it."

She gulped, scarcely able to comprehend what he could possibly mean. She nodded, only because Tom didn't look like he'd move until she responded in some way. With one hand still firmly circling her arm, he opened the waiting room door and led her down the hall. He knocked on a door.

A nurse in blue scrubs appeared a moment later.

"We're here to see Michael," Tom said.

The nurse seemed to be expecting them. She led them past a panel of monitors walled in by a glass partition into an open ward. Only one bed was occupied.

Kate's legs gave out, but Tom immediately curled his arm around her waist and held her close to his side until she regained her composure. "Thank you," she whispered, unable to tear her eyes from the man in the bed.

Tubes and wires ran from under the blankets to machines and an IV at the side of the bed. His hair, matted to his head, was completely gray, not at all how she remembered, but she'd know that red whiskered chin anywhere. A memory of how her dad used to tickle her with his whiskers against her neck flowed over her. How had she not recognized him sooner?

Tom prodded her forward and eased her into a chair next to the bed.

Tearing her gaze from her dad's swollen lip and the jagged line of stitches on his forehead, Kate slipped her hand into his.

His gold wedding band still encircled his finger. Did he know Mom had died?

He must have. For all Kate knew, he'd remarried. How could he have stayed away all these years? Didn't he love them?

She tamped down the unwelcome flood of questions and rested her cheek against the back of his hand, tears streaming over his fingers. "Why, Daddy?" The words ripped from her throat, yet they came out as the barest of whispers.

Still, Tom's gaze shot to the nurse now sequestered behind the glass partition.

Kate pressed her lips to her father's leathery hand. "I've missed you, Daddy. Please don't die." She swallowed the tears pooling in her throat. "Please don't leave me. I don't think I could stand to lose you again when I've only just found you."

Tom rubbed a warm hand across her back. Meant to be reassuring, supportive, she knew, but something hot and ugly boiled inside her, and she arched away from his touch. He'd knowingly kept them apart. He'd cost her precious time with her father.

She'd never—NEVER—be able to forgive him.

Tom stood outside the ICU door and closed his eyes. He'd rather have Kate pound her anger out on his chest than be forced to watch her tortured expression, hear the despair in her voice, and have his attempt to comfort rebuffed.

He prayed he hadn't just made the biggest mistake of his life. Her father had been convinced he'd be a dead man if

GPC learned he was still alive. And from all appearances, he'd been right.

And if someone from GPC saw Kate talking to him, she'd be next.

Before telling her, he'd reasoned that he could set her father up in another witness relocation program . . . if he survived. But what about Kate?

Now that she knew who was in that hospital bed, he'd never be able to pry her away from him. She'd want to go with him. She'd have to give up her research.

Tom pressed his fingertips to the corners of his eyes. He'd have to give up Kate. What had he been thinking?

Movement at the end of the empty hall caught his eye—the flap of a suit jacket as its owner jerked back from view. Tom checked the other direction, and seeing no one, ran after the man who didn't want to be seen.

His shoes squeaked on the tile, sounding like a wailing police siren in the deserted hall. He rounded the corner, but the guy had already disappeared. He could have been anyone. A doctor. A visitor. The hair on the back of Tom's neck bristled.

A killer.

He hurried back to the ICU and, knowing Kate wouldn't be willing to leave on his say-so, whispered his request to the nurse.

As he stood at the door, the nurse went to Kate. "I'm sorry. Visiting hours are over now."

Kate clutched the woman's arm. "I can't leave him. Please."

"You can't stay, I'm afraid. But you may come back tomorrow."

Kate dug in her purse, then handed the nurse a business card. "Please call me immediately if there's any change in his condition."

"Of course." The woman slipped the card into her uniform pocket without glancing at it.

Tom couldn't risk the nurse identifying Kate as next of kin. So as the nurse returned to her desk, he lifted the card from her pocket.

Kate turned toward the door and for a moment looked as though she might walk right past him.

"I'll drive you to my sister's," he said, grateful she didn't have transportation of her own.

With a single nod, she strode past him out the door.

Her red-rimmed eyes wrenched at his heart. "I'm sorry," he whispered, catching up to her in the hall.

For a long time she didn't say anything, just kept putting one foot in front of the other like a soldier obeying orders. A soldier whose world had just been decimated by a long-buried land mine.

As they left the glaring lights of the hospital and stepped into the darkness, Kate's shoulders slumped. Tom longed to fold her in his arms. Instead, he guided her toward his car with a light touch to her back, his senses hyperalert for signs of anyone watching.

Two women in nursing uniforms stood chatting near a staff entrance, puffing on their cigarettes. A male talking on a cell phone sat in a late-model Ford two rows over from Tom's car. The man didn't look their way. The street was quiet.

"Why?" Kate asked so quietly that Tom almost didn't hear her.

His heart clenched. Why what? Why had he kept the truth from her? Or why had her father? "Let's talk in the car." Tom clicked the car remote and motioned her inside. The extra seconds he took to round the front and climb in beside her weren't nearly enough time to compose a response that sounded remotely acceptable.

After he pulled onto the road, she listened in silence as he recounted her father's story.

Kate gasped. "Mom knew he was alive?"

"At first, yes. And I'm sure she hated hiding the truth from you as much as I have. But it was the only way to ensure all of your safety."

"Maybe then." Her voice shot higher. "But I'm not a child anymore."

"This isn't about being a child or not. It's about witness protection. They have no-contact rules for a reason." Tom let out a sigh. "It wasn't easy for your dad to walk away from the life you had together. But he would rather die a thousand deaths than see you hurt."

"Hurt. *Hurt?* Losing my dad at ten years old hurt. Watching my mom's life eaten away by depression hurt. Finding out I've been lied to and deceived by the people I thought I could trust hurts." She curled her arms against her chest as if to stay the pain and turned toward the window and the blackness beyond.

"I'm sorry," he whispered, but he knew with heartbreaking certainty, it was too little too late.

24

Kate squinted at the morning light seeping past the curtain edges and rose onto her elbow at Tess's whispered "How are you doing?"

Thanks to Tom's warning to not mention her dad, she'd been forced to be as secretive with his sister as Tom had been with her. So she couldn't pour out her muddled emotions in an attempt to sort them out. Instead Tess had misinterpreted her blubbering last night as a breakup with Tom.

Kate swiped at a tear. Okay, not a total misinterpretation. "Head still hurts."

"I called the research station and told them about your concussion and that you probably wouldn't make it in today." The empathy in Tess's voice made Kate feel all the worse for not telling her about her dad.

An engine rumbled in the driveway.

"I'll go see who that is," Tess said. "You go ahead and sleep in as long as you like."

After Tess shut the bedroom door, Kate got up and hurriedly

dressed. She needed to get back to the hospital to see her dad before Tom showed up and tried to stop her.

As she pulled up the sheets and smoothed the bedspread, the sounds of voices drifted up the hall—male and female.

Tess's husband must have gotten back from his buying trip. Kate folded her nightclothes and tucked them into her bag to stall for time and give Tess and her husband a few moments of privacy.

"What's up between you two?" Tess's sharp question caught Kate's attention.

Tom? She inched open the door.

"I know it's none of my business, but she's my friend too, and she was an emotional wreck."

"Wouldn't you be if some creep attacked you?" Tom growled.

"Yeah, but she didn't even talk about the attack."

"What did she talk about?" A nervous edge vibrated through Tom's voice.

"Mostly she muttered about you. How you weren't the man she thought you were."

Kate groaned. She hadn't meant to say as much as she had. She'd just been so . . . so . . . mad. Mad at Tom for not telling her the truth sooner. Mad at Mom and maybe even Gran and Gramps for lying to her about what really happened—at least as much as they knew about. And mad at her dad for leaving, for caring more about punishing a corrupt company than being with his family, for being in a coma when they'd finally been reunited.

She grabbed a tissue from the box next to the bed and sopped up her tears.

"She's still in bed," she heard Tess say. A true friend.

Protecting you. Isn't that what Tom did for you? What you did to Tess last night? Kate shut out the voice in her head.

"Have her call me when she wakes up, okay?" Tom said, followed by the sound of the front door opening and closing.

Kate edged aside her bedroom curtain. Her yellow Bug sat in the driveway. Tom must've been delivering it. He marched down the driveway to his dad's gray sedan idling at the curb. As he opened the passenger door, he glanced back at the house.

Kate jerked back from the window and steeled herself against his tormented expression.

He couldn't understand. How could he? His father sat in the seat beside him, while hers lay dying in a hospital bed.

This was all that stupid pharmaceutical company's fault. Why'd they ever have to come here? Tom had let her see her father last night, but she knew that deep down, he hadn't wanted to, that he wouldn't want to again.

Please, Lord, don't let it be too late for me to be reunited with my father.

Peace eluded her. Tom's revelation had eaten through her heart like a plague of locusts, and she wasn't sure there was a sprout of hope left. She picked up her suitcase and tiptoed down the hall.

Tess appeared at the kitchen doorway, drying her hands with a tea towel. "Were you going to sneak off without saying good-bye?"

"No, I—"

"Tom wants you to call him before you go anywhere. There are muffins if you're hungry."

Kate dropped her bag at the door and followed Tess to the kitchen. "Thanks for putting me up last night."

"No problem. What are friends for? I guess you saw Tom brought your car?"

Kate nodded and forced herself to eat, not really tasting the food.

Tess set a steaming cup of tea in front of her and sat down. "Whatever Tom did to upset you last night, he seems genuinely sorry."

"I know." Kate sniffed to stave off tears. She did know, but that wouldn't stop him from continuing to do whatever he thought he needed to do to protect her. And in his mind, that meant keeping her as far away from her father as he could.

"So you'll call him?" Tess brought her cup to her lips, watching Kate over the brim.

"Yes."

Tess arched a brow.

Her new friend could read her too easily. "Eventually," Kate clarified. After all, people were less likely to notice her hospital visit if she wasn't under a detective's watchful guard.

"He cares about you, you know?"

"I know." She popped the last of her muffin into her mouth and quickly washed it down with her tea. "I need to go."

"I thought you were taking the day off."

"Changed my mind. I can't mope around all day."

Tess grinned. "That's the spirit." She rose and added Kate's mug to the dishwasher. "If you want to talk, Kate, you can call me anytime, okay?"

Kate gave her a warm hug. "Thanks. You're a good friend."

Conscious of Tom's warnings, Kate kept a close eye on the vehicles around her as she drove to the hospital. She parked in a private lot a block from the hospital and then took the long way around to the hospital's side entrance in case someone was watching for her.

Instead of using the elevator, she took the stairs up to the burn unit. Before exiting the stairwell, she even peeked out the door to see if any sketchy characters were loitering in the hall. No one.

She tapped on the window at the nurses' station.

A middle-aged woman in a crisp white uniform dipped her head to look over the top of her reading glasses. "May I help you?"

"Yes, I'm here to see Michael—" Kate swallowed. She couldn't say Baxter. Was he still going by Beck? Or some other name? Maybe not even Michael. No, that's what Tom had called him last night. She was sure of it. She pointed toward the unit, praying the nurse hadn't noticed the hesitation.

"Are you a relative? Only next of kin are permitted in."

"Yes, I'm his . . ." Kate faltered. Tom's warning—*No one can know you're his daughter*—blasted through her mind.

"I'm sorry," the nurse said, coming around the nurses' station looking ready to shoo her off the floor. "You'll need to wait until—"

"No," Kate blurted. She couldn't wait. He might not live to get out of this unit. But if he did wake up, she intended to be here. "I'm his niece. I'm just so upset. The accident was such a shock."

The nurse's eyes narrowed as if she didn't quite buy Kate's story. She'd always been a terrible liar. But surely the Lord would forgive her for lying to be able to see her dad.

A second nurse motioned to the first from behind the glass partition. She had a phone in her hand.

"Excuse me a second," the woman ducked back into the nurses' station, then reemerged thirty seconds later. "I'm sorry. No one can see the patient at the moment, doctor's orders."

"But he shouldn't be alone. I should be with him."

"I'm sorry," she repeated and scurried back behind her glass wall.

Kate wanted to scream. Rattle the locked door that stood

between her and her father until they let her in. *Lord, this isn't fair.*

Staring at her reflection in the glass, she tried to think of another way. Would a police detective be able to change the doctor's mind? She wasn't ready to face Tom again, even if deep down she knew that he'd been trying to do the right thing. But he was her only hope.

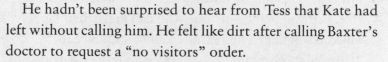

He hadn't been surprised to hear from Tess that Kate had left without calling him. He felt like dirt after calling Baxter's doctor to request a "no visitors" order.

Okay, he hadn't been shocked Kate didn't want to talk to him, but the fact his sister would snitch on her did surprise him. Clearly she was as worried about Kate as he was. Hopefully now if she went to the hospital—and he was 99 percent certain that's exactly where she went—she'd then turn to him for help.

Truth was, he would've insisted she be under guard if doing so wouldn't endanger her more by drawing attention to his knowledge of the connection between the attack on Kate and her father's accident.

He studied the pictures included in the accident report. If he wanted to keep Kate safe, he needed to figure out who attacked her. Tom zoomed in on the debris left behind on the road. Debris that might point to the type of vehicle the other driver had been in.

Hutchinson tapped Tom's desk. "Just got a call from Lawton's neighbor. Vic finally made it home. We need to pick him up."

Tom pushed back his chair and rose. After everything else

that went down last night, he'd completely forgotten about the Lawtons. "How did Mrs. Lawton react to the charges?"

"Shocked. Said she didn't know how those files got on her computer."

Tom snorted. "Of course not." As they stepped outside, Kate's yellow Bug pulled into the parking lot. "Give me a minute," he said to Hutchinson, then opened her car door. "I thought you'd call."

Anguish shadowed her eyes. "I want to see my"—she glanced at Hutchinson climbing into his car and lowered her voice—"Mike, and you're the only one who can make that happen."

Hutchinson pulled up beside them in a squad car.

"Give me another minute," Tom said and refocused on Kate. "I can't right now."

Determination flared in her eyes. She pulled her keys from the ignition and climbed out of her car. "Then I'll stick around until you can."

"Stick around?"

"Yes." She leaned into him. "You know, like glue."

"But I have an arrest to make."

Her face lit up. "For the hit-and-run?"

"No, sorry." His chest tightened at the instant disappointment in her eyes. "A suspected counterfeiter."

Her eyes widened. "Who?"

"Vic Lawton, who I'm also pretty sure was behind the attempts to frame you." Which twenty-four hours ago would've been the best news he could have given her.

"Then I *should* go with you." The excitement returned to her voice, and with it, a sliver of hope that she didn't hate him. "If you're right about him framing me, then just the sight of me with you will have him quaking in his boots."

He knew what she was doing—promising to drive him crazy until she got what she wanted, but she actually might be right about Vic. "Okay, you can ride with me."

Her jaw dropped, but she snapped it shut again almost immediately. "Okay."

Cupping her elbow, he guided her toward his car. "I need you to drive separate," he said to Hutchinson. "Miss Adams is coming along." Tom pretended not to notice his I-hope-you-know-what-you're-doing look. As long as she was at his side, he didn't have to worry about what other trouble she might get into, and that alone would help keep his mind focused on Vic's interrogation.

A few minutes later, he pulled to the curb in front of the Lawton house. "Wait here," he said to Kate, not sure how Vic would respond to a cop showing up on his doorstep.

Kate made no move to get out anyway. She probably hadn't counted on him taking her up on her offer. She glanced around the neighborhood, then at Vic's pickup in the driveway, a couple of lawnmowers and weed-whackers strapped in the back.

He tried not to notice how vulnerable she looked.

When Vic didn't respond to the first knock, Tom directed Hutchinson to cover the back, then pounded harder. "Vic, it's the police. Open up. We know you're in there."

The door jerked open to reveal Vic half-dressed in faded jeans, a T-shirt in his fist. He was unshaven, although he smelled like he'd bathed in aftershave, and his hair was still damp. Dark circles ringed his eyes.

"I knew it," Vic muttered, turning from the door, his shoulders slumped. "I knew it sounded too easy." He sunk to the sofa, planted his elbows on his knees and cupped his head in his hands.

Tom stared at him, speechless. He hadn't expected this level of remorse. Most criminals made at least one attempt to deny guilt. Not wanting to miss the opportunity to take full advantage of his remorse, Tom read him his rights.

At the sound of Hutchinson stomping onto the porch, Vic glanced up, dragging his fingers down his whiskers. The color drained from his face. "I should've known you'd be behind this." Vehemence crept into his voice.

"What's that supposed to mean?" Kate demanded.

Tom's gaze snapped to the open door, eyes flaring. "I told you to wait in the car."

"Is he dead?" Vic asked, his voice hollow.

Tom whirled his attention back to Vic. "Is who dead?"

Vic's eyes widened. Red streaked up his neck and back into his cheeks. "Why are you here?"

Tom pinned him with a piercing gaze. "Why do *you* think we're here?"

"I don't know. You jolted me out of a deep sleep."

The guy didn't look like he'd slept all night.

"I missed a payment on my truck. I figured you came to repossess it. I can't do my job without it, you know. That's why I was upset." He slouched over again, gripping his head.

"The police don't repossess trucks, Mr. Lawton. What sounded too easy?"

His attention snapped back to Tom. "What do you mean?"

"A minute ago, you said you knew it sounded too easy."

"Why are you messing with me? If you're going to arrest me, just get it over with."

"For missing a car payment?" Tom fished. He knew it was unconventional, but unless he missed his guess, Vic's remorse went a lot deeper than passing a few phony bills. He just prayed

Kate didn't clue in. Tom whispered to Hutchinson to check the passenger side's fender on Vic's truck and report back.

Unfortunately, Hutchinson's hasty exit piqued Kate's attention. She tracked his movement through the front window and let out a strangled gasp. "It was you!"

25

Kate's legs turned to jelly at the sight of Hutchinson examining Vic's truck. She sank into the nearest chair. "Why?"

Tom clasped her shoulders and urged her to stand. "You should wait outside."

Kate shrugged off his hold. "He ran my—"

"Vic." Tom's loud voice drowned out her protest. "Why were you in the woods off Hollow Road last night?"

Kate pressed her lips together, realizing what she'd almost done.

Vic tugged his T-shirt over his head. "There wasn't supposed to be anyone there. He didn't say anything about anyone else being there."

"Who didn't?" Kate blurted, earning a scowl from Tom.

"I don't know who he was. Just some guy. He saw the odd jobs sign on the side of my truck and asked if I'd be interested in digging up a few plants for him."

"On someone else's property?" Kate's voice pitched higher.

Tom put a heavy hand on her shoulder.

She glared at him. "He can't just traipse onto anyone's property and start digging up their plants."

"Then what were you do—?" Vic suddenly clamped his mouth shut as if realizing what he'd admitted.

Kate's breath caught as his explanation sunk in. Someone knew about the plants. It had to be GPC. Who else? Her eyes stung at the thought. Her father gave up everything to keep the plants out of their hands. And now . . .

"Can you describe the man who hired you?" Tom asked.

Vic shrugged. "He wore a fancy suit, drove a fancy car, and offered me a thousand dollars."

"A thousand dollars," Kate blurted. "You'd—"

Tom's hand returned to her shoulder, his fingers digging in more insistently, as he leaned close to her ear. "Let me ask the questions, or you'll wait outside."

She surged to her feet and out of his reach. Crossing her arms, she stood in front of the window. Outside, Hutchinson was taking photos of Vic's front fender. *A thousand dollars.* "What kind of a man runs someone off the road for a measly thousand dollars?" she muttered under her breath.

"I panicked when I saw Miss Adams. I knew she'd snitch on me if she saw me there. I didn't see the other guy at first. But Miss Adams had a spade too. I figured she was trying to cheat me out of my money. You can see that, right?"

"Sure," Tom agreed.

Kate clenched her fists. She kept her mouth shut, though. Technically she'd been there to steal a plant too.

"I didn't hurt her bad." He jutted his hand in her direction. "You can see for yourself." His eyes speared her. "You don't understand what it's like. You with all your highfalutin education, working up there in your government-funded ivory tower, not even willing to pay a little out to have your lawn mowed or a room painted, while guys like me can barely scrape together enough to pay the mortgage, let alone put food on the table."

"That's why you printed the money? To put food on the table?" Tom interjected before Kate could comment on the giant flat-screen TV in the corner that could've covered a few bills.

Vic inhaled sharply and looked around wild-eyed. "Where's Izzy and Trish?"

Tom pulled out a pair of handcuffs. "Your wife was arrested for counterfeiting."

"No!" Vic surged to his feet, shaking his head violently.

Kate backed into the corner, and Tom instantly stepped in the gap, motioning Vic to calm down.

He collapsed onto the sofa, clutching his head. "Izzy didn't have anything to do with it. I clean the newspaper offices on Saturdays. I knew her computer password. It was all me. She doesn't know anything."

"What about the letter to the editor? The text message to the mayor?" Tom asked.

Vic jabbed a finger in Kate's direction. "She was blasting off her mouth against the one company that might offer a decent job to guys like me around here. Someone had to do something."

"To discredit her?" Tom said as coolly as if he were asking about the weather.

"You charging me for that too?" Vic asked hopelessly. "Might as well. I'm going to spend the rest of my life in jail anyway, aren't I?"

Vic snatched up a family photograph and tenderly outlined

the faces of his wife and daughter. "I didn't mean to kill him. I just wanted the plants back. I wasn't lying about the truck payments. If I lose the truck, I'll lose my business."

"He's not dead," Kate whispered, a shard of pity for the man piercing her heart.

His head shot up, his eyes brimming with hope. "He ain't?"

"He's in critical condition," Tom said soberly. "And these plants, where did you deliver them?"

"I didn't. I . . . I . . . broke the window with a rock." Vic's hand clenched as if holding an imaginary rock. "He looked at me like he was memorizing my face, and . . ." Vic slammed his fist against his leg. "When I saw what I'd done, saw the blood dripping from his head, I . . . I . . ."

"Ran," Tom filled in.

Vic rubbed at a spot on his faded jeans. "I drove around for hours. Then came home and showered and showered, but I couldn't get rid of that awful feeling. I swear I didn't mean to hurt no one."

Kate hardened her heart against her growing pity for the man. The man who beat her father with a rock and left him to die. Tears blurred her eyes as Tom handcuffed Vic and handed him over to Hutchinson.

Tom cupped her shoulders, gently this time. "C'mon Kate, time to go."

She blinked her eyes clear. "What happened to the plants?"

"It's okay, honey."

"It's not okay," she cried. "He almost killed my—"

Tom turned her toward him and crushed her in his arms. "I know." He stroked her back, making soothing noises, and as much as she didn't want to lean on him anymore, she couldn't stop herself from crying all over again.

Tom's heart ached at the silent torment on Kate's face as she sat at her father's bedside. Most people would be ranting at God for twenty years of separation and the unconscious state that kept her father from really being with her even now. Part of Tom wished she'd rant at him for keeping her father's secret so long.

He touched her shoulder. "Can I get you anything?"

Her head turned his way, but her gaze seemed unfocused. "All these years, I convinced myself he was innocent despite how things looked. But I was afraid to search too hard for the truth for fear I was wrong. I just wanted to believe that somehow God had a higher purpose in everything that happened."

"Maybe he did. Your family experiences fueled your interest in herbal research, especially in finding a cure for depression, right?"

She turned back to her father's bed as if expecting him to stir. The heart rate monitor marked the time with a steady beat. She drew in a ragged breath. "Deep down I think I blamed myself for his arrest the same way I did when Mom got into one of her funks. I'd think if I could just be a better daughter, she'd be happy."

Tom rubbed Kate's back. "It was never your fault."

She shook her head. "We weren't enough for Dad."

"That's not true. He loves you very much. He wanted to tell you himself."

"Then how could he choose punishing a stupid company over being with his family? He sacrificed his life and our future together for what? GPC didn't suffer."

"But we don't know what plans he might have thwarted."

"He kept the plant from being used to heal people. How is that good?"

"Maybe that's not what GPC planned to use it for. It's not always easy to know the right thing to do."

"Being honest is a good start."

Tom winced, suspecting she was talking about him as much as her father. "Even if the truth will endanger people?"

"The truth got Jesus crucified. Minimizing collateral damage may sound noble, but sometimes you just need to trust people to act responsibly, rather than take the decision from their hands."

Tom pressed his lips together, but the image of Ian's burning car preyed on his mind, and he couldn't remain silent. "My partner died because I put loyalty to him above duty. Trust me, I know how hard these judgment calls can be to make, and even harder to live with."

Her gaze dropped to the bed, where she held her father's hand in her own. "I know you didn't want to keep my father's secret from me," she whispered. "But . . ."

He had.

Her body trembled, but she wouldn't welcome his comfort. Not this time.

Unable to bear watching her torment any longer, he slipped into the hallway. He took a seat where he could keep an eye on her father's door and all the entry points to the unit and pulled out his cell phone.

No new messages.

He tried calling his NSA buddy again. If anyone could arrange some cross-border cooperation to get Kate's father safely out of harm's way, Zeb could. Tom had no idea who he could trust in the local police station, let alone among the elite group of officers who could pull off the kind of shell game he was proposing.

Zeb picked up. "I got your message," he said immediately. "I should've known when you got yourself entangled in that Molly Gilmore case that you'd be a thorn in our side."

"What's Gilmore got to do with anything?"

"You're kidding, right?"

Was his affection for Kate—Gilmore's intended victim—that obvious? Tom glanced at his watch. They'd already been here too long. "Just tell me if you can make it work."

"Yeah, it's taken care of."

"Where will you put him?"

"Better if you don't know, don't you think? Especially if whoever hired Vic Lawton figures out who your victim really is."

"Yeah, you're probably right." Except no way did he intend to let Kate think her father had died. Not again. He just prayed Vic had told the truth about not mentioning Kate's being in the woods to the guy who'd hired him. Since the burlap sacks were never found, chances were he'd lied about not taking them. At least if the goon had gotten what he wanted, he shouldn't give them any more trouble. Not the outcome Baxter would've wanted after twenty years of hiding, but probably safer for Kate.

A commotion erupted in the glass-walled nurses' station. The two nurses bolted into ICU.

Tom's heart sank. "I gotta go." He clicked off the phone and dashed back into the room. Kate flung herself into his arms. He held her close, thanking God that she wasn't shutting him out. "I'm so sorry, Kate."

She lifted her head from his chest, her face beaming. "It's

good news." She swiped at happy tears with her sleeve. "His eyelids fluttered. He's waking up."

Tom's gaze shot to the nurse checking Baxter's vitals. "We see this sometimes. I'm afraid it doesn't necessarily mean anything's changed."

"He's getting better," Kate insisted.

Tom's arm tightened around her shoulder. "C'mon, we need to go."

"But—" She pulled away and leaned over her father's bed and kissed his cheek. Her hand slipped over his. "I love you, Daddy," she whispered close to his ear. "Please, come back to me."

Tom gently caught her shoulder to urge her away. As they turned toward the door, a face disappeared from the window. Tom's heart rammed into his throat. It was Peter Ratcher. He was positive. And he'd seen Kate.

"Wait here," Tom said to her and charged out. The hall was empty. He raced to the stairwell. No one. He checked the one at the other end of the hall, scanned the parking lot from the window. Nothing.

Pulling out his phone, he rushed back to get Kate.

Zeb picked up on the first ring. "What's going on? Why'd you hang up so fast?"

Outside the ICU door, Tom paused at the heart-wrenching sight of Kate huddled over her father. "Ratcher knows. The move has to happen *now*."

Driving from the hospital with Kate, Tom pulled into the three-car lot of a little-used trailhead. "We need to talk."

"Who did you see outside the hospital room?"

"Do you want to walk?"

"No." Her fingers twisted in her lap. Her leg bounced.

349

"Yeah, okay." She sprang out of the car and wrapped her arms around her waist, watching him. "Tell me what's going on."

The sun slipped behind a cloud as he motioned toward the trailhead. The parking lot was empty except for them, but he scanned the trail ahead and surrounding forest for any sign of listening ears, then matched her step. "We need to move your dad."

She whirled toward him. "Move him where?"

"Away from here. You can be sure the guy who hired Vic will want to know what your father's interest in the plants is. Or worse, put an end to it."

Her face went ashen. "You can't take him away from me."

Her plea hit like a punch to the gut. "Peter Ratcher saw you in your father's hospital room."

The panic in her eyes confirmed she knew exactly what that could mean.

Tom cupped her shoulders. "Every minute you're with your dad increases the risk these goons will figure out who he really is and come after you too."

"But it was *Vic's* idea to run my father off the road. Not whoever hired him. Maybe—"

"This isn't a debate." Tom softened his voice. "It's all arranged."

"No, you have no right!" She spun on her heel and marched back toward the parking lot.

He caught her arm and jerked her to a stop. "I didn't have to tell you, Kate. I could have let you . . ."

"What?" Pain flared in her eyes. "Keep on believing he was already dead?"

"No." Tom looked away. He hadn't thought he could feel any worse. "Let you believe he was dead again."

"What?"

A bird took flight at her cry.

Tom glanced around. Hearing and seeing no one, he explained, "That's how we plan to hide the move. Fake his death."

Her jaw dropped and she just stared at him.

"It's the perfect way to get the heat off him, and you." He'd managed to keep her name out of Vic's file. The man had been more than happy to *not* have an assault charge added to his list of crimes. Which just left Peter Ratcher to deal with.

"I don't care about me."

"Well, I do." His voice caught.

Her mouth opened, then closed again—and let out a soft huff. "Other people know I've been in those woods."

"Grandma Brewster has no use for reporters, and I doubt Nagy or his son will say anything with charges hanging over their heads."

"What about his real estate agent and the guy he was showing the property to?"

Tom's gut churned. The interested buyer could be who'd hired Vic. "But you didn't think they'd seen you looking at the plant, right?"

"No, Grandma B made up a story about collecting colts-foot." Kate shrugged. "They acted like they believed her."

Tom prayed it hadn't been an act.

"Patti and Jarrett and Betty know about the plant too."

"But not where you found it." Tom grazed the back of his fingers down her cheek. "Kate, you're not going to change my mind."

"Then I'll quit my job and go with my dad."

As much as he'd like nothing more than to squirrel her away

in protective custody, at her father's side was the least-safe place for her to be. "What about your research?"

"My dad is more important."

Tom caught her hand. "He'd want you to stay. He was so proud of you, the work you're doing."

She blinked away the moisture clinging to her lashes. "He told you that?"

"Yes. He loves you very much." Tom swept the hair from her cheek and tucked it behind her ear. "Too much to risk your safety after all the years he sacrificed to ensure it."

She took a step back, hugging her waist.

Tom slowly lowered his hand. "We'll get through this, Kate. We'll figure it out."

"Like *we* told me Dad was alive. Like *we* can trust each other. There is no *we*. Just like there is no trust. Take me home."

Epilogue

Suppressing a sigh, Kate arranged the welcome home muffins she'd baked for Verna. They should have been for her dad.

Since he'd been secreted away, all Tom had told her was that he was still in a coma. She wasn't sure she could believe him, because Tom knew she'd move heaven and earth to see her dad again if he awoke.

Pushing the thought aside, she headed across the yard to Verna's. The crisp smell of autumn was already in the air, even though it was barely September.

Late summer dandelions in Verna's lawn had gone to seed and been spread into a snowy blanket by the evening breeze. Strange that Vic hadn't mowed it today. He always mowed it on Tuesdays, and Verna had been one of his few clients who hadn't fired him since he was released on bail last week. He couldn't afford to skip the job.

Or maybe he could, considering that to make bail, he obviously had a benefactor with deep pockets. GPC Pharmaceuticals, she suspected.

Despite how Vic had tried to frame her, she felt a little sorry

for him getting mixed up with the likes of GPC and really sorry
for his wife and daughter, but she was having a hard time forgiving him for what he did to her father. To think she'd been
seconds from finding him when Vic hit her with that shovel.

That familiar empty feeling threatened to swallow her again.
Drawing a deep breath, she knocked on Verna's door. She
couldn't let Verna see her melancholy when they were supposed
to be celebrating her homecoming.

"Kate," Verna squealed like she was eight instead of eighty
and pulled her into a hug. Whiskers twined around her legs,
as happy and healthy as ever. "Come in, come in. Would you
like a glass of lemonade?"

"What, no tea?" Kate quipped then instantly realized her
mistake. "Oh, I'm so sorry. I didn't mean—"

"Nonsense. Only natural you should ask." A faint blush
colored Verna's cheeks. "The truth is, a warm cup of tea just
doesn't comfort me like it used to."

Yeah, Kate could relate. Ever since Molly Gilmore tried
to finish her off with tainted tea the way she'd done Daisy,
Kate hadn't enjoyed a cup quite the same way either. She set
the muffins on the coffee table next to the lemonade pitcher,
wondering if she would again once Molly was finally back
behind bars where she belonged. Of course, the way it was
looking, that would be at least a year away. And that was not
something she wanted to think about today.

She poured the lemonade and handed Verna a glass. Verna's
silver hair was glossy and newly styled in short curls. She didn't
look nearly as frail as she had. Amazing what cutting a little
toxic tea out of the diet could do. That and the TLC she'd
gotten at the nursing home. "You look wonderful."

"I feel wonderful. The Lord worked everything out." Her

gaze drifted to the photos lining the hallway, and the light in her eyes dimmed. "Well, almost everything."

As much as Verna's son deserved to rot in jail as he awaited trial, Kate knew Verna would miss him.

Verna took a seat beside Kate on the sofa. "So, what's been happening in your life?"

"Oh"—Kate sipped the lemonade and thought about how much she missed her father—"I've just about finished the research project Daisy and I had been working on before she died. Next month I'm scheduled to present it at a symposium in DC."

"You must be excited."

Kate waited for the giddy feeling to bubble up inside her as it had when she and Daisy first realized the importance of their discovery. It never came. Her discoveries didn't seem to matter anymore. Certainly not enough to justify being separated from her dad.

The front door opened. Kate whirled in her seat, Tom's warning to be cautious screaming through her head.

"Lucetta, come join us," Verna called from her place on the sofa.

Lucetta set down a small suitcase and took three steps before her gaze slammed into Kate's and she stopped. "Oh . . . it's you."

"Nice to see you again," Kate said as sweetly as she could manage. She hadn't seen the woman since their argument over the photo of her mother's supposed murderer.

The truth will set you free.

The thought—the Scripture—came out of nowhere.

Lucetta's gaze was glued to the floor.

"Join us," Kate urged, suddenly feeling ashamed for her

negative feelings toward the woman. Lucetta didn't know what really led to her mother's death any more than Kate had known what had become of her father. How could she blame her for lashing out at the sight of Dad's picture?

The urge to reveal the truth they'd both been denied these last twenty years suddenly overwhelmed her. Except Tom had warned her to tell no one. And even she still didn't know the whole story.

Lucetta perched on the armchair next to Verna, and they chatted about the new live-in arrangement Verna had proposed.

Kate finished her lemonade and contemplated cutting her visit short. She didn't understand why Tom refused to tell her where her father was. It had been two weeks and there'd been no threats, no mysterious phone calls, no one following her.

Not that she didn't appreciate Tom's concern, and the state-of-the-art security system he had installed in her house. She glanced out Verna's living room window at the darkening sky as his words—*the alarm only works if you remember to turn it on*—whispered through her mind. She jerked to her feet. "I need to go. I"—she glanced at the plate of muffins—"I think I forgot to turn off my oven."

She hurried to the door as Verna thanked her again for stopping by.

"We'll visit again soon," Kate promised. It wasn't as if her social calendar was jam-packed. If she didn't count church on Sundays, it'd been pretty much nonexistent since she'd stopped seeing Tom.

She stepped onto Verna's porch, and at the sight of Tom's car in her driveway, her traitorous heart leapt. She was still working at forgiving him. She spotted him on her front porch, reaching for the doorknob.

"Looking for me?" She called out, her heart jumping for an entirely different reason—the scolding she'd get if he found the door unlocked.

His attention jerked her way, a look of sheer panic on his face.

"What's wrong?" She ran toward him, and his expression morphed to relief.

He swept her into his arms and buried his face in her hair at her neck. "Am I ever glad to see you." His voice came out kind of husky, like he had tears in his throat. His hold tightened, and because she felt silly standing there with her arms dangling by her sides, she slid them around his waist.

She'd forgotten how safe she felt wrapped in his arms. She slipped her hands between them and pressed her palms against his chest. "What's going on?"

The fierceness of his embrace suddenly raised another specter. She gulped down rising panic. "My dad?"

"No." Apology lined his face and her pulse slowed. "I'm sorry. I didn't mean to scare you like that." He clasped her hand and tugged her toward the house. "Let's go inside." He scanned the street and neighboring yards before turning to the door.

He didn't seem to notice that it was unlocked and the alarm was off even though she'd been next door when he arrived. Clearly he was rattled by whatever he had to tell her.

She didn't like him coming inside. His presence filled the small living room, and his woodsy scent would linger, tormenting her for hours. She had been so lonely these past two weeks. Of her own choosing, sure. But seeing him, and his family, only made her miss her father—what they could have had—all the more. "What is it?"

Tom slid the deadbolt home, then caught her hand again and drew her to the sofa.

Not ready to sit so close, she bypassed the sofa and sat in the armchair.

A frown whispered over his lips as he sank into a seat opposite. "Vic is dead," he said without preamble.

"What?" Shock ripped through her even as some part of her brain told her she should be glad. The man had nearly killed her father.

But the worry in Tom's eyes said there was more to it. "We think it happened sometime last night. His car went off the ravine at Turner's Hollow."

She gasped. "The same place he rammed Dad's car off the road."

Tom leaned forward, resting his forearms on his thighs, and rubbed the thumb of one hand over the other. "Given the location and timing and lack of evidence to the contrary, the investigating officer is calling it a suicide."

The air stalled in Kate's chest. He killed himself because of what he'd done? *Oh, Lord, if only I'd forgiven him. Would he still be alive?* Her chest burned.

Tom's warm touch startled her out of her thoughts. "Breathe."

She inhaled, easing the pain in her chest only a fraction. "I'm so sorry. I know the Bible says we're supposed to forgive those who wrong us. And I would have gotten around to it eventually. I know I would have."

Tom touched two fingers to her lips, his touch undeservingly gentle. "This isn't your fault. In fact, I don't believe it was a suicide."

"What do you think it was?" She held her breath, remembering the sheer panic on his face when she hadn't answered his knock. He thought she was in danger.

More danger than before.

"I think he was murdered by the guy who hired him to dig up the plants."

She dug her fingers into the seat cushion to try to still the trembling that overtook her.

"So far nothing about Vic being hired has come out in the news. They no doubt wanted to keep it that way."

She choked. His poor wife and daughter.

"Rumors of Vic's heightened depression after your dad 'died' created a perfect setup to make his death look like suicide."

"But you have no proof?" She couldn't mask the desperate hope in her voice. As much as she didn't want Vic's death to be suicide, she didn't need a PhD to know what Tom feared. She swallowed but couldn't dislodge the lump in her throat.

She was next.

Julie's Favorite Muffins

1¾ cup	whole wheat flour
1½ tsp	baking powder
½ tsp	nutmeg
½ tsp	salt
¼ tsp	cinnamon
⅓ cup	sunflower oil
¾ cup	milk
1	medium egg
⅔ cup	granulated sugar

Topping Ingredients:
¼ cup	melted butter
¾ cup	granulated sugar
1 tsp	cinnamon

In a large bowl, mix the first five ingredients. In a second bowl, whisk together the oil, egg, milk, and sugar. Then add the liquid ingredients to the dry, stirring only to combine. Spoon batter into paper-lined muffin pans and bake in preheated 350° F oven for 20 minutes or until toothpick comes out clean.

For topping, mix the cinnamon into the sugar. While muffins are still hot, dip tops in melted butter followed by the sugar and cinnamon mix.

For an added surprise, fill muffin liners half full, add a teaspoon of your favorite jam, and spoon batter over top.

Acknowledgments

Working with the Revell team on this series continues to be a fabulous experience. A huge thanks to each one of the many, many staff members who have a part in getting my books into readers' hands. You are tremendous encouragers and a delight to work with.

Thank you to Eileen Astels, Wenda Dottridge, and Amber Perry for your insightful suggestions at the critiquing stage, and to Kathy Pilkington, the NRP officers, and Meridian Credit Union staff who answered all my power of attorney/ guardianship, counterfeiting, and police questions and some I forgot to ask.

My deepest thanks go to the Lord for bringing all these wonderful people into my life and for inspiring the stories I write, and most especially for blessing me with incredibly supportive family and friends.

And thank you to you, my readers. I've said it before but can't say it enough: with more books than ever vying for your time, I feel truly honored that you chose to spend a few hours reading this one.

Sneak Peek

Book 3

1

Squinting against the bright grow lights, Kate Adams slipped into her fruit cellar in the back corner of her basement and shut the door behind her. She couldn't risk anyone discovering her little greenhouse. Enough people had already died.

The humidity in the room squeezed her chest. She hated to think of the mildew problems it would cause, but it was a price she'd happily pay if it meant getting her dad back.

Ignoring for a few minutes the paint job awaiting her upstairs, she pressed her fingers into the soil of the nearest pot to gauge its dampness. She smiled at the sight of a few new buds. The plants her dad had missed digging up were thriving in the tropical microclimate she'd re-created since sneaking back into Verna Nagy's woods for them. A big part of her didn't want anything to do with the plants that had cost her twenty years of separation from her father. But after Detective Parker's "executive decision" to send Dad back into hiding, figuring out what gave them such extraordinary curative properties might be her only hope of ever seeing him again.

The thought of Dad alone, lying in a coma somewhere, preyed on her mind night and day. If only that guy hadn't driven him off the road in a rash attempt to recover the plants, they might be enjoying a sweet reunion even now. *Why, Lord? I don't understand why you brought him back into my life, only to take him away again.*

No answer came. Not that she'd expected one. Lately, it felt like even God had abandoned her.

Guilt niggled her at the irreverent thought. As much as it felt like it, her dad hadn't really abandoned her by faking his death twenty years ago. He'd been trying to protect her the only way he thought possible. And as for God, hadn't Daisy taught her to trust in the authority of his Word, not emotions that surged and ebbed like the tide?

The Bible said God would never leave her or forsake her.

She let out a sigh and rubbed her knuckles over the ache in the vicinity of her heart. If only every other person she'd ever trusted hadn't lied to her face or hid things from her—big, monumental things, like the fact her dad was alive—maybe she'd have an easier time taking God at his word.

Shoving aside the thought, she snatched up her spray bottle and misted the succulent dandelion-shaped leaves. "What's your secret?" she whispered to the plants as she deadheaded a spent aster-like flower.

She could scarcely imagine what could be so special about this plant that a multinational pharmaceutical company would burn down a remote Columbian village to control it. So special that her father would sacrifice a lifetime with his family to keep it out of their hands. So special that all these years later, his former employer, GPC Pharmaceuticals, would track it down to Port Aster and kill a man to safeguard its existence.

Kill her, if they found out she had it.

Her chest squeezed tighter, cinching off her breath. With GPC still vying to partner with the research facility where she worked, she didn't dare tell anyone about the plants.

Detective Tom Parker least of all.

If he'd separate her from her comatose father to ensure her safety, he'd never allow her to experiment with the plant responsible for Dad's fate. But if she could figure out what was so special about it, maybe she'd have the leverage she needed to force them to let her see him.

Did Tom already know why GPC wanted the plant? Was that something else he'd kept from her? Like the fact her father was alive?

She jerked the mist bottle's trigger. Anger at Tom's betrayal still blindsided her every time she thought of him keeping her from her father. "For her own protection," he'd said. And she appreciated his concern. She sincerely did. But she couldn't trust him not to do the same thing again.

The doorbell sounded.

She froze. Who'd come around on a Saturday morning? Especially this early?

Glancing down at the painting clothes she'd tugged on first thing, she palmed the perspiration from her brow. *Pull yourself together. No one's gonna suspect you're up to anything.*

The doorbell chimed a second time.

She closed the fruit cellar door and hurried upstairs, still puzzling over who could be here. Tom would call first. *Unless . . .*

Her steps quickened. Had he finally brought good news? That her father was out of his coma, that she could see him again?

She peeked out the peephole and her chest deflated. She

turned off her security alarm and unlocked the deadbolt. "Patti, what brings you by on a Saturday?" Kate did a double take at her lab assistant's faded jeans and the ratty T-shirt straining at her ample hips. Since Patti started dating the mayor's son, Kate hadn't seen her in anything that wasn't designer fashion. "What's wrong?"

Laughing, Patti pulled her long, dark hair into a ponytail and snapped on an elastic. "Nothing. You said you were finally going to paint your bedroom this weekend. I came to help."

"Really?"

"Don't sound so shocked. I do know how to paint."

"No, I—" Kate motioned her in and relocked the door. "I just assumed you'd be hanging out with Jarrett. You two have been inseparable lately."

Patti shrugged. "A girl's got to spend some time with her girlfriends. Right?"

Kate nodded, speechless. Patti was her assistant, her co-worker. She'd never really thought of her as a girlfriend. A shadow crossed Patti's eyes, and a niggling suspicion struck Kate that there was more to the visit than a little altruistic bonding.

Kate shook off the thought. Goodness, she'd grown as cynical as Tom! "I'd love some help. Thank you." She led the way to the empty room. "I laid old bedsheets over the carpet so I wouldn't have to worry about paint splatters."

"Smart idea." Patti grabbed the stepladder and set it up along the far wall. "I can do the top and bottom edges with a brush if you want to handle the roller."

"That would be awesome." Kate poured half of the lemongrass green paint into the paint tray, then set the can on the ladder's holder for Patti's easy access.

Patti started in immediately, saying little, except that she liked the color.

Kate loaded her roller and concentrated on making long, smooth strokes. "You seeing Jarrett later?"

Patti shrugged.

"Did you two have a fight?"

"No, nothing like that," Patti said. Only her brushstrokes grew jerky, as if it was *exactly* like that.

A real girlfriend would commiserate with her. But Kate couldn't. She'd be happy to see the pair break up. She didn't trust Jarrett. It was too coincidental that he'd started dating Patti at the same time Kate took her on as a research assistant, especially when his mayor father was so set on helping GPC partner with the research station.

Patti jabbed her brush into the paint can and glanced Kate's way. "Whoa. You might want to wear a ball cap. You're speckling your hair green."

"Red and green. Terrific. I'll be all set for Christmas." Kate set down her paint roller and ran her palm over her long waves. Yup, she could feel little wet spots.

Patti muffled a giggle.

"What?" Kate pulled away her green-smeared hand and groaned.

"At least it's not speckled anymore." Patti returned to her painting, still chuckling.

Kate went to the bathroom and washed out the paint as best she could, then squashed a ball cap over her hair. By the time she got back to the bedroom, Patti already had the top of three walls edged. "Wow, you paint like a pro!"

"Thanks." She climbed down to move the ladder and swayed precariously.

"Watch out!" Kate dropped her roller and lunged for the ladder, scarcely stopping it from toppling, along with the can of paint.

Patti stumbled off the bottom rung and struggled to recover her balance. "I'm sorry." She pressed her palm to the side of her head. "I don't know what's wrong with me. I keep getting these bizarre dizzy spells. Last night I tripped up my porch steps."

"No harm done, but you really should see a doctor. Have it checked out."

Patti dropped her hand and straightened. "I don't think it's that serious. Probably just low blood sugar or something."

"Then let me get you a glass of apple juice."

Patti retrieved the roller Kate had dropped on the bedsheet. "That's okay. I can get it. How about you finish edging the top of the wall and I'll take over the roller?"

"Okay, but"—Kate pried the roller from Patti's hand and set it in the tray—"first get yourself that juice. There's a bottle in the fridge."

Patti saluted and headed down the hall.

Kate climbed the ladder and continued painting where Patti had left off. But when Patti still hadn't returned by the time she reloaded her brush for the fourth time, she called out, "You okay?"

When she didn't respond, Kate dashed down the hall. An empty juice glass sat on the table, but Patti was nowhere in sight. Kate skidded to a stop at the top of the basement stairs beside the kitchen. "Patti?"

Halfway down the steps, Patti whirled at her name. "Ahhh!" Her arms windmilled, and for a sickening millisecond the sheer panic of knowing she was going to fall and not being able to stop herself blazed in her eyes. She tumbled backward, catching

370

her heel on the tread, and slammed her head on the cement floor, half her body sprawled on the steps.

She shifted awkwardly and her screams escalated.

"Don't move!" Kate raced down. "You might have broken something." *Oh, no.* Kate swallowed the bile that stung her throat at the sight of Patti's badly broken leg. She was lying at such a horrible angle. Kate prayed her leg was all that was broken.

Patti collapsed back against the floor. "I can't believe this. I saw you'd left a light on, and"—she gasped for air in short, painful sounding gulps—"I was just coming down to turn it off for you."

Kate's gaze shot to the fruit cellar, her breath caught in her throat. The door was closed like she'd left it. But no light that she could see seeped around the edges.

Was Patti lying? Had she really gone in? Had she seen the plants?

❧

The abandoned Potter farmhouse sat a quarter mile in from the road. Tom Parker parked at the end of its overgrown driveway, not willing to risk busting an axle to save himself a walk. He checked his gun in his shoulder holster and shrugged into his sport coat before climbing out. Calls about a squatter weren't normally his territory, but he had a hunch this particular squatter might be the missing teen he'd been trying to track down.

He scanned the horizon for any sign his arrival had been noticed. The young Conner family, who'd made the call, lived north of the property. Their youngster stood on a tire swing, pointing Tom's way. Shading her eyes, Mrs. Conner followed the direction of her son's finger. Tom waved, then radioed dispatch to alert them, in case Mrs. Conner mistook him for another trespasser thanks to his unmarked car.

A weed-infested field lay south of the Potter house, bordering Patti Goodman's property with its six-foot high walled perimeter. If this squatter wasn't his missing teen, he could be someone scouting out the wealthy estate she'd recently inherited.

Too bad it was Saturday. Questioning Kate's research assistant about any suspicious activity she might have noticed on the adjoining property would have been a great excuse to stop by Kate's work.

A sense of sadness crept over him, followed by the memory of her parting words: "There is no *we*."

He kicked the dirt. Yeah, wake up and smell the weeds. Stopping by wouldn't change anything. If he weren't the *only* connection to her father—as tenuous as that connection was—she probably wouldn't talk to him at all. Never mind the danger he believed she might still be in.

Despite his certainty that GPC must have recovered the plants Vic Lawton stole from her father, the pharmaceutical company was still vying for a stake in Port Aster's research center. And Lawton's murder proved that they didn't leave loose ends.

He returned his attention to the task at hand. Multiple bicycle-sized ruts through the grass confirmed someone had been around. He scoped the area for any evidence he might be walking into more than he bargained for, like some gang's hideout. A cool breeze whispered through the timothy fields. A murder of crows, perching on a dead tree, cawed noisily as if to warn of his arrival.

But no shifting shadows at the windows betrayed a response to the birds' alarm call.

He tried the front door. It held fast, and from the look of the crusted edges, it hadn't been opened in years. He peered through the dirty window. An old sofa, its stuffing puffed out the corner, sat in the otherwise bare main room. A staircase with ratty carpet curling on the treads stretched to the second level. In the dim light, it was impossible to tell if anyone had traipsed across the floor recently.

Tom strode around the house, glancing in windows, then yanked on the metal screen door at the side of the house. It fell off its top hinge, and before he pushed open the inside door, the reek of animal waste bit his nostrils. A dilapidated table and two chairs sat in the center of a floor layered in years of dust and raccoon dung. But man-sized scuffs across the dust-covered floor leading into the adjoining hall betrayed a recent intrusion.

"This is Detective Tom Parker. Anyone here? I just want to talk to you."

A skittering inside one of the kitchen cupboards answered his call, nothing more. Holding his breath against the oppressive stench and dust, he moved from one room to the next, checking closets. There were definite indications someone had wandered through the place, but nothing to suggest anyone was living there. Tom grabbed the stair rail, glanced up the open staircase, and tested the bottom step.

His cell phone rang. He cocked his head toward the top of the stairs, thinking he'd heard movement. The phone rang again. Seeing his dad's name on the screen, he punched it on. "Yeah, Dad. What is it?"

"I was listening to the police scanner. An ambulance was just dispatched to Kate's house."

His pulse torpedoed into hyperdrive. "Did you catch any

details?" Giving the stairs one last fleeting glance, Tom hoofed it back to the door.

"No, but I'm on my way over now."

"Thanks, Dad. I'll be right there too." Tom bolted outside just as a motorcycle roared up the overgrown driveway.

Tom took cover behind a porch pillar, his hand settling on his gun.

The bike swerved to a stop at the foot of the porch, kicking up a cloud of dust.

"Hold it right there," Tom shouted.

The driver yanked off his helmet, revealing dark hair and blue eyes Tom would know anywhere—Jarrett King, the mayor's son. "What's going on, Detective?"

Leaving his weapon in his holster, Tom refastened his sport coat. "What are you doing here?"

"My girlfriend lives next door."

Right. Patti Goodman. How could he forget, after catching the pair nosing through Kate's house a little more than a month ago? Was a month all it'd been? Tom glanced at the yellowing fields of early September. Seemed like a lot longer with Kate avoiding him most of the time.

Jarrett tucked his helmet under his arm. "I saw the car at the end of the driveway and got curious."

Tom started toward him, peeling a business card from his wallet. "The neighbors called in a possible squatter. Has Patti mentioned seeing anyone hanging around this place?"

"No." Concern rippled Jarrett's brow. "Are we talking kids or someone she needs to be worried about?"

"I don't know yet." Tom handed him the card. "I have an emergency I need to get to. If you notice anyone around the place, give me a call."

"Will do." Jarrett yanked on his helmet and wailed out of the driveway before Tom's long strides ate a quarter of the distance.

But instead of turning south toward Patti's, Jarrett turned north. So why had he really happened by?

Outside her house, Kate spun from the departing ambulance to a car screeching to a stop behind her. Tom's car. Her heart leapt to her throat at the sight of him climbing out, looking as handsome as ever with his dark hair newly trimmed. She swallowed the thought of how she used to enjoy inhaling its clean, fresh scent. "What are you doing here?" she blurted, although his dad's arrival two minutes after the ambulance's should have prepared her.

Tom's blue eyes sparked as if she'd asked in Swahili. "A 911 call to your house, Kate?" he said, exasperation oozing from every word. "Where do you think I'm going to be?"

Her heart made another traitorous leap. She could always count on him to watch out for her. If only his protectiveness hadn't cost her so much that just the sight of him made her feel the loss swallowing her all over again.

His gaze traveled up her paint-splattered clothes. "What's going on?"

"Oh." Pricked by the thought of the plants he didn't know she had, that he didn't know existed, she waved her arm mindlessly toward the house. "Nothing you need to worry about. Patti was helping me paint and fell and broke her leg."

"I'm sorry."

Kate dug her car keys out of her pocket. "I need to go to the hospital."

"You might want to clean up first." She jerked from his touch on her cheek, then felt foolish when he presented a lemongrass-green-smeared fingertip.

She swiped at her cheek with her shirtsleeve, trying to ignore the flutters triggered by his touch.

He jutted his chin toward Patti's car blocking hers in the driveway. "If you give me the keys, I can move her car out of the way for you while you change."

Kate glanced helplessly down the now-empty street and groaned. "Patti took her purse with her."

"No problem. I can give you a lift to the hospital," he said, sounding far too happy about her problem.

"Uh . . ." Not a good idea. If her insides were already doing gymnastics, a twenty-minute car ride together would be pure torture. She'd probably end up confessing to digging up the plants and everything.

And he'd take them away, just like he took her dad, and she'd never figure out what was so special about them, let alone gain enough pull to get her dad back. She shifted from one foot to another, squinting at her blocked car. "Aren't you supposed to be working?"

"I'll take an early lunch," he said, sweetening his it's-no-big-deal shrug with a wink.

Oh, she was in big trouble.

Tom's father emerged from the house. "I emptied your paint tray into the can and sealed it up and washed your brushes in the basement."

"The basement?" She swallowed a gasp, but Tom's eagle eyes still narrowed. *Not good.* When Keith arrived and volunteered to clean up her paint supplies so she could follow Patti to the hospital, she hadn't thought about him going

376

downstairs and possibly noticing the grow lights on in the fruit cellar too.

"Yeah, I didn't think you'd want me cleaning paint in your kitchen sink."

"No, of course not." Realizing she was fluttering her hand way too nervously, she pressed it to her side. "Thank you."

Keith gave Tom a look she couldn't read, but that made her stomach churn. Did he know? Would he tell Tom? "Um . . . I'll just go get changed real quick." She hurried inside, dead-bolted the door behind her, and raced downstairs. Her pounding heart roared in her ears as she opened the fruit cellar door. At the sight of the grow lights still burning, she blew out a breath. *Thank you, Lord.*

She charged back upstairs and snuck a peek out the front window. Tom and his father were in deep conversation. *Okay, that might not be good.* She quickly washed and changed and raced back outside. "Ready," she said, breathlessly.

The smile that crinkled the corners of Tom's eyes as he held open his passenger door for her sent a too-nice zing right to the center of her chest. Oh, boy.

He hadn't even turned the corner before diving into the questions she'd dreaded. "Dad said Patti was at the bottom of the basement stairs, but all the paint and brushes were upstairs. So why was she going downstairs?"

"Uh . . ." Kate wished she knew. She clutched her thighs to still her fidgeting hands. Tom was far too adept at reading her body language. He was bound to suspect she was hedging. Patti had no business going downstairs. Maybe she was just going to turn off the light, like she'd said, but Kate wasn't sure she believed her. "I guess I accidentally left a light on." She tried not to squirm as the word *accidentally* came out of her mouth.

Tom glanced from her lap to her face. "Hey, it's not like you pushed her. It's not your fault."

Softening at his caring tone, she tried to relax, except one look at his deep blue eyes and her anxiety only morphed into guilt over how nice he was being. Of course it was her fault. She was harboring a fugitive plant in her basement and not telling him about it.

He reached across the seat and squeezed her hand. "I'm glad *you're* okay. I was afraid GPC had gotten to you."

She stiffened at his touch. GPC *would* be after her if they knew. And Tom would have a hairy canary fit if he knew.

"Kate, you have to know that I'm doing everything I can to figure out a safe way to reunite you with your father."

"I know," she mumbled, feeling even worse that he'd misread her reaction and taken it personally. But she couldn't explain. Instead, she gave his hand a quick squeeze and then pulled away, retreating further to her side of the car. She'd been deprived of her dad her whole life, for safety's sake. Now that she knew he was alive, she intended to do whatever it took to be reunited, safe or not.

Tom parked near the ER, and as he guided her toward the entrance with a gentle touch to her back, she tried not to think about the last time they'd visited the ER—the night Vic attacked her in the woods, the night he rammed her father's car over a ravine, the night she learned the truth Tom had been hiding from her.

A soft cry escaped her at the memory of the precious few hours she'd had with him before they'd whisked the father she'd thought dead for twenty years into hiding yet again. As if he'd read her thoughts, Tom's hand rubbed soothing circles on her lower back.

She arched away from his touch, willing her anger at the unfairness of it all to dispel the impulse to turn into his arms. She didn't have time for a pity party. Patti needed her.

The ER doors slid open and the bright lights hurt her eyes. Jarrett, looking way too pale, pushed through the door separating the waiting room from the patients.

Kate ran to him. "Is she okay? How did you know she was here? Have you talked to the doctor?"

"I called him when you were changing," Tom whispered.

Jarrett raked his fingers through his hair. "The doctor said she has a displaced fracture, and because of the swelling and pain, they may need to put her under to set it. First they're sending her for a CT scan of her head. She hit it pretty hard."

"This is all my fault." Kate sunk onto a chair along the wall. "As soon as she told me how dizzy she'd been feeling, I should have told her to rest."

"You knew she was dizzy?" The urgency in Jarrett's voice made Kate's heart race. "Did she suspect what caused it?"

"She said maybe low blood sugar."

A nurse carrying a clipboard joined them. "Are you Kate? Miss Goodman said you'd be able to tell me the policy number for your work's medical insurance."

"Oh, yes." Kate dug into her purse and produced the card. "The group policy number is on the top. I guess you'll have to call for her personal number."

The nurse tapped her pencil in a quickening staccato as she studied the card. "You work at the research station?"

"Yes."

"Doing the same sort of research as that woman who recently died from drinking her own herbal tea concoction?"

Kate sprang to her feet. "Daisy was poisoned! How—"

Tom's heavy hand on her shoulder stifled the indignant retort she'd been about to blast the nurse with.

"Of course, I'm sorry. I had read in the papers that poisoning was the new theory," the nurse said apologetically. Kate had to dig her teeth into her bottom lip not to shout, "It's not a theory!"

"I just thought," the nurse went on, "that if she drinks different herbals, they might explain the dizziness, since she said she had it before she hit her head."

"I thought the doctor ordered blood tests," Jarrett cut in.

The nurse handed Kate back her card. "Yes, but if you can think of anything she might've consumed that could explain the dizziness, please let us know."

As the nurse walked away, Tom pulled up a seat beside Kate. "This scenario sounds too uncomfortably like your friend Daisy's."

Kate's heart pummeled her ribs. "You think someone poisoned Patti?"

"No, I—"

"Daisy had complained of dizziness a few times before . . ." *Oh, no. Oh, no. Oh. No.*

Tom gently clasped her arms. "It's okay. Take deep breaths."

"It's not. *It's not!*" Kate whipped free of his hold. "What if they poisoned Patti to get to me?"

Sandra Orchard is an award-winning author of inspirational romantic suspense, whose novels include *Deadly Devotion* and several Love Inspired Suspense titles, including two Canadian Christian Writing Award winners and a *Romantic Times* Reviewers' Choice Award winner. Sandra has also received a Daphne du Maurier Award for Excellence in Mystery/Suspense.

In addition to her busy writing schedule, Sandra enjoys speaking at events and teaching writing workshops. She especially enjoys brainstorming suspense plots with fellow writers, which has garnered more than a few odd looks when standing in the grocery checkout debating what poison to use.

Sandra lives with her husband of more than twenty-five years in Ontario, Canada, where their favorite pastime is exploring the world with their young grandchildren. Learn more about Sandra's books and check out the special bonus features, such as deleted scenes and location pictures, at www.sandra orchard.com. While there, subscribe to her newsletter to receive subscriber-exclusive short stories. You can also connect with Sandra at www.facebook.com/sandraorchard.